The City

Valerian Pidmohylnyi

THE CITY

A NOVEL

Translated with an introduction by
Maxim Tarnawsky

50 years ▪ 1973–2023

 HURI

Distributed by Harvard University Press
for the Ukrainian Research Institute
Harvard University

The Harvard Ukrainian Research Institute was established in 1973 as an integral part of Harvard University. It supports research associates and visiting scholars who are engaged in projects concerned with all aspects of Ukrainian studies. The Institute also works in close cooperation with the Committee on Ukrainian Studies, which supervises and coordinates the teaching of Ukrainian history, language, and literature at Harvard University.

An earlier version of this book in Maxim Tarnawsky's translation previously appeared in *Ukrainian Literature: A Journal of Translations*, vol. 4, 2014, and vol. 5, 2018.

This translation was edited by Oleh Kotsyuba with assistance from Michelle R. Viise.

ISBN 9780674291119 (hardcover), 9780674291126 (paperback), 9780674291133 (epub), 9780674291140 (PDF)

Library of Congress Control Number: 2023942584

LC record available at https://lccn.loc.gov/2023942584

Cover image and collage of maps on the endsheets by Romana Romanyshyn and Andriy Lesiv, Art Studio Agrafka, agrafkastudio.com.

The following historical maps of Kyiv were used for the design of endsheets of the hardcover edition and the reverse side of the cover of the paperback edition: "Plan˝ gor. Kieva s˝ ego dostoprimechatel´nostiami, prilegaiushchimi okrestnostiami i ukazaniem˝ N°N° tramvaev˝ i ikh˝ napravleniia" (Kyiv: Litografiia S. V. Kul´zhenko, 1913); "Kijew. Bearbeitet v. Vermess. Abt. 16, Heeresgr. Eichhorn, nach topogr. Erkundungen und Fliegerbildern, Juli 1918. Maßstab 1:20000" (N. p.: N. p., 1918). File source: Tours de Kiev, www.toursdekiev.com.ua.

Book design by Mykhailo Fedyshak, bluecollider@gmail.com

Publication of this book has been made possible by the generous support of publications in Ukrainian studies at Harvard University by the following benefactors or funds endowed in their name:

Ostap and Ursula Balaban
Jaroslaw and Olha Duzey
Vladimir Jurkowsky
Myroslav and Irene Koltunik
Damian Korduba Family
Peter and Emily Kulyk
Irena Lubchak
Dr. Evhen Omelsky
Eugene and Nila Steckiw
Dr. Omeljan and Iryna Wolynec
Wasyl and Natalia Yerega

You can support our work of publishing academic books and translations of Ukrainian literature and documents by making a tax-deductible donation in any amount, or by including HURI in your estate planning.

To find out more, please visit
https://huri.harvard.edu/give.

Contents

Valerian Pidmohylnyi's *The City*

Maxim Tarnawsky

In 1920, in the central Ukrainian city of Katerynoslav (now Dnipro), nineteen-year-old Valerian Pidmohylnyi published his first book. It was a small volume of nine stories with a very big title: *Works: Volume 1*. A year later, he was in Kyiv, the capital of the Ukrainian People's Republic, taking the first steps toward a career as a professional writer. These were heady times, not only for the aspiring young writer but for the Ukrainian nation and its culture as a whole.

In the nineteenth century, Ukraine may not have existed as a state, but the roughly 25 million Ukrainians certainly did. They were split unevenly between two imperial powers, Austria-Hungary and Russia. As with other stateless Slavic nations, much of Ukrainian history in the nineteenth century consisted of cultural activity designed to promote and assert national identity. In the Russian Empire, where the majority of Ukrainians lived, this national awakening was met with repressions: there, the very existence of a Ukrainian nation and culture was perceived as a threat to the empire. But the political turmoil of the early twentieth century and the double calamities of WWI and the October Revolution brought the empire to its demise and opened the floodgates for a flowering of Ukrainian identity in both politics and culture. Between 1917 and 1919, a succession of Ukrainian governments claimed authority in Kyiv, before being overrun by Bolshevik military forces. Yet, unlike Ukrainian armies and politicians, Ukrainian culture and identity had substantial power and broad support. In the chaotic aftermath of wars and revolutions, in the absence of imperial restrictions on Ukrainian identity and the use of the Ukrainian language, Ukrainian culture — its literature in particular — flourished.

The 1920s were a period of growth and adjustment in Soviet Ukraine. In politics and the economy, it was two steps forward, one step back. But in literature, it was full speed ahead. A massive cohort of new writers, too young to have been active before the war, was suddenly writing and clamoring to get published. Literary journals were being established, publishing houses were growing, and literary groupings and organizations were forming and re-forming, battling each other for public attention. Most surprising of all, there was now a public whose attention was worth seeking. Four vital changes had occurred since the early years of the century. The upheaval of war and revolution and massive human displacement, particularly of young men who had served in the military, meant that the uneducated, provincial Ukrainian peasants of nineteenth-century folkloric illusions had become worldly, inquisitive, and experienced individuals. Specifically, they had been transformed socially in three different ways, becoming literate, urban, and nationally conscious. A fourth dimension of societal development was the emergence of women on the cultural landscape as creators and consumers, which brought about significant changes, not least in their treatment as subjects.

The results of these changes can be seen in the outpouring of new literature in the 1920s. As the various wars finally came to an end and other problems like famine and cholera subsided, Ukrainian culture poured out into a receptive society as if from a dam breach, at first slowly and then in a massive torrent. Of course, not all of this flood was great literature. There were plenty of authors whose literary ambitions lacked substantial foundation. But there was also genuine talent in abundance. And, most importantly, there was diversity. Where Ukrainian literature of the late nineteenth century had mostly kept to a familiar pattern of heartfelt, realistic depictions of a variety of social ills, in the 1920s it spread into a very wide range of topics, genres, styles, and forms. The novel, a genre that usually prospers where there is a good market for literature, was flourishing. Novels were appearing with subjects as diverse as prostitution in Kyiv and chemical plants in New York. There were novels about future world revolution and novels about the seventeenth century. There were novels about factories, farms, children, women, airplanes, motion pictures, exotic places and strange people, science, politics, sex, philosophy, and literature — or all possible combinations of the above in one work. There were detective stories and thrillers, family dramas, social dramas, and closet dramas. There was even pulp fiction.

This remarkable explosion of creativity lasted for about a decade. By the early 1930s, Stalin was conducting show trials of Ukrainian intellectuals and censorship was tightened. Soon, writers were being arrested and sent to the Gulag, or worse. The period when culture had been able to flourish later became known as the Executed Renaissance (*Rozstriliane vidrodzhennia*, after the title of an anthology published in Paris in 1959). The attack on Ukrainian culture was part of a Soviet attack on all things Ukrainian, including the nation itself, deliberately starved in a man-made famine in 1932–33. Such was the world of Ukrainian culture in which the ambitious young author of *Works: Volume 1* set out to make himself a place in the literary pantheon.

Valerian Pidmohylnyi was born on February 2, 1901, in a village called Chapli, then part of the Russian Empire and now absorbed into the city of Dnipro in southern Ukraine. His father worked for a landowner as a manager of his estate. Valerian attended a village school and, in addition, learned French from a tutor the estate owner had hired for his own children. Little is known about his life just after WWI. His KGB file said he was a supporter of Symon Petliura, a leader of the Ukrainian liberation movement. Some of his early stories focus on military events, but that was true of most writing at this time. What is clear is that he started writing when he was young and his early stories focused on young men finding their place in a hostile and confusing world. He also translated the French poet, journalist, and novelist Anatole France. But writing and publishing in the south of Soviet Ukraine was not sufficient to satisfy this ambitious writer — he was headed for the big city, Kyiv.

The welcome he received there was mixed. The Kyiv he arrived in faced outbreaks of disease and hunger; many intellectuals were leaving the city to settle in surrounding villages, where they could become schoolteachers and get paid with food. In Pidmohylnyi's case, that village was Vorzel, where he met and married the priest's daughter, Katria Chervinska. Kyiv also did not welcome his authorial ambitions. The arbiters of ideological purity wouldn't publish his work, as publishing was entirely state-controlled, so he sent it abroad, where it appeared in the publications of the anti-Soviet Ukrainian diaspora, a step that raised further ideological suspicions against him. But with the about-face in policy that came with the implementation of the New Economic Policy and then Ukrainization, his fortunes improved dramatically. Within a few years, a number of his stories were published in Kyiv journals, and three small collections of stories appeared as separate books. Together with new-found friends in Kyiv — Ievhen Pluzhnyk, Hryhorii Kosynka, Borys Antonenko-Davydovych, and others — he formed a literary grouping that adhered to a fellow-traveler — that is, apolitical — position. Before long, they were in charge of an important Kyiv journal, *Zhyttia i revoliutsiia* (Life and revolution), with Pidmohylnyi as editor. Ukrainian literary life in Kyiv was now vibrant and contentious (as well as politically charged), and Pidmohylnyi was part of the action. But during the early 1920s, something was missing — the novel. Breathlessly emotional short stories, particularly about the recent years of wars and revolutions, were easy to create and thus abundant. A longer and more sober view took time to develop. And then, by the late 1920s, suddenly, everyone was writing novels. Pidmohylnyi's contribution to this stream was the work you are about to read: *Misto* (The city; 1928).

The novel was popular and cemented the author's reputation as a leading intellectual author. Pidmohylnyi rode a crest of popularity, and even traveled to Paris, Prague, Berlin, and Hamburg on a trip organized by the Commissariat of Education. He was also translating a great deal, mostly Guy de Maupassant and Anatole France. But the times were, once again, changing. His second novel, *Nevelychka drama* (A little drama; published in English translation by

George S. N. and Moira Luckyj as *A Little Touch of Drama*
in 1972), was serialized in the journal he edited, but it did
not appear in book form. Stalinism was taking hold. Pidmohylnyi was dismissed from his position as editor of the
journal. He moved from Kyiv to the eastern city of Kharkiv,
then the capital of Soviet Ukraine. No longer being published as an author, he worked tirelessly on translations
to support his wife and son. From Kharkiv, he witnessed
the progress of Stalin's dramatic attack against Ukraine:
show trials, Holodomor (the Great Famine), the suicides
of Mykola Khvyliovyi and Mykola Skrypnyk, among other
leading figures. Like most intellectuals, he was, no doubt,
waiting for the midnight knock on his own door. It came
on December 8, 1934. He was charged with membership
in a fabricated terrorist organization. He was interro-
gated and tortured for a month, sentenced to ten years'
imprisonment, and transported to the prison camp on
the Solovetsky Islands in the White Sea, in Russia's north.
On November 3, 1937, following a re-examination of his
case, he was secretly executed. In this, he shared the fate
of hundreds of other Ukrainian writers at that time.

Valerian Pidmohylnyi's *The City* is a landmark event in
the history of Ukrainian literature. First and foremost,
it is an exceptionally good novel, well written by a master
craftsman in full control of the texture, rhythm, and tone
of the text. The quality of the writing is, of course, tied to

the author's talent. But writing is also an acquired skill, and this novel displays better writing than Pidmohylnyi's earlier works. Much of the difference derives from the authors he was reading and translating — the nineteenth-century classics of French prose and some contemporary authors. The lessons learned can be summarized in three categories: construction, style, and themes. The basic plot of *The City* is clearly lifted from Guy de Maupassant's *Bel Ami*, which Pidmohylnyi had translated into Ukrainian. Maupassant's novel is about a young man from the provinces who rises to worldly success as a journalist in Paris by manipulating a series of powerful and influential women. Pidmohylnyi's hero, Stepan Radchenko, is not quite as corrupt or manipulative as his French counterpart, but he, too, achieves success as a writer through a succession of romantic encounters with women. It's not just the overall plot that is borrowed — many scenes, tropes, and devices are, as well. One example is names. Maupassant's Duroi renames himself Du Roi, to sound more aristocratic; Pidmohylnyi's Stepan becomes Stéfan — with stress moved to the first syllable — because, he wonders, "Wasn't he a king or something?" a reference to the sixteenth-century Polish king Stefan Batory (150). Both men are given pet names by their lovers — Bel-Ami for Georges and *bozhestvennyi* ("the divine one") for Stepan. Devices such as these and discipline in chapter construction give the novel a shape familiar to readers of Western European literature.

Style is also a lesson that Pidmohylnyi learned from his French models. Although Pidmohylnyi is writing in an age of modernist literature, his prose lacks some of the features that characterize modernism. If modernist prose is embodied by the writings of James Joyce, Marcel Proust, Virginia Woolf, and Mykola Khvyliovyi, and if modernist prose is experimental, ornate, subjective, densely allusive, and inscrutably complex, then Pidmohylnyi's novel belongs somewhere else. That somewhere else is, in fact, realism. Of course, Pidmohylnyi does share some features characteristic of modernism: irony, skepticism, and a retreat from blind faith in the rational powers of man. His writing is certainly not a throwback to the ethnographic realism that characterized Ukrainian prose in the nineteenth century. But in its clarity, precision, simplicity, and materiality, the style of *The City* is far closer to Honoré de Balzac, Guy de Maupassant, Gustave Flaubert, and Anatole France than to André Gide, Franz Kafka, Samuel Beckett, or William Faulkner. What distinguishes Pidmohylnyi is the fact that he writes about things, not emotions. For instance, we observe the number of pockets in a pair of trousers but not the experience of pain or joy. We walk the streets of a real city which we can trace on a map, and we flounder in the alphabet soup of various newly-formed Soviet institutions. The author exposes human psyches through actions rather than a stream of consciousness. His sentences have a logical structure, and his narrative is held together by development rather than association: X causes Y and leads to Z. Language is used as an instrument of sense, not ornamentation. Words appear in their basic meanings, not through prisms of symbols, sounds, or allusions. Even where the author allows himself an allusive and symbolic image, he hides it beneath a veil of visual reality. For example, in approaching Kyiv on a steamship at the beginning of the novel, Nadiika notices a sailboat with three boys and, with them, a girl in a veil who seems like someone from old fables. Old fables, indeed: her name is Lybid, the boys are her brothers, Kyi, Shchek, and Khoryv, and we are witnessing the legendary story of the founding of ancient Kyiv that is told in the Rus' Primary Chronicle. Yet it is not necessary to make this connection in order to enjoy the text: It could just be some folks enjoying a sunny day on the river.

As this example shows, Pidmohylnyi's realism does not come at the price of ignoring allusions, symbols, or emotions; they are built into the fabric of the text. Emotions in particular — the whole gamut of human relations — are a vital part of this novel. There is probably no other writer in Ukrainian literature whose characters are so completely informed by Freudian psychology, which Pidmohylnyi knew and wrote about. Repression and the subconscious are evident everywhere. But psyches are revealed through the actions of characters, not through self-analysis or the narrator's descriptions. Where modernists say things, realists show them.

The thematic palette of this novel is very wide, and only some of it comes from the French realists. Balzac and Maupassant did not invent the theme of rural conquest of urban space, but it is their example that has brought that theme into modern literature, and this novel in particular. Eugène de Rastignac and Stepan Radchenko are cut from the same cloth. But Stepan exists in a Soviet world, where rural-urban relations are not just a sociological curiosity but an ideological platform. The propaganda of the time called it "coupling," and Pidmohylnyi turns it into a joke in the novel. Yet here the topic has various dimensions, including Ukrainization, the official policy of expanding the role of Ukrainian language and culture in an otherwise Russified urban setting. Radchenko is a perfect choice for this function, but his general behavior, like that of his French cousins, is far from ideal, although in his case the iniquity is largely limited to his relations with women. He date-rapes Nadiika, crushes Musinka, and humiliates Zoska. However, unlike Maupassant's hero, he does not commit these offenses for the purpose of social advancement. His faults are emotional and instinctual, not purposeful or calculated. Indeed, his ascent in his career as a writer and in his material conditions are almost accidental: they are not the reward for his misdeeds.

Pidmohylnyi's depiction of Ukrainian literary life in the 1920s is, of course, unrelated to his French realist models. Some of this description is just realistic satire,

with vaguely recognizable figures and a searing indict-
ment of the personal rivalries, incompetence, unpro-
fessionalism, and ridiculous bureaucracy that characterized organized Soviet Ukrainian literary life. But it's
also an uplifting chronicle of the success of Ukrainian
culture and literature in Kyiv and all of Soviet Ukraine
in the 1920s. Ironically, the foolish hijinks of literary life
and improbable trajectory of Radchenko's literary career
are proof positive that Ukrainian literature had finally
arrived and taken its rightful place in Ukraine. Unlike the
martyrs and saints who struggled against repressions
in the Russian Empire to keep the candle of Ukrainian
writing flickering, Radchenko is part of a chaotic horde
of wannabe big shots trying to express themselves in
poetry and prose. Ukrainian literature, like every strong
national literature, is a disorganized mess within which
the unexpected gems of culture and talent can develop.

Perhaps the most important quality of this novel
is its profoundly philosophical core. The chief idea is
signaled in its two epigraphs. Man is both physical and
spiritual, instinctual and intellectual. This disharmo-
ny characterizes our existence in the world, where our
intellectual side expects rational order, whereas the instinctive natural world follows its own principles. The
result is alienation and disorientation, the basic principles of existential philosophy. In this, Pidmohylnyi is
much closer to his modern European counterparts than
to their nineteenth-century realist forebears. Nothing

is certain anymore. The first sentence of the novel tells us so: "It seemed you couldn't go any farther" (7). Of course, you can go farther, but it is not clear in advance where you are heading. This is a very complex problem involving reason and irrationality, and one that I have written about elsewhere.* Here I shall merely state that Pidmohylnyi sees unpredictability and uncertainty everywhere — that's why so many games of chance appear in this novel.

Pidmohylnyi's *The City* is many things, but, at its most basic, it is a novel about Kyiv, a great and ancient Ukrainian city that he lived in for barely a decade. It sits, as the novel makes clear, at the very heart of Ukrainian culture and identity. As I write these words, Russia is conducting a genocidal war against Ukraine. Kyiv is slowly being destroyed, because the Russian goal — a Ukraine that is not Ukrainian — cannot be achieved as long as Kyiv exists. We can only hope the Russians fail.

March 2022
Toronto

---

*   Maxim Tarnawsky, *Between Reason and Irrationality:*
The Prose of Valerijan Pidmohyl'nyj
(Toronto: University of Toronto Press, 1994).

THE CITY

Man has six qualities: in three he resembles an animal and in the other three he resembles an angel. Like an animal man eats and drinks, like an animal he procreates, and like an animal he expels waste; like an angel he has reason, like an angel he walks upright, and like an angel he speaks in a blessed language.

    Talmud, Avot (Aboth) tractate.

    [*Hagigah* 16A, in the *Mo`ed* seder]

How can one be free, Eucrites, when one has a body?

    Anatole France, *Thaïs*.

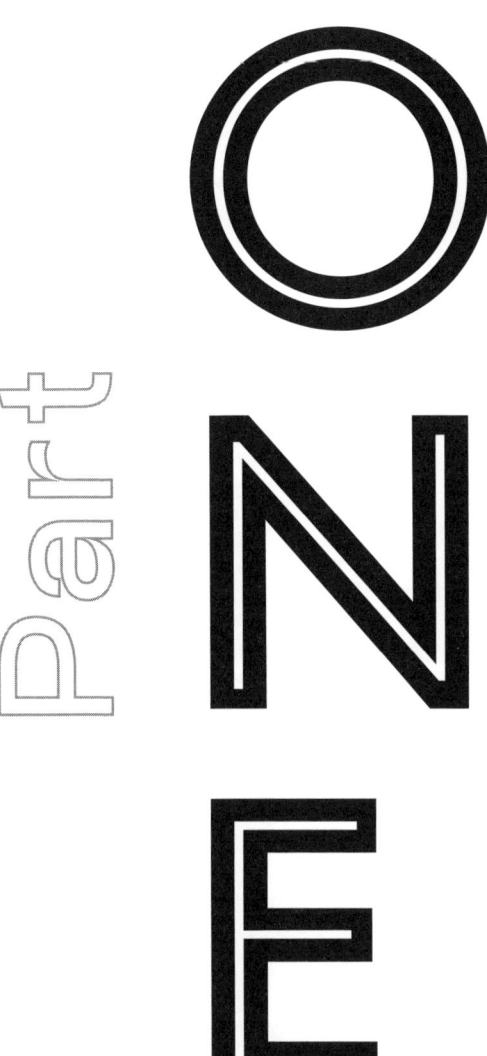

Part ONE

Chapter One

I t seemed you couldn't go any farther. Ahead, the Dnipro appeared to stop in an unexpected cove, surrounded on the right, on the left, and straight ahead by the yellowish-green banks of approaching autumn. But the steamboat suddenly turned and the long, smooth streak of the river stretched out to the barely visible hills on the horizon.

Stepan stood by the railing on the deck, his eyes unconsciously diving into the distance as the even strokes of the paddle-wheel blades and the dull sound of the captain's voice at the megaphone sapped the strength from his thoughts. They, too, stopped in that hazy distance where the river imperceptibly disappeared, as if the horizon were the final limit of his desires. The young man slowly looked at the near banks and was somewhat confused. At the bend, on the right, appeared a village, previously hidden behind the bank. The August sun wiped the dirt from the white houses and highlighted the black paths that ran into the fields and, turning blue like the river, just disappeared. And it seemed that this disappearing blue path joined the heavens in an endless field and returned by a second branch to the village, bringing to it some of that vast expanse. A third path rolled down to the river and carried back to the village the freshness of the Dnipro. The village slept in the midday sun, and there was a secret in that sleep amidst the natural elements that nourished it with their strength. Here, near the shore, the village seemed to be the tangible creation of the expanse of space, the magic flower of earth, sky, and water.

His own village, the one Stepan had left, also stood on a bank and now he unconsciously searched for some similarity between his own village and this one that happened to appear on his great journey. With happiness, he felt that this similarity was real and that here, in these houses, as in the ones he had left, he would have felt at home. With sadness, he watched the village melt and fade with every stroke of the engines, until the trail of grimy smoke hid it completely. Stepan sighed. Perhaps this was the last village he would see before the city.

In his soul, he felt an indistinct agitation and dizziness, as if in his own village and in all those he had seen he had left not only the past, but his faith in the future as well. Closing his eyes, he surrendered to the sadness that cradles the soul.

When he straightened up from the railing, he saw Nadiika. He hadn't heard her approach. He hadn't called her, but he was happy to see her. Quietly, he took her hand. Without raising her head, she shuddered and stared at the fan-like wake created by the prow of the steamboat.

They lived in the same village, but before now they had barely known each other. That is, he knew that she existed, that she studied hard, and that she did not go out. A few times he had even seen her in the Village Hall, where he was in charge of the library. But here they met as if for the first time, and the coincidence of their destinations cemented a bond between them. She was on her way to study in the big city, as he was. They both had travel papers in their pockets and before them lay a new life. Together, they were crossing the frontier of the future.

Actually, her prospects were somewhat more certain. She bragged that her parents would provide her with food. He was hoping for a stipend. She would be living with some girlfriends in their apartment. He had a letter from an uncle to a merchant he knew. Even her personality was more energetic, while he seemed withdrawn and lethargic. In the course of his twenty-five years he had been a sheep hand, then just a boy, then a rebel, and finally the administrator of the village bureau of the Robzemlis Trade Union of Agricultural and Forest Workers. He had only one advantage over her: he was bright and did not fear the entrance exam. Over the course of the day on the steamboat, he had managed to explain to her many of the more complex principles of the social sciences, and she had listened with rapture to the enchanting sound of his voice. Stepping away from him for a moment, she would experience a sudden boredom and new, still unexplained economic problems. But when he'd begin explaining them, she would want him to speak about something else, about his expectations, about how he had lived before they knew each other. However, all she would do was thank him for the helpful pointers, adding with assurance, "Oh, you'll get a stipend! You're so knowledgeable!"

He smiled. It was pleasant to hear praise and faith in his abilities from this blue-eyed girl. Indeed, Nadiika seemed to him to be the prettiest of all the women on the steamboat. The long sleeves of her gray blouse were more appealing to him than the bare arms of others. Her collar left visible only a narrow ribbon of flesh, while others shamelessly uncovered their shoulders and the incipient curves of their breasts. Her shoes were round, with moderate heels, and her knees weren't always jumping out from under her skirt. He was attracted by her unpretentiousness, which nicely complemented his own disdain for artificiality. His reaction to the other women was a mixture of contempt and fear. He felt that they weren't noticing him, or perhaps they were even scorning him for his faded field jacket, reddish cap, and threadbare pants. He was a tall, tanned, and well-built young man, but the short soft hairs on his face, unshaved for a week, gave him a slovenly appearance. He had bushy eyebrows, large gray eyes, a wide forehead, and sensitive lips. His dark hair was swept back in the style worn by many villagers and now adopted by some poets.

Stepan kept his hand on Nadiika's warm fingers and gazed pensively at the river, the curving sandy banks, and the solitary trees on the shore. Suddenly, Nadiika straightened up and, waving her hand, pronounced, "Kyiv isn't far now."

Kyiv! The big city, where he was going to study and live. It was that modernity that he must infiltrate to realize his long-cherished dream. Was Kyiv really close? Flustered, he asked, "Where's Levko?"

They looked around and saw a group of villagers who had spread out their lunch on the stern. On the cloak they had spread out as a tablecloth lay bread, onion, and *salo*—cured fatback. Levko, an agronomy student from Stepan's village, was sitting and eating with them. He was smooth and fatter than his height warranted, so in days gone by he would have made an ideal village priest—now, an exemplary agronomist. A villager himself from many generations back, he would be perfect at helping the villagers with a sermon or some scientific advice. He studied very diligently, always wore an overcoat, and, above all, liked to hunt. After two years of hunger and want in the city, he had formulated and developed a basic law of human existence. From the slogan popular during the Revolution, "whoever doesn't work, doesn't eat," he developed the corollary, "whoever doesn't eat doesn't work," and he applied this thesis at all times and in all circumstances. The villagers on the steamboat eagerly shared their simple meal with him, and, in return, he told them some interesting things about Mars, about farming in America, and about radios. They were amazed, and cautiously, with some derision and secretly disbelieving what he had told them, they asked him questions about these wonders and about God.

Levko came up to his young colleagues, smiling and swaying on his short legs. Smiling and being in good humor were his essential qualities, the measure of his attitude toward the world. Neither poverty nor education had managed to kill off the good nature that he had developed under the quiet willows of his village.

Stepan and Nadiika were already tying up their things. Just one more turn of the rudder and at the end of the sandy hills on the left side of the river emerged the gray outline of the city. Before the extended pontoon bridge, the steamboat let out a long cry and this piercing noise echoed painfully in Stepan's heart. For a moment he forgot the desires he was fulfilling and stared longingly at the stream of white steam above the whistle, which signaled the end of his past. And when the whistle suddenly stopped, his soul became quiet and lifeless. Somewhere deep inside he felt the foolish pressure of tears, totally inappropriate to his age and station, and he wondered that this moisture had not dried up during hard times and hard work, but instead had hidden and now stirred, unexpectedly and pointlessly. He reddened from embarrassment and turned away. But Levko noticed his distress. He put his arm on Stepan's shoulder.

"Don't worry, my boy," he said.

"It's nothing," answered Stepan, embarrassed.

Nadiika was showering Levko with questions—he had to identify every hill, every church, just about every building. But Levko proved to know little about the area. True, he could name the Lavra Monastery and the statue of Volodymyr, but he could not say for sure whether the hill on which the statue stood was called Volodymyr's. In Kyiv, he circulated in a limited and well-defined circle bounded by Lenin Street, where he lived, and the Institute. He almost never deviated from this path, except that three times each winter he would go to State Cinema No. 5 to see some American films, and every once in a while he would go hunting along the Kyiv–Teteriv line. Therefore, he was incapable of satisfying Nadiika's curiosity, which festered unchecked. The jumble of buildings, so brittle and comic from afar, charmed her, and her smile betrayed joy at the prospect of living in them.

But her attention was soon torn away from the city. She was watching the motorboats that thumped briskly along the river, and the rowboats, in which half-naked, tanned athletes exercised their muscles, smiled, and swayed on the waves of the steamboat's wake. Daring swimmers dove almost under the paddle-wheel itself, yelling merrily. Suddenly, like a white illusion, a three-masted schooner passed by the steamboat.

"Look, look!" yelled the girl, captivated by the unusual triangular sails. On the deck of the sailboat were three boys and a girl in a veil. She seemed a water nymph from old fables. She was beyond envy.

Closer to Kyiv, traffic on the river increased. Ahead was a beach, a sandy island in the middle of the Dnipro, where three motorboats ceaselessly ferried bathers from the harbor. The city flowed down from the hills to this shore. From Revolution Street down the wide stairs to the Dnipro rolled a colorful wave of boys, girls, women, men—a white and pink stream of moving bodies anticipating the sweet comfort of sunshine and water. There were no sad faces in this crowd. Here, at the edge of the city, began a new land, the land of primordial happiness. The water and sun welcomed everyone who had just abandoned pens and balance scales—every young lad as if he were Kyi, every young lass as if she were Lybid. Their pale bodies, oppressed by clothing for so many months, were now released from prison and blossomed into bronze languor on the hot sand, like savages lost on the banks of the Nile. Here, for a moment, they were resurrected into primal nakedness, and only their flimsy bathing suits marked the passage of a few millennia.

The contrast between the dour buildings on the shore and this untroubled bathing seemed to Nadiika both shocking and enchanting. In these opposites, she recognized the breadth of urban life and its possibilities. The girl did not hide her excitement. She was blinded by the multicolored costumes, the range of body colors, from pale pink, only just exposed to the sun for the first time, to dark brown, well baked by the intense summer sun. She repeated avidly, "O how pretty! O how pretty!"

Stepan did not share her excitement at all. For him, the spectacle of a naked, thoughtless mob was deeply displeasing. The fact that Nadiika, too, was willing to join this silly, mindless herd affected him negatively. He said, gruffly, "Foolish caprice."

Levko looked at the people with more compassion. "They sit in their cubbyholes all day and go nuts."

Having climbed down to the shore in a crowd, Stepan and his friends stepped aside to let the other passengers go ahead. Nadiika's excitement had withered. The city, which had looked sun-bleached and airy from afar, now hung over them, dark and heavy. They glanced around timidly. She was deafened by the cries of petty-trade women, whistles, buses clanging on their way to Darnytsia, and the rhythmic gasp of a steam engine at a nearby mill.

Stepan rolled a cigarette with his cheap tobacco and smoked it. He had a habit of spitting after lighting up, but here he swallowed the bitter tobacco and dust-flavored saliva. Everything around him was strange and alien. He saw the shooting gallery, where air guns were being fired, stalls with ice cream, beer, and kvas, petty-trade women with rolls and seeds, boys with irises, girls with baskets of apricots and morellos. Hundreds of faces floated past him, some happy, some serious, some troubled. Somewhere a woman was yelling because she had been robbed. Children at play were making a racket. This was how it usually was here, and how it was when his feet were still treading the soft dust of the village, and how it would continue to be. And to all of this he was a stranger.

All the passengers had dispersed. Freight was being unloaded from the steamboat. Half-naked stevedores were climbing the long ramps with crates, bags, and fruits. Then they carried carcasses of beef and rolled smelly, tarred barrels off the boat.

Levko led Stepan and Nadiika, showing them the way. At Revolution Street, their paths diverged: Stepan was headed into the Podil, the other two into the Old City.

"You can move in with me, if there's any problem," said Levko. "Did you write down the address?"

Stepan quickly bid them farewell and turned right, occasionally asking passersby for directions. At a bookstore, he stopped in front of the display window and began to examine the books. They had been dear to him from an early age. Even before he learned to read, still just a child, he would page through the only book that graced his uncle's study—an ancient journal of some kind, with endless portraits of the tsar, archbishops, and generals. Yet it wasn't the pictures but the rows of evenly spaced black marks that had caught his eye. He didn't even remember how hc learned to read—accidentally, it seemed. Then he would pronounce the words with delight, although he still didn't understand what they meant.

He stood for a long time by the window, reading the titles of the books one by one, the names of their publishers, and their dates. Some, he thought, would be useful to him at the Institute. But the mass of volumes, among which he recognized only one that he had read, made a strange impression on him. They seemed to embody everything that was strange, everything that frightened him, all the dangers that he had to overcome in the city. Contrary to reason, and to all his earlier calculations, desperate thoughts—at first formulated as questions—began to assault him. Why did he have to come here? How was he going to live? He would wither here. He would return home a beggar. Why didn't he sign up for the education courses in the provincial town near his village? What was the point of these childish dreams of Kyiv and the Institute? The young man stood before the modest Podil bookstore, which to him appeared so brilliant, and seemed to be wavering whether he should return to the dock.

"I'm just tired after the long trip," he surmised.

This fatigue also accounted, he thought, for the weariness of his muscles and the unwillingness to move that overcame him here. But he considered himself a messenger charged with an unusually important but alien assignment. His old desires suddenly felt like someone else's commands, to which he was surrendering but not without a quiet resentment. He went on under the power of his momentarily faded but still tenacious dreams.

He found number 37 on Nyzhnii Val Street, opened the gate, crossed the yard, stepped up to the veranda, and knocked on the worm-eaten door. After a moment, the door was opened by a man in a waistcoat with a short beard and graying hair. This was the fish merchant Luka Demydovych Hnidyi, who, in the early years after the Revolution, when the cities were poor and hungry, set up the base of his commercial enterprise in Stepan's native village, Tereveni, where he invariably stayed at the home of Stepan's uncle. Now the fish merchant was to repay these past favors, although times had changed and the past was not so pleasant that anyone willingly recalled it. He glanced at Stepan apprehensively over the top of his glasses, nervously tore open the envelope, glanced at the letter, and silently walked into the house, reading it.

Stepan was left alone in front of the open door. His bundle was eating into his shoulder, and he put it down. He waited a few moments and then sat down on the porch himself. The street before him was empty. In the time since he had arrived, no pedestrians had appeared on the street, only a wagon had rolled by with the driver barely holding the reins. Stepan started to roll a cigarette, focusing all his attention on it, like a person who wishes to fight off insistent but irrelevant thoughts.

Slowly he licked the edge of the cheap, thick cigarette paper, carefully sealed his creation, and then admired his work. The cigarette came out surprisingly straight, with a sharp point at the end to make it easier to light. He put it in his mouth and, pushing aside the tail of his jacket, he reached into the deep and only pocket of his pants—on the other side, the tailor had not wasted extra material, assuming quite correctly that there were people for whom one pocket was sufficient. Following this tailor's example, nature could save an eye or an ear on many a person, as the myths about Cyclopes suggest. Rummaging through the treasures in his pocket—a knife, an old coin purse, an unexpected button, and a handkerchief—he pulled out a box of matches, but it was completely empty. He had used the last match on the dock. Stepan threw down the box and crushed it with his boot.

Because he couldn't smoke, Stepan wanted to smoke all the more. He got up and went over to the gate, looking around for a passing smoker. But this Podil street was, as before, deserted. A row of low, old-fashioned buildings stretched to the riverbank, where it ended in dilapidated, long-unpainted shacks. A solitary poplar, denuded by age, reached up awkwardly in front of a window.

Suddenly someone on the porch called him by name, and he shuddered as if caught committing a crime. It was Hnidyi calling him.

"I shall live here," thought Stepan, and this thought seemed as strange to him as the poplar he had just seen.

Yet Hnidyi did not lead him into the house, but deep into the yard, to a shed. Stepan walked behind him and stared at his back. The shopkeeper was somewhat hunchbacked and had thin legs. He was not tall, but his skinny legs seemed long and stiff. And a thought occurred to Stepan: How easy it would be to break such legs!

At the shed, Hnidyi turned the lock, opened the door, and said, "You'll stay here."

Stepan glanced over Hnidyi's shoulder into the tiny nook. It was a small carpentry shop. By the wall was a workbench; on the shelves above lay various tools. On another wall a flimsy window cast its shadow into the room. There was a scent of sawdust and fresh wood. The youth was so surprised by his new quarters that he even asked, "Is this it?"

With keys jingling, Hnidyi turned his glasses toward him. "You won't need it for long, will you?" His face was all wrinkled. There was something of a victim in his eyes.

Stepan timidly entered and put his things in the corner. Bending down, he caught a glimpse of his neighbors through the cracks between the boards of the partition—a pair of cows calmly chewing their cud by a manger. A barn! That's where he was supposed to live! Like an animal! Like cattle! He felt his chest tightening and blood rushing to his face. He straightened up, red-faced and insulted. Stepan looked at Hnidyi's pale face, behind which there seemed to be neither desire nor idea, and, with a sense of his own superiority, said, "Give me a match—I need a light."

Hnidyi shook his head. "I don't smoke... And you be careful, too—there's wood here."

Hnidyi closed the door and for a while the jingle of his keys was audible in the distance. Stepan paced about his nook in long strides. Each step was a threat. He had not expected this kind of humiliation. He was prepared for hunger and poverty—but not livestock. True, he had tended cows once. But now, after the Revolution, after all the uprisings, some shopkeeper—this stick-legged nothing—has the right to shoo him off into a barn?

The little window in the shed grew darker with the sudden nightfall of this still-summery evening. Stepan stopped and looked out. Above a row of identical roofs, a factory smokestack stretched into the sky. Black plumes of smoke blended imperceptibly into the gray-blue dusk, as if penetrating the sky to reach into the depths of the universe.

His cigarette had already torn open between his fingers and the tobacco was spilling onto the floor. He rolled another and stepped out into the yard. So he'll go into the house, find the kitchen, and get himself a light. What's there to be ashamed of? After all, they're people, too! But there was a youth sitting on the veranda, and when Stepan bent over to get a light from his cigarette, the youth said, "Have one of mine."

Stepan was surprised, but he took the cigarette. Inhaling the smoke, he took a closer look at the youth, who was carelessly exhaling rings of smoke. When Stepan thanked him, the fellow nodded as if he were deep in thought and would be sitting here until morning.

Stepan lay down on the workbench in his room and enjoyed the fragrant smoke of the cigarette, which was intoxicating him. He closed his eyes and dreamily concluded that everything was fine. The fact that he was in a barn now seemed merely comical. He knocked twice on the wall to the cows, laughed, and opened his eyes. Above the smokestack in the window hung a bright new moon.

Chapter Two

Outside, the sun had risen when Stepan awoke and got up on the workbench. His body was numb from lying on the bare wood, but he paid no attention to this languor and rubbed his eyes with apprehension. Today was the day of the entrance exam. Had he overslept? Remembering that the exam was scheduled for one o'clock, he felt calmer and stretched. His neck ached and he rubbed it with his hand.

A quiet, monotonous gurgling came from beyond the partition that separated his quarters from the stables. The cows were being milked. This calmed him completely—it was still early. He sat on the workbench, his hands on his knees, and his uncombed head bowed down in recollection. Yesterday's details stretched before him in a bright thread. Perhaps it was back in his days as a stableboy, lying in the field and weaving whips or baskets, that he had developed this habit of self-reflection.

Now, remembering the previous day, he was disappointed with himself. He noted a certain inner hesitation, a small, albeit fleeting, uncertainty—in short, what is known as faintheartedness. But in his own mind he had no right to that feeling. He was part of that new force called from the villages for creative work. He must courageously take his place among those who would replace the rancid past and courageously build the future. He was now ashamed of that fragrant cigarette—it was like some young gentleman's castoff.

Stepan tossed back the hair falling on his forehead and quickly began to dress. He shook out his field jacket, rubbed his pants with his elbow to knock off some of the dust, and untied his packages. They held some food, a military overcoat in the old tsarist style, and a change of underwear. Having emptied one sack onto the floor, he used it to wipe his shoes; then he spit on them, and buffed them again. Now he was thoroughly prepared.

Rather than wash now—which was, in any case, impossible—he decided to bathe in the Dnipro after taking the exam and turned his thoughts to breakfast. His supplies included three flatbreads, almost twenty pounds of wheat flour, maybe four pounds of salo, a dozen cooked eggs, and a bag of buckwheat. Unexpectedly, a couple of potatoes rolled out of his sack, and our boy laughed aloud at this find. He laid out all his edibles on the table and, for the sake of order, untied his field kettle from the sack and set that beside them. He was about to cut some bread when he remembered morning exercise. He definitely wanted to start his day normally, the urban way, as if he were already completely at home in his new surroundings. It was important to give yourself a routine straight off. Discipline and order were the best guarantors of achievement!

Stepan got up and looked around for an appropriate object for his exercise. He picked up the bench and lifted it a few times, admiring his agility and muscle tone. Putting it down, he was still not satisfied. Feeling his biceps lovingly, he jumped up and, taking hold of a low joist, began doing pull-ups with ever-increasing speed and enthusiasm. When he finally jumped back down to the floor, crimson with effort and satisfaction, he turned toward the door and saw a woman with a milking pail in her hands. She was staring at him with a frightened, troubled expression.

"I slept here," he muttered. "I have their permission."

She was silent. Stepan felt unsure of himself—not because he didn't have his jacket on or because during his exercise his shirt had come out of his belt like a little child's. No, for him clothing was only a safeguard against the cold. But he understood that, in this instance, the exercise had exceeded proper limits and turned into a silly game unbecoming of his dignity or position. And then this milkmaid will likely wag her tongue and say that he was trying to climb into the loft in order to steal something. He tossed back his hair and, considering the conversation closed, wanted to get on with his breakfast, but she entered his room, looked at his things, and put the milk pail on the ground.

"Was it very uncomfortable sleeping here?" she asked in a sad, listless voice, running her hand over the workbench.

"N-Yeah," grumbled Stepan unhappily.

But she wasn't leaving. What does she want, exactly? What is this—some kind of inspection? He took on an unmistakably dour appearance.

"I'm the lady of the house," the woman explained, finally. "Would you like some milk?"

The mistress! And she milks the cows herself? Sure, now it's not so easy to boss around the organized proletariat! Of course, from a milkmaid—one of his own—Stepan would have accepted the offer of milk, but if it's an act of charity from the mistress—no thank you!

"I don't want milk," he answered.

But the mistress, without waiting for his answer, was already pouring him some.

"You can wash in the yard, there's a faucet there," she added, taking up the milk pail.

Stepan looked after her. She had a thick, round back—abundance was evident in her shape. He angrily put on his jacket and buttoned it. He sliced off some salo and started his breakfast, his thoughts turning to his exam. He had nothing to be afraid of. Math—he had an excellent command of it. To test himself, he recited the formula for the area of all geometric figures, binomial expressions, and the relations of trigonometric functions. And, although he was unwittingly remembering precisely what he knew best, he was nevertheless pleased with the clarity of his knowledge. About the social sciences there was no concern at all. He had listened to so many lectures back in the village, and he had read the newspaper every day. And all this was in addition to his social background, his revolutionary credentials, and his professional work. All in all, he was well-armed on the educational front.

A look through his documents also left him content. In this pile of papers lay his entire life over the last five years—a rebel under the hetman, fighting the White bands, cultural and professional work. He even read some of it with interest. What couldn't you find here! There was his capture, imprisonment, and escape from execution. There were demonstrations, agitation, resolutions, the battle with ignorance and with homebrew. And how pleasant it was to see all this documented with seals, stamps, the straight lines of a typewriter and the clumsy squiggles of semi-literate hands.

Stepan got up energetically, put his documents in his pocket, sharpened a pencil with his pen-knife, and prepared some paper. It was time to go. Covering his food with a sack, he stopped by the milk. He was, in fact, very thirsty. Salo and bread really need something liquid. And the milk would go rancid in this heat, anyway. He grabbed the cup, emptied it with one gulp, and threw it contemptuously on the workbench. Even a scrawny lamb will yield some sheepskin.

He stepped out into the yard, latched the hook on the door, and set off down the street. Before going to the Institute, he wanted to stop in at the trade union offices to see about possible jobs. Today, for some reason, it was easy for him to find his way around the city and he gave it little mind. Troubled with the important matters of settling down in a new place, he observed himself more than his surroundings.

Among the hundreds of offices at the Palace of Labor Stepan barely managed to find the division he was looking for—Agricultural and Forest Workers. Considering his business sufficiently urgent, he decided to go straight to the director of the division. It turned out he must wait, but this didn't trouble him excessively: first, it was only ten o'clock, and second, he was sitting on a bench waiting along with other visitors, an equal among equals. Borrowing his neighbor's newspaper and wasting no time, he became familiar with the most recent developments in the international situation, and, judging them to be propitious for the Union of Republics, went on to the "Village Affairs" pages. Here, he found captivating reading. Learning that in the village of Hlukhari, at the request of the village council, an unreliable agronomist was fired from his job, Stepan sorrowfully reflected, "That's what we needed in our village! But our people just sit like bumps on a log."

He diligently read about pilfering at the village co-operative in Kindrativka, about the battle against home-brew in the Kaharlyk region, and about the exemplary breeding station in the town of Radomyshl. Each fact and figure he compared to his own village, and in the end concluded that its situation was, by and large, no worse than anywhere else.

"We need cultural cadres, that's what we need," Stepan reasoned. He was glad that he had abandoned the thatched roofs only temporarily, for three years. After that, he would return well-armed to do battle with homebrew, pilfering, and the inertia of the local administration.

At last it was his turn to speak to the director of the division. Stepan crossed the threshold anxious that the face he would encounter in the chair behind the desk might be too unfamiliar, along with soft furniture and a carpeted floor. After all, this was Kyiv! But his first glimpse set his mind at ease. The office furnishings were not much different from those of the regional committee, which served simultaneously as an office for all the regional administrators. Except maybe the sofa against the wall: such a luxury would have been unthinkable out there, but even if there had been a sofa, there likely wouldn't have been a free spot to sit down on it.

The director of the division was a straightforward man—but after hearing out Stepan, he was very surprised. Didn't Stepan, an experienced employee of the Agricultural and Forest Workers' Trade Union at the regional level, know where such matters were handled? First, he must register with the local office as a transient member, and then take his place with the others in the job lottery. There was a well-established and well-known procedure for matters of this sort, and you couldn't just go about wasting your time and the valuable time of busy administrators on things like this.

Stepan left his office somewhat perplexed. The director hadn't told him anything he didn't already know. But—that was the "usual" procedure. Stepan had secretly hoped that in his case an exception would be made—at least on account of his active participation in the Revolution and his exemplary service in the trade union. Besides, he had been sent off to obtain a higher education and deserved consideration ahead of the others. Yet the director hadn't even asked to see his documents. That was unfortunate. But after all, you had to admit that this way was even-handed and fair. No one should receive special favors.

Stepan found the job lottery desk and discovered that it only operated on Wednesdays and Fridays. This happened to be Monday. Such was the procedure, and no changes could be made, even for the newly arrived. A bulletin had been sent to all the regional centers, the clerk told him. What's more, she pointed out to him the list of documents necessary to register for the lottery, and Stepan realized, to his horror, that he was missing some of them and could not immediately produce them.

As hopeful as he had been entering the Palace of Labor, he was equally gloomy leaving it. It immediately became evident to him that he would find no job here. He was only one among hundreds. While he collected the necessary documents, others would get all the jobs. And then, was there really any sense in entering the lottery? They'd tell him that he was here to study, not to work. He should have government support. He should be looking into stipends. That, indeed, was how it should be. He did not blame anyone.

Out on the street, he suddenly had an idea. What if he just walked into some larger institution? Perhaps they just happened, by sheer coincidence, to be looking for a young, savvy accountant or registrar? Just walk in and ask—it's not a crime. At worst they'll say no and he'll leave. And what if it works? This idea excited him. In his heart, he had a strong sense of his destiny—it's natural for everyone to consider himself the only creature under the sun and moon. He turned in the direction of a large veranda over which hung a large banner, "State Publishing House of Ukraine," and quickly made his way to the second floor. In the first room a few young men were engaged in conversation on the sofa, a typewriter was clattering in the corner, tall bookcases lined the walls. Stepan stopped for a moment and then went on, assuming a carefree manner to avoid being stopped too soon. His eyes searched for a sign that said "supervisor," which he didn't find until he reached the third room. He was ready to grasp the doorknob when the man sitting nearby examining a pile of manuscripts suddenly said, "The supervisor is not in—what's your business, Comrade?"

Taken aback, Stepan mumbled, "I've come on business," and retreated with equal carelessness. Near the exit he heard words that were obviously said about him, "Probably brought a bag full of poems."

And then there was laughter. At the door, Stepan turned and saw the person who had spoken, one of the young men sitting on the sofa, a dark fellow in a gray shirt with narrow stripes. Going down the stairs, he mulled over these puzzling words.

"What poems? What do poems have to do with anything?"

But his enthusiasm did not abandon him. And, although in the second institution he was again unable to get through to the supervisor, and in the third he was shown a list of dismissed employees in the very first room, he nonetheless entered a fourth. The director was in his office and received Stepan.

There was soft furniture and a huge, massive clock on the wall, but the director was young and not an ogre. Destiny was smiling on Stepan. The director invited him to sit down and listened him out to the end. Then, he lit a cigarette, and said, "I've learned this on my own skin. I'm a Red director, after all. Promoting employment for the worker and peasant youth is our most important task.

That's the only way to cure the ills of our society. We know that it's only the young who will have the strength to build socialism. Come back in two or three months—"

Leaving this commercial institution, Stepan could hardly hold back the insult he felt. The director's gracious welcome exasperated him to the core. He sensed that all doors would close before him like that—some with no hope and others with saccharine politeness. Two or three months! With one *chervinets* and three flatbreads! In a pigsty at the mercy of a merchant! Shoving his hands into the pockets of his jacket, Stepan pushed his way through the crowd of pedestrians, avoiding any eye contact. It seemed everyone was ready to pronounce a harsh judgment of him—a failure.

The clock on the building of the district executive committee stopped the bustle of his unhappy thoughts. It was a quarter to twelve and the exam began at one o'clock. Hurriedly asking for directions to the Institute as he went, Stepan forged ahead. The clarity of his immediate goal—the exam—quickly settled him down. If he failed the exam, what need would he have of any job? But, in his heart, he was powerfully sure of passing the exam and imagining the other possible outcome gave him a sweet sensation, like a pleasant joke. In rhythm with his confident steps, he easily quieted his agitated thoughts. It was silly to imagine that he need only show up and everyone should be bowing to serve him. He must understand that he has entered into a pattern of life that has been unrolling for hundreds of years. There are no more good fairies and magicians, and there never were any. Only endurance and hard work can accomplish anything. And the dream of gaining a place in the city machinery by a single assault now seemed childish to him. He explained to himself that first he must write the exam, earn a stipend, and study, and the rest would follow. There are student organizations, guilds, cafeterias. For this, one must be a student. And, you must remember—there are thousands like you!

In the corridors of the Institute there was such a mob that Stepan was swept up in spite of himself. Falling into the mighty stream of humanity, he could only let himself be taken he knew not where or why. Only when the stream dispersed at an auditorium was he able to ask where the exams would be taking place. It turned out that they were to take place exactly here, and that they were about to begin. But Stepan was no sooner calmed by this news than his neighbor asked him, "And you, my friend, have you gone through the screening committee?"

Screening committee? No, Stepan had heard nothing of it. Is it required? Where is it? The third floor?

Forcing his way through the crowd with all his might, Stepan reached the stairs and ran up to the third floor. And what if he was too late and the committee had closed down? Searching for employment, indeed! Red with shame and agitation, he entered the screening committee room—no, they were still in session. He was written down as number one hundred twenty-three.

Four hours later, Stepan had cleared the screening committee and was assigned an examination session the day after tomorrow. Hungry and disenchanted, he headed home sluggishly. He understood perfectly that a screening committee was an absolute necessity and that you could not possibly examine in one day all of the five hundred candidates sent off to the Institute. But logical explanations did not stir his sympathies. He began to understand that order is pleasant only when you willingly apply it to yourself, but altogether unpleasant when it is applied to you by someone else. He was tired out. The empty day tomorrow frightened him.

Descending down to the Podil, he turned to the Dnipro to have a bath, as he had planned in the morning. Along the way he bought a box of matches, and, although he very much wanted to smoke, he was afraid that it would make him nauseous. First he would bathe, then have a bite to eat, and only then would he indulge in a cigarette. But he had no luck with bathing. This could only be done on the beach, which is to say he would have had to take the ferry over to the island. That cost five kopecks by rowboat, ten by motorboat. Two kopecks for the matches plus five—that would make seven kopecks! Such expenses were beyond his means, since, besides his expectations—which, after all, might come to nothing—he had only one chervinets, that is, ten *karbovanets* to protect him from the misery and misfortune that might beset him in the city. Perhaps he would have to return home to the village—he would need money for the ticket. He doggedly persuaded himself that such things had to be kept in mind.

At first, he had the idea of following the shoreline far out of town, where he could bathe in a deserted spot before returning to his nook. But his body was exhausted: hunger was spreading a terrible languor through his muscles, and he decided just to wash up. Stepan took off his cap, unbuttoned his collar, and, looking around sheepishly, dipped his hands into the water. His body shook. The water felt so slimy and unpleasant. But he forced himself to wash, dried himself with an oily handkerchief and slowly went back to his Nyzhnii Val Street.

In his nook, everything was as he had left it. Stepan forced himself to swallow a couple of eggs and greedily rolled a cigarette. But he couldn't even smoke—the dryness in his throat and awful spasms forced him to throw away the cigarette and crush it under his boot. Utterly worn out, he took off his field jacket, spread it on the workbench and stretched his entire length on the boards, with his legs dangling off the end. Without any effort to focus his thoughts, he stared dumbly at the dusk in the window. The same chimney was spreading a blanket of smoke across the gray sky.

Chapter Three

After lunch the next day, Stepan set out for Levko's. Only yesterday he would have found it unpleasant to encounter an acquaintance, but today he wanted to see someone, to have a conversation. In the morning, he took some bread, salo, a few potatoes, and some buckwheat and wandered off along the riverbank a long way out of the city. He had gone quite a distance, maybe three kilometers from the harbor, searching for a spot where there weren't any people. A few times he was ready to make his camp but then suddenly he would come upon a fisherman or a petty-trade woman waiting for the ferryman. It was hard to avoid your fellow man here, but Stepan patiently walked on, leaving even his view of the city far behind the bend in the river.

Finally, he reached a small cove between steep banks where it was peaceful and deserted. Here, he took off his shoes and field jacket, cut down two thick branches, and set up his pot. He gathered some dry grass, started the fire beneath his pot, rinsed the buckwheat, peeled the potatoes, and diced the salo. The gruel was cooking. Stepan put a few more sticks on the fire, undressed, and lay down on the bank in the warm morning sun. From afar, the monastery chimes rang out every quarter hour, and this ringing, along with the gentle lapping of the water, brought the young man peace and sadness.

Then, abruptly, he got up and jumped into the water. He swam, rolled, dove, and yelled for joy. Afterwards, wild with hunger, without even getting dressed, he sat down to his gruel. It had thickened and was slowly bubbling. With a sharpened stick, he impulsively hunted the potatoes and pieces of salo and swallowed them without chewing. Then, having no spoon, he greedily dipped pieces of bread into the thick mass of buckwheat and shoveled them into his mouth. In a moment, the pot was empty and its sides were polished clean, down to the last grain. And the diner himself lay nearby on his jacket, covered with his shirt. The heat was weighing down his eyelashes. He fell asleep before he could even have a smoke.

He awoke just as easily. Over his head the color of the sky was slowly changing, and a shiver that seemed to come out of the river ran across his body. He was now lying in the shadow of a hill behind which the sun had passed. The chill had awakened him. He got up, rubbed his eyes, and mechanically began to dress. This pointless sleeping had left behind a muddiness in the mind and a weariness of the muscles.

Later, Stepan sat down on the riverbank in the sun, which had long passed noon. Here, in the clear silence of the last days of summer, he was overcome with a painful feeling of solitude. He did not know its source or exact name, but every one of his thoughts dragged behind it a sticky weight and eventually broke off, empty and defeated. This was his first experience of such inescapable helplessness, and it breathed into his soul a dark premonition of death. His eyes stretched across the water to that place where he had grown, struggled, and desired. The wind-swept, deserted, sandy riverbanks that stretched before him reminded him of the peacefulness of the village and added to his sorrow. On the other side of the hill he could sense the city, and himself as one of the countless unnoticed bodies amidst the stone and the orderliness. On the doorstep of what he desired, he saw himself as an outcast who had abandoned the springtime and fields of blooming flowers of his native land.

Immediately he thought of Nadiika. The memory of her that was hiding within him seemed to suddenly blossom in the passionate longings of his loneliness. She had been hiding from him, coquettishly, but now she emerged from that concealment, fragrant and cheerful. The erstwhile touch of her hand sent a living fire through his veins. He recalled their meeting on the steamboat and the words she had spoken, seeking in them the assurance he yearned for. Her every glance and smile was now illuminating his soul, clearing there the twisted paths of love.

"Oh, you'll get a stipend. You're so knowledgeable!"

Yes, indeed! He was gifted and strong. He knew how to persevere. Where obstacles could not be pushed aside with a good push of the shoulders, he would wear them away with patience. Days, months, even years! Let her but lean toward him—together they would enter the gates of the city as conquerors!

"Nadiika," he whispered.

Her name itself meant hope, and he repeated it as a symbol of his impending victory.

Stepan returned home quickly, captivated by a single thought—his sudden girlfriend. She had erased all of his troubles, like a true enchantress, by becoming herself the most important objective that had to be attained. The desire to meet with her was so compelling that he determined to visit her right away.

At home, while he was straightening his field jacket and polishing his shoes with the spit-softened sack, hesitation began to engulf him. It was true that Nadiika had been very sweet to him on the steamboat and had invited him to come visit. But she had also been very happy—didn't that mean she already had a boyfriend? But he quickly corrected this frightening thought. After all, Nadiika was in this city, as he was, for the first time. Maybe she had met someone and fallen in love in the two days since they had arrived? That love could spring up suddenly he knew from his own experience. Perhaps she had even seen something in him, but now what could he, a homeless wretch, use to strengthen her feelings for him? So he'll go visit her as a pitiful villager in the midst of the boisterous city. And what will he say? What can he bring? He wants to lean on her but women themselves seek someone to lean on.

Stepan weighed his options at length, sitting on a bench, and decided to visit her only after he had passed the exam. He would come to his beloved as a student, not as a village bumpkin. He would say, "Here's what I have accomplished and what I am worth." This settled him down, but he could no longer sit at home, so he decided to visit Levko.

Fortunately, he found Levko at home. The first thing that struck Stepan was the absolute orderliness in the student's humble quarters. The furnishings were far from ostentatious: a small painted chest, a simple table, a folding bed, two chairs, and homemade shelves on the wall. But the table was covered with clean gray paper, the books on it were arranged in neat piles, the trunk was topped with a red-and-black checked tablecloth, the window was adorned with an embroidered curtain, and the bedding was neatly folded away. Up above hung the largest and most important decoration and the inhabitant's prize possession—a shotgun and leather cartridge case. The evenly hung line of portraits on the wall—Shevchenko, Franko, Lenin—each draped with an embroidered cloth, projected an atmosphere of quiet, deliberate contemplation. Envy and consternation overcame Stepan as he entered this tidy apartment.

The inhabitant himself was in an undershirt, working over a book at the table, but he welcomed his guest sincerely, sat him down on one of the chairs, and began to inquire how he had managed to set up his own affairs. Stepan could not subdue his shame. He replied, briefly, that he had set himself up well, that he was living in a room that was free during the summer, where the family expected to settle a distant relative in the fall. He had nothing to complain about, for the moment. He expected to earn a fellowship soon and would move into an apartment, likely in the building of the Committee for the Improvement of Student Housing (KUBUCh), as soon as he was registered as a student. The entrance exam was tomorrow, and he wasn't at all worried about it. Besides, he could count on some recognition for his participation in revolutionary activity.

"And what about you? You have a nice place?" asked Stepan hesitantly, full of respect for Levko.

Levko smiled. This apartment was paid for in suffering. When he was assigned to these quarters a year and a half ago, the owners had greeted him as if he were a wild animal. They refused to give him water, and they locked the washroom. They were an elderly couple, both former teachers. The husband used to teach Latin in high school, but since Latin was now cut from the curriculum, he worked in the archives for three chervinets. Later, they had slowly got to know each other. Now they were friends. They drank tea together, and, if he really needed to cook something, they let him. They were nice people, but very old-fashioned.

"You'll see for yourself in a minute," he said. "We'll all have tea together."

Stepan started excusing himself—he wasn't hungry! But the student didn't listen to him, slowly put on his shirt and, without even tying his belt, sailed out of the room.

"Well, here's the tea! Let's go," he announced happily.

He dragged the embarrassed Stepan by the hand, with the latter only pretending to resist, since he truly wanted to meet people from the city and to get acquainted with them. Levko could not substitute for the real thing, since he, too, like Stepan, would return to the village eventually after spending some time in the city, perhaps not accidentally but still only temporarily. Flustered, but with a firm resolve to observe and listen more than to speak, he entered the room of a real urban person—and a former high school teacher at that!

The room presented a strange collection of the most diverse things, which seemed to have come from various other rooms, huddled here in terror, and become petrified. Since there was absolutely not enough room for all of them, they stood in an odd crowd along the walls or simply in the middle of the floor. The edge of a wide double bed peeked out from under a short screen. Its head abutted a bookcase, in which faded brown cardboard covered the panels where glass had once been. A large wooden sideboard with high relief carving stood next to the bookcase and prevented its doors from opening properly. The top of the sideboard leaned against the wall, without which it would lose its balance. Farther along the wall, under the window, were shelves full of sheet music, although there was no piano in the house. At an angle to the window, which was partially obscured by its edge, stood a tall, mirrored wardrobe—the only thing that retained its original, clean appearance. Symmetrically across from the bed stood a tall, worn Turkish divan. On its wide back, topped with a long wooden surface, a gramophone, surrounded on both sides by even piles of records, raised its lonely horn toward the ceiling.

In a corner just by the door stood a small black stove, a "bourgeois," whose function was to heat the room in the winter, while in the summer it was only used to cook meals. A wide chimney-pipe, attached to the ceiling, stretched directly from the stove to the middle of the room, then turned and wound its way to the wall, where it disappeared above the bookcase. The room was big, but diminished by all the objects it contained, leaving hardly any space in the middle for a small card table, which served as the dining table and seemed lilliputian next to its colossal neighbors. The tea was laid out on it in a sooty blue teapot, with four cups, a bowl of sugar, and a few slices of bread on a plate.

Levko introduced the owners. Andrii Venedovych was a lively old man whose face was overgrown with gray hair. His hands and gracious bow betrayed a certain pomp and self-respect. His wife, however, was missing a few teeth, so Stepan could not make out her words of welcome. This hunchbacked woman with a dry-skinned face and trembling hands invited everyone to sit down in her incomprehensible gurgle and began carefully to serve the tea.

Andrii Venedovych praised Stepan for his intention to study but criticized the current educational programs and the fact that the old, experienced teachers had been dismissed. Suddenly he asked, "Do you know Latin?"

Stepan felt uncomfortable as the object of the owner's undivided attention and blushed. He honestly admitted that he knew a Latin language had once existed but had never studied it, since it was no longer needed. These last words jarred Andrii Venedovych. Latin not needed?! Well, this young student had better know that only the classics will rescue the world from its current obscurantism, as they had earlier rescued it from religious blinkers. Only by returning to the classics could humanity revive its clear perception, full nature, and creative drive.

The former teacher's voice rose and resounded with passion. With ever greater enthusiasm, Andrii Venedovych inundated Stepan with names and aphorisms whose meaning and importance were completely lost on his young visitor. He spoke of the Golden Age of Augustus, the genius of Rome that had conquered the world and still shone in today's darkness with a bright beacon of salvation. He spoke of Christianity, which had betrayed and devoured Rome but was in turn conquered by it during the Renaissance. And he spoke about his beloved Lucius Annaeus Seneca, Nero's tutor, the incomparable philosopher hounded by challenges and intrigues, who, when sentenced to die, met death by his own hand, cutting his veins, as befit a sage. He spoke about Seneca's tragedies, the only Roman tragedies that have survived; of his Dialogues, among which he could recite *De providentia* by heart. And they dare to accuse this Seneca, who combined stoicism and Epicureanism in a synthesis of the highest degree, this genius of Roman genius, of being in communication with the apostle Paul, that shallow follower of the prison religion that toppled Rome!

It was getting dark in the room, and, in the dusk, the Latin instructor's voice resounded like a prophet's. He addressed Stepan time and again, and the young man was taken aback despite himself. But noticing that Levko was peacefully sipping his tea, he found the courage to drink his own cup in spite of the owner's prophetic voice. The lady of the house sat unnoticed, her narrow shoulders nearly disappearing behind the stout teapot.

"I may be old but I'm energetic," announced the old man. "I'm not scared of death. Because my spirit has classical clarity and tranquility."

Back in Levko's room, Stepan said, "The old man is overwhelming."

"He's a bit psychotic, with his Latin language," answered Levko, "but he's a good-hearted person. And he's helpful. He's smart. He knows everything."

On his way out, Stepan asked, "And what about this Latin? Is it really useless?"

"Completely," laughed Levko. "Why do you think it's called a dead language?"

He led his visitor out to the stairs and encouraged him to stop by again, even just to say hello.

Chapter Four

Walking down Lenin Street to Khreshchatyk, Stepan had much on his mind. The visit to Levko's had strengthened him. He told himself that Levko's path was his path, too, and involuntarily he felt a touch of jealousy regarding his friend. He couldn't imagine anything better than such a handsome little room. Levko will work quietly and steadily there. He'll pass all the necessary exams, earn his certificate, and return to the village a new and cultured person, and, with his return, he would bring new life to his village. Stepan, too, must follow this course. He now clearly felt the weight of his responsibility, a feeling he had lost for a moment when he first set foot on this foreign, urban soil. The memory of the send-off he was given back in the district wafted over him like a warm breeze. How could he even for a moment have forgotten his friends, left behind with no hope of escaping the backwoods? He smiled by way of sending them a greeting.

His first acquaintance with city folk was also pleasant. First there was the skinny shopkeeper, whom he could crush with two fingers; second, the half-crazy teacher dismissed from his teaching, with his Latin and his peccadilloes. About the first Stepan did not trouble himself to think much—a simple NEP-man whose wife milks the cow in the morning and in the evening puts on her silk gown and sips tea with her friends. The shopkeeper—he's just a coward who trembles like jello over the fate of his house and store in which he has invested all his life and dreams. Stepan happily discovered for himself the cultural emptiness of the owner of the barn where he was now forced to take residence, rather than in the apartment that so far inhabited his consciousness only as a disembodied idea. What could there be in this shopkeeper's soul, besides kopecks and marinated herring? What feelings could he possess? He existed only so long as he was permitted to exist. A freak—nothing but weeds or trash that disappears without a trace or afterthought.

The teacher was more interesting. He thought about things and had a purpose in life. But that room—Stepan had to laugh remembering it. He could imagine the destiny that awaited this gentleman. No doubt the teacher had at one time been the owner of a large and comfortable apartment, but the Revolution had, in one housing requisition after another, cut off room after room, chasing him and his unrequisitioned and unsold property into this cramped little corner that resembled an island after an earthquake. The Revolution had also destroyed the high school where he had taught children of the bourgeoisie how to exploit the common folk and it had thrown him like a rat into the archive, where he could burrow among the old papers. He was still alive, he was still ranting, but his future is extinction. In fact, he was already dead anyway—as dead as that useless Latin language.

So there they are, these city folk! They're nothing but the dust of the past that needs to be swept out. And that was to be his goal.

With these cheerful thoughts Stepan reached Khreshchatyk and found himself in a crowd of people. He looked around and saw the city at night for the first time. He even stopped. The shining flames, the rattle and chimes of the streetcars that converged here and then ran off again, the hoarse howl of the buses whose large carcasses rolled so easily along the streets, the piercing cries of the individual automobiles and the shouts of the carriage drivers along with the dull clamor of the wave of humanity—all this suddenly shattered his concentration. On this wide street, he encountered the city face-to-face. Leaning against the wall, hemmed in by the shameless surges of the crowd, the young man from the country stood and watched, letting his eyes wander along the seemingly endless street.

He was shoved by girls in light blouses whose thin cloth blended into the bare skin of hands and shoulders; by women in hats and veils, men in jackets; hatless boys in shirts with sleeves rolled up to their elbows; soldiers in heavy, stifling uniforms; chambermaids holding hands; sailors from the Dnipro fleet; teenagers; the raised caps of engineers, the light overcoats of dandies, and the grimy jackets of vagabonds. His eyes rested on hands that in the twilight seemed to him to be touching women's breasts, on interwoven elbows, on thighs squeezed against each other. His gaze rested on heads with hair neatly trimmed or braided in ponytails; necks straight and upright or curved sensuously on someone's shoulder. Before him passed couples captivated by each other; careless singles—sidewalk Hamlets; groups of boys chasing girls and throwing them the first flat words of friendship, which unexpectedly acquired provocative sharpness; businessmen returning late from the office, in no hurry to arrive at their boring homes; elegant ladies casting superior glances at the men and shrinking from an unexpected touch. His ears heard the indistinct clamor of interwoven conversations, sudden exclamations, occasional curses, and that sharp laughter that starts in one place and then rolls, it seems, from lips to lips, igniting them in sequence like signal flares. His entire soul was consumed with unbounded enmity toward this mindless, laughing stream. What else were all these heads capable of, except laughter and courting? Could there be a spark of an idea in their hearts? Could their thin blood sustain passion? Could there be a sense of purpose and duty in their consciousness?

Here they are—these urbanites! Shopkeepers, brainless teachers, ignorantly carefree dolls in fancy costumes. They should be swept away! They should be crushed, these worms, to make room for others.

In the twilight on the street, he sensed a trap. The pale glow of the streetlights, the string of shining display windows, the glare of the cinema—these were all will-o'-the-wisp in the urban swamp. They are a fatal attraction. Their illumination is blinding. Above, on the hills where the rows of buildings meet the rushing cobblestone street, in the darkness that dissolves the sky and stone, were enormous reservoirs of poison and colonies of snails that poured out at night into this ancient Khreshchatyk valley. And if only he had the power, he would, like a sorcerer from a fairy tale, call forth thunder against this gray, heavy mud.

Stepan began to force his way disdainfully through the crowd, pushing every which way, without regard for any protests, blunted and desensitized like a believer in the midst of a witches' sabbath. Beside every cinema, he was spun about in a whirlwind. Hundreds of feet were shuffling here, hundreds of torsos were bumping together, hundreds of eyes were staring. From wide vestibules decorated with bright posters and giant signs, row after row poured forth, spreading out or bunching up depending on the force of the opposing streams. The shows were ending and within these establishments an exchange of substances was taking place. Paddling his way out of these treacherous streams, Stepan thought gloomily, "Watching pretty pictures!"

He passed without stopping the sumptuous displays in the store windows, where waves of silk and muslin changed color under the lights and fell in soft waves from display stands onto the windowsill, where on glass shelves lay gold and shimmering stones, mounds of aromatic soaps amid vials of mysterious perfumes, countless packages of cigarettes with colorful labels, Turkish tobacco, and amber pipe stems. Walking past, he threw contemptuous glances—fire and ice—at these objects. The electric store stopped him, however. Behind its reflecting glass colored bulbs were flashing on and off, creating strange, lifeless flowers in the crystal of the mirrors of the display. And Stepan thought bitterly: why not take these lamps to the village, where they would bring real benefits, rather than mere amusement. Oh, the insatiable city!

He didn't recognize the bookstore at all. Could these really be those same familiar books, so dear to him, lying in this window, stretching endlessly beyond its edges in the reflecting mirrors at either end? Why were they, too, being paraded before the scornful gaze of the witless mob? Were theirs the eyes that would delve into the depths of these books, these repositories of important ideas, destined to set the world in motion? They had no right! This was mockery! He felt pity for these dishonored treasures, demeaned by the stares of the ignorant—a bountiful harvest trampled by a lust for amusement.

"Anything to make a sale," he thought.

He was so deep in thought that when he set off again, the clamor of the street seemed even wilder. In this noise, he heard both laughter and a threat to all those who would rise up against the shops and the lights. Tomorrow this street would spill out into the offices of businesses and institutions, it would flow into all the workplaces, filling all the jobs large and small, so that wherever he might come knocking, the doors would be closed.

"Damned NEP-men," he thought.

On the corner of Sverdlov Street, he was momentarily stopped by a crowd. He glanced up the incline where the streetcar was rising. There was an unexpected calm here, a sudden haven from the storm, where the crowd turned, died out, and evaporated, dispersing into individual figures. He watched the streetcar disappear into the distant gloom as it crested the hill, and in this bluish band of dusk beneath the streetlights, between the vague rows of motionless buildings, he felt the strange beauty of the city. The bold lines of the street, its crafted symmetry, the heavy perpendicularity on either side, the majestic slope of the cobblestone pavement throwing sparks from beneath falling horseshoes, revealed to him a stern and unfamiliar harmony. Still, he hated the city.

Past the greedy doors of beer-cellars, from which drunken music blared onto the street, past the archway that enticed people to the lotto-hall and the crocodile head over the entrance to the casino, he walked by the

Regional Executive Committee building and slowed down. In the evening, the section of Khreshchatyk between Komintern Square and Revolution Street was a desert, where only lonely prostitutes could be seen passing the time beneath the dark verandas. Behind him the valley of Khreshchatyk was abuzz. On the right came music from the Proletarian Garden. On the left, human shadows were rustling on Volodymyr Hill. Even the streetcars here seemed less intrusive.

For the first time this evening, Stepan tore his eyes away from the earth and raised them to the heavens. A curious trembling overcame him when he saw the crescent of the moon overhead amid the stars, the same moon that shone for him in the village. The tranquil moon, a rural wanderer like himself, companion of his youth, confidant of his adolescent dreams, subdued in him the anger that had been provoked by the street. The city must be conquered, not despised! A moment earlier he had been crushed, but now he was envisioning endless possibilities. Thousands like him came to the city, huddled somewhere in cellars, barns, and dormitories, and went hungry, but worked and studied, imperceptibly undermining its corrupt foundations and replacing them with unshakeable new ones. Thousands of Levkos, Stepans, and Vasyls were laying siege to these nests of NEP-men, squeezing them, and tearing them down. Fresh village blood was pouring into the city to change its substance and appearance. And he was one among these thousands, whose destiny was to conquer the city. The city-orchards and village-cities that were promised by the Revolution, these wonders of the future about which books had given him only a dull impression, were for him at that moment very close and comprehensible. They were the challenge of the future, the noble goal of his education, the result of all that he had seen, done, and would accomplish. The life-giving power of the soil that coursed in his veins and his mind, the powerful winds of the steppe that had given him birth added passionate clarity to his fantasy about earth's shining future. He dissolved in this boundless dream, which captivated him immediately and completely. This dream was his fiery sword, with which he conquered everything around him. Descending down Revolution Street to the grime of Nyzhnii Val Street, he was ascending ever higher, to the passionate twinkling of the stars.

Chapter Five

The city is a wonder. On the outside, it's all hustle and bustle—life in the city, it seems, bursts forth like a mountain spring, with the energy of lightning. But inside, in the dim offices of various institutions, it drags along like an old wagon, entangled in thousands of rules and regulations. Stepan felt the blows of this urban formalism at every step, and no matter how he tried to excuse them with objective reasons, they did not become any less irritating for his efforts. Having learned from his previous experience, Stepan arrived on the appointed day for his exam two hours early, to allow time for waiting in line. Today, he was convinced, the formality of his attendance at the Institute would be settled, and he would have full rights to visit Nadiika with the distinguished, although invisible, badge of a student. True, the impressions of the previous evening had, for a time, replaced the image of this beloved figure. Returning home, he had sat up for a long time, smoking and thinking about the city, its destiny and true purpose. But in the morning he awoke as always, eager and full of youthful energy, which, like a life preserver, kept him from drowning in the uncertainties that had unexpectedly engulfed him. Somewhat accustomed to his new lodgings, he boldly asked the lady of the house for a bucket and washed himself thoroughly. And then again the recollection of Nadiika flooded his soul with its warm turbulence.

"The examination," he thought happily. "That's the primary thing!"

Having an uncontrollable inclination to analyze his own thoughts and actions, he scolded himself amicably for yesterday's anger and vague apprehension. Dreaming was a waste of time, he lectured himself: actions were needed—ceaseless activity to overcome all obstacles, with all one's energy focused on the next hurdle. The first of these hurdles was the Institute. He must gain admittance to the Institute and not fool around with all kinds of dreams, no matter how noble. Indeed, the examination seemed to him to be a hurdle that, once cleared, would gain him a queen and a kingdom. He prepared for it as if he were a famous warrior setting out on a campaign that would earn the victor the keys to the magic cave of treasures. And, because he was inclined to conquer his enemies with one great effort, once and for all, he was unpleasantly struck by the fact that the examination would last two days—a written exam today, an oral one tomorrow. The notice that contained all this information in a few short lines of text was entirely unconcerned with his idealistic enthusiasm, his youthful passion to solve all problems immediately. And he had to surrender to these meager lines.

Stepan sat down on a window ledge and prepared a cigarette—tobacco was a true friend and a comfort in all of his difficulties. But even this small pleasure was denied him by another small notice on the opposite wall. He spent two hours in boredom, carelessly observing the mob of his future friends and thinking about himself. He sensed, although indistinctly, a change within himself. He could not but observe a new fire starting to burn inside him, but one that was fitful, that trembled with every breath of an external wind. In the morning, he had been happy, but now he was overcome with a sadness that was impossible to contain. Yet he was surely not worn out by any work, nor had any accident befallen him. And was it not but a few hours ago that he had told himself to be steadfast? These unfamiliar vacillations in his mood worried him. He was beginning to understand that the unsophisticated village existence that he had known heretofore, where all problems had been simple and overly practical, was entirely different from his new life in the city.

Among the possible essay topics on the exam, he immediately chose "The coupling of the city and the village." After preparing a mental outline of his essay, he wrote quickly and easily. He elaborated his principal arguments extensively, examining both the economic and the cultural needs of this partnership, and illuminating its goals and desirable consequences. The village cultural activist, with a firm Marxist understanding of the importance of economic preconditions, was reawakened in him. The assignment captivated him completely—reading over his own sentences, he forgot that he was writing an examination. "The coupling of the city and the village is a bold step toward the construction of our future orchard-cities," he concluded, and turned in his finished exam a full hour before the scheduled deadline. Evening was falling. After wandering aimlessly along Shevchenko Boulevard, he decided that he should indeed visit Nadiika, who was staying with some friends near the covered market.

The house she lived in was one of those ancient little homes that can be found unexpectedly on Kyiv's side streets right next to six-story masonry buildings. The rusty green roof, the wooden window-shutters, the old-fashioned fenced-in yard in front of the windows, and the rickety stairs to the uneven porch were evidence of a greater antiquity than that allowed by the law on stolen and lost property. But Stepan was happy to see this shack, next to which his own shed seemed less miserable—a girl who lived here could, quite properly, be his.

Nadiika lived with two girlfriends from her village who had set out into the wide world a year earlier and had rented so-called "quarters" in this old-fashioned home. One of them, Hanna, or Hanusia, was enrolled in sewing courses, preparing to replenish the ranks of the army of seamstresses whose profession had fallen into such disfavor during the years of war communism and barter economy, when everybody washed and cooked for themselves and sewed nothing at all, but now, in the NEP years, needed rapid replenishment, in accordance with the growth in demand and fashion. She was a quiet girl, driven out of the village by the hardships of a large extended family—driven out forever, with no hope of returning under the tattered, thatched roof of her parents. She was sincere and defenseless, somewhat romantic and forbearing, like all poor girls who harbor within them neither real passion nor reliable strength. Her companion, a successful farmer's young daughter, was completing, in accord with her plans, a typing course and had been searching a half year now, with no success, for a suitable position and an appropriate partner, one with some accomplishments. She dressed with pretension and extended her little finger when raising a teacup. Her name was Nusia, which is to say Hanna, as well, but to a higher degree. Of the two beds, neither of which could be called a double bed, one belonged to Nusia, who was unwilling to compromise her possession in any respect, so that Nadiika always had to double up with Hanusia, who was always agreeable to everything. These two beds and a table, typewriter, sewing machine, and haggard chair were the only markers of material possessions in the girls' apartment; the other decorations had more of a spiritual character: portraits and pictures that Hanusia had naively plastered on the walls, straining to add some domesticity to the empty rooms. She had adorned the portrait of Lenin that hung in the center with a big sign in uneven letters: "You have died, but your spirit lives on." In the corner, she had hung an icon of Saint Nicholas the Miracle-Worker that was hardly noticeable at first sight. Of all the pictures, only one belonged to Nusia: a naked Galatea raising her arms and breasts to the heavens. It hung over Nusia's bed and disturbed Hanusia with its indecency.

Outside the door, Stepan could already hear male voices, and his heart sank. He was not in the mood for happy people, and he wanted to speak to Nadiika alone. But there was no other option, so he opened the door. The situation looked worse than he had imagined: there was a bottle on the table and the beds were pulled up around it to seat the three girls and three boys. Stepan's interest cooled, but then he noticed Levko and understood the situation. Those two were the boyfriends of Hanusia and Nusia, but Levko was just here for the company, and so Nadiika was free, free for him, since she was the first to get up from the table and welcome him. He was introduced to the two friends and sat down with them. Although he had eaten nothing all day and was hungry, he categorically refused to eat or drink. To eat at the expense of these two strangers—this party was surely their treat—was something his honor did not permit. Levko was a different matter: he sat in the corner, like a father at a wedding, and wasted few words, since his mouth was busy the whole time. He just smiled and gazed at the company. The life of the party were the two other fellows, who were displaying all their wisdom and wit for their ladies.

Hanusia's suitor was one of those village fellows who appear in the city like a wandering meteor—visiting the theaters, obtaining free passes everywhere thanks to the "coupling the village and city" campaign, attending all the public debates and soirees and applauding endlessly there, annoying girls on the street, sneering at everyone, cursing everything; and then, after a year, returning to the village, taking up farming and growing wild again in one month. They turn out to be family despots and political conservatives. The trump cards of this fellow's behavior were his salacious anecdotes and suggestions, which disorganized Hanusia's dreamy soul and broke down her already weak resistance. Compared to this wit, the other fellow was the model of probity. He, too, paid little heed to education, his chief goal being to latch on to a secure job; if that could be done without a diploma, then higher education should be cut off as a useless appendage, much like the worm-like protrusion of the appendix. Nostalgic for the beautiful turbulent years when it was so easy to get ahead, he knocked on all doors with a villager's steely determination and took advantage of every fortuitous acquaintance, until at last he landed himself a position as an instructor of club work, to which he clung with hands, teeth, and both his feet. But, examining his life through the prism of the ancient village stereotype, which puts certain, very specific expectations before a young man setting out on an independent path, the brave young instructor was intent on adding Miss Nusia as a partner in his future official successes.

The conversation had stopped momentarily on account of the appearance of the new personage and now resumed its course. The topic was Ukrainization.

"Now take, for example," remarked the instructor, "club work. It's serious business. The workers are already fidgety, they complain about the drought of interesting leisure activities. And add to that the language classes. I mean, a drama club, and maybe a choir—but then whoa! Stop! That's a break with the masses. It's tough for the Party with this Ukrainization policy."

He put particular emphasis on "Party," a word, he felt, that had a magic influence on any sentence in which it appeared.

"Will the villagers be Ukrainized, too?" asked Hanusia, hesitantly.

The instructor gave a faint smile.

"It turns out, they'll need it, too. After all, what kind of a Ukrainian can a bumpkin be?"

Stepan could not endure this anymore. He burst into the conversation energetically.

"You are mistaken, Comrade," he said to the instructor. "Ukrainization is meant to strengthen the coupling of the village and the city. The proletariat must be..."

But Yasha, the young villager who was on tour in the city, laughed suddenly and threw a jeering glance at Stepan and Nadiika. It was his habit to delight in his own witticisms even before he uttered them.

"He-he! So you two are coupling, too?"

Nadiika turned red, while Stepan, offended on both his own account and on hers, turned sullenly silent. What could he say to this insolent fellow, who considered himself the master of the situation, waving his arms about, pinching his Hanusia, and winking all around? He couldn't fight him here! Hunger and antipathy to this company were leading to nausea. So, this was the vanguard of village society, erstwhile conquerors of the cities? And why was Levko so calm, as always? Was he like them, too? Was it the eternal fate of the village to be the dull, hopeless slave that sells himself for employment and food, at the expense not only of his goals but of his dignity, as well? Perhaps this was the path that awaited him, too, this swamp that would suck him in and digest him, transforming him into a servile supplement to the rusty system of life's usual course? He sensed that life's terrible steel springs, which had flexed on the ruts of the Revolution, would now be straightened again. Perhaps life was nothing more than this unstoppable train. Could no engineer alter its course along the rails on which it was destined to travel between the familiar, gray stations? One thing was certain—hop on, no matter what or where it was going. Weren't they symbolic, those famous freight cars of the recent though half-forgotten days, where hucksters fought for room, kicking and cursing each other, climbing onto the roofs, hanging off fenders and bumpers with their treasure sacks full of crumbs, living in filth and misery but with an unquenchable desire for life, with dreams of girlfriends, pies, and moonshine? And, if there was such a mass of those mongers then, what of today, when there were no longer any food blockades, tribunals, or requisitions—when they were free to make use of entire caravans for their goods and the soft upholstery of train coupes for themselves?

Plunging into these unhappy thoughts as if peering into a bottomless pit, Stepan mechanically picked up the heel of a loaf of bread and began to chew it. The village was receding from him. He was beginning to see it in a distant perspective which left only the schematic outline of a living organism. He felt afraid, like a person beneath whom the ground has just shaken.

Meanwhile, the conversation, having wandered over various topics, turned to the ones that inevitably result from the very slightest infusion of alcohol even among the most virtuous people. Women's committees, marriage, love, and alimony appeared on the lips of the guests and the room filled with Yasha's laughing, "But I tell you, the woman will always be on the bottom!"

"Oh my God, what is he saying?" cried Hanusiathe most likely target of Yasha's prediction.

Stepan felt Nadiika's worried gaze and, raising his head, looked into her eyes. She smiled at him, but, in this smile, was the longing that comes to a girl in love, clouding her eyes and weighing down her hands with an insuperable weariness. Her heart had already opened like a seed in loose soil, sending out its first pale shoots to the surface under the influence of the eternal sun, which melts the snow and wakens thousands of seeds from the depths, without any responsibility for the winds they may encounter in its kingdom.

Levko was dozing, bent over the table. He wasn't hungry, today he had passed another exam, and he had every right to be happy. Nusia was leaning her elbow on the knee of the instructor, who had lit his pipe and was contentedly blowing smoke in front of himself. Yasha had his arm around Hanusia, who had acquiesced after a few feeble protests.

"How 'bout a song?" he suggested. "Hanusia, you begin."

Hanusia raised her head and started singing, dragging out the words for a more sorrowful effect:

"To Ukraine the wind will blow,

Where my sweetheart I left low …"

In a moment, the song brought everyone together. Yasha, becoming serious, offered support in a lyrical tenor that, incomprehensibly, lived in his prosaic throat.

Nature had not endowed Stepan with the musical gifts of his nation and, once again, he felt himself a stranger in this company. He felt the senselessness of his position here, where he was a silent dolt who had opened his mouth only once during the whole evening, and even then unsuccessfully. But he couldn't go, either. He wanted to say something to Nadiika. She was sitting next to him, and the passionate but unfulfillable desire to touch her hand—to hear from her lips words addressed only to him—gnawed at him. She was waiting for him, he could see this in her every glance. And he was waiting for her. Nevertheless, other thoughts were continually obscuring her image, pushing her away from his dreams, although he was unaware of these involuntary betrayals.

As he left, he said to her, "I'll come tomorrow."

"Do come!" she answered, and her easy familiarity filled him with a magical warmth.

"Nadiika, I'll come tomorrow," he whispered. "Expect me, Nadiika."

He went home quickly, consumed by a feeling in which he expected to find comfort and confidence.

Chapter Six

"**G**ood! Very good!" said the professor.

Stepan came out from the exam. A crowd of curious students waiting for their own turn surrounded him. "How was it?" "What questions did they ask?" "Is it brutal?"

He had passed the exam. Tomorrow, his name, too, would appear beneath the glass where the names of the accepted were posted. For the next three years, these walls would be his shelter. He must see about the scholarship. He must write and tell the friends back home in the village about this success. The exam had been conducted in groups of five, and Stepan had listened in amazement to the answers of the four before him. Would they really admit them to the Institute? In any case, he was head and shoulders above them. His knowledge was firm and broad, without gaps or thin ice. He proved to himself the value of his three years of tireless work in the village, without rest or vacation, when the urge to study had overcome him. The last ounces of the milled grain he had earned and all the coins he had saved had been turned over to the teacher, or for books and paper. He had forsaken everything, had become an oddball and a recluse, spending his nights by a lantern dreaming of formulae and logarithms, while his friends laughed at him behind his back. Only someone strong in spirit could have managed the work he had undertaken, and he had accomplished it because he had a clear notion of what he wanted. He wanted to pursue higher education. Fearfully and devoutly he had dreamed of the day this would happen. And now, that day had come! The only thing missing was the joy that should have accompanied such a momentous event.

He cheered himself with words of all sorts, turning his mind to his serious and worthwhile goals, but he could not drown out the misgivings in his soul or fill the void that had arisen there once the exam was off the agenda. The fact that he had passed the exam with great distinction had somehow disenchanted him, instead of bringing him satisfaction. The immediate goal was attained, and beyond that there appeared before him an endless road without any milestones. Preparation for the Institute had taken three years. Now it would be three more at the Institute itself. And what then? The prosperity of the village and the happiness of the people were, after all, far too distant goals to serve as the primary aim of his energies. He was strong, but he needed a fulcrum to move the world.

Stepan exited the large building, whose exterior was being painted in bland gray and white tones more suitable for one of the former institutes for the education of aristocratic young ladies than for an institution of the economic superstructure. Looking up at the high scaffolding and the painters dangling from the roof on cables and smoking cigarettes, the young man was taken aback by the soft colors that were replacing the harsh revolutionary paint on buildings, posters, and magazine covers. And that gray-haired professor at the exam had used the term "comrade" so freely, as if it had never been for him a symbol of violence and looting. He had digested it, pared down its rough edges, and pronounced it now without any apparent discomfort.

The young man went to Nadiika's, struggling to understand his disappointment and low spirits, although such searching seldom points to the true source of ideas and feelings. People deceive themselves more often than they tell themselves the truth owing to tiny and imperceptible—even to the person most interested—factors that cause enormously important changes in the soul, just as invisible bacteria influence the physical condition of the body.

"I'm sad," he thought, "because I want to see Nadiika. I'm suffering because I've fallen in love with her."

Once again her name, which he whispered to himself, resounded as a happy echo along the dark corridors of his thoughts. She was a sun for him, its rays suddenly emerging from a gap in the clouds. Again and again, he would lose her, then find her anew.

He didn't want to come in, even though Hanusia was the only other person there, her sewing machine clattering away. So Nadiika tied on a kerchief and they walked out into the gray shadows of the early evening. The girl had also passed her exam to the vocational college and cheerfully told Stepan how she had almost flunked the political fundamentals part of the exam:

"...And then he asks me—this curly-haired guy—what is the RadNarKom? Well, I know the RadNarKom and the VUTsVYK inside out, so I say it's the Rada Narodnykh Komisariv, the Council of People's Ministers. And who is the head of the RadNarKom, he goes on to ask me. I'm as confident as ever and shoot back immediately: Chubby! And they start falling all over themselves in laughter. Not Chubby, miss. It's Chubar!"

Stepan chuckled.

"Nadiika, isn't it wonderful to be together!" he said.

She threw him a fiery look, one of the kind whose attraction and promise are greatest when they themselves are most innocent. Every note of her excited laughter reverberated with love. Her courses would begin in a week, and she had to travel home to get the rest of her things and some food. On hearing that he, too, had a free week,

74   THE CITY

she suggested secretively, "We'll go together, won't we? I'll come out to meet you by the willows, the ones near our garden."

"I can't go, Nadiika," he answered gloomily. "I need to settle the details of the scholarship."

All the joy left her voice.

"I won't see you all that time?"

"You'll come back, Nadiika."

He had fallen in love with her name and repeated it often. It was already dark as they, along with other couples, climbed Volodymyr Hill where, in a quiet corner, the statue still held its cross, now blessing the Kyivans bathing on the beach. During the day, this was where children played with balls and hoops, tired office workers relaxed, and students read their wise books in the shade. At night, this was the promised land of love for chambermaids, soldiers, youths, and all those who did not yet comprehend the benefits and comforts of lovemaking within four walls. Love abhors witnesses, but, in a city, they're everywhere, even under tree branches in a park.

They wandered up and down the winding paths in the dense twilight. The accidental touch of their bodies through thick clothing provoked shivers, and their hands eventually intertwined in a tight clasp. Their love was blooming like a late flower in the intoxicating breaths of near autumn. Somewhere, nature's white gown was already being woven and the icy nails of its coffin were being forged, but here, the last gust of warmth, tinged with the thick scent of decay, was melting and soldering their hearts together into one heart, throttled by the flow of a new, combined blood. Words evaporated on their lips unsaid and the wind from beyond the Dnipro touched their bodies with a passionate tickling.

They stopped by the barrier above the cliff and watched fireflies on the hillside street crawling toward each other, up and down the incline, until they unexpectedly passed each other at the point where they would have collided. Below them, the great river was a dark ribbon in the valley, its outline marked with streetlights and the fires on Trukhaniv Island. Below, on the left, through a shimmering haze, flickered a carpet of lights in the Podil.

"Do you love me, Stepan?" she asked abruptly.

"Nadiika, my dear," he whispered listlessly. "My dearest Nadiika, I love you..."

He wrapped his arm around her waist and she put her head on his shoulder, trembling from the humidity above the river and the warm moisture in her eyes. He softly stroked her hair, subdued by a feeling that leaves emptiness in its wake.

In the morning, Stepan came out to the port and waved his cap for a long time in response to her kerchief. She took with her his greetings to the village, a few delegated tasks, and a letter to one of his friends at work. It was a long letter, with more questions than information. About himself, he said only that he had written the test, was hoping for a scholarship, and was temporarily living with friends. But under the influence of the recollections that overcame him, he was acutely interested in the conditions at the Village Hall, about the series of lectures that he had arranged before his departure, about attendance at the film series, and any new performances. He completely forgot that it was only a week since he had left the village. In particular, he asked about the work of his successor. The library, his child, so to speak, which he had built from the remains of the collections of a number of rich landowners, consisted of 2,178 volumes that he had personally cataloged, numbered, and shelved according to their subject. It was the largest rural library in the district, and every single volume carried the stamp of his diligent work.

"Remind them to make sure they pick up the Lenin display from the district office," he wrote. "I paid 7 karbovanets, we owe 2 and a half more. The emblems and banners that the girls embroidered are stored in the big wardrobe—I left the keys with Petro. Ask the girls to weave red and black ribbons together as a decoration—at the Institute here, the portrait is draped with ribbons like that, and it looks very nice. I haven't made any friends here yet. I met two fellows from some village—they're so distracted and apathetic, it makes you sad. It will be tough to get enough to eat, but I'll manage somehow. Write to me about everything. I might be able to come for Christmas. Stepan."

When the steamboat disappeared from view, he sat down on a bench and rolled a cigarette. The dock had emptied of all visitors. The boys who sold sunflower seeds and seltzer were arguing among themselves for no reason. One of them asked him for a light and said, "Your princess has left. It's tough without your princess."

Stepan smiled at the words and serious expression of this expert. He, too, could leave tomorrow, if he wished. It would even be the wise thing to do, instead of loitering half-starved on the streets of the city. Classes probably wouldn't start for at least a week, anyway. But something was holding him back, some kind of anticipation and a hidden unwillingness to go back home, even for just a few days. His letter was sincere only in appearance. It seemed to him that a whole eternity had passed from the time he had left the village. His expression of such detailed interest in matters over there in his letter was merely an attempt at deluding himself—convincing himself that the past still held significance for him, that he was living in it and for it.

At one o'clock, he found his name, as expected, in the list of those who were accepted. He submitted a scholarship application to the SotsZabez Student Support committee and stopped by Levko's place to borrow some books, because there was a whole week of free time ahead. But Levko's library was too limited and eclectic: aside from some agricultural textbooks, he had all the issues of *Literaturno-naukovyi visnyk* for 1907, Ivan

Nechui-Levytskyi's *The Clouds*, and the Collected Works of Fonvizin. Stepan tied all of these together with some string, adding a textbook on agricultural economics that just might prove useful at the Institute. In addition, Levko advised him to do what he himself had never gotten around to: see the city. Pulling an old map of Kyiv from a drawer, he passed it on to the Stepan as a guiding star.

This advice intrigued Stepan. After some bread and salo for breakfast, he would grab an issue of the *Visnyk* and set out for the whole day, systematically visiting all the places that were marked with symbols and accompanying explanations on the map. In the space of three days, he visited the Lavra, descending into both the far and the near caves where, in the narrow and very low-ceilinged stone passageways, there was a string of glass-enclosed coffins of the saints, and where pilgrims' candles flickered and smoldered in the heavy dense air; he stopped by at Askold's grave, now a neglected cemetery where he read on the gravestones the names of people who had once lived but had left behind nothing of themselves except these names on a plaque; he wandered the winding alleys of the former Tsar's Garden and sat with a book above the cliff overlooking the Dnipro; he stopped by the Sophia and Volodymyr Cathedrals, centers of church activity imperceptibly churning beneath the lofty domes; he viewed the Golden Gates, the former entrance into great Kyiv. He took in all the large bazaars—the Zhytnii, Yevreiskyi, and Bessarab-ka. He meandered near the train station; he traveled the Brest-Litovsk highway to the Polytechnic Institute. He wandered through Demiyivka into the Holosiyiv Forest, rested at the Botanical Gardens, and spent thirty kopecks (not without some hesitation) to enter the Historical Museum and the Khanenko Museum, where he was enthralled by the ancestral weapons, ancient furniture, decorative panels, and colored china, which most attracted his eye. The shiny colors and fine designs enchanted him and attracted his hands. He stood in front of the display for a long time, noting every small detail, firmly inscribing each one in his memory. Everything new that he saw fit easily into his mind in ordered layers, tied by thousands of threads to what he had read and to what he could surmise. And everything new elicited a new desire. Of the monuments he had circled on the old map, for the most part only the pedestals remained. Actually, he had seen the figures of Iskra and Kochubei—they lay with broken limbs along the riverbank, beside a forge. Only Bohdan, untouched, sitting on his proudly prancing horse, pointed his mace northward, either as a threat or with the intention of lowering it.

Stepan gave his most diligent attention to the Podil, the area of the city where he himself lived. His own eyes confirmed that it wasn't only people whose passing is marked with faded inscriptions: entire eras of history pass almost without a trace, leaving here and there only indistinct suggestions of their former glory. The shining hub of the Middle Ages, with the Academy and famous monasteries, was now transformed into a small market square, the haunt of tradesmen and foul-mouthed petty-trade women, the center of domestic manufacture for soap, cartridges, leather, vinegar, and shoe black.

In the evening, returning from his excursions, Stepan would descend directly to the Dnipro in a remote spot, bathe and then wearily make his way home. After his evening ration of salo, which had become his only sustenance, he would sit outside by the shed and have a smoke. The Hnidyi home seemed dead. If there was any life in it, it was imperceptible from outside. Not a sound emanated from it and its door opened most unwillingly. At night, the lights inside would silently turn on. In all this time, Stepan had only once caught a glimpse of the owner coming home from his shop. His wife still milked the cows twice a day but no longer offered any milk to Stepan. But every evening, the same solitary young man who had offered him a cigarette on the first day came out on the porch for a smoke. He sat and smoked, then disappeared into the house again. Stepan felt a reflexive sympathy for him, since the young man seemed just as lonely as he himself was. But he didn't find the courage to walk up and speak to him. Stepan went to sleep early, since he didn't have any light, and slept late, compensating for his meager diet with rest. He put off any thoughts of searching for new quarters for the winter until his scholarship came through. But the question came up abruptly and unexpectedly on its own.

One evening, the skinny-legged shopkeeper himself walked over and greeted Stepan, sitting down beside him on a stump of firewood. Looking sideways through his glasses he asked, "Have you found yourself a place?"

Stepan had fully anticipated this unpleasant conversation and had a ready answer—he would move out in a week. He'd get his scholarship (that was certain!) and then he'd move out. The shopkeeper grunted. He had a proposal: Stepan could stay with them. He could sleep in the kitchen (there's a bed there) and get breakfast, lunch, and dinner. In exchange, he would look after the cows, bring in the water (the faucet was outside), and, in the winter, he would be responsible for the firewood. Nothing more! On these terms, the shopkeeper was willing officially to declare Stepan his nephew at the housing registry. When it was Stepan's turn to answer, he thought for a minute, mostly out of self-respect: what was there to think about? He immediately calculated that he would have food and a warm room, while the scholarship would be left over for clothing and textbooks. The work wasn't hard—something better was hard to imagine. He answered slowly and seriously, "Well then, I'll stay."

Hnidyi got up. "Well, you may as well move in," he said.

Within a half hour, Stepan had abandoned his shed and settled into the kitchen, where a small bed stood next to the stove, a cheap wooden clock clattering above it. The shopkeeper's wife, Tamara Vasylivna, handed him a gas lantern, a glass of milk, some bread, and a piece of roast meat, with which he celebrated his new quarters. After the workbench in the shed, the mattress felt like the tsar's own featherbed. The next morning, he began his service as dairyman, water-carrier, and wood-chopper.

Chapter Seven

On Sunday, when Nadiika was due to return, Stepan made a general appraisal of his clothes. He sewed on a few uncertain buttons, using the needle he had made a habit of carrying around during his years of living alone; he shook out his field jacket, and polished his boots with a sack. He had been wearing his suit for three years now and the fabric had discolored in the sun; but this was sturdy stuff meant for an officer and would not wear through for at least three more years. Then he shaved very conscientiously before a small warped mirror that hung in the kitchen—in the previous week, he had developed quite a beard. Feeling fresh, youthful, and handsome after these preparations, Stepan left the house with a spring in his step, heading in the direction of the covered market.

Two days in his new quarters had calmed and strengthened him. Like a treasure trove discovered after bland and crusty fasting, the warm meals freshened his insides and his thinking. Yesterday, taking advantage of some hot water left in the pot, he had done his laundry, dried it in the sun, and ironed it. He knew how to do laundry, how to iron, cook, and even mend boots. Reassured by the security of his new position, he took two of his now superfluous dry flatbreads to the bazaar in the morning and sold them for 10 kopecks. He didn't like to let anything useful go to waste. He could not be accused in any manner of disorder or dissipation, and the 10 kopecks—a hryvenyk—he spent to buy twenty cigarettes was an indulgence that even the poorest of beggars would have allowed himself on the day that his much anticipated and much desired sweetheart was due to return.

By Stepan's calculation, the work around Mr. Hnidyi's home amounted to no more than an hour and a half or two hours per day. There was plenty of time left for the Institute and for studying. Add the scholarship and, for now, he had a solid foundation for further endeavors. He accepted this change for the better in his circumstances as something appropriate: he had been expecting it without knowing where it would come from, since, despite his doubts and hesitation, he was confident of his good fortune. Like a young hunter in the forest, trembling before the wild beast but confident of his steady hand, he was ready to meet the success that fate held out for him, even if occasionally that fate stuck out its tongue.

Nadiika had indeed returned, but the girls' apartment had the usual guests—the instructor and young

Yasha—so there was no opportunity to speak with her, if he did not want to betray his feelings in front of these sneering skeptics. Stepan dejectedly lit a cigarette, but, in giving him a letter of reply from his village friend, Nadiika gave Stepan such a heartfelt look that he immediately cheered up and drifted into a soft warm languor. Putting the letter in his pocket, he thought, "Dear Nadiika! My beloved, my only Nadiika!"

Yasha, who kept up on all the announcements and posters, suggested they go to a literary evening that was taking place that day in the auditorium of the National Library and was sponsored by the Cultural Committee of the local chapter of the All-Ukrainian Academy of Sciences. Yasha didn't remember which literary organization would be appearing but assured everyone that admission was free and that there would be plenty of opportunity for cheers and good laughs.

"They're pretty nutty," he said. "Some of them even have some hair on their upper lip already."

Nadiika tried to claim fatigue in order to stay behind with Stepan, but Yasha cut her short. "Kissing gets boring faster than you think."

Everyone set off for the literary evening.

They arrived an hour later than the announced starting time, but they still had to wait for a half hour. The delay was not an expression of the public's distaste for literature but rather of the general state of affairs, one of the consequences of a deep distrust of civic life.

Scattered and hounded into his burrow, the inhabitant is quite unwilling to crawl out, so when he is told to come at one, he comes at two, having licked his paws for another hour.

The wretched Yasha planted his own person directly between Stepan and Nadiika, cutting off their path for interaction and leaving Stepan no option but to look around at the audience and the auditorium. The seats in the National Library auditorium were divided into two categories according to the class principle: in front were the seats for the selected few, in back were benches for the common folk, mostly students. Behind the benches there was enough empty floor space to allow standing room for those who could not find room even on the benches. The feeble voices of authors who, for the most part, have no skills in reading or speaking in public, reach the ears of listeners back here as completely indistinct mumbling, and the standing audience must find its amusement in the mere appearance of the literary performance, the figure of the author who is reading, and his friends who sit at the table on the dais smoking, writing notes to one another, yawning, and making inspired facial expressions. This back gallery gives the greatest applause not to those prose writers who spread out their manuscripts on the lectern and read at great length, but instead to the poets who walk out onto the center of the dais and recite from memory with great feeling and gestures, because these are more dramatic and they change frequently. The first two rows of seats were reserved for the most select: the critics and authors, the literary leaders and pleaders who come with their wives and friends and cannot sit farther than the second row to avoid disgracing the dignity of literature itself, because an idea can only be honored in the person who represents it. And some of them actually sat in the front rows because they were these representatives, while others considered themselves to be such representatives because they were sitting in the front rows.

Among this literary beau monde, Stepan noticed the young fellow who had mentioned a bag full of poems when Stepan had visited the State Publishing House of Ukraine. Although this recollection was indeed quite painful, he asked Yasha who the young man was.

"Oh, that's Vyhorskyi," answered Yasha. "A poet, of sorts. He writes poems."

This was the first literary evening of the current season, so there were many spectators and admission to the auditorium was not nearly as free as the poster had indicated. The tradition of public literary readings had developed in those years when there wasn't even enough paper for cigarettes and writers were given the task of "going out into the streets." Literature had been forced to become a spectacle and the writer a public performer, but this tradition is now dying out and we can breathe a fond "Amen" over its casket. Literature, after all, is a book, not a recitation, and performing it in public is as strange as reading musical works without a piano.

When the authors had taken their appropriate seats around the table on the dais, the head of the Cultural Committee of the local chapter of the All-Ukrainian Academy of Sciences opened (or unveiled) the evening with a few moving words about literature and its current goals, expressing an appropriately hopeful sentiment. But Stepan didn't hear what was being spoken. Unrelated thoughts were increasingly occupying him, replacing the works and the audience in his perception. He was thinking about the authors themselves, about their walking out in front of other people, and about how those people listened to them. They had detached themselves from the crowd, taken their appropriate place, and everyone knew them by name. They write books, these books are printed, sold, and cataloged in libraries. Back in his distant Village Hall, he himself had marked with the library stamp a book by this Vyhorskyi whom he saw here. Here was the author himself. Stepan was jealous of these authors and he did not hide this from himself, because he, too, wanted to detach himself and become one of the selected. He was almost insulted by the laughter and applause given to these happy few, and each new author that appeared by the lectern posed the same painful question for him: Why wasn't this him? He wanted to be each of them, whether novelist or poet.

The presentation of works at a literary evening is only a warm-up for the main event—the discussion and evaluation. The audience likes these discussions, but not because they participate. The discussion is a bigger spectacle than the reading, with a larger body of participants and more spice. But, as a general rule, no one wants to be the first to speak. After all, the last speaker has the pleasant opportunity to belittle all his predecessors and thus seem the wisest. Specialists in literary criticism who maintain their reputation by never being satisfied with anything proudly refuse to proclaim their esteemed opinion and must be asked over and over, like dignitaries at a public dinner. All in all, everyone prefers to laugh at everyone else rather than offer others grounds for laughter, but once someone has spoken, the stream of speakers grows like an avalanche. Wisdom is contagious.

At the first evening, quite naturally, everyone wanted to express himself, and so the innocent lectern became a scene of fierce verbal warfare, where all possible tools for convincing one's opponent were manifested: mockery, wit, torment, inventories of an author's ancestors with the aim of revealing among them a *kulak* or a bourgeois, citations from the author's previous works where a contradictory idea was expressed, and so on—matters interesting to the spectators but sad for literature. All the speakers, regardless of their convictions, adopted these beautiful and chaste methods, each justifying himself by observing that his opponents forced them to do so. After a half hour, a veritable knightly joust began on the dais, where Don Quixotes in armor forged of quotations or with bare hands battled against immortal windmills to the howls and applause of the satisfied spectators, while Sancho Panzas displayed their intellectual prowess, cultivating dreams of becoming governors of literary islands. These contests always ended in a draw, which allowed everyone to consider himself the lone victor.

At the beginning of the discussion, Stepan, wilting from internal trepidation, contemplated what *he* could write, *what* he could write about, and *how* he could write it. He examined all the events of his life that might be of interest to others, and joyfully latched onto some while hopelessly abandoning others, sensing their banality. But he had taken the first step and had immediately shown the essential skill of a writer: the ability to separate oneself into layers, to examine oneself through a microscope, categorize oneself according to possible themes, to treat one's own "I" as material. However, Stepan was hopelessly confused by his own self, at times feeling his own emptiness and, at other times, an excess of sensations that he could not bring under control.

Anguished, he raised his head and glanced at the current speaker whom the audience was giving more attention than previous speakers and he, too, began to listen. This one was speaking melodiously and with wit, placing emphasis on appropriate words, underlining sentences as if he were mounting them in shining frames. To the extent that he was able, he threw out a pithy word to the audience, evoked laughter, adjusted his pince-nez, and set off on a new inspiration. From his lips poured quotations in all languages, literary facts, demi-facts, and anecdotes. His facial expression evoked the anger of an insulted deity, the misery of a scorned dwarf, his torso curved and straightened in harmony with his authorial gestures. His words formed into lumps of malicious dough, which he rolled into leaf-shaped dumplings, sprinkled with baker's sugar and glazing, embellished with marmalade roses, and then he paused for a moment to admire his own creation before serving up these delicacies for consumption.

"Who's that," Stepan asked Yasha, impressed with the confectionary art.

Yasha was amazed at the limitless depth of Stepan's ignorance. This was Mykhailo Svitozarov, the most renowned of critics. For the first time that evening, Stepan joined the rest of the audience in a storm of applause that drowned out the words of the eminent critic.

At twelve midnight, the head of the Cultural Committee of the local chapter of the All-Ukrainian Academy of Sciences closed (and covered up) the evening, saying a few moving words to the effect that somehow things would work themselves out, that there wasn't really any fatal crisis, and three cheers for literature. The evening ended and the field of battle was cleared without the help of first-aid battalions, since literary corpses do not lose their peripatetic functions.

"They sure did go at each other," exclaimed Yasha on the street. "I love to watch. This one gives the other one a whack and that one gives the first a double whack."

"Their writing is inferior, that's the issue," said the instructor solemnly. "I'm reading Zagoskin at the moment. Now there's a writer!"

"And I like Benois," said Nusia.

Hanusia was silent. Literature had robbed her of four hours, and tomorrow morning she must rise at dawn to complete an order.

Nadiika walked behind with Stepan, telling him the news from the village. He was sullenly silent. By the porch she whispered to him, "Come tomorrow."

Stepan walked home enraptured by a single thought, having surrendered to it completely, down to the very last cell of his brain. The desire that had arisen and had now taken hold of him dominated him completely, consumed all his energies for its own purpose, blocked out the rest of the world, making him like the woodcock that hears only its own song. The youthful spring of his consciousness, which heretofore had fluttered only weakly, acquired tension and began to expand, giving motion to hundreds of gears and levers. Yes, Stepan must become a writer! He saw nothing frightening or unusual in this intention. Within a couple of hours it was completely familiar, as if he had nurtured it for years and, in his nervous apprehension, he saw a sign of his talent, a display of his inspiration for creative work.

He had already chosen a topic: he would write a story about his old jagged razor that nicked him mercilessly every time he shaved. Here was its extraordinary story.

Back in 1919, he had hidden in the forests with a rifle during the uprising against the Denikin forces. They were a small platoon, maybe twenty men, making their way to the main insurgent camp near Cherkasy. That night they had been surrounded, but unsuccessfully—the entire platoon had managed to slip out, escaping one by one to nearby villages, to wait for a more opportune time. Having hidden his rifle in a recognizable haystack on a field, Stepan had wandered the road a free citizen, but he was captured and delivered for interrogation. He insisted so patiently and naively to the gentleman officer that he was just an innocent young man from that village over there that the officer let doubt creep in and gave orders to a Circassian to escort Stepan to the village. There, he was to determine whether Stepan really lived in the village and why he was wandering in the field—and should the story prove false, to execute him before the assembled villagers to spread fear and serve as a lesson for all.

Yelling frightening threats, the scruffy, black-haired soldier in a fur hat mounted his horse, lassoed Stepan for security and led him in front, promising to shoot him like a rabid dog at the first attempt to escape. After a mile Stepan, swearing by his parents and all that is sacred that he was a peaceful villager, as a sign of his good character offered his severe captor the razor that he always carried in his boot leg. The Circassian became persuaded of Stepan's innocence, whipped him across the back, and told him to run off as fast and as far as his feet could carry him. But Stepan knew their merry tricks too well and stood in place until the Caucasian had ridden off so far that he could no longer put a bullet in Stepan's back. The strangest thing, however, came a week later, when the rebels finally regrouped and successfully gave battle to the Denikinites. Stepan noticed the Caucasian's corpse on the battlefield and pulled his own razor from the dead man's pocket. This adventure was intriguing in its own right, but Stepan deepened it and gave it a nearly symbolic significance.

In his story, the razor first belonged to a front-line officer, the embodiment of the tsarist regime, but that officer was killed at the beginning of the Revolution and the razor passed on to the victor, a supporter of the Provisional Government. From him it went to a Petliurite, who soon lost it to a Red partisan, who momentarily gave it up to a Denikinite but quickly got it back, this time permanently, as its lawful owner. The fate of his razor was being elevated to the level of a history of the Civil War. It would be a symbol of the battle for authority. But this canvas needed to be embroidered with shiny threads and decorated with substance and action, so that the idea would truly come to life. Along the way home, he considered various episodes and details, basing them on his military experience.

The wooden clock in the kitchen showed 12:15 when Stepan entered the house, quietly lit a lamp, grabbed some paper, and sat down at the table to write, drowning in a torrent of images and words. At 2:30, he finished, put the manuscript away without reading it, lay down, and, after a few more minutes of vivid recollections, sank into sleep like a stone.

Chapter Eight

After cleaning up around the cows and completing all his domestic obligations according to a definite regimen he had worked out, Stepan read over his story and was left wholly satisfied. A wonderful story! Thoughtful and wise. And he had written it! He lovingly turned the pages—material evidence of his talent and a guarantee of future fame. After correcting a few blemishes, and writing out a clean copy, he considered the story's further fortune. First of all, he must sign it, attach it to himself with a unique name. He knew that some writers choose a different name, a so-called pseudonym or pseudo-name, like monks who renounce the world and their very selves, and everything that defines them. This is what Oleksandr Oles had done, for example, but Stepan found this path unappealing. In the first place, his surname was not one that would bring any shame—it was even very contemporary, if you like—and, in the second place, what was the point of hiding? Let everyone know that Stepan Radchenko writes stories, that he is a writer, that he reads his works at the Academy and is greeted with applause. Let there be a copy of his book in the Village Hall library, and may the friends he left behind there marvel and envy his achievement!

But as he was about to put down his signature, he hesitated. While his surname raised no objections, his name itself—Stepan—was troubling. It was not only too plain but somehow tarnished and coarse. He thought for a long time, torn between preserving himself entirely in his signature and making it more sonorous and sparkling. He went through a whole stack of names looking for a worthy successor, then suddenly he lit upon a wonderful idea: to simply make a slight alteration in his own name, to give it the required dignity while changing only a single letter and moving up the stress. He made his choice and signed the story, becoming not Stepán, but Stéfan, thus giving himself a new christening.

The fate of every literary work is, if possible, to be published, to find its way to its reader, and to captivate him. Stefan Radchenko, the writer, held out great hopes for himself and trusted even more in his own abilities to achieve them. In his own mind, his story would surely find a place on the pages of some journal, and it would happen soon. From his experience in the Village Hall library, he knew only of the journal *Chervonyi shliakh*, published in Kharkiv. That's where he should send his story. But his desire to hear someone else's opinion of his story without delay convinced him that he must give it to a qualified reader this very day. But to whom? Why, Mykhailo Svitozarov, of course—the critic who had spoken so beautifully yesterday from the lectern, captivating everyone and garnering such applause. He was the one, the only one! He was very knowledgeable about literature, surely he was very sensitive to all the latest developments, particularly the ones with fresh new ideas. Surely he would want to offer his support, advice, and guidance to a beginning writer! After all, this was his obligation and duty. In the overheated imagination of our young writer, the figure of this critic became a benevolent divinity who would most graciously accept the proffered literary offering.

Stepan resolved to visit the critic. True, he did not know his address, but his creative instinct promptly suggested that he might discover it at the address bureau. How convenient to live in a city! All the various conveniences! Having asked Tamara Vasylivna where that bureau was located, Stepan set off for it before lunch and, for ten kopecks (one hryvenyk), he learned which path to take to the literary heights.

After lunch, he stepped out of the gate with the sure stride of a person who has found his own place in the great jungle of the modern world. He passed one city block after another, carelessly stopping in front of store windows and posters, to show himself that he was not

in a hurry. On Volodymyr Street, across from the Khmel-
nytskyi monument, he entered a park and sat down
on a bench among the children playing there, who were
jumping, running, and throwing a ball. Their joy infect-
ed him. Catching the ball that happened to roll up to his
feet, Stepan threw it so high—as high as the buildings
themselves—that the kids yelled and cheered, all except
its owner, who worried that her toy would never return
from the great womb of the heavens. But the ball did
fall, like a bomb from under the clouds, eliciting a new
explosion of wild joy. Everyone jostled to give Stepan
their own ball to see it fly into the sky. Taking three into
his hands he began to toss them all together, like a circus juggler, completely enchanting his young admirers.

In their company, he enjoyed a sweet moment without dark-tinged thoughts about the future or memories
of the past. He felt the strange flood of existence that
gives satisfaction all on its own, without recourse to
hopes or plans. He felt like a bird resting in flight on outspread wings, capturing with its small eye the lush earth,
a flower opening its petals in the morning, spilling its
sweet scent to greet the sun.

Having said goodbye to the kids, who yelled after him as he left, he went on. Everything around him
pleased his eye: the old bell tower of Saint Sophia, the
streetcar, and the uneven street lined with chestnut trees.
By the opera he stopped to listen to some Ukrainian
songs performed by two women and a blind old man,

representatives of those artists who were "going out into the streets." From there, he turned onto Ncstor Street, guided by his desires and the directions he was given at the address bureau. The closer he came to the precious building, the more he felt—not anxiety, but the feelings of a woman who must undress before her doctor. Hastily, he prepared the words he would say: "Excuse me, I have written a story, and I've come to you so that you could listen to it."

No, better this: "Excuse me for bothering you, but I would like to have your opinion of a story I have written."

The building where the great critic lived was itself great, with two separate wings surrounding a courtyard. Guided by his intuition, Stepan climbed up to the fifth floor in the first building, but the last apartment there had the number fifteen, instead of the required eighteen. After making inquiries in the courtyard, Stepan entered the second building with growing anxiety. Knocking on the door with his fist, he waited, his heart pounding louder than his knock. He knocked again, frightened by his own compulsion.

"Who do you want?" asked a woman who opened the door.

"Excuse me for bothering you," Stepan began, not recognizing his own voice. "I would like to see..." he stopped, forgetting the name. "I would like to see ... the critic."

"The critic?" asked the surprised woman, holding her capricious housecoat across her breast with her hand.

"That is, he writes essays," explained Stepan, weakening under the burden of the cross. "Mykhailo ..."

"Do you mean Mykhailo Demydovych Svitozarov? The professor?" the woman said, relieved, and let him enter. "Yes, yes. This way, please."

She led him along a dark corridor while he trembled like a young thief breaking into a home for the very first time.

"Misha, someone's here to see you."

The young man entered the room where the great critic sat at a table by the window, writing. The critic did not raise his head. Stepan stopped at the edge of the rug that lay on the floor and timidly cast his eyes along the large bookcases lining the wall. A pious shiver chilled his heart in this holy of holies, and he was ready to stand there for an hour, or two, even forever, absorbing the feeling of greatness and languor.

Finally, the great critic finished pouring his thoughts onto the paper and cast an inquiring glance at the youth, who felt the gaze like a frighteningly sharp point pricking his skin.

"Excuse me," he said, bowing. "Are you Comrade Svitozarov?"

Conscious of the pointlessness of such a question, he tried, to the degree it was possible, to swallow the inappropriate word "comrade."

"I'm Svitozarov. How can I help you?"

"I've written a story here—" Stepan began, but stopped when he saw an unpleasant grimace on the critic's face.

"I have no time," the critic answered. "I'm very busy." This disparaging answer stopped Stepan dead in his tracks. In the despondent chill that enveloped him, he understood only one thing: there was no desire to listen to him.

Since Stepan didn't move, the critic deemed it necessary to repeat himself, emphasizing every syllable: "I–am–ve-ry–bu-sy!"

"Goodbye," Stepan muttered glumly.

Walking out of the courtyard, he wandered about on unfamiliar streets, carrying in his heart the unbearable weight of helpless anger. He had never felt so demeaned and destroyed. The proud words of that bookworm fell on him like shameful spittle. So he doesn't have time—well, let him set a time for an appointment. Even if he refuses to help, he could at least suggest where to turn for advice. And what right does he have to speak *like that*? Oh yes, he felt cut to the quick by that pompous manner, that aristocratic manner of a literary gentleman.

Walking with his head bent low, he fancied indefinite thoughts of revenge. He could crush that snail and break his ostentatious pince-nez, and drag him around on the floor, since the superiority of his own muscles was beyond doubt. And, because this was the only kind of revenge he could think of, the realization of his powerlessness depressed him even more. Once again, he could sense awakening within himself the peasant from the village, with a dull antipathy to everything that was above him.

Finding himself near a park, he went in and sat down on the furthest bench. After a while, he looked around and recognized his surroundings—it was Golden Gates Square, with a fence around the two piles of crumbling stone from which it took its name. Overcome by a rising flame of all-consuming hatred, he muttered gruffly and with a wry grimace, "Golden Gates, indeed!"

The unexpected wound clouded all of the young man's thoughts. He could not escape the sense that he had left his home as an August Stefan but was now returning a mere bumpkin Stepan. He looked glumly at the silhouettes of passing figures and saw in each of them a secret potential enemy.

The green leaves on the trees were darkening, the splash of the fountain was growing stronger in the twilight, and a thick evening was descending from above the foliage. Suddenly, the lights turned on. In his remote corner, Stepan was long since all alone. The daytime visitors—fathers with newspapers and mothers and nannies with strollers—had melted away along with the last rays of sunlight. In their place came nocturnal moths, and those who chased them.

Stepan stood up, took up his story, and tore it to shreds.

"May you be damned," he said.

He set off toward Nadiika's, although it was all the same to him whether he saw her or not. He would have gone to her after a victory, so he decided to go after a defeat as well. She met him happily in her kerchief on the corner of her street, where she had been strolling, hoping to see him.

When she saw him she raised her head and laughed eagerly, but he greeted her coolly.

"Hello, Nadiika."

They walked over to the Tsar's Garden, and the girl laughed and cheerily described the first day of classes at the vocational college. He clenched his teeth. Classes had probably begun at his Institute as well. Well, let them begin! He immediately closed up within himself and looked out onto the world through self-imposed grates. Nadiika's laugh was unbearable to him, her cheerfulness offended him. Suddenly he felt an antipathy to the girl arising within him and the sensation was pleasant.

"And what does Semén write," asked Nadiika, not yet sensing his mood.

"He doesn't write anything at all," he answered. And, truly, he did not know, because he had not yet read the letter from his friend in the village.

Nadiika looked at him, perplexed.

"Stepan, dear, you're strange today," she said cautiously.

He didn't answer, and they reached the edge of the Tsar's Garden in silence. This silence offended the girl and she stopped, holding back tears.

"If you don't love me, I'll go home."

Stepan yanked her by the arm.

"I *love* you. Let's go."

He felt his power over her and wanted her to submit. All his animosity was focused on her and, had she resisted, he might have hit her. But she went along meekly.

When they reached the top of the hill, a blue rocket flew up from below and went out with a quiet crackle. It was a fireworks display. Pink, blue, red, and green flames whistled and streaked into the sky, describing bright arcs against the dark background, exploding and then falling back down to earth in a shower of sparks.

Stepan got out the last of his cigarettes and lit it.

"They're all pigs," he grumbled and spat.

Nadiika was enchanted by the new experience, the play of colors and fire, and she had forgotten for a moment about her cheerless boyfriend.

"Who?" she asked in confusion.

"All of them watching over there."

"We're watching, too," she cautiously observed, frightened by his voice.

"You think they're doing this for you?" Stepan asked harshly.

She sighed. He turned his back to the fireworks and walked away. Nadiika silently caught up with him and glanced at his face. It was disinterested and cold in the intermittent glow of the cigarette.

In a few minutes, they ended up in the thicket where the alley ended and the path along the cliffside began. Here, dark bushes breathed a moist, gloomy calm, like that of a cellar. Stopping beside the ravine, made deeper by the darkness, they looked across to the other side where groves of tall trees stood like dark giants were frozen in a fearful silence. The silence everywhere harbored anticipation and desire, as before a storm, and the noise of the city below echoed like distant thunder.

Stepan's cigarette went out, and he threw it impatiently into the ravine. Then he turned to the girl who met his gaze with joyful expectation.

"Dear Stepan," she asked, leaning over toward him. "Why are you so ... angry?"

Suddenly he took her in his arms and squeezed her breasts into his own chest with a passion sharpened by anger and humiliation. For this forceful embrace, she was willing to forgive him all his previous inattention. She took his head in her hands and wanted to pull it closer and kiss him, but he continued his motionless squeezing, weakening her with his embrace. The girl pressed her hands against his shoulders, trying to push him away, but, groaning in pain and feeling suffocated, she dropped her hands, sensing suddenly that he was crushing her and bending her down, that her knees were giving out and the dark clouds of the sky were floating before her eyes.

She fell outstretched to the ground, chilled by the tingling touch of air and grass on her uncovered thighs, squeezed by the dumb weight of his body, as it jerked and divided and penetrated her.

Afterward, they sat on a bench above the river, which ran silently below, a play of lights reflecting on its waves. Cutting through the clouds and leaves, the white moon rose in the west, casting cold tinsel onto the waters.

The urge to smoke tormented Stepan as his fingers shredded an empty package of cigarettes.

"Why are you silent?" he asked Nadiika, tossing the shredded package into the ravine.

She embraced him longingly and hid her face in his knees.

"You do love me?" she whispered.

He raised her up and pushed her off.

"I *love* you. Why ask?"

She then began to cry—loudly, gulping and choking as if the flood of tears she had held back had burst out in a ruinous torrent. Stepan looked around.

"Don't cry," he said harshly. She wailed and cried on, losing her presence and her will in the flood of tears.

"I'm telling you—stop it!" he said again, jerking her by the arm.

She stopped, but a muffled cry again burst out, enraging him.

"In that case, I'm leaving," he said, rising. "It's your fault," he yelled. "You—you're to blame!" And he left, full of longing and anger.

Chapter Nine

L ife is frightening in its unrelenting continuity, its unstoppable drive. It doesn't adjust for a person's greatest suffering. It ignores a person's greatest pain. A person can struggle among life's thorns, but life will continue. It will pass right by, along with its acolytes who yell for all to hear, in fear or in awe, that there can be no roses without thorns. Life is that ubiquitous scoundrel who answers the tattered beggar's pleas with a shove, a slap, or a stick, and then moves on, smoking his cigarette without even turning his gold monocle in the victim's direction. Shacks for the living sprout up immediately on the ruins of an earthquake to accommodate the survivors who ceremoniously tossed the crushed victims into the ground, but the graves are soon overgrown with grass, and the veils of mourning fall from faces that have long wished to smile.

At 37 Nyzhnii Val Street, there was no sign of the glacier that had crushed the spirit of one of its inhabitants. The cows were cleaned and fed, and sufficient quantities of water had been brought indoors for everyone's needs and wishes. Every indication pointed to good order, nothing signaled any changes, and a lost coin would have been more noticeable here than some fellow's lost peace of mind.

The prudent shopkeeper had already begun to put in a supply of wood for the winter. For a moment, the sleepy yard of the Hnidyi home awoke to the sounds of cursing delivery men and squeaking logs. Indistinct gray workers appeared, of the kind that hang around the bazaars and on corners with saws and axes, waiting for clients who will purchase their labor. A team of workers typically consists of two adults and a youth who only carries the split lumber, in keeping with the child labor protection rules. Stepan joined in helping them, assured that this would not influence their negotiated wage. All day, he eagerly cut and split the logs, swinging an axe with great anger, as if the logs were his mortal enemies. He handled the logs as if they were the branches of a vine, he talked with the villagers about their work and their lives, about their needs, the level of cultural activity in their village. But, when they left, he felt guilty about his hollow words and insincere interest. It wasn't the first time he had observed a change in himself, but previously he had turned his thoughts away from this change. Now he had to admit to himself honestly that he was estranged from the village. It had faded in his recollections like a lantern fades in the light of day, but it hung over him as a rebuke, as a source of concern.

In the evening, lying on his bed, exhausted by the logs and by his thoughts, he suddenly remembered the letter from his friend in the village—he still hadn't read it. Stepan retrieved it from his pocket, where it had aged like an old document. There, after commenting on the state of affairs in the village, his friend continued: "...it always seems that you've only left for a short time and that you'll return in a few days. We got used to having you here. Work continues, more or less, but you know our guys—as long as you keep your hands on the reins, it's all right. And now Oleksa Petrovych is being transferred to the district. It's strange—whatever is good around here runs away from us. I guess it makes sense, it's only misery that keeps people here. We're tied to this place like a curse. And, when someone leaves, believe me, it makes you feel so sad, you feel like crying. Sometimes I'd start thinking that it's time to get married already—but that's just another pipe dream. You say you'll come home for Christmas. We'll have a talk. But I don't think you'll actually come. There's nothing here for you, no wife, no kids. Out there, at first it's lonely, but there's plenty of work, interesting work, and you'll soon forget us and make new friends. But do try to write..."

Every word of this letter hurt him by its simple, glaring truth. He could not contradict a single word. Holding the letter in his hands, he closed his eyes and whispered, "I won't come. I'll never come."

He called himself a traitor. This was the behavior of a renegade who had robbed his own parents, and he expected them to curse him. But as soon as he began to berate himself, he lost sight of the object of his disgust. It disappeared under the force of an unknown power, which methodically transformed his reproaches into pointless outbursts. Why, after all, did he consider himself a traitor? Plenty of people leave the village! Cities grow at the expense of villages—that's normal, completely normal. Furthermore, his higher education would be in economics. Once he finished that, he would obviously not be returning to a village. Living in the city was his destiny. And what had really changed in him? He was the same person he had been before. Everything was fine. He had food and shelter, in a day or two he'd get his scholarship. Where was the problem?

And then, like an indistinct pain, like nausea, like a terrible nightmare, a memory emerged—one he had passionately tried to destroy, to eradicate, and whose traces he had attempted to remove from his consciousness until it grew over in a barely noticeable scab, bleeding only occasionally—the memory of Nadiika. This girl, who had only recently been so attractive to him was now a nightmare. His love had turned into a counterfeit banknote, received amid confusion and bustle and then thrown away as trash, with anger at being so deceived. She was from the village, which had now faded for him. She was a brief episode in the transition that had overtaken him, although a painful episode, a difficult one, with little justification. What about her? He gritted his teeth and whispered insolently, "If not me, then some other guy."

He was ready to yell this from rooftops to rid himself of the gnawing pangs that would not yield to his willful commands. But he had to cross her out of his life, to crush her image within himself, to remove this constraint that bound him like a chain on a prisoner's leg. He had glimpsed freedom through the grates on the window, and he now felt a secret hostility to anyone who was a witness to his past. In changing his plans, he was burdened by the power his old friends held over him. He could not force himself to return the books he had borrowed from Levko, even though he had read or at least skimmed them. It would be agonizing to meet a person whom he had earlier considered an ideal worthy of emulation but had then suddenly been revealed in his emptiness. In his eyes, Levko had shamefully become, together with Yasha and the instructor, essentially a member of the threesome that now symbolized the dullness of the village, its dumb backwardness, its vile inferiority. It sees no possibilities, or doesn't look for them, or doesn't need them. And Levko's neatly arranged room, the object of his jealousy, now seemed like a blind mole's burrow.

After a few days of solitary despair, he forced himself to visit the Institute. Yes, he had been awarded the scholarship. Instead of being happy, he felt offended. Only eighteen karbovanets! They said it would be twenty-five. He had secretly hoped for even more: there are, after all, scholarships for fifty, even for the full one hundred! Classes had started already, but he had forgotten to bring pencil and paper, so he figured it was pointless to attend one today. And he wasn't really inclined to go to class right now.

Back on the street, he was overcome with an unusual concern. He made frequent stops at advertising kiosks, announcements, film posters, and shop windows, scrutinizing them with the same attention that he had once given objects at the museum, and with a certain piety and excitement. He was particularly attracted by the illustrations. A giant poster for the circus in three vivid colors—red, green, and light-blue—announced that a well-known and unusually dextrous clown and acrobat would soon be appearing and, as incontrovertible evidence of this, there was an image of him along with the circus troupe, and another separately, on the ground, and yet another high up, in the unreachable expanse of a high dome.

"This is very interesting," thought Stepan.

From an adjacent advertisement, he learned that the Taras Shevchenko Theater was offering a concert series by a world-famous violinist, who gazed down at him with a friendly smile from the gray poster.

"Excellent!" Stepan said approvingly.

And, at the State Cinema No. 1, a beautiful film with a big-name actor was playing. Examining the mysterious eastern costumes worn by actors in the still photos from the movie, he had an acute sense of just how unfashionable his own field jacket, yuft boots, and crumpled cap were. The famous actor was generously displayed in tails with a turban, in tails without a turban, in the cloak of a raj, on foot and on horseback, alone and in a duet with his sweetheart, and in a chorus of his admirers. Silently but sullenly, Stepan moved away from these photographs.

Next, he stopped by a bakery window where, in a poetic arrangement on white doilies, in delicately painted boxes, on china plates and vases, were displayed sweet and unspeakably delicious treats. His sad eyes devoured this heap of wafer and almond tortes, rum babas, glazed nuts, mounds of chocolate, layers of colorful candies, and pastries of various form and content without knowing their names but understanding full well that they were not donuts, muffins, or cupcakes. He fingered the twenty kopecks in his only pocket but did not dare enter the store. Instead, he bought himself a couple of pastries on the street from a lovely girl who had the honor to sell them but never to eat them. Taking these slippery products of the sugar industry in his hands, he impetuously gulped them down, telling himself sternly, "Quiet! I, too, want to indulge."

To him, it was like a First Communion, which leaves in the faithful a sadness for the blood consumed and a hope for eternal life.

Before a ready-made clothing store, Stepan examined the suits with an expression as if it were merely a matter of choosing which one would look best on him—in a fine material and well-tailored, of course. The price tags did not bother the handsome boy at all. They were far beyond his means—he might just as well choose the most expensive suit, since he couldn't afford even the least expensive one. He was free to imagine himself the undisputed owner of these treasures, which would make him handsomer than the movie star, more talented than the violinist, and more dextrous than the circus acrobat. He could change suits as he wished at any moment, trying on top hats and ties, with matching handkerchiefs and socks, because there is no law that prohibits making use of someone else's property in your own imagination. And, in that moment, Stepan came to understand the magical power of clothing, which had long since stopped being a means of covering the body and had acquired a wider and more noble function—to adorn and enhance it. Perhaps he would create something of genius if he were dressed right now in a high-collared English shirt, short narrow slacks, and pointed shoes. But, in fact, he did not create anything, because he could not rid himself for one moment of the awful realization that none of the items in the window belonged to him nor ever could. He sighed but kept standing there, sinking with his gaze into the fabrics and the silks, like a diver trying to find pearls but coming up only with algae.

He was getting tired of the fruitless gawking when a woman in a batiste blouse that betrayed the edge of her camisole walked up to the window. Leaning her bare arms against the railing, she carelessly surveyed the color wheel of ties, perhaps even choosing one to make her lover an elegant, pleasing, and not overly expensive present, one that would satisfy both the heart and the wallet, since the latter expands and contracts, just like the former. This lady was perfumed with a strong Parisian fragrance, and its scent wafted around her like an illusion. It engulfed Stepan in a sweet fog, exciting him, and his nose widened, greedily inhaling the unfamiliar, fine scent, which poured through his veins like an intoxicating smoke. He smelled this woman as one smells flowers, breathed her as one breathes in the freshness of spring, the tar of a pine forest, the morning mist rising from the earth. Only the first wave was somewhat disagreeable to him, like the unaccustomed smoke of a cigarette that soon becomes a craving. Alongside this woman, he experienced the swooning dizziness that people experience at great elevations, recoiling from danger but also captivated by it. And, when she had gone, he gazed after her with a brazen and reverent eye. Shuddering, he thought that this skirt could also rise, no matter how white, that he might also take possession of this fragrant body, as of all others, and immediately the thought struck him as savage and frightening. But this Kyiv woman, daubed with Paris, smoothed out the scab in him that belonged to Nadiika, rendering it a pale and inconspicuous bruise.

At home, he wandered in the yard, suffocating in the crazy dreams that beset him. They weren't even dreams but senseless, ridiculous hallucinations. Jumping from one in mid-stream, he latched on to another, sucked it, tasted it, and then cast it off, too, with countless other and better ones to choose from. Here, he was a people's commissar, driven around in an automobile, making public speeches, which thrilled him to the very marrow. He welcomed foreign delegations, conducted negotiations, introduced strange laws that changed the face of the earth and, after his death, modestly unveiled a monument to himself. Then, elsewhere, he became a great writer whose every line tolled around the world like a prophetic bell, agitating people's hearts, especially his own. Or, abandoning great deeds, he would endow his face with captivating beauty, dress in the choicest suits, and conquer women's hearts in droves, breaking up marriages and running away with his lovers across every conceivable frontier, except the one of his imagination. Or he would saddle a rebel horse, break out the hidden sawed-off rifles, and lead a band of mindless men in a siege of the city, where he would shoot his way into these shops, pile his wagons high with these suits, these delicacies and these pastries, and force a perfumed woman beneath him, like a captive. This was the image that captivated him most. Clenching his powerless fists, he whispered in anger and desire, "I would loot and pillage, and pillage some more!"

His fantasies were inexhaustible, his imagination untiring, his vanity unconquerable. He held in his hands a magic stone that trembled and burned, revealing all of the world's wonders. And that stone was he himself.

And when reason, that wearisome preacher, that desiccated sage who cannot understand desire, would fearfully begin its miserable sermon, he resembled a toy ship on the waves of a real ocean, and all of his wailing sounded like the complaints of a homeowner trying to mend a broken water pipe by asking it to stop leaking.

That night, he had a dream. He was walking through a lush garden along a straight alley shaded by trees on whose branches elongated fruits, like bananas, hid among the leaves. Looking to one side, he saw a gazebo that he hadn't noticed before and walked into the shade of the grapevines growing around its walls. The unfamiliar woman who sat there did not even raise her head. Hesitating, he stopped at the threshold and then noticed that she was beckoning him with her finger. Looking closer with ever greater amazement, he observed that she was wearing nothing but a nightshirt, and beneath her feet was a pond in which she would be bathing. Suddenly, she fell back, face up, and a breeze lifted the rest of her covering. Savagely he threw himself on her, but no sooner had he touched her than he fell into a thick dense puddle and awoke from the pounding of his heart.

For a long time, he stared into the darkness before him. According to folk wisdom, a naked woman in a dream foretells unavoidable shame.

Chapter Ten

The only relief Stepan had these days from his difficult trials was his contact with the Hnidyis' son, Maksym—the same fellow who had treated him to a cigarette back in the penniless days of his first acquaintance with life in the city. This young fellow, barely older than Stepan, was easygoing by nature, dreamy and restrained, with a soft voice and a truly deep and sincere smile. His expressions and manner evidenced the mature equilibrium of a person who was satisfied with his life and easily carried his destiny on his shoulders. It was precisely this tranquility that attracted Stepan to the landlord's son, whom he had at first disparagingly labeled a young gentleman. In his own confusion, he instinctively gravitated toward anything self-assured, and he secretly envied Maksym's good fortune.

For his part, Maksym was well disposed and attentive to the village boy. Two years earlier, he himself had finished the Institute where Stepan was just beginning. While his own recollections of his studies bordered on the painful, he endured conversations about specific programs, professors, and the various incidents of student life.

"Where do you work?" asked Stepan one day.

"At the Leatherworkers' Collective," answered Maksym. "I'm a pretty decent accountant. And that takes some inborn talent, to be sure."

"What kind of talent?"

"Attention to detail, most of all. And a kind of self-sacrifice, if you will. It's a peculiar world. That's why there are so few real accountants."

Stepan nodded. Since he had an active imagination and the skill to grasp everything immediately, as well as a propensity to take an interest in everything, he suddenly understood that noiseless world of invoices and vouchers, where life's variability fits into monotonous formulas, developed in advance, where numbers replace events and people. He sighed, unconsciously longing for the carefree tranquility of documents.

"Does it pay well?" he asked, after one of the frequent pauses in their conversations.

"It's pay scale 16, with 25% benefits. It amounts to about 140 karbovanets."

Stepan could hardly hold back his amazement. For him, one hundred karbovanets seemed an amount beyond his most fervent desires, but a hundred plus forty more was a true marvel of immeasurable wealth. He asked naively, "So why aren't you getting married?"

This question made Maksym visibly uncomfortable. Hesitating a moment, he answered indistinctly, "You see, that's a complicated thing. And not at all a necessary one. You see, a fellow grows up and naturally starts thinking that it's necessary to get married. It's a tradition of sorts."

Suddenly he laughed and added, "And, if you want, I can give you the textbooks. I kept them all after I finished the Institute. Though since then they've published new ones."

But Stepan was in no hurry to take advantage of this gracious offer, since he was not very interested in any books at the moment, not even the most erudite ones, except the open book of his own life, whose most recent pages he skimmed incessantly every day. Unable to find what might be called happiness, particularly one that was his alone, finding there nothing but monotonous days—whether because there really were no brighter memories, or because such memories are the unique privilege of old age, where they replace hope, or maybe because he was deliberately blurring them to crave the future all the more—he understood the past as a dull and difficult path along the ridge toward a precipice, which had brought him to the edge of a cliff in the mountains, to an abyss that he must either jump across, risking a swift fall to its base, or else return to the unhappy valley from which he had begun. Standing at the edge of the abyss, he felt the terrible determinacy of life, which leaves a person so little choice. It began to seem to him that his own path, in keeping with the general rule, had been ordained far in advance, and that the wide avenues that he seemingly chose for himself were actually narrow alleys, along which he was wandering blindly. The children's game of blind man's bluff, where a group of pranksters tease and poke an individual who is blindfolded while avoiding being caught by him, now became for him a symbol full of the deepest meaning, a representation of the essential condition of man in the world. Experience told him that he who snatches for the least and prepares for the grab with a patient, siege-like strategy will capture the most. Having fallen through thin ice on a number of occasions and gotten cold and wet in these unhappy immersions, he wanted to be careful, and so he temporarily came to a complete halt, viewing any movement as potentially dangerous.

The next evening Maksym called Stepan into his room in the house and insisted on giving him the old textbooks. The homeowner's son was in an unusually excited mood, talking a great deal and laughing frequently. Giving Stepan the books along with some advice, he cheerfully added, "See, you were surprised that I make what seems to be so much money but am not getting married. No doubt you think I'm lonely and don't know what to do with my money. But look here," he pointed at his library. "I have lots of books. I like to buy them, and read them, too. And, you know, there are those who buy books but don't read them! Buy them and put them on a shelf. That's silly, don't you think? Plenty of things are silly. You're still young—I don't mean you're foolish. Not at all. But someday you'll see that reading books is far more interesting than doing the things that are described in them yourself."

He sat Stepan down in a chair by the writing table, lit a lamp that stood on it, and extinguished the electric light on the ceiling. Shadows stretched into the corners of the room. Stepan's gaze swept from the illuminated circle on the table to the gloom beyond, which seemed to give objects and words greater significance. Maksym sat down across from him.

"And then," he continued, "it never turns out the way it does in a book. You laugh, but it's true. This, too, you'll understand some day. I'm not saying 'such things never happen,' only that 'it doesn't happen that way.' In a book everything is gathered together, polished, ordered, and made prettier. In the real world, things are the way they are, but in a book it's the way it should be. And tell me, what's more interesting? Let's say you go to a photographer and say, 'Take a picture of me that makes me look handsome.' You send the picture to some friends who have not seen you in a long time and maybe never will. Now tell me, do you think it's better if they see you in person? I'm not saying you're some kind of ogre—it's just an example. Would you like a cigarette?"

He held out a leather cigarette case to Stepan.

"And this, too, is where the money goes: I like good tobacco. You know, in the years of war communism, everyone smoked that cheap tobacco. Not me! You won't find cigarettes like these anywhere. Nothing but the finest tobacco, scented with opium."

"But it's bad for your health," objected Stepan, lighting a cigarette.

"Everything is bad for your health! Breathing is bad for your health, because it burns up your blood. So don't breathe, perhaps you'll live longer. You probably think that, if you avoid doing harmful things, you'll live longer. But think this way: 'I'll do the harmful things and maybe life will be more satisfying.'"

"Life is interesting even without opium," said Stepan. "Here, in the city, I tell you, what's important is having money, a job. Oh, to have some money! But opium, that's for those who don't have a reason to live—the empty ones, the sick."

"Splendid! What an analytical mind you have!" Maksym replied. "Do you think a person's strength can be measured in foot-pounds? Can you measure the fullness of life in kilograms? You're naive! When you first mentioned marriage, that's what I thought—you're naive."

"So you think everyone who gets married is naive?"

"It's not those who are married that are naive, but those who think they need to get married. No—those who get married are not naive at all. They're unfortunate, if you really want to know. Have you ever in your entire life seen a single happy marriage? Be honest! No? I haven't either. What do you think of such a state of affairs? You want me to show you something?" he asked conspiratorially. "But it's a secret."

He retrieved a small box from the drawer and opened it. On a velvet background lay a flat golden ring with small diamonds around a large ruby.

"Do you like it?" he asked, excited. "You know whom I'll give it to? My mother. Today is her birthday. Don't imagine we'll have company. We don't celebrate birthdays in our family. We live so quietly, no one ever comes over—did you notice?"

Stepan timidly took the jewelry in his hands and examined it, holding it in his palm. The diamonds sparkled, throwing sparks into the ruby, which it swallowed in a dull, bloody glow.

"It's very nice," he said, carefully putting the ring back into its box.

"You'd probably like to give something like that to your mother, wouldn't you?" Maksym continued. "Well, I know you're an orphan. If you want, I'll tell you something more. The only reason we took you in is because you're an orphan. We don't like strangers, we're used to being on our own. We wouldn't have taken you in for anything. But when I read in that letter that you had no parents, I spoke up right away and said we should take you in. Anyone who doesn't have a mother deserves help."

"Thank you," mumbled Stepan, experiencing warmth, shame, and a bitter pain at the revelation of this charity.

"Don't thank me or I'll get offended. I'm sorry I told you about this. But I really was thinking about you. And I suggested turning over the household chores to you. Surely that's better than hanging around a dormitory, and Mother also benefits from the help. But don't go expressing your gratitude. Just forget about it—forget all about it."

Then Maksym showed him a few of the treasures of his book collection: wonderful editions from the Petrine era, Ukrainian publications with engravings from the first half of the nineteenth century, and an enormous collection of postage stamps in five thick albums—the result of tireless collecting that had begun in his childhood. He told Stepan about the World Association of Philatelists, which he had been a member of for many years and through which he now conducted an intensive correspondence with fellow collectors in all corners of the world, supplying them with valuable stamps from the time of the Revolution.

"You know," he said, "I would have a place to stay all over the world—Australia, Africa, the Malay Islands, if ever I traveled there. The rules of our association require hosting any fellow members. But I've never been outside of Kyiv," he added.

From Maksym Stepan brought back to the kitchen a whole pile of textbooks on statistics, economic geography, and commercial accounting, and put them all aside for future reference. Whenever he made a new acquaintance, he promptly noted that person's inevitable ludicrous qualities and thus lost some of his respect for him. So it was with the generous Maksym, whom he designated a strange fellow, perceiving in him a similarity to the crazy teacher he had met at Levko's a few weeks earlier.

"People are strange!" he thought. "And what do they need? To live a simple life, but no—they're always seeking a convolution."

This was what he thought, despite the convolutions he himself was hopelessly seeking, since a person is absolutely incapable of living a simple life.

But what struck Stepan most was the mention of his own orphanhood, which had unexpectedly brought him such a benefit. Indeed, his mother had died, as people told him, when he was only two years old, and no recollections of her were saved in his memory. Thus, going through the pain and suffering of childhood, he had sought solace in dreams, gliding across steppes and forests, reaching out into the boundless distance. Later, he even lost the perception that his mother had ever existed in the same way that other women exist and give birth. Now the strange, filial tenderness that resonated in Maksym's voice awoke in him an aching longing for the woman who would have been dearest and closest to him. If only he had a mother he would not be so lonely. With grief, he recalled the fate of mothers in the village who cowered in the corners of their son's homes as mere extra mouths to feed, disdained by their grandchildren and daughters-in-law, and he imagined all the more clearly how he would have loved and honored his own. But she was lost to him forever, without a trace, and the sudden realization of this loss underscored his alienation in the world, where he lacked the most basic, first relationship, as well as the most basic hope for the future. Lying down to sleep, he somehow grew smaller, curled up like a child under the influence of his feelings. The unquenchable thirst for a mother awakened in him the sensation of her former caresses and singing over his cradle. He passionately recreated his imaginary mother, whose beautiful features suddenly transformed into the harrowing face of death.

In the morning, mostly because of the books he had brought yesterday, which admonished him by their presence, he decided it was time to stop playing the fool. Grabbing a pencil and some paper, he finally set off for the Institute. But the sights and sounds of the streets and people, particularly the loud ringing of church bells, objectively convinced him that today was Sunday. He had completely lost count of the days, and the situation amused him immensely.

"What a knucklehead," he thought about himself. "Well, tomorrow I start studying."

But he miscalculated by one day, discovering through his own experience that Monday is an unusually difficult day and not a good one to begin important matters. On Sunday night, an unexpected incident occurred, of the kind that leaves an indelible imprint on the character of an individual; an ember that continues to glow, despite multiple layers of subsequent ash, like the flame of a lantern, marking the dramatic turning points of a person's development.

That evening, Stepan resolutely sat down to read attentively the introduction to statistics, an astoundingly insightful science that unerringly calculates the likelihood of any person falling under the wheels of a streetcar, dying of cholera, or becoming a genius. But Stepan did not quite get to those instructive chapters, and when the wooden clock, the chief decoration of his quarters, indicated that the time was ten o'clock, he felt it was his right to sleep and thus resolve all outstanding questions from the previous day.

He fell asleep, and awoke at a quiet rustling by the bed. He instantly opened his eyes and, in the gray shadows of the room's only window, saw a white figure, enormous in the haze of his somnolent eyes. He sat up and asked in confusion, "Who's there?"

A thief? An illusion? A nightmare?

But the figure was coming closer, and Stepan didn't so much recognize as instantly guess that it was the landlady. What had happened? A fire? A sudden death? But before he could formulate a question, he felt the touch of a sizzling hand on his face, his neck, his chest. And then two hands. The halting, irregular breathing was getting closer, leaning over, and stopped on his own lips in a dry, ravenous imprint. The woman's hands slid around his waist, and on his chest he could feel the touch of soft, warm, and trembling flesh. Seized with incomprehensible fear, Stepan jerked away and pressed against the wall, eager to melt into it and disappear altogether.

"What are you doing? What's with you?" he muttered, gasping. His entire body stiffened in terror. His arms froze in ossified fear. He was breathing heavily and loudly, gasping for the cool, sharp air.

She went away quietly, and Stepan, as in a dream, heard the door gently close. Life was slowly returning to his limbs, his heart was steadying. He tried to move and cautiously stretched out, face up, on the bed. His legs were still trembling and blood throbbed in his temples. Slowly, as his terror subsided, he was realizing what had happened.

"What? How can this be?" Stepan blathered, flexing his hands.

Along with his presence of mind came the recollection of the kiss that he had broken off, of the contact with his chest and the embrace of her naked arms. Naked! Now, belatedly, he understood! Her entire body, her excited, submissive body, was separated from his by no more than a nightshirt. And he had pushed it away, like a coward, instead of diving into it, discovering in its depths a hidden, energy-sapping warmth. What had stopped him? Sin? A sense of wrongdoing, or injustice to someone? Conscience? What did he care for this clingy rubbish, these sharp needles scattered along life's roadways, the stupid morality of superstitions? No, it was only childish fear—there was no other explanation that he could fathom.

His blood, having cooled somewhat, was now again inflamed and pulsed through his veins. His young heart was beating at a full, youthful throttle. His inventive fantasy was creating images in his mind that would seem distasteful only to others but, in the flame of one's own imagination, were not subject to review by conscience. Overcome with a flaming desire for satisfaction, he carefully got up, trembling at the touch of the cold floor. On tiptoe he approached the door that led to the Hnidyis' bedrooms. Quietly he tried to open it, but it barely moved, only as far as the hook inside would allow. Thoughtlessly, Stepan was about to knock on the door, but his upraised hand fell limp. After all, it was his own fault.

The room was suffocating him. He stepped out onto the veranda in his underwear and sat down with his elbows on his knees. The cold air did not diminish his agitation. Fear and tension left a dull pain in his heart. Remorse for his sin—for the failure to commit the sin—gnawed at him, persistently, dreadfully. He called himself a dope, an idiot, a coward, and a loser. And not only because his unsatiated body had filled with bitterness, but also from the unexpressed deduction that possession of this lush woman, who was above his reach and more mature than he, could strengthen his spirit and temper his will, as sometimes happens after a victory that shows the hero himself what he is worth.

In the morning, Stepan, nervous and fidgety from a sleepless night, glumly hung about the yard, smoking cigarette after cigarette, depleting his supply of cheap tobacco. Although it was now a weekday and the Institute was open to accommodate his desire to study, the mere thought of school evoked a terrible disgust. Who cares about the Institute? Compared to last night's incident, studying would be simple and easily achieved. But the desire for this woman, about whom he wouldn't have dared to even dream yesterday, had been transformed into an aching thirst with an exotic, irresistible flavor, and had become, in the end, a burning issue of personal selfishness. The instant he imagined that this woman might not be his, anger welled up in him and brought to his lips the most insulting words. Adulteress. Debauchee. Even whore.

He was, however, quite capable of falling on his knees to beg her to smile at him at least once, to give him the smallest sign. But on meeting him in the kitchen, she was no different than she had been yesterday, the day before yesterday, a week or two weeks before. She did not betray last night's visit by the slightest of gestures. This seemed to him the very nadir of hypocrisy, the deep depravity of an overly self-indulgent female.

She had come to him. That was indisputable. So why this proud dissimulation? That was unclear. Would she come again? He understood perfectly that he had offended her by his behavior, that he should do or say something—but what? But how? He didn't know and he didn't dare, fearful of spoiling his chances by a word or gesture that ruins everything instead of fixing it.

Quietly, without being heard, he entered the kitchen where Tamara Vasylivna was cooking lunch. She stood with her back to the door, and Stepan entered unnoticed. Hobbled by the consciousness of his own mortification but simultaneously overwhelmed by an aching, almost beggarly desire, his eyes, alternating between pleading and voracious appetite, devoured the lines of her back and legs. And when she turned around and saw him, he observed on her face her suffering and enmity, which, appearing for a moment, hid behind an expression of immutable tranquility. But for him, that was enough to catch a brief glimpse into her soul.

"Come tonight, come," he whispered, even too quietly, although there was no one who could have heard his words, since everyone else was always out of the house in the morning. Not a muscle moved on her face under his careful scrutiny. She turned around and Stepan bolted out of the house, angrily slamming the door.

He did not come home for lunch, not without hope of thus signaling his despair. He returned home late at night, having spent the whole day wandering by the

Dnipro, and he lay down to sleep immediately, again hinting at his readiness. The hours dragged on in endless eternities, the ceiling and indeed the entire house of the peaceful merchant were in imminent danger of collapse from the explosion of his impatience, and when she at last did come, Stepan welcomed her with all the fire of youthful passion and that enormous store of energy that he had brought with him to the city.

Chapter Eleven

The last days of summer were exploiting their remaining privileges. At the end of September, mornings turned cloudy, while in the afternoon the sun came out, filling the air with spring mirages and holding back for a while the falling leaves. But at night, the winds tore them off and blew them around the streets, adding more work for the streetsweepers. Across these yellowish doormats, the city stepped out into a period of activity, awakening from its summer doldrums. The seasons—educational-cultural, cabaret, and theatrical—opened in a feverish frenzy. Various learned and semi-learned societies came to life, as their members returned from holidays and vacation homes. The bookstores and libraries, lethargic in the summer season, when the mind is enfeebled, filled with customers and patrons. Exhibits were opened, and lectures were read on the most serious topics of economy and morality. The proper life of the city was beginning—the springtime of its creativity—generally enclosed by walls, and yet without limits.

With great enthusiasm, Stepan, too, partook of this impulse. Actually, he had hardly missed anything by skipping the first weeks of classes at the Institute. Only now had all the professors returned and the hand-printed schedule become an actual one, particularly in the work of study groups and resource centers that begins with an unavoidable period of organizational activity. On the whole, he walked into class to find everything ready, and he could immediately roll out his studies at full speed on the tracks that had been already laid to meet the academic plans. He signed up for practical sessions in statistics and historical materialism, and he attended lectures regularly—indeed, he was so absorbed in his studies that he barely got to know his classmates. They were of interest to him only as coworkers. But, for them, within a half-month, he had become a reference book on Institute events, changes, and programs, because no one was better informed than he about all these matters. His notebooks with lecture notes were in such demand that they were typed up in multiple copies. Particularly in the fields of the theory of probability and higher mathematics, he immediately rose to the level of a recognized master, one of the select few who could see through the maze of formulas and propositions to the essential ideas that become the unfailing signposts in the labyrinth of external complexity.

In the evenings, having quickly run home for dinner, Stepan sat for two hours in the statistics laboratory, calculating endless rows of crop yields and death rates to establish the coefficient of correlation between them, and then spent two more hours in the library preparing for his presentation on Greek Atomism. Every spare moment at home he devoted to studying languages—English and French, of which up to now he knew only the alphabet used in mathematics. This was the largest gap in his knowledge, and liquidating this deficit was an overriding imperative for him. Stubbornness and persistence were reborn in him, and these qualities were strengthened rather than depleted by greater application. Each day that passed was filled to the brim with content, leaving no room for doubts or hesitation. Stepan was developing his strengths, burning brightly, because such was his nature: he could take the oars in a race and move the boat without resting, until, in the end, the oarlocks themselves would give out.

The strange relations that evolved between him and the landlady did not hinder him at all. During the day, he somehow forgot all about them, since by her behavior Tamara Vasylivna herself severely limited their daytime contact. No allusions. No privileges. Only business, everything aboveboard. Nor did Stepan attempt to transgress these limits. Indeed, he liked this reticence in his unexpected girlfriend. As if she were afraid of the light that eats away at secrets like acid. Their encounters always maintained the magic of surprise. Theirs was a peculiar, comic, but pleasant kitchen liaison between a young man and a wicked mother, a quasi-sentimental domestic romance hallowed by the unchanging night and the ticking of the cheap clock on the wall, a romance with a sudden beginning, a passionate plot line, and a boring ending. And yet, sometimes, perhaps in some trivial gesture or word, he suddenly detected in his visitor a hidden virtue that aroused his respect and undermined his previous understanding of her as a licentious woman always chasing men. At such times, he succumbed to a fearful anxiety, and this relationship, which he explained in such simple terms, began to seem entirely incomprehensible to him. He would ask, feigning extreme naiveté: why, with what purpose, by what cause, for what reason?

"Because you're my little love," she would say.

But he wouldn't allow himself to use the familiar pronoun with her and called her "Musinka," as she suggested.

Occasionally, while reading a book or working, he would be tempted to laugh in amazement and happy satisfaction. How strange the world was! He had appeared in this merchant's family God knows how, attached himself to them somehow, and now look what he's doing—and not even intentionally, without any effort on his part. It turns out somehow that the things you seek escape you, but what you don't expect happens all by itself.

Sometimes, in passing, he would think of Hnidyi and Maksym. He hardly ever came across the former. He was sort of friends with the latter but didn't see him very often either. Were they catching on? No, clearly not—since there were no changes in the internal, closed, and dreary life of this strange family. As for himself, he certainly would have noticed something, caught a stray glance or inadvertent allusion. His conscience told him that everything would be discovered, discovered soon, and things would end badly. These probable results—even without any mathematical calculations—made an unpleasant chill run down his back. But the voices of alarm were quickly silenced in the whirlwind of academic enthusiasm, which rarely gave them a chance to be heard.

Nor did he trouble himself too much with questions of terminology. Was this love? All right—it could be. It was funny, but possible. Who has the courage to say what is love and what is not? Shoes can be worn out, torn, patched, warped, and orthopedic, but they're always still shoes. Why does love need new footwear each time? Sometimes it walks in bast shoes and sometimes in slippers. In any case, secrecy and prohibition inflamed Stepan's excitement—excitement of the kind that completely replaces affection in young men—and the satisfaction of his desire gave birth to feelings of tenderness and gratitude. Under their languid influence, Stepan even kissed her hands, and these were the very first hands that had earned such regard from him. He was acutely aware of the thrill that her touch infused in him, of that explosion of active energy that her kiss ignited, like an electric spark. She wove herself into his life as an invisible, secret but powerful influence, allowing him also to discover in her a woman who does not alternate among a variety of trivial emotions and does not force herself to meet specific expectations. Next to her, all the girls he knew were affected dolls who imagined the act of giving themselves to someone as an accomplishment, a self-sacrifice, and an irrecompensable service.

Slowly initiating the young man into the mysteries of love, she taught him to value a kiss, which heretofore had seemed to him a mere plaything, as well as the whole intimate web of arousal that mankind has developed in the period from the Stone Age to the present. Stepan quickly mastered the accelerated course in this field of human experience, passed on from one generation to the next without textbooks or instructional guides—freeing himself from his books, the baby blankets that swaddled his thinking. Because nights gave him the sensation of thoughtless and therefore authentic living, free from all prescriptions and stipulations, unconstrained by requirements or explanations. At night, the sedulous eye of control and objections was closed, the odious voices that invited, pleaded, and commanded fell silent, and, having rid himself of them, he could feel the wanton liberty and insolent power of life, which breaks through thousands of obstacles to deliver its eternal magic.

There was nothing artificial in her knowledge of love, although the word "love" was her favorite joke. Yet suddenly, in the midst of caresses, Stepan would sense in her a commitment, something unspoken, the heat of an internal flame that scorched him and frightened him. At such moments, he told himself that he would never leave her, that he could not live without her. He was ready to suggest that she leave her family and make a new home with him on the foundation of the scholarship he received at the Institute. But a moment later, she was joking again, and again he did not feel the pull of any obligations. He loved her jokes, he loved the happy, tender pet names that she bestowed on him, which everyone likes to hear, although they're silly. He loved the scented cigarettes she always brought, stolen from her son, and the careless and pointless conversations that they enjoyed together. Musinka never spoke of anything serious, she never troubled him with her soul, and he should have been most grateful to her for this favor, since knowing another person's soul is too great a burden for one's own.

A month of carefree tranquility went by, working days and amorous nights, deepening and burnishing his consciousness. The wearying rains and gray mists had begun, but his army overcoat, unpacked from storage, saved him from the weather, while his heavy yuft boots were completely waterproof. In these garments, his body felt as peaceful and comfortable as his soul felt in his body.

All his worries fell silent, without any great effort on his part, and he was moving forward, full steam ahead, like an arrow shot from a taut bow. An awareness of this disposition brought a blessed order to his mind, impregnating it with the clear thinking that bears no resemblance to the malignant glitter of dreams. Poisonous, selfish, worldly illusions abandoned him and thus simplified his life, because he now understood that he must cross many a stream before he could draw his own conclusions. A dangerous inclination to incomplete induction, when the young man, on the basis of the first two decades of his sojourn on this earth, years both laughable and naive, attempted on his own to formulate the basic rules that govern life in this world, knocking his head against the wall of reality time and time again, was now replaced with a judicious intention to make life's acquaintance gradually and to accumulate within himself a sufficient quantity of life's facts. He became serious, somewhat proud, and acquired the appearance of a clever young man who, although still young, already knows a great deal, understands everything, and can explain to everyone the what, the where, the how, and the why.

At the Institute, Stepan was making progress with giant strides. Aside from his studies, he was becoming more prominent in the social affairs of students, who were at the time largely indifferent and mistrustful of collectivism because of its obligatory status in the community. People only recognize the sweetness of those fruits that are forbidden, and the biblical parable on this topic would be very instructive for politicians. In any case, those for whom public life was an instinctive choice unrelated to circumstances found the student population of those days an unplowed if somewhat infertile field. After a few appearances at student forums, Stepan was elected as the administrator of the student office of the Robzemlis trade union and a member of the Institute's KUBUCh committee. He was swamped and extremely busy, barely able to fit into a single day all of his personal and community responsibilities.

For the theatrical event being organized by KUBUCh in the Institute's auditorium as a fundraiser for impoverished students, it was decided to include, in addition to the invited performers, a talent show. Stepan decided to submit his story "The Razor," which was lying around in manuscript without any purpose, to the event committee for its consideration. Having received their approval, Stepan cleaned and sharpened it for shaving the masses, and read his work on stage before the audience.

He was nervous only for a moment. Then he suddenly calmed down and, sensing the growing attention of his listeners, found his rhythm as a reader. He read the story through to the end in a steady and well-balanced voice, avoiding unnecessary changes of pitch or pauses, and received as much applause as the invited tenor from the opera. Even more, since a flower was thrown to him—though it did not reach the stage and fell sadly on the floor. He did not deem it necessary to retrieve this first branch from the laurel wreath of his future fame.

His reaction to his own success was very negative and, when Borys Zadorozhnii, one of the participants in the talent show and a student in his last year, warmly complimented him on his story and asked if he had written anything else, he answered grumpily, "I don't have time for such nonsense."

"That's a shame," said Zadorozhnii. "What's awaiting us after we graduate? They'll herd us into a factory or behind a cash register, and that's it. You'll soon be overgrown with moss. But writing stories, that's a fine thing! As for me, I spend every free moment I have reading."

Stepan thought differently. Stories were just empty amusement, entertainment. You could survive just as well without them. And a small discussion began between them about literature, in which Stepan was the detractor and Borys the committed defender.

Nevertheless, at home, before a week had passed, he had written two more stories. The student Zadorozhnii who had so warmly welcomed his story became—was it precisely for this reason?—his close friend, to whom he eagerly turned for advice and sometimes even visited at his apartment. This cheerful and talented student's biography was full of difficulties and disappointments. He had made the mistake of being born the son of an Orthodox priest, whose death some ten years ago had failed to erase the stain on his son's character. Twice he had been thrown out of the Institute for his class origins, and twice he had been reinstated, because his personal past was in fact without blemish. After five years, he had reached his third year in the program and got a job as a night watchman in a dormitory. He considered himself the most fortunate person in the world.

That spring Borys would finish the Institute with a specialization in the sugar beet industry. Stepan felt a friendship toward him and a deep faith in his aesthetic taste. Thus Borys became the intimate confidant of his literary efforts and the first—and sympathetic, no less—judge of his literary works.

"Listen to this," he said, unfolding a pile of papers.

Borys listened and approved.

"This is just something I threw together," said Stepan.

He threw together a half-dozen stories about rebels. He wrote them easily and quickly, a little carelessly, but with enthusiasm.

"So, why are you marinating them?" asked Borys. "Send them off to a journal."

"You don't understand!"

And Stepan told his friend how he wrote the first story, how he even thought of changing his name to a more dignified Stefan, and how the great critic had burst his bubble.

"Literature is a delicate thing," he added with sincerity. "If you don't have the talent, don't even start. That's why, I think, there are so few writers."

Borys did not agree.

"So you think it is like a professional appointment?"

"Yes, sort of."

"You're a fool."

"So be it."

Borys laughed.

"So how did you come up with Stefan?"

"Wasn't there a king or something?"

From that day onward, Borys called him Steffi.

One evening, Stepan was concentrating on calculating currency conversions, estimating how many gold rubles there would be in an Indian rupee if the rate of conversion to pounds sterling were known. While Stepan was in this state of disconnection from the moment and the environment, Maksym entered the kitchen very agitated.

"I need to talk to you," he said icily.

Maksym's voice was trembling and the lines on his forehead quivered nervously. An expectation of something very unpleasant swept over Stepan. Guiltily, he anticipated the subject of the conversation.

"You are a nocturnal thief," said Maksym, standing across from him by the table.

"What?"

"You are a nocturnal thief," Maksym repeated dully, leaning against the table with his hands. "You're a thief."

Stepan got up, frightened by Maksym's quiet, sullen tone.

"What's this about?"

Suddenly Maksym bent over and, raising his arm, awkwardly and angrily hit Stepan in the face with his hand, striking him, in his haste, not on the cheek but directly on the mouth. This blow to the lips was not very hard but it was deeply offensive, and Stepan felt it like the sting of a whip on naked flesh. His face reddened like a wound, and his whole body erupted. He jerked forward and threw himself at Maksym, overturning the table with his leg and knocking Maksym onto the bed.

He beat him with his knuckles, with his chest, and with his head, in senseless rage and extreme anger. Then he stopped and sat up, blinking to erase the red spots circling before his eyes. He threw back his tousled hair and, legs shaking, threw on his overcoat and cap and left the house. He walked out without buttoning his coat, mindlessly splashing through puddles, shaking in anger and mortification. That swine had hit him in the face! Maybe he should challenge him to a duel? Swords? Pistols? Hah—what a knight-defender of his mother!

With drunken satisfaction he recalled how he had beaten him, choked him, twisted him, kicked him, and, at the same time, he regretted that he had cut off the punishment so quickly. He should have killed the snake! Made mincemeat of him! Because it was not just the insult that Maksym had given him that enraged him, it was the ruined tranquility, the financial ruin, and the loss of his mistress. And, the more he realized the extent of his catastrophe, the greater his emotional enervation grew—a mindless, crippling, gnawing hatred. He was entirely consumed with a boiling rage. Had someone bumped into him at that moment, he likely would have hit him.

Running out heedlessly down the familiar path to Khreshchatyk, Stepan had to stop and consider where he would sleep the next few nights. Actually, there wasn't any choice, and he set out for Borys's place on Lviv Street, behind the Sinnyi Bazaar. Brisk walking tired him and calmed him somewhat. His muscles ached from the emotional upheaval, and he was yawning from nervous exhaustion. Because it was late, he had to knock for a long time: although Borys was out guarding offices, Stepan, as a familiar guest, was allowed into his room. Borys's absence pleased Stepan and he expected that, by morning, he would invent a sufficiently plausible reason for his visit. He found some bread, ate it, and immediately went to sleep, cursing Maksym for disrupting his life.

In the morning, Stepan went to the Institute and it wasn't until evening that he ran into Borys, to whose place he had to return since he had nowhere else to go. His mood was as black as tar—he had spent the whole day walking around in a huff, but he cheerily told his friend that his landlords were entertaining a houseful of family visitors and so he had to give up his place there for a while.

"Why don't you just stay here permanently?" said Borys. "As you know, I'm hardly ever at home at night. It's a dog's life, but it's better than dying of hunger. I've tried that before—it's not pleasant."

But, instead of jumping at such a convenient offer, Stepan graciously declined because he was infused with a secret expectation that somehow everything would get straightened out and he would return to his comfortable nest. How? He didn't know. A great "somehow" lived within him, a deep faith in his destiny, which had not been very hard on him up until now. Would Musinka really have to carry water herself? He could not fit such a barbaric possibility in his head. Or would Maksym—may his soul rot in hell—really tend to the cows himself? But he had to admit that the Hnidyi household had prospered without him in the past and could do so again. Musinka would cry a little and then she would find a more convenient lover. Such thoughts drove him into a deep despondency. He decided to wait. For what? Maybe Musinka would write him a letter—but she didn't know the address. And he didn't dare write to her—he was even ashamed, since, no matter how you spin it, he had retreated from the field of battle, albeit as a victor.

For two days a longing for Musinka gnawed at him, mostly because he was distanced from her against his own will. He couldn't stand it when things didn't go his way. After another two days, however, he was reconciled to his situation and likely would have stayed at Borys's had it not been for a new difficulty, which dashed his plans once again.

That evening, before setting out on his watch, Borys noticed his unhappy demeanor.

"You're overworked, Steffi," he told him. "Even a steam boiler can crack from too much pressure, and that's cast iron. It was Karl Marx who said that the working man deserves a rest."

"Yes, I see that myself," said Stepan, caught up in his work.

"The best relaxation is a woman's company, or, to put it plainly, a party. Somebody took me to one recently, and I'll take you there, too. All we need is half a bottle and something to eat, like sausage. It's not far to go for fellows like us, just up to the Krytyi Bazaar. It's not exactly a house, not exactly a barn—heaven knows what it is, but there are five girls."

"Five?" asked Stepan.

"A whole handful! And one of them, a real-life Beatrice. So fair and quiet—but you know, still waters can rupture a levee. What's her name? Natalka? No. Nastia? No. Well, whatever... On one condition—she's mine."

"You can have them all!" said Stepan glumly. "I don't have time for girls."

"Do as you please, but even scholars say it's good for the metabolism."

After Borys had left, Stepan thought long and bitterly. That there were five girls rather than three was easy to explain. He himself had heard Nadiika say that they would take in two more girls for the winter to help with the cost of firewood. No less certain was it that Borys was thinking of courting Nadiika. And besides, if he stayed on here, Borys would keep dragging him there. Furthermore, Borys would keep telling him how the courtship was coming along. Any allusion to that girl was enough to make Stepan feel physically ill. What would happen if she came up time and again in Borys's conversation? An instinct for self-preservation prodded him, telling him that it would be dangerous to expose himself to so much pain.

That evening, he felt hostility toward girls, a sad hostility over what had been lost and could not return, but now, from a distance, had acquired an ever greater attractive force. Could she possibly fall in love with Borys? For a moment, he felt an urge to stay at Borys's place, to stay deliberately and go with him to the parties to prevent him from getting Nadiika, to rub this conceited chump's nose in the dirt. Step on his tail a little, so he couldn't say, "This one's mine." But his soul was too weary to take up such a challenge. He had a different, more important challenge before him. Picking up a book he said complacently, "Let him have her."

He decided to move to the KUBUCh dormitory, bitterly disillusioned that the city was, after all, not big enough to avoid meeting certain people.

Chapter Twelve

This was the first morning that the most dogged student at the Institute, Stepan Radchenko, did not appear for class. Drearily, lost in thought, he walked along Revolution Street to Nyzhnii Val Street to get his things, to remove from the home where he had found refuge the last traces of his stay there. He had specifically chosen the morning to do this, since Musinka was at home alone at that time. Although his anger at Maksym had burned out and extinguished, and Hnidyi himself would hardly find the courage to say something—mostly he played the role of a non-speaking extra in this strange family—nevertheless, it would have been unpleasant to see them. And they, too, would probably not want to meet him, and he certainly did not want to cause people any discomfort.

The door was unlocked, and he walked into the empty kitchen. For a moment he considered grabbing his things and disappearing forever. But he rejected this as shameful—he was not, after all, a thief. Besides, when he entered this kitchen where everything was familiar, when in the corner he saw the bucket with which he had carried so much water, the table on which he had scribbled so many sheets of paper, his books and notebooks still lying where he had left them—he felt a painful pang of regret that he must actually abandon all this. And why? He felt that he was the victim here. But all these objects were merely the background for the traces of a passion visible only to him. All of these things reminded him of his connection to a woman who had given him so much and such rich satisfaction. He realized in their midst that, even if this feeling was not love, it had not yet been exhausted: its depth reached out for many more nights, the loss of which would surely be his ruin. Suddenly he felt that, in losing her, he had lost his spark, that the forced separation would throw him back into the despair that he had been battling all week with a subconscious hope that he might return to her and possess her again. Shaking with agitation, he knocked on the door to her room and then without waiting knocked again.

When Musinka appeared, Stepan thirstily looked into her face, seeking there any signs of joy or delight at his reappearance. But her face was tranquil, as always during the day, though somewhat tired and pale. Then, without greeting, he said sharply, "I've come for my things."

She smiled, and with that smile increased his irritation.

"I don't want to bother you," he cried. "Maybe you've grown tired of me. Maybe you sent Maksym yourself to get rid of me."

"Maksym has gone," she said.

"Gone?"

"He's left us. He'll live on his own."

Terror gripped Stepan.

"He said, 'Mom, promise you'll get rid of that vagabond, and then I'll stay, and everything will be as it was before.' I said, 'He's not a vagabond.'"

Stepan ran up to her, grabbed her hand, and kissed it passionately.

"No, no, Musinka. I am a vagabond," he said. "I'm awful, and I should be run off. I love you, Musinka—forgive me."

She replied listlessly, "Forgive? You? For what?"

He kissed her neck, the corners of her lips, her eyes, her forehead; caressing these familiar spots, he embraced her piously and sensually. And she, as if awakened, threw her arms around his neck, and pulling back his head, looked into his eyes with wild desire.

That night she said to him, "I knew you'd come back."

"How?"

"I'll tell you later."

"I, too, was sure, despite everything, that I'd come back. I was coming for my things, but, somewhere in my soul, I knew that I would be back with you. Kiss me. Aren't I handsome?"

"There you go, my love," she laughed.

He fell silent.

"What are you thinking about?"

"About... about the other half of your household."

"You didn't think about that before?"

"Very little, actually. I was scared to ask, Musinka. Everything turns out so strangely. It turns out that I don't know my own self."

"And you never will."

"Why not? I've learned many lessons already. And how much I've endured. The city bewildered me. I was drowning."

"And now you're drying out here beside me."

He heard so much pain and derisive mockery in these words that, inadvertently, he flinched, suddenly and unexpectedly coming to the realization, previously beyond his reach as something hidden and frightening, that his Musinka had had a life before she began to exist for him: that years, decades of the lost past, had unfailingly led them toward each other, their paths crossing here, in this kitchen. And, at that moment, more clearly than ever before, he sensed (the way that an intent stare makes one suddenly look over their shoulder) the quiet and inexorable force of destiny that shapes the ordinary convergence of beings who, though complete strangers yesterday, will become friends, lovers, or enemies tomorrow, and it struck him as mysterious and frightening.

Now he was afraid because he did not know what she was thinking. He clasped her hands in his own.

"You won't abandon me?"

"You'll never let anyone leave you."

"Is that why I returned?"

"What do you think, my little one?"

He leaned on his elbow and lit a cigarette. Her words were somewhat unpleasant to him. They carried an echo of a knowledge of life that he still found unattainable, as well as a hint of gloomy irony.

She remained silent. He continued smoking, lying on his back.

"This was an unhappy week," she said.

"For me, too," he answered.

"For you, too? But how old are you?"

He wanted to protest.

"I am forty-two," she said. "I'm old. You're going to say that's not very old? Oh, my dear little one, in a year, I'll be a real old bag, you'll hardly recognize me if we meet. But once, a very long time ago—you can't even imagine how long ago—I, too, was young. Do you know what happiness is? It's like ether. It can evaporate in a moment. But pain persists, on and on, without end."

"That's true," he said, "I've noticed that myself."

"People say that life is like a bazaar. And so it is. Everyone has their goods to sell. Some make a profit, others take a loss. Why? Because no one wants to die. You must keep selling, even if at a loss. After that, anyone can call you a fool. The seller who miscalculates is called a fool. But people are very different. Books tell us: this is a human being, with these qualities, and so forth. We have all kinds of sayings about people, about all human beings, and you might think we know what a human being is. Somewhere I read that there's even a science of souls called psychology. The author claims that people don't run because they're scared but are scared because they run. But what's the difference to the one who's scared? He doesn't know anything anyway. Do you understand?"

"You're probably thinking of idealist psychology. Today, psychology is built on entirely different principles. Introspection has long been discredited as a methodology."

He put his cigarette butt on the table, extending his arm for this purpose, and turned onto his right side.

"So, what happened then?" he asked, "You were young, and then what?"

"Nothing very interesting. I had two brothers and two sisters. They died. Who knows why I survived and they didn't. Strange, isn't it? We lived here—this is my building. We weren't rich, but we got along. My father was a small merchant. And now listen. He had a friend—they grew up and went to school together. My father dealt in iron goods, his friend sold fish. His friend did well. He built himself a big five-story building in Lypky, he went into wholesale and put away a few million. My father still traded iron here. He didn't envy anyone. But when four children of his died, he somehow withered. All his plans were lost. And then my mother died. I was left alone. I was scared of my father—he was so dour. He didn't notice me. He said nothing for days, weeks even. I didn't have any friends. No one visited us. In school, the girls teased me and called me a nun. Then late one evening, when I was seventeen, that friend of my father's showed up with his son..."

"That's your husband?"

"Yes, that was Luka. I remember his father had a civilian medal on his chest. I can recall every day of my life, from when I reached consciousness as a child—it's frightening to remember your entire life. As if you were standing guard over yourself. My father said, 'Tamara, I'm going to die soon. You should get married.' I said 'Yes, Father,' and kissed his hand. His hand was cold. He really did die two months later. That was when I first saw how distant people are from each other. Father was buried with honors because everyone liked him. They put me in a black dress and led me by the arms behind the hearse, Luka on one side, my aunt on the other. I glanced over to the sidewalk and noticed people stopping, taking off their hats, asking who was being buried, and then going on about their business. When I saw this, I stopped crying. I felt ashamed to be crying in front of people who were going about their business. I imagined that they would go home and relate over dinner that some fellow was being buried and his daughter was crying wildly.

After that, my tears dried up forever, though there were plenty of reasons to cry."

She stopped and leaned back against the cushion. The serenity of her words had gradually bewitched Stepan, and the more he fell under the spell of her story, the less he could say himself. Cautiously, he pulled out another cigarette and lit it.

"Don't shine that in my face," she said. "I haven't yet told you anything about why Luka, who had maybe seen me once somewhere by chance, came to get engaged to me. I didn't learn this until later. You can be certain that if anything's unpleasant, they'll always tell you about it eventually. Sooner or later, intentionally or not. So this is how it was. Luka fell in love with a girl who was also a merchant's daughter, and the affair reached the engagement stage. But the father or mother of the girl, I don't remember which, was careless enough to say that it was a great honor for the Hnidyi family that they were letting them have their daughter. So old Hnidyi immediately took Luka by the hand, and that same evening he brought him to our place. Luka hated him but acquiesced. You can imagine the fate that awaited me. In a word, Luka said that, since I had ruined his life, I would at least need to cheer him up a little."

"Why didn't you leave him?" asked Stepan.

"Oh, he took care of that. All the doors were locked and the windows on the fourth floor were left wide open. How he wanted me to commit suicide! But he was scared to kill me himself. I was waiting only until my father died. But after his death, Luka changed his attitude toward me. He stopped beating me, he completely forgot about me. I rarely even saw him. Of course, people told me exactly where he was and with whom he was living. And I kept living just for show. Do you know what dreams are for those in pain? They're a curse. But what dreams I had! The harder it was for me, the happier I became. I knew the most unusual worlds. I traveled to the evening star, the one that rises at twilight, where I lived in exotic orchards, with quiet murmuring streams in an endless autumn. I dreamed only of autumn. And the love I enjoyed there! Later, I had a son."

"Maksym?"

"Yes, Maksym. I wanted him to have a different name, I wanted ..."

"What name did you want?" he asked.

"You'll be surprised—I wanted him to be named Stepan."

"Why"

"I didn't know back then, but later I figured it out. I had enough time to study myself, to uncover every thought. In the end, you see, I began to wonder at myself. I did not have the kind of self-love that other people have, but I was very close to myself. Do you understand? Self-love means being divided from yourself, but it's also possible to merge with yourself. In that case, you can no longer love yourself—or better yet, there's no way to love yourself. And then you're not scared of your own self and your own thoughts. So here's why: when I was maybe twenty years old, a tradesman was working in our home. One evening, I fell asleep over a book and he carried me to my bed. While he was carrying me I woke up, but I pretended to still be asleep, so he wouldn't put me down. I closed my eyes—it was both frightening and pleasant. Later, I had such an urge to ask this Stepan to carry me around that I would flee the house in shame. I tried in various ways until I finally succeeded in getting Luka's father to take him into the store, and I didn't see him anymore."

Stepan felt a vague uncertainty. Could this really be her, his smiling Musinka, always cheerful and merry? Suddenly he felt uncomfortable that this woman, whom he thought he knew well, had her own secrets, unconnected to him.

She went on. "And then came the Revolution, and it destroyed all his millions. Luka went gray in a week, and we were chased out of Lypky to this place. That's when he noticed Maksym and me. One day, he came into my room and asked, 'Tamara, do you hate me?' I said, 'You don't exist for me.' He began to fear me. He was scared to look at me. He began to wear blue glasses. And Maksym was growing up. Maybe it was my own fault—I loved him madly. Sometimes I thought he would be abducted. I stood guard over him night after night. When he started going to school, I would die of fear—I missed him so much. He grew up to be quiet and gentle. He collected butterflies, insects, then, later, postage stamps. He loved to read. Every evening, he would tell me about everything he had seen and done in school, everything. I helped him study as long as I could. When he became a teenager, I was overcome with grief. He would be pulling away from me soon, he would have to. I was heartbroken, I cried. He didn't understand. Once he came up to me and said, 'Mom, I'll never leave you.' 'That's impossible,' I said. But he replied, 'You'll see. Have I ever deceived you?' And indeed, he did not deceive me."

She fell silent, falling under the spell of her own words, overcome with the sadness of her own story, as if hearing it for the first time from a stranger's lips. Because when it takes shape in words, a recollection acquires a previously unknown reality. In the interplay of sounds, it acquires a sharp edge very different from its peaceful existence in silent thought.

He, too, remained silent, smoking, and looking out the leaded window, listening to the ticking of the clock over his head, which in the silence seemed to have accelerated. But his thoughts were hard at work, receiving and internalizing what he had just heard and what he needed to accept. The distant horizon of her past, the long dark corridor of time, illuminated here and there by the words she had spoken, first astounded him with the mysterious complexity of its turns and branches, but then dimmed and faded before his eyes, replaced by the growing smirk that forced itself onto his lips. So, what's the point? What was so strange in this banal story about an unhappy marriage, in this familiar urban story that gets repeated everywhere and anywhere under the low roofs of residential areas near cities where life consists of nothing more than love and tranquility? A merchant's submissive daughter, an unfaithful and tyrannical husband, autumnal dreams, motherhood followed by pride in a handsome child, clutching at the remnants of life, a sickly need to find at least some meaning in that life before it descends into old age, when the last, tearful, mindless flame erupts in a woman's blood. This was neither new nor rare. And yet he felt renewed energy from the unexpressed thought that he somehow had managed to squeeze into her squalid life, to reorganize and control it. When he appeared, everything changed. That was most important to him. Suddenly, embracing her and taking command of her, he whispered, "Musinka, you do love me a little, don't you?"

The handsome and bright boy's life, disrupted for a week, crossed the next threshold, and resumed its steady and surging flow. Whether at the Institute or at home, he felt marvelous, with too much work in school and in his community activities to give serious thought to any matter, particularly an unpleasant one. And Musinka, such a delicate woman, did not poison his satisfaction in possessing her with any painful reminders. Within the subdued home of the Hnidyis, which had managed to expel one of its residents, everything was peaceful again, decomposing, dying a slow death that might take months or even years, yet emitting through its doors a fresh shoot from the random seeds in its manure. Within this rotting nest, a wayward chick was shedding its immature feathers and resolutely learning to spread its wings. And, indeed, after this remarkable event, the young man could not help but feel himself the master of not only the kitchen, but also of the rooms beyond, which he never entered in the exercise of his invisible authority. Having caught a momentary glimpse into Musinka's uncovered soul, the inevitable consequence was that he immediately sent out his roots into this new area, established himself, and made himself at home there, freely soaking up the nutritious juices that can be drawn from a woman's body before it decays. He enveloped her and fed his vitality by possessing her, and her cheeks burned in a feverish blush from the flame that consumed her while it warmed and nourished him, like the fruit that swells until it must fall away from its branch.

Winter should long since have arrived, as the reports from the Ukrainian national weather bureau affirmed, but it was delayed for reasons beyond the control of science. A timid snow would fall in the morning, only to melt on the cobblestones, leaving a watery mud that was not harmful to Stepan's yuft boots but was very troublesome to the street kids, those urban outcasts without waterproof footwear, who therefore needed to relocate to their winter quarters in manholes and trash dumps. In the endless slush, people seemed as gray as the mud on the streets. Then one day something strange happened, and the snow, squeezed by the frost, did not flow down the streets to the awaiting sewers, and the city majestically unfurled its white arteries and proudly raised its forehead. Showered with white flakes, it was reaching the apogee of its industriousness, hardening and contracting so that, come spring, it could throw off its wedding veil and begin its gradual wilting. This was the time when the windows of buildings were not extinguished until late, and inside, around tables—those altars of the new paganism—sat attentive two-legged owls, gestating, birthing, and raising administrative, operational, artistic, and scientific plans. It was the time when sleighs glided along the icy streets, when music from the bars grew louder, when revolutions of the roulette wheel accelerated, when buses donned chains and women donned fantastic boots, and when students wrote their first reports at institutes and in life.

Chapter Thirteen

S pring is brought to the city not by sparrows but by wagon drivers who, with the blessing of their collective farms, begin to break up the trampled snow on the streets, load it onto their sleighs, and haul it off where it can melt without affecting the welfare of the city. Before these harbingers of warmth arrive, not a single bud on the trees along the boulevards dares to fluff up and open. That would be a pretentious transgression against local laws and a barbarian assault on the foundations of civilization.

The awakening of nature did not pass by without affecting Stepan's soul, which resembled an extremely sensitive plate, suitable for instant photography. Nothing highlights the artificiality of a city like spring itself, melting the snow but uncovering dead cobblestones rather than the expected plants. Stepan still longed to smell the moist breath of the earth, to bury his gaze in the endless greenery of open fields, in the black rows of fluffy soil. All around him he saw the terrible subjugation of nature. The trees on the streets and behind fences in the yards, like animals in cages or a zoo, sadly stretched out to him their swollen limbs. So, what did the change from cold to warmth mean here, besides an appropriate change of clothing? What was there to remind one of the steam rising on the steppes and the happiness of the man who feels the fertile earth beneath his harrow? There, spring was the trumpet of a shining god, the luminous oracle of happiness and work. Here, it was but a trivial, though pleasant, episode: the disappearance of streetside sand boxes and the renewed running of the suburban trains. The city rolled over in the sun, like a giant pampered cat, squinting its innumerable eyes in the sun, stretching and yawning in satisfaction. The city was preparing to rest.

But Stepan's springtime recollection of the village, brought on by the warm temperatures and rains, did not have sufficient strength to really subdue him. He was mournful about his childhood, and wistful about the past, which, at some distance, acquires a charm unrelated to its quality, but he hoped that this quiet grief would dissipate, like a thinning fog. Or maybe these were just the dregs of those indistinct appetites and unformed desires that are stirred up in the heart by springtime, whispering flattering words about the future, stoking a greater thirst, promising change and a new direction. Spring awakens and confounds the soul with various seeds that germinate more often into tough wormwood than delicate roses. Because life is a verbose and loud lottery with colorful posters, enticing billboards, and a sophisticated advertising campaign that promises extraordinary winnings, silently ignoring the fact that, for each winning ticket, there are thousands of thin and empty bits of paper on which their holders have staked their only hopes.

At the Institute, spring meant exam fever, a disease that affects only students. It begins slowly with a lengthy period of latency that can be characterized by a heightened concentration, as well as a tendency to create outlines and underline passages in textbooks. But the first symptoms of a full-blown pathology follow the posting of an announcement on the professor's door, after which the disease passes into the typhoid stage, with fever, nightmares, and insomnia, reaching a crisis in the examination hall, where all the complications and possibilities of a relapse are revealed. Having received a grade of "good" in the serious disciplines, such as political economy and economic geography, Stepan reflected on the Ukrainian language requirement and decided to get that out of the way, too. These were the only classes he had not attended, and he did not intend to waste much time preparing for a Ukrainian language exam, assuming, with very substantive foundation, that this was the language that he knew and used very well, even wrote stories in, and that he himself was precisely one of those Ukrainians for whom this language exists;

therefore, he had every reason to believe he could pass this exam, all the more so because, in his career as a rebel, before he had hoisted the red flag, he had for some time held the flag of the autumnal steppes and sky. But one can trip even on his own native doorstep. Stepan cowered at the first explosion from the heavy artillery of voiceless vowels and the laws of Ikavism, while rapid bursts of fire from the nominal and verbal cannon forced him into a shameful retreat, with the firm resolve to capture this unexpected fortress at all cost.

Armed with copies of the very best language textbooks from the library, he abandoned all others and, that very evening, began to explore and study them. Heretofore, he had known only the Russian terms for grammatical concepts, and he pronounced their Ukrainian equivalents with a strange trepidation, seeing that his language had also been dissected into chapters and paragraphs, its laws summarized and rules established. He immersed himself in these matters with ever-increasing interest and satisfaction. Simple mundane words seemed somehow deeper, more meaningful when he mastered their component parts and the secret of their declensions. He fell in love with them, appreciated their function, and was overcome with respect for them, as if they were important dignitaries whom, from his own ignorance, he had previously treated as plain folk.

So, one month later, having mastered Olena Kurylo's weighty tome and studied the history of the language according to Shakhmatov and Krymskyi, he stood before a professor at the Institute who, not recognizing the student before him, marveled at the depth of his knowledge.

"You see how useful it is to listen to all my lectures," he said. "But I must say how rarely I have the satisfaction of testing a Ukrainian who knows his own language."

"Unfortunately," Stepan noted, "the majority think it is sufficient to be born Ukrainian."

"Yes, yes," answered the professor. "But I must admit that I persecute them mercilessly. I'm very happy you avoided that."

Their conversation developed and the professor asked Stepan about his origins and his circumstances. Stepan depicted the latter in the bleakest of colors, since his arrangements really had begun to seem miserable to him. He described cleaning up around the cows as something dreadful, as if it involved dangerous work with African lions, and his kitchen as so dirty and stuffy that it might have been the cell of an anchorite monk in the thick of a dark forest. The good professor took pity on him and said, "You seem to me to be a talented and serious student, and I'll try to help you. I must admit, I don't have that many students who listen to my lectures and whom I have not failed in an exam at least once."

After this, the professor wrote a note of recommendation to the head of the Bureau of Instructors of the Ukrainization Program and also promised to speak to this eminent person himself. Then he added, squeezing

Stepan's hand, "I expect that there you will be transformed from a student into an instructor."

Early the next day, Stepan appeared before the Areopagus of Ukrainization, where an informal examinational conversation took place *between* or *among* the members of the board and *he* or *him*, depending on the linguistic theories of each of the members of the board. Once it had been established with certainty—based on the defendant's confession—that, according to all the relevant authorities of grammar, infinitives were to never be split, and sentences were not to end in prepositions, even if there seemed to be good reason for them to. Having spent some time analyzing the prohibitions against dangling participles, it was concluded that, as a matter of fact, the theory that it seemed likely that, in many cases, various and sundry expressions could often be deleted from a sentence with no discernible effect on its meaning was true. Finally, after explaining why the word *which*, that is a non-restrictive pronoun, should be distinguished from the word *that*, which is often—mistakenly—used in its place, and why it is better to maintain verbal parallelism on both sides of the word *than* than not, Stepan was proclaimed a Knight of Ukrainization of the first order, with a payment scale of one karbovanets and eighty kopecks per academic hour.

Taking down his address and writing out a certificate for him, the elegant administrator of the Bureau of Instructors said, in a friendly manner, "Comrade, I expect that, within a week or two, you will receive an assignment in some company and,"—he added with a pleasant smile—"turn in your field jacket for something more appropriate. The biggest problem with Ukrainians is that they don't know how to dress."

Stepan himself was perfectly aware of how accurate these words were. Indeed, his worsted wool clothing was not only old but quite uncomfortable in warm weather, and it was high time to change it. He had often thought of this while dressing in the morning and undressing at night, when he came into closer contact with these rags and became convinced how poorly this exterior covering suited his abilities. And actually, it wasn't the lack of money that held him back—he had managed in these seven months to put aside about a hundred karbovanets from his scholarship—but an embarrassment before his own sensibilities. Although his field jacket and boots had become a moldy costume for him, they still had the power of tradition. Changing his wardrobe seemed too audacious an undertaking, one that required a significant justification.

His horizon was expanding. To have three hour-and-a-half classes in some institution every week, getting a whole chervinets, that is, raising his monthly earnings to almost six chervinets—for him, this was no joke but a limitless expansion of his possibilities. These calculations excited and comforted him, and then the springtime agitation would not leave him even for a minute, churning from day to day into a seductive worry that draped his beautiful eyes in anxiety. It was increasingly wearisome to return home, and he spent evenings sitting in the library until closing time, immersing himself in books far deeper than any studiousness would require. In the morning, remembering that he was obliged to clean out the dung from the stalls and give the cows fresh hay and water, he began to lie around in bed, getting up at the last moment; sometimes, he hit the meek animals with a stick in anger, although they always greeted him in a friendly manner. With growing irritation, he imagined that, for the entire summer, when the Institute was on break, he would be chained down in his kitchen, since he saw no need to show up in his village. The Podil, and particularly Nyzhnii Val Street, this god-forsaken little hole in the ground, a suburban thicket, were no longer attractive to him, and the distance to the Institute, which he hadn't even noticed before, now seemed overly tiring.

Besides, anticipating his future wealth, he foresaw a real possibility of becoming better acquainted with urban culture—going to the theater, cinema, exhibits, and talks—but the distance to the center of the city meant he would be wasting a great deal of time on needless walking back and forth, discouraging him from taking part in these activities and thus hindering him from freely communing with the benefits of civilization. And, in consequence of these unhappy reckonings, Stepan was filled with disaffection, which poisoned his academic achievements, discolored his expectations, and diminished his energy. Suddenly, he imagined that he was exhausted, and he secretly attributed a portion—maybe even the largest portion—of his exhaustion to Musinka, whose passion was needlessly, it now seemed to him, consuming his strength, worthy of higher and more valuable uses.

The Bureau of Instructors did not mislead him. Within a week and a half, he received an offer in the mail to take over a class at the Housing Administration from Comrade Lanskyi who had announced his intention to give up teaching. That night, Stepan shared his good news with Musinka, but her reaction was not very supportive.

"What do you need these lessons for?" she asked. "Do you want for anything here?"

"But it's almost two karbovanets for forty-five minutes!"

"Your studies will suffer because of them," she said. "Those two karbovanets will cost you the Institute."

"Never," he answered and, sensing a deeper suspicion in her words, he added bitterly, "I'm not going to play with cows all my life."

"Yes," she sighed. "You're right."

He was silent and continued smoking. Abruptly he added, "I'm tired. In the evenings my head hurts."

"Does it hurt? This wise little head? No, my shopkeeper's joy, it is your heart that's bored and filled with longing. How long will it keep beating? But Musinka will never hold you back—when she becomes unnecessary, she'll never—"

"Musinka, you're insulting me," he said. "I will never forget you."

"I see—you're already saying farewell. Those are always the final parting words: 'I will never forget you.' Your soul is like a slate tablet—rub your finger on it and you erase what was written there."

He would have preferred to listen to her jealous anger than to the soft bitterness of her words, which troubled him precisely by their accuracy. And, wanting to convince her and himself of the impossibility of a separation, he embraced her in the throes of a simulated passion, attempting to recreate the ardor of their first meetings.

The next day, he had to be at the offices of the Housing Administration at 3:30 pm. Up until 11:00 am, he leafed through several textbooks and prepared his introductory speech. He wanted to begin his classes with a certain degree of grandeur, knowing full well how important first impressions can be. No less did he understand that appearing in the clothes he now had before an audience that he needed to win over was tantamount to playing on an untuned piano—even the finest symphony would turn into a cacophony of sounds. He needed to transform himself in the name of Ukrainization—this basic premise finally overcame his earlier hesitation. Gathering his savings, he set off for the store whose window had arrested him half a year earlier, its grand finery filling him with envious daydreams. Now he flew into it on the wings of his cash, fluttered and circled within it like a nimble sparrow, and in three-quarters of an hour he walked out with a sizable package containing a gray demi-season trench coat of indifferent quality, a similar suit, a pair of shirts with button-down collars, a Caucasian silk tie, green enameled cufflinks, and three colorful handkerchiefs with checkered edges. After further purchasing a gray cap, pointed shoes of chrome-tanned leather and matching galoshes, he spent the remainder of his wealth on good cigarettes and took the bus to Revolution Square in the Podil, because he needed to hurry. This bus had the honor of carrying him on his very first bus ride and the good fortune of pleasing him completely.

Musinka, who was cooking dinner for three in her *ménage à trois*, was very surprised to see him in the image of a youthful Santa Claus, carrying so many parcels, but he only asked, secretively, for permission to use her room for a half hour, because it had a mirror. There, he completed his transformation, easily adapting himself to the requirements of his new clothes, since his quick eye had often observed on others where everything belonged. Only the tie gave him trouble, unwilling to tie itself, but with brilliant insight he eventually achieved the desired effect. Examining himself from head to foot in the mirror, he froze in excited satisfaction, as if he were seeing and recognizing himself for the first time. His energy, flagging from secret anxiety, was immediately restored when he saw his tanned face set off against the white collar and the powerful arc of his chest beneath the close-fitting jacket. In rapturous delight he observed his high open forehead, welcoming the reason hidden behind it, and he slowly raised his hand to his hair, to smooth it, to stroke it, to caress his own self and thus show his love for his own person.

With an eager new spring in his stride he stepped back into the kitchen and stopped in front of Musinka, who could not hold back a joyous cry on seeing this butterfly that had emerged from its chrysalis. She hugged him and kissed him, forgetting in her fervor that she had less right to do this now than ever before. Then she stepped back a little, and her more careful observation completely confirmed her first impression—the young man was devilishly handsome, poised, and seductive.

"Your eyes are laughing," she exclaimed.

Hers were also laughing, in part. He, too, was looking her over from the heights of his European wardrobe, seeing in her signs of fading as much as she saw him in bloom. Never before had he noted so painfully her scrawny cheeks marbled with thin wrinkles, her anemic lips and sagging breasts. Her girlish smile was a grimace on her aging face, and he could not suppress the haughty thought that, if she had been worthy of a first-year student at the Institute, she was certainly not worthy of a full-fledged language instructor.

At the appointed hour, he ran into his predecessor, Comrade Lanskyi. Looking at him carefully he asked, "Aren't you Vyhorskyi, the poet?"

"True," grumbled the man, unhappily. "But we've been Lanskyis from the time of my great-great ancestors."

Then they talked about the business at hand. It turned out that the poet was leaving this class in pretty bad shape. He could not even say for sure what topics they had last covered in class.

"On the whole, I don't actually believe that studying is of any use," he finished, "especially the way I teach."

"OK, we'll go over the material from the start," said Stepan. "But tell me, if it's not a secret—why did you choose to use a pseudonym? I don't understand. You have such a beautiful name."

"It's not a secret at all," answered the poet. "You see, at first, I signed my poems with my real name, and no one wanted to publish them. Then I invented a pseudonym, and they were accepted."

"Can that really happen?"

"Of course it can. Besides that, there's another reason. It's too big a responsibility to sign your own name. It's like an obligation to live and think the way you write."

"That's not impossible, is it?"

"It's possible, but it's boring."

Stepan offered him a cigarette.

"No, thank you—I don't smoke," said the poet, "but I do drink beer."

The new suit gave Stepan unusual boldness, surprising even him.

"Comrade," he said, "I write, too, you know."

"You don't say?" the poet said sadly. "What do you write, if I may ask?"

Stepan cheerfully told him not only about his stories but also about his experience in visiting the critic, which now seemed to him a pleasant anecdote.

"I know him," said the poet. "A little wasp that tries hard to inflict painful stings. If you like, give me your stories—I promise to be attentive. But you must bring them to me this evening—12 Mykhailivskyi Lane, Apartment 24. I'm leaving tomorrow and I'll take them with me."

"You're leaving? Where?"

"I'm not sure yet. I have three hundred karbovanets and I'll try to get as far as possible for as long as possible. I'm sick of this stupid city."

"Sick of it?"

"Aren't you? Just wait, you'll see. It will reveal itself to you. This one in particular. You know what our city is? It's a historical corpse, rotting for centuries. It needs to be aired out."

But the bell rang, signaling the end of the workday and ending their conversation, which Stepan had found of considerable interest. Together, they entered the large room where the classes were held after work hours. The office workers sat in a group around tables that had been pulled together, across from a large piece of linoleum, which served as a blackboard for the class. After introducing his replacement, the poet left and Stepan, standing by the table, loudly, confidently, and energetically, like a nightingale singing its very first song, gave his lecture on the benefits of the Ukrainian language, in general and in particular.

Chapter Fourteen

Only a first-year student can truly appreciate the meaning of the term "perfect score," which represents something of an imaginary, magic island, unreachable even by silver-tongued poets. In any case, Stepan Radchenko was the only one in his circle of friends who achieved this result, that is, he earned perfect grades in all the courses he had taken during the year. This achievement cost him an enormous expenditure of energy, particularly since he was also giving Ukrainian-language lessons three times a week and needed to spend considerable time preparing, as his theoretical knowledge did not quite meet the practical needs of the institution where he was called upon to enlighten the tired office staff who wanted to eat, not conjugate, and who had only a very dim understanding of the enormous obligations to the Ukrainian nation that had fallen on their shoulders.

The days he taught his classes were all the more difficult for Stepan because he needed to change his clothes.

He couldn't risk showing up at the Institute in a tie, lest he provoke unnecessary questions or, heaven forbid, lose his scholarship. This was a giant headache for him, but he kept up the same annoying routine without fail: leaving home first as a poor student and then as a well-groomed instructor, with the appropriate changes in his facial expression, gestures, and gait. He was singular, but in two incarnations, each of which had its own separate function and goals. Man could not invent multi-personed gods without himself being heterogeneous, because, as a strange combination of striking contradictions, he needed an embodiment for each of them, and the inclination to create a single, great god with a small devil was an indication of the normalization of the human being—that is, a shriveling of the imagination. Mankind does not break down into so-called good and evil, into plus and minus, no matter how convenient this might be for public use.

Having fallen into the state of uncertain balance between his brown field jacket and the gray suit, Stepan was not worried by the duality of his existence, being sufficiently hardened against the minor superstitions that frighten the conscience and poison the lives of weaker individuals. In the process of development, he had risen above them. Over the previous winter, he had been convinced by personal experience that an individual should view the world and himself in a more forgiving spirit, because in life, as in an ice storm, one can fall and even knock down someone else quite accidentally, fully unexpectedly for both one's self and the other person.

All of this running around and the stress at work would perhaps have exhausted him, except that he finally resolved to find a new apartment, to open up new possibilities whose very existence was the most important stimulating factor for him. This decision promptly cleared away all of his springtime gloom and changed his attitude toward the cows and toward Musinka. Knowing that he would soon be rid of them forever, he began to show them the graciousness of a host whose unwanted guest has finally picked up his hat. Meanwhile, he inquired among his friends about rooms and viewed a few, but they all involved either renovations or the buyout of a lease. He did not want to spend the money, knowing full well that his resources were insufficient to allow for an apartment that would be fully commensurate with his tastes and dignity; he preferred to take something worse until his situation improved, rather than spend money on something middling.

At the end of June, the Institute fell completely silent. The last examination session had ended, the corridors emptied, and there were just small groups of students finalizing their documents for summer leave. But Stepan still went there often to deal with community matters. It was in the small room assigned to the KUBUCh that Borys Zadorozhnii, the friend whom he had lately been avoiding, ran into him.

"So this is where you've buried yourself," exclaimed Borys. "Why did you disappear so suddenly?"

"I was busy," answered Stepan, pointing to the account books.

"Busy-shmizzy—it's not right to forget your friends. Remember what Shevchenko said, 'He who forgets his friends is punished by God!' Well, it's a good thing I found you."

"Were you looking for me?"

"I certainly was. You see, I'm all done. I've finished the Institute."

"I have two more years," sighed Stepan. "They say they're going to add another year to the program."

"I suffered for five years, and it was nothing. But here's the point: I'm moving out and I'm looking for a decent person—"

"I'm dying to find a room!"

"And you're wondering why I was looking for you! Let's show some gratitude here. But don't think I'm leaving for a professional appointment somewhere. Nope, I'm taking the academic route—staying on with the department at the Institute. And I found myself a big, sunny room."

"You're a lucky stiff."

"There's got to be some reward for all my misery. But you, my dear Steffi you don't know the most important thing. I'm getting married."

"The same one?"

"Yup, the same one—the fair-haired one. I can't control myself when I think about it. You understand—it's love."

Stepan gave him a congratulatory hug, feeling a strange sense of relief, as if a great weight that he had been carrying all this time had fallen off his shoulders.

"Now, if I could just find someone to marry Musinka," he thought.

That evening, they settled the details. Stepan said to his friend, "At my place, it's always so noisy and busy, there are always guests visiting my hosts, it's too much to put up with. You've really done me a big favor. I'm very grateful to you, Borys."

Borys warmly squeezed his hand.

"It's really nothing, don't thank me," he said with feeling, dropping his joking manner. "It's a great pleasure for me now to do something nice for someone. I give a kopeck to a beggar, and I feel good. I feel like thanking him for taking it."

"You're getting all starry-eyed, my friend," Stepan observed.

"Maybe because I'm head over heels in love. Don't laugh. Love is real. I'm beginning to believe in eternal love. Really!"

Borys gave Stepan his new address and invited him to come over in a couple of weeks, after they were settled in at their new place as a couple.

"Well, that would be dangerous," thought Stepan. Then he said aloud, "I'll move in tomorrow."

On parting, after a slight hesitation, they embraced.

After Borys left, Stepan shrugged his shoulders. What a strange fellow, this Borys. He couldn't imagine that the feelings might be mutual. He recalled Nadiika's face for a moment, her eyes that used to smile for him, and he came to the ultimate conclusion that she could love only him, Stepan Radchenko, and no one else. Although they were not apparent to others, he had special rights to her and, if he called her, she would have to come immediately. Stepan felt as if he had some kind of power over his friend's happiness and was allowing him to make use of it.

Then he felt sorry for Borys. The fortunate are, after all, just like the sick, and they need careful attention. Happiness, in the final analysis, is a disease of spiritual short-sightedness: it's possible only under an incomplete calculation of circumstances and an incomplete understanding of things. Sharp vision is also a problem, like blindness, and the most unfortunate people are astronomers who see dark spots on the surface of a bright sun.

Agitated, in part by the meeting with a happy person and even more by the inevitability of parting tonight from Musinka, Stepan was cheerless and could not fully appreciate the satisfaction of his long-hoped-for change of apartments and the beginnings of his independent path into the beautiful world. Although he cheered himself with Musinka's words promising not to stand in his way when she became unnecessary, he was not at all sure she would admit that she was unnecessary at precisely the same time that he reached this conclusion.

He sighed and killed time until it was dark, even growing angry at the thought of a possible unpleasant scene, considering all the work he had done for the Hnidyi family.

Indeed, when he, feigning levity, announced the news, it broke over Tamara Vasylivna's head like a thunderclap. For a moment she bent over and Stepan feared that she might be fainting. That would be a real mess.

And then she whispered so softly that he could barely make out her words: "You'll leave... that's all right. You have everything before you. Just stay until the fall. You'll leave in the fall. The leaves will be falling, the evenings will be quiet. Then you'll go. Let this be your little sacrifice. You have everything before you: life, happiness, youth. You have everything, I'm only asking for a crumb. Is it so hard? Are you so stingy? You don't want to tend the cows? All right, we'll get a hired man. You want to move out of the kitchen? All right, take one of the rooms. What do you want? All right then, not the fall, just one month. One week. One day—but not right now, not now!"

He let her express herself, and then, wrapping his voice in sorrow and pity and struggling to express his deep sympathy for her pain, he said, "That's just how it turned out with the apartment, Musinka. I'll still come to you."

Abruptly, she pushed aside the hand he had raised to embrace her.

"And you're a liar, too!" she exclaimed. "You want to deceive me. I take this one in off the street, like a little bastard, and now he's giving me charity!"

However uncertain his situation was, he understood these words as a terrible insult. He? A bastard? He had earned top honors, the "perfect score." He had entered the second year at the Institute. He was active in community work. He wrote stories that had caught the eye of a well-known poet. And he's a bastard!? Maybe it's time he stopped screwing around with this old hag. But before he could articulate an answer worthy of his offended self-respect, Tamara Vasylivna was patting him on the head.

"Don't be angry, Stepan," she said, so meekly that he felt appeased. "This hurts me. But all this is nonsense. Tomorrow you will go. Tomorrow, in a week, in two—it's all the same. I'll have to endure it. My dear little one, you don't even understand what there is to endure. You'll leave, whistling as you go, and that's that. I won't cry, either. Only those who expect happiness cry. I'm all alone. Maksym has left. And he'll never come back."

She laughed, quietly, and sniffled.

"Remember, I told you about myself?"

"Sure, what?"

He would be happy to listen to her entire life story from the beginning, as long as she didn't speak of tomorrow's separation, although, at the moment, he didn't anticipate that her story would be very interesting.

"I didn't tell you the most important thing... I never loved anyone."

He didn't quite understand what she was saying.

"You were the first one I ever loved," she went on. "Before, I didn't dare, because of my son. How I hated him sometimes! You don't even know how beautiful I was. My clothes scorched my flesh, I slept without a nightshirt, it burned me. That was a terribly long time ago. And then, you came."

She kissed him on the forehead quietly.

"I didn't believe in God. That is, I had once believed and, when I saw you, I began to pray again. It didn't help. I came to you as in a nightmare, and you pushed me away. I left. Then you called me, and I came. My will was broken."

She squeezed his hands in her own.

"Tomorrow you'll go, and you'll keep going for a long, long time. You'll pass by many people. Maybe I, too, will still have many days, only I won't ever meet anyone again. Many empty days, if I can sleep at night. I will tear them off like sheets from a calendar and there won't be anything written on the other side. And then death will come. That's frightening. Say something, anything!"

He shuddered. There was something unspeakably difficult and hopeless in her words. Again, they drifted into a whisper, pushing him into an endless distance; they fell on his soul like drops of warm oil, softening all the calluses there, smoothing out all the wrinkles and folds, awakening a calm and happy sensitivity.

"Well, Musinka," he said, lost in thought, "You must do the talking. I can't say anything. I don't know anything. I don't know what will come of me. But one thing I have learned—we don't live the way we want to, and we can't help but give pain to others. That much I have understood. Sometimes it's nice, like now. Quiet, peaceful. What you have done for me, no one else will ever do. Musinka, you know this. I did not give you much thought when you were with me, but I will always remember you when you're gone."

Gratefully, kindly, she kissed him, but when, feeling encouraged, he wanted to answer with more than a kiss, she pushed him away.

"Let's not steal from ourselves, my love."

She embraced him and began to cradle him quietly, indistinctly singing, rocking him to sleep with gentle kisses to his eyes and forehead. Stepan soon fell asleep, wearied by events and the warmth of his own kindheartednesses.

In the morning, he didn't awake until eight, and he lay in bed for a long time. Then he washed up and knocked on the door to the bedrooms. Getting no answer, he entered quietly. No one was there. As if no one had ever lived in these rooms. He stood for a while in Musinka's room, which resembled a young girl's bedroom with its white duvet and the embroidered curtains on the windows, and then he returned to the kitchen, laden with distant memories. He drank the milk that had been left out for him, performed his duties to the cows one last time, and brought in some water. Now he was free, and he began gathering up his few possessions.

After some consideration, he lit the stove. As the logs ignited, he changed into his gray suit and then began to burn his field jacket, his pants, and the sacks he had brought from the village. The boots would not burn, so he threw them into the trash. All that was left were his notebooks, books, and underwear bound up in his bedroll.

He tied up all his things into two bundles, locked the door, put the key under the porch, as always, and left with the two parcels in his hands, carrying in his soul sadness, the bitterness of his first encounter with life, and troubling hopes.

Part TWO

Chapter One

Stepan returned from his morning swims in the Dnipro at nine thirty. He went out to the river at seven and spent two hours lying on the sand in the soft sunlight, which slowly turned his body into that of a brown Atlas. Such were the details of the invariable, if unwritten, daily schedule that he had developed on the second day after settling in his new apartment and adhered to without fail, thus marking the beginning of his new life.

For the first time in his life, he was free of the hardships of inadequate means. He was entirely satisfied with his living arrangements, somewhat impulsively considering himself a hardy tree, capable of taking root in any soil. Following village habits, by summer, he had again economized a few dozen karbovanets, living frugally, drinking two glasses of milk every morning, having lunch in the NarKharch Union of People's Food Service and Dormitory Workers cafeteria, and then, in the evening, returning there again for another modest meal. He did not keep even a slice of bread at home, fearful of mice and roaches and instinctively concluding that consuming food, as well as discarding it, is not appropriate in a room where you work and sleep, and that civilization in its unceasing progress had created for these purposes specific places of public use whose value was not identically understood for both functions, although in practical terms they were of equal value.

The only indulgence he allowed himself was smoking really good tobacco. He did not economize on that, since, if it was unpleasant to treat a friend to inferior cigarettes, it was even worse to smoke them yourself. The serious work that he began over the summer, when his affairs at the Institute had ended and he had moved to these new quarters, obscured for him all the seductive posters about world-renowned films, the most famous singers and actors appearing in the theaters, as well as the most raucous entertainments and amusements taking place in parks and along the Dnipro. Deliberately and willingly, he had condemned himself to solitude within these walls, where the only decoration was a wilting palm in one corner, a relic of the former bourgeois owners that was handed down to each successive tenant, reminding them of the unfortunate history of this world. Under its yellowed leaves, he undertook the systematic labor of transforming his own person.

He had observed in himself a quality he found most strange and even frightening, and whose real causes and natural origins he did not understand. Instead of building him up with new knowledge, his first year at the Institute, brilliantly accomplished from all perspectives, had, it seems, resulted in the destruction of the wisdom that he had brought with him from the village. Suddenly, he felt that his brain was dressed only in the most shameful rags, and this feeling troubled him, since it degraded his dignity. Most of all, he was troubled by deficiencies in a field that was not even part of his Institute studies at all but a personal and somewhat sensitive matter—namely, literature. It had become his closest and most important concern, for reasons that he did not really want to analyze in detail, justifying his enthusiasm, instead, with the substantial argument that a familiarity with literature was the primary characteristic of a cultured person. From his voluminous reading back in the village, he had remembered a whole host of names, titles, and plots, but all this was like a neglected library, where the books have not even been put up on the shelves. So he began to arrange them in his head, just as he had once done in the library of the Village Hall.

After his morning bathing, the hours from ten to three were for reading. Then, until five, various minor chores—teaching lessons at various offices, exchanging books at the library, eating lunch, and resting; then two hours to study languages, alternating between

English and French every day; and afterwards, until ten, Ukrainian literature. Finally, some free time for a walk along the streets or in a park, supper, and then sleep from eleven to seven. This was the regimen that he followed like a supreme law carved by a divine hand on stone tablets. At moments, when something within him rebelled against such a regimented life, he scolded himself and cursed in the foulest language, knowing full well that a betrayal in one instance was a betrayal forevermore. But, in the evening, after a walk and a fitness regimen that followed the functional system of Dr. Anokhin, when he lay down to sleep, he felt that his thoughts were unusually clear, and he experienced the sublime pleasure that was the cornerstone of Epicurean teachings.

In two months, he had covered as much material as can be covered by a talented young man who is willing to expend all his forces on the capture of this single fortress. He experienced almost no fatigue, refreshing his powers each morning with water and sunlight and exercising his muscles each evening with rhythmic calisthenics. A few weeks after introducing this schedule, however, he felt a need for at least a little rest after his work on languages, and after careful consideration in a special deliberation, having given himself an opportunity to be heard both "for" and "against," he approved the resolution to permit Stepan Radchenko to lie down for ten minutes after language study. And these moments became the happiest time of the whole day. They came between seven and eight o'clock, when evening extends through the window its ephemeral warm hands, reaching down from distant heights, rising up from the depths of the earth, and carrying into the home the soothing tranquility of immeasurable space, silently joining the soul with the expanse of the universe. Drowning his gaze in a corner of the room, he observed as objects dissolved in the creeping dusk and walls disappeared in a thick bluish glow. Ten minutes of this lethargy, and then he suddenly jumps up, turns on the electric light, harshly breaking the magical charm. Books open. Silence. Intermittent scratches of pencil on paper.

Sustained by the saturation of his own mind, he did not feel a need to interact with other people, those distant figures whom he occasionally encountered. Their lives now seemed to him comically simplistic and unworthy of any attention. He was becoming a wild recluse in his room, although he ascended the peaks of civilization every day. Having reduced his own life to a mechanical process, he wanted to see the same in others, as he gained more wisdom than one ought to allow oneself to gain.

At eleven o'clock on this day, after a morning that had augured nothing new, a knock on his door disturbed his concentration. Damn it! Who dares disturb him at this sacred time? But it was only a letter, whose arrival surprised him even more than an uninvited guest. From whom? Shrugging his shoulders, he tore open the envelope. It was from the poet Vyhorskyi, who had taken his stories. He trembled as if in that very moment his future life was being determined and the wisdom of his fanatical efforts was being judged. An unexpected burning, a sudden confusion forced him to sit down and hastily scan the letter, searching for the necessary phrases. Here—here they were: "They are wonderful stories, to be sure." Suddenly, the letter was no longer interesting, as if he had instantly ingested all of its contents.

Stepan threw the letter on his bed and began pacing the room in agitation, like a person who has awakened in a strange setting. "They are wonderful stories, to be sure," his soul sang out these words, and he realized that, while he had forgotten about his stories, his entire life revolved only around them, in expectation of this unforeseen letter. Swallowing the burning sensation of joy, he stretched out and picked up the letter again. Unwittingly focusing on the beautiful sentence in the middle, which stood out from the entire text as if it were laid out in a diamond mosaic, he lit a cigarette and, leaning back carelessly in his chair, began reading.

"I stopped for a short layover in Simeyiz and remembered that I owe you a letter. And what do you think jogged my memory? A couple was walking by and 'he' was complaining about Ukrainization. The poor fellow brought his offended Russian selfishness even here, to this resort town. So here I am at the post office, and you must thank that Russian vacationer, because I don't willingly write letters—they're one of the most foolish things invented by mankind. Whenever I see a 'Post and Telegraph Office' sign, I think, 'Here's the enemy of mankind.' You don't yet know how pleasant it is to run away as far as possible from those who know you, to a place where no one cares about you and you don't care about any of them, and you can be anything you want to be and no one is going to demand an accounting from you. And to encounter at such a moment the mechanisms of communication! It's barbaric! In any case, to my credit, this is the first letter I'm writing, and I've already walked through the Caucasus and now I'm walking along the southern coast of Crimea. I'm all alone but full of enthusiasm. My plan is to walk the western coast as well. I'm not tired, and there's still a great deal to do. I'm writing, but not about the sea or the monasteries. About the city! And your stories are all rural. They are wonderful stories, to be sure. Their faults only point to future accomplishments. I read them back on the train and sent them out to journals when I reached Katerynoslav. It would be good if they both appeared together. That would be an unpleasant surprise to our literary critics who specialize in the aria about the crisis in literature. I don't know how to finish a letter. Nor how to write one. Vyhorskyi."

Stepan got up impulsively, lost in thought. He grabbed a shirt and rushed out into the street, slowing his movements so as not to attract attention. Along the way, he stopped in a couple of bookstores, but they did not carry periodicals. What do you mean, you don't carry periodicals? He sullenly walked out of the shops. It wasn't until he reached Volodymyr Street that he had any success. Which journal are you looking for? All of the ones that had issues last month! Stepan greedily surveyed their contents and, with a trembling hand, set aside two of them. His own name, printed alongside those of others, gave him such a start that he did not immediately understand what to do with the journals. Eventually, taking himself in hand, he purchased them and stepped out of the bookstore.

Where to now? He couldn't imagine what else was left for him to desire. Within him, a sharp burst of emotion settled into a sweet, calm, and intoxicating fog. He did not want to go anywhere. He stood in front of the shop window, forcing himself to look at the books displayed there, but feeling only the tension of his fingers on the pages in his hands. Suddenly, pulling away from the glass, he left quickly, driven by a fervent desire to sit somewhere alone and read, over and over, the stories he had written.

In the park where he had once watched children playing ball, he hid himself in a remote corner and opened the publications to the pages where his works were printed. Carefully, he examined the paper and the style of the printed letters and then began slowly to read, like a newly literate reader consuming his first book. At first, he did not recognize his lines in their new, external appearance, and he felt uneasy. This uneasiness increased even more as he connected with his own writing. He read, trembling with exhilaration and fear, and the works he had created now produced in him a new being, allowing him to experience the joy of the complete oneness of his person, erasing any duality of the soul between internal and external components. He became unified and powerful, and if an unexpected tremor arose in him, it was only a response to his own greatness.

He read for a long time, and sat even longer, weaving indistinct dreams that led, time and again, to the indisputable fact that he had become a writer. If he had been capable of writing these stories, it was evident that he would be able to write many more, and better ones.

His dreams grew brighter, transforming into thoughts. He was beginning to realize that, secretly, without ever admitting it to himself, he had been certain that someday this moment would arrive, and this certainty had been invisibly guiding his life. Even before reaching the first rung of the literary ladder—not yet having seen his works in print—he had begun to study literature in order to strengthen his position on that rung. He was fascinated by the secret processes of the soul, which knows more and sees further than the poor mind, which often merely sanctions already approved resolutions, like those English kings that reign but do not rule. The idea that all this might not have happened was something he acknowledged like the shadow of an incapacitated threat whose possible effects on his life he could not even imagine. But this thought, although disarmed, was too horrible to linger on for long.

After lunch, having decided that today marked the beginning of a new era in his life, he decided to start a diary. Having written a few uncertain lines in a notebook, he needed to put a date under what he had written. Glancing up at the calendar, he was surprised and forgot all about the diary: today was exactly one year to the day since he had arrived in the city. How short it had been, this year! How strangely and quickly it had flown by. So, he decided to treat this doubly remarkable day as a holiday and to mark it with an appropriate leisure activity. His shoes and trousers, with their slight bulges at the knees, were scoured once again, although cleaning them every morning was one of the rules of his strict regimen. At six o'clock, he changed his collar, put on his jacket, and, without a hat, as usual, left his room.

The street greeted him with a soft evening rustle as he measured its surface with strong, energetic strides, as if his legs were fitted with new steel springs. He walked without hurrying, haughtily raising his head as a mark of his superiority. His consciousness of this superiority had firmly implanted itself in his mind and added sparkle to his eyes and a peaceful dignity to his actions. This very process of proud walking, the flawless motion of each gear and lever of his own complex machine, gave him such intoxicating satisfaction that he didn't even consider where it was his legs were taking him.

Reaching Khreshchatyk, he bought a newspaper, sat down at a table in an open-air café, and ordered coffee and a pastry. With incomprehensible and unexpected refinement, he crossed one leg over the other and lazily stirred the aromatic liquid, all the while glancing obliquely at the hundreds of faces passing on the sidewalk and taking in the variety of colors and activities on the street. Then he opened the newspaper to the events announcements.

"Another pastry," he called out to the waitress who was walking past him.

A concert of the symphony orchestra at the Opera won him over, mostly because he had never been to such a concert and, hopping on the bus—although the Opera was only two blocks away—he reached Volodymyr Street. He bought an expensive ticket—it had to be an expensive one—and walked around the circular gallery, taking delight in the spectacle of constantly changing faces, figures, and attire. The crowd had a strange effect on him. Its motion and sound aggravated his already sensitive nerves, as if he were for the first time seeing so many people and feeling his own relation to them. He experienced the joy of existing alongside his fellow beings, united with them in shared activity. He wanted to laugh when he saw others laughing. The diversity of these unknown beings was closer to him than all those he had previously known.

Peering further into the depths of the enchanting crowd, composed, it seemed, of the finest specimens of the human race, he found a woman. Slowly focusing his gaze, he passed through the transparency of her clothing, expanding the naked flesh beyond her arms and shoulders, sensing the pleasing firmness of her legs in the thin stockings that disappeared beneath the scallops of her dress. The crowd exuded desire like a blossoming tree in early spring sends forth its matrimonial scent. It oppressed with the power of its sensuality, hidden within these hundreds of beings, who seemed to be the refined incarnation of one giant male and one giant female, with passions worthy of their giant bodies.

He listened to the concert inattentively, distracted by impressions of the crowd. He, too, was a full member of this crowd, but he could not even speak to anyone. He was surprised at the insult he felt at his own alienation. Beyond doubt, all these people were cultured individuals who read journals, and many of them would consider it an honor to make the acquaintance of a talented writer. Yet they were separated by a very unfortunate boundary that made him a foreign body that had only accidentally entered into this smoothly functioning organism. Oh, if only he had a single acquaintance. But now he was like a ghost, perhaps a well-educated one, but nevertheless one incapable of taking part in the joy of material existence. He was lonely, and the months of solitary effort were now turning against him.

During the intermission Stepan loitered gloomily in the gallery. The crowd had so easily taken him down a notch and so thoughtlessly destroyed him that he began, in the end, to pity himself, grasping at any sliver of high esteem that he could still ascribe to himself. After all, nothing much had happened: he had simply become a little too emotional. He was a writer, after all, and that was indisputable, and he need not concern himself too much with all these mugs around him. There probably wasn't anyone among them who could write a publishable work.

Seeking any kind of comfort for his alienation, Stepan approached the kiosk of an instant lottery that had been set up in all theaters by the Committee to Aid Children. Here, he had the right to speak, if only for money. Since the lottery to aid homeless children was not very popular among the spectators, the pretty salesgirl greeted him very graciously. Would he like a lottery ticket? They're twenty kopecks, please. Stepan glanced at the wine, candy, make-up, penknives, decorated boxes, and other trivia that was ready to belong to anyone who might win it, and, reaching into the box, pulled out a ticket, which, on examination, proved to be completely blank.

"I'll take another one," he said.

But the purpose of the lottery was to aid children, not to hand out a bottle of port to each customer for two coins.

"One more," Stepan continued.

After the fourth blank ticket, he was attracting the attention of a number of people, drawn in by the lottery girl's beautiful laugh and the figure of an intrepid philanthropist.

"But they're probably all blank!" said the budding young writer with theatrical despair after the sixth ticket, to the amusement of a sizeable audience whose curious stares he felt on his back with great satisfaction.

"Oh no, you're just unlucky. You're probably lucky in something else," answered the salesgirl coquettishly, pouring out her charm in front of Stepan for the benefit of the charitable committee.

With the ninth ticket he turned toward the onlookers with a nervous blush on his face and, unfolding the ticket, held it high over his head. A roar of satisfied laughter rose from the crowd—this ticket was also blank.

With a conqueror's delight, Stepan surveyed the ocean of heads before him that was filling the passage, blocking the movement of people who were joining the crowd as they learned that this tall fellow was buying his twenty-third ticket without any results. Off to the side, the shining helmet of a firefighter could be seen moving toward the crowd.

"I'll buy a ticket!" called out a woman's voice unexpectedly and, while Stepan was rummaging in his pocket, a diminutive girl put her hand into the perfidious box. She won a baby pacifier and ceremoniously turned it over to Stepan, accompanied by the joyful shouts and applause of the onlookers, who were hurrying back to their seats. The intermission was coming to an end.

Stepan paid even less attention to the second half of the symphonic concert than he had to the first. Whether from shame or excitement, his face was hot. It was foolish to act so silly in front of the crowd. And an even greater misery gnawed at his heart: of the five karbovanets with which he had left home, he now had only two silver coins. The pacifier gave him the greatest misery, and he quietly threw it under his chair. May it be damned! And what benefit was there from all this spending?

After the concert, Stepan walked out of the Opera in a dour spirit and stopped by the portico to light a cigarette. This doubly remarkable day in his life was ending without any uplifting feeling.

"Can you give me a light?" He heard a familiar voice and saw the girl who had participated with him in the lottery. For an unknown reason he was overjoyed and flustered. As if he had seen someone he had long expected, with whom the brightest hopes were associated. Graciously lighting her cigarette with a separate match, he began to walk alongside her.

"I've got the cigarette lit already," she remarked when he followed her as she turned on to Lenin Street.

"I want to thank you for your present," said Stepan, after a moment's thought.

"You're welcome. You can suck on it at your leisure."

He glanced at her, surprised by her peevish tone. This skinny little thing, hardly up to his armpits and topped off with a flattened hat. Stepan was dissatisfied with this disparity between them but, nevertheless, carefully took her by the arm when it came time to cross the street. She threw him a sideways glance, pulled back her arm, and walked on with her firm, almost military, stride.

"Why are you silent?" she asked, turning into Gimnazia Passage.

"And what's your name?" asked Stepan uncertainly.

"And what's it to you?" she answered sternly. "My name is Zoska," she added, softening.

"Zosia…" Stepan began.

"My name is Zoska, you hear—Zoska," she cut him off impatiently, going toward the door.

Stepan followed her, vaguely expecting the staircase to be dark, allowing him to steal a kiss there and thus recompense himself for the misery at the concert and the money wasted there. But, as if guessing his intentions, the girl sprang up the stairs to the first floor hurriedly and pushed her key into the lock.

"Bonjour," she said, disappearing behind the door.

Chapter Two

Finally, after many corrections and crossings out, the sheet contained only a few words, and was evidently completely acceptable:

"Dear Comrades. In the last issue of your journal, you published one of my stories. Please write and let me know if you would like any more stories. I can send some. My address: Kyiv, 51 Lviv Street, Apt. 16. Stefan Radchenko."

And yet, on further reflection, he felt that the fact that his story had been published in the journal was so obvious that mentioning it in his letter would be unnecessary, so he crossed out the relevant sentence. Reflecting even further, he determined that it was insulting to his own dignity to promote his own stories, so after the final redaction his letter was entirely acceptable to him:

"Dear Comrades. My address: Kyiv, 51 Lviv Street, Apt. 16. Stefan Radchenko."

Making two separate copies of this text, he addressed the letters to the journals, one in Kyiv, the other in Kharkiv, and felt a deep and liberating relief.

Then he got up and paced around his room. It was near eight o'clock in the morning—half of the second floor, which included his room, was only just getting up. From the kitchen, past a number of closed doors, he could hear the hiss of three gas stoves, corresponding to the number of families that were squeezed into the remaining four rooms of this apartment. He didn't really know his neighbors, since he spent most of his time alone in his room and did not meet them in the kitchen, the usual site of domestic meetings, acquaintances, and arguments. He never even touched this nerve center of activity, with its cooking stove, table covered with chopping scars, greasy cabinet, and collection of pans, pots, colanders, and ladles along the wall. Even to wash up in the morning he walked down to the Dnipro, which deprived him of the opportunity to come into contact with his cohabitants and to observe them in their natural state. After all, the code of customary behavior allows people to enter the kitchen in their housecoat, if they are women; without a jacket, if they are men; or sleepy and disheveled, regardless of their sex. Sharing the same roof brings people together not so much because they can demonstrate their finest qualities to one another but rather because they cannot hide the dirtier sides of their lives, which, unfortunately, are more significant. Every apartment is a small group of conspirators who silently grant mutual exemptions from the decent behavior that they would otherwise demand of anyone who did not have the honor of living with them.

Stepan listened to this morning symphony of domesticity all the more carefully because he had never actually heard it before, since he was never at home in the morning. The ceaseless slamming of the doors, the yelling of the breadwinners who were rushing to their jobs, the angry responses of the women, the shrieks of children being sent off to school, and the incessant wail of infants bore witness to an income level of between fifty and one hundred karbovanets a month, a level associated with the intellectual proletariat, otherwise known as city dwellers or the bourgeoisie. These umpteen cubic meters of air locked between walls, ceiling, and floor were the unsung home of the youthful aspirations, beauty, hope, and rose-colored expectations that mattered in this world, and the young man, although he considered himself an incomparably higher being than the average person, reflected sadly and with a secret fear: "What are they living for, actually? Today, tomorrow, a month from now—it's always the same thing. They're nuts."

At nine o'clock, when the working men had left for their jobs and their wives for the bazaars, the apartment sank into a relative silence, which, after the earlier clamor, seemed absolute. Sitting down at his table under the beneficent branches of the old palm, Stepan pulled a packet of papers written in pencil from a corner of the drawer and began to sort them carefully. These were the working copies of the stories he had written last winter, three completed and one just started. They were longer than the ones that had been published, but they shared the same themes—revolution and rebels. In addition, they all shared another quality, one which had already been evident in his first story, "The Razor," and had emphatically continued in all of Stepan's further stories, crystallizing his understanding of the civil war as a gigantic mass uprising in which individuals were invisible particles leveled in the larger whole and mindlessly subordinated to it, and where people were depersonalized in a higher will, which had stripped them of their own life and, along with it, all illusions of independence. Thus, quite naturally, the heroes of his stories became things in which the mighty idea was superficially embodied. Indeed, all by themselves, the carriers of the action in his stories became a derailed armored train, a burnt-out estate, or a captured station that had all stood against the human collective as distinct individuals. There had never been such summary executions, and corpses had never fallen as meekly as they did in the works of Stefan Radchenko, because, as he tuned his ear to the groans of the derailed armored train, the author forgot about the cries of the living beneath its shattered carcass.

By evening, he had completed the unfinished story, surprised by the heaviness of his hand in writing. Pages he had earlier written in an hour now cost him half a day of intense concentration, with unfortunate interruptions when the pencil refused to write altogether. He ended up crossing out what was written, grinding to a sudden stop from full speed after reaching a word that didn't really fit but also wouldn't allow itself to be replaced. His expertise in language turned into an unmitigated enemy. His mind, weighed down with the burden of his reading, with the stylistic examples of the masters, and with heightened expectations from every turn of phrase, was constantly holding back the free flight of his inspiration. His literary taste, sharpened by the finest works of literature, revealed countless blemishes in the construction of his story. Twice he had to rebuild the plot of the work, abandoning what he had thought up and adding completely unforeseen elements. On finishing, he felt an angry satisfaction, like a rider who has finally subdued a horse that has repeatedly thrown him to the ground.

He devoted two days to making a clean copy and superficial corrections, leaving his home only to eat and to teach his language classes. He even neglected his hygienic bathing in the Dnipro. A day later he received a reply from the editorial office of the Kyiv journal, one just as brief as his letter: "Please drop by at the editorial office between 11 and 2 o'clock." The "please" was very gratifying, but he did not visit the editorial office. He was held back from such a step by a strange combination of modesty and pride. Nothing, however, held him back from washing up and tidying his clothes as carefully as possible and setting off for Gimnazia Passage, to the building where the girl Zoska lived.

In truth, he did not feel a great desire to meet with her, but solitude had become burdensome and the need to have some fun after working on the stories led him out to where he might at least hear a living word—and, if it came from a girl, all the better. Of course, it wasn't words alone that interested him. The physical longing for a woman had not left him since he had abandoned Musinka, and the more completely he closed off any practical possibilities of satisfying this longing, the more completely it captivated his imagination. For a few minutes before falling off to sleep, as a just reward after the learned books, he allowed himself to toss around in his imagination a few of those things associated with lovemaking, and these imaginings were very gratifying, despite their immodesty. He would drift off to sleep wrapped up in invisible embraces that did not release his willing body until morning, leaving behind an unquenchable desire to convert them into reality. And his dreams were deeply immoral, revealing his goal in stark simplicity, dredging up material from his days as a wanderer, when relations with women were not adorned with even the most elementary seemliness, since, in their very essence, they were absolutely unseemly.

The seductive tormentor of all champions of spiritual values, that sleazy devil, ceaselessly stoked the flames of the wild fire in Stepan's blood, and, if he succeeded in containing it within the limits of his imagination, then that itself was a considerable virtue.

About Zoska herself, however, he had no particular intentions. He even thought that, through her, he might make some further acquaintances and thus expand the narrow confines of his solitude and imagination that were beginning to suffocate him. With such thoughts in mind, he cleared his nose and throat and knocked on the door, which was opened by the girl herself.

"What do you want?" she asked, having opened the door.

"I wanted to see you," answered Stepan.

"I did not give you permission," she answered sternly. But then, a moment later, she added, "Not here. Wait outside, and I'll be right out."

Before he could say a word, she closed the door. Stepan went out on the street feeling offended, since he considered himself on all counts—mental and physical—deserving of a better reception. What a snob! Nevertheless, he strolled along the sidewalk, mindlessly reading the signs on the door identifying the inhabitants. Zoska did not make him wait long, and soon stepped off the porch in a jacket and hat.

"Look at what I bought myself," she said, showing him a small riding crop. "Nice, isn't it? A remarkable one."

"It's very nice. Unusual," said Stepan, examining it.

"Do you know how to use it?"

"Just please don't hit me," he said, seeing her take a swing.

"It's for a dog—a Pomeranian, like the one we have. So, where's the pacifier?"

"I threw it away."

"The one I gave you as a present?!"

She stopped, mortified.

"No—no," said Stepan, fearing that she would leave, "I'm joking. I put it away in a drawer, at home."

"Bring it to me," said Zoska, "I'll attach it to the riding crop."

I guess I'll have to buy one. And a pacifier suits her, Stepan thought, glancing at her childish features.

A quarter of an hour later, Stepan was ceremoniously buying tickets for front-row seats at the cinema, expecting this expenditure to set a firm foundation for their further friendship. He reasoned, quite logically, that when a girl gets something from a boy, she begins to owe him something, too.

With knightly chivalry he let her into the cinema lobby ahead of him and graciously strolled around with her examining the posters and film stills.

"Look at this moron," said Zoska, pointing with the crop at a young man riding a horse in one of the stills. "In movies, you should ride in an automobile, not on a horse like a policeman."

Stepan was puffed up with pride—this was the first time in his life that he was with a real girl in a public place. His only regret was that she was swinging the crop too much and looking around, instead of paying attention to him. Nevertheless, she was sure to have a deep appreciation for the fact that it was he who had brought her here.

When the lights in the theater went out and images began to flicker on the screen, Stepan took her small hand and squeezed it. The girl did not respond but she also didn't pull back, so after a few minutes he put her hand on his knee and covered it with his palm, having decided, cautiously, to stop for the moment at that. After the last scenes, Zoska exclaimed, "What a wonderful film! Apollo, buy tickets for the next showing."

"My name is Stefan," said Stepan, offended. "Sit here. I'll get the tickets."

He quickly returned with the tickets, secretly fearing that she might run away.

"Oh, you're just divine," said Zoska.

But no sooner had the film begun than she proclaimed wearily, "Phooey, this stinks. I want to go home. It's stuffy in here."

On the corner of her street, she expressed another wish.

"I want to take a boat ride."

"As you please," answered Stepan. "It's such a quiet evening, we can go somewhere far."

"As long as it's on our street."

"But where's the water?"

"Create it!" cried the girl plaintively.

His patience ran out and, discreetly looking about, he kissed her.

"How boorish!" she cried.

"I love you," mumbled Stepan helplessly.

"I did not give you permission," she said as sternly as possible, walking away.

"Zoska, when will I see you?" he asked as she was leaving.

"Never," she said.

But Stepan only smiled at this word, and he went home filled with a variety of pleasant feelings. Zoska's decisive "never" only cheered him. Indeed, it gave him hope for another meeting very soon, perhaps even with important consequences, since it was not difficult for him to figure out that this girl was a capricious double-dealer who didn't know what she wanted. That gave a great deal of latitude to a person with constant desires. He was particularly pleased with her habit of saying that she had not given permission after the matter was already accomplished. Such a prohibition was, as everyone knows, not much of an obstruction.

All in all, he liked the girl more than he would have thought only a few hours earlier. When he touched her for an instant on the street he felt a restless change—experiencing at first hand the truth that a woman's body, just because it is small, does not lose its attractive features. On the contrary, in the paucity of its dimensions, he felt some special, sophisticated charms bred by the city, since such a body simply could not exist in a village environment. It was precisely this urban quality in her that attracted him, inasmuch as becoming a true city dweller was the first goal of his ambition. With her, he could go to all the theaters, cinemas, and performances. With her, he would achieve familiarity in urban society, where, of course, he would be accepted and honored.

At the Institute, classes had no doubt already begun, and he promised himself over and again to show up there. One morning, while dressing, he actually decided to make that happen forthwith. Then, suddenly, he asked himself, "Why should I go there?" And he did not find a suitable answer. At first, he was surprised, then gratified, and, embracing his own decisiveness, he spent the day feeling himself a conqueror. What do I need the Institute for? Stepan Radchenko is a fine fellow even without a diploma.

Fortune was generous, showering him with gifts from its ancient horn, visible on posters in all the bakeries. Within a week he received an answer from the editorial office of the Kharkiv journal along with a check for eighty-seven karbovanets. The letter was not unexpected, but the money was a complete surprise. Literature, it turned out, was not only a noble pursuit, but a lucrative one as well—that is, it was doubly worthwhile.

Stepan indulged himself in writing a long letter of reply about receiving the money. He would have been happy to write endlessly, if that had been required by the mail, that wonderful achievement of human culture that not only allows people to communicate at a distance from each other, and not only delivers journals with published stories but also delivers money.

The letter from the Kharkiv journal was very interesting, indeed. In it, the virtues of his stories were briefly but clearly noted, and he was invited to send more, even several, if possible, so that a collection of between three and six printed signatures in size might be assembled. This last line confused him. What is a printed signature and, what's more important, will the stories he already has fit into these "three to six printed signatures"? This needed to be determined, along with other questions about the printing process that had arisen in his mind. That a page is composed of individual letters was well known from that place in the history textbook where Gutenberg's invention is described, but on the question of how, for example, books could include illustrations and portraits, history was silent. So the young writer decided that he would buy the appropriate technical guidebook, and from it he learned what a printed signature is and how many characters it contains, and what is meant by proofs, cicero, quads, leading, and Linotype. He paid particular attention to all things connected with portraits: zincography, half-tones, three-color printing, and offset presses. The information about portraits he stored in his memory for later use, but the definition of a printed signature was immediately applied to his own six stories as a practical exercise, with the determination that, since they contained 207,194 characters, they fit very neatly into the category "from three to six printed signatures."

He then assembled them neatly, renumbered the pages, and wrapped them in clean paper, inscribing on it in nice large letters: "Stefan Radchenko. *The Razor: A Collection of Short Stories*." He bound the whole with string, as he had once done with his report on the Silbud, and turned the package over to that marvel, the post office. He did not send any letter, since he considered silence the most dignified reply.

Chapter Three

Theater has completed the circle of its development. In the constructivist method of staging—a method in which emphatic gesture and intonation by the actors manifest the singular, focused character traits of dramatic personages, or in which there is a preponderance of crowd scenes and conventional situations where descriptive placards and the mere skeleton of stage decoration designate the setting, allowing it to develop on any number of planes—the contemporary theater has risen to the highest level of its development, achieving communion with its original source: the religious spectacles of antiquity and the Middle Ages. Theater's future is laid out in a continuous repetition of its past, an accelerated replaying of now-familiar stages of development with an admixture of innovations, but no longer with that great ferment of progress that alone can give life to the arts. The main trunk of theater—governed by the all-encompassing, unique, and inviolable laws of development, whose presence in the diversity of life's processes the genius of man can discover but not alter—has sent forth from its roots a lateral stem whose growth resembles the trick of an Indian magician who, within the space of a minute and directly in front of his onlookers, can make an entire tree sprout from a seed.

Twenty years ago, relegated to wooden shacks on the outskirts of circuses and bazaars, where it shared in the typical smells of barns and cheap commerce and earned the disdain of higher society, the press, and public opinion, the cinematic seedling was transplanted to the central streets, to sumptuous establishments with sparkling decorations, large lobbies, and symphonic orchestras and, blossoming there into a mature flower, it immediately garnered a stunning acceptance. Realizing possibilities of illusion that were impossible in the theater and a full range of action for the actors, it reduced the stage by one whole dimension but expanded it into infinity and threw onto it the full flood of reality, without depriving it of any authenticity. Having taken away the action's voice, it made it comprehensible to all nations and tribes, and thus, turning contradictions on their head, like an accomplished dialectician, it strengthened and won over to itself the opinion and the hearts of mankind.

The variety of characters, countries, and times thrown on the screen by the wand of the silent magician awakened in the young writer Stefan Radchenko that tickling sensation of combined happiness and oppression that overpowers a person somewhere in the middle of the steppe when the night hums with inaudible whispers and bedevils the eyes with deceptions. When the lights went out in the auditorium, and the first bars of music were heard, he was enveloped in just such a mood of observation, and quietly, under his breath, he would repeat the title of the movie, as if it foreshadowed the plot. Then he would dive into the images on the screen with the enthusiasm of an explorer, shuffling his feet when a subtitle he had finished reading remained on the screen too long, and sometimes, engrossed by a pithy or tragic scene, he clenched the fingers of his hand, which had its permanent place on the knees of his girlfriend, Zoska, who was his constant and invariable companion. She whispered in pain, "That hurts, divine one."

But in these moments, like a true god, he was far from her, united with the moving figures made of projected light, who captivated his fervent imagination and took it with them in their travels, experiences, and adventures, where he smelled the scents of the gardens he was seeing and heard the shots as smoke billowed from rifles. Often, on returning home, he did not light a lamp but, in the dark glow of his window, recreated the images he had brought home with him of beautiful actresses, clothing their seductive shadows in flesh.

But more often and more sadly, standing in front of that window, he thought about the girl Zoska, who called him "divine" as if laughing at the powerlessness of his endeavors. In the three weeks of their acquaintance, their relationship had been stuck on the same level, as if they had bogged down after a propitious beginning, and the young man felt powerless to budge them toward a higher plateau. His rainbow plans were overturned by nature. An unexpected autumn covered the city with a gray and damp covering, wrapping the days in damp mists, rains, and ugly fogs. Sharp winds with sudden gusts bent the branches of the chestnut trees and tore off their still-green leaves. Cobblestones and roofs resounded from the cold teardrops, which then flowed down gutters in innocent streams, pouring out into the streets along the sidewalks, where the channels in the asphalt formed puddles that never dried out, whose surfaces trembled from the raindrops. Drivers hid beneath the taut cabs of their carriages, lined up in a black thread on the corner, their horses with bowed heads, seemingly forgotten. Street hawkers of cigarettes huddled on porches along with newspaper vendors; stores with artificial mineral waters, kvas, and fruit soda took down their colorful street signs; and the cheerful chatter of the petty-trade women peddling Rennet apples and Bartlett pears died away. Moisture and tedium saturated the air and the people.

This angry weather abruptly interrupted the sweetly scented season of parks and walks along the river into the bosom of nature, where, in the quiet and deserted tangle of bushes, lovemaking can reach its natural culmination. Nature closed down its convenient shelters, but no rain was capable of dousing the flame that overcomes the human heart without regard not only for age but also for time, contrary to the hearts of other animals, who have a designated period when they are in the mood for love.

After some futile attempts to get into Zoska's room, and a few rejected invitations to his own room, Stepan had to acknowledge the cinema as the only venue for his meetings with the girl, meetings that were hopeless, since his enthusiasm for art could not substitute for the disappointment of his desires. And this disappointment only further bolstered these desires, becoming for him a difficult trial by endurance. In the evening, he now lost the ability to fall asleep quickly, instead tossing and turning with eyes closed, and, in the morning, he awoke exhausted by his difficult dreams where, it seems, his cheek began to swell interminably or his arm grew longer and longer, and, sometimes, he was tortured by nightmares in which corpses would gather into a single mass and sway before him in the air, like bodies hanging from a gallows. He abandoned all his work and books; he continued giving his lessons at various enterprises as if they were a penance he could not escape. Each day, he waited in agitation for the evening, longing for it, preparing for it, awakening to live in the evening, only to have it end in perpetual expectations and inconsequential dreams.

There were also, however, some victories. She agreed to call him by the informal, second-person pronoun, rather than the formal one, but she drew no conclusions from this. Furthermore, she was a smoker, and wore her hair cut short, but even these unmistakable—in his estimation—signs did not help him in anything. She expertly kept him at a distance, and only when he began to mope did she allow him to kiss her, which she never reciprocated.

"I love you," he whispered with more passion than sincerity, leading her along the familiar path between the cinema and Gimnazia Passage.

"Ah," sighed Zoska. "There is no such thing as love. All that is just something people invented."

"If you don't love me," he asked, "why do you go out with me?"

"Because you're paying for my ticket!" she replied in astonishment.

This answer offended him deeply, but he kept silent, since he had to acknowledge to himself that he was somewhat scared of her. She was fickle and wrapped up in strange, otherworldly whims. In a single evening, she might want to fly in an airplane or fire a canon, or be a musician, a professor (any kind would do), sailor, or shepherd.

"Ah, I would like to be a shopkeeper," she would say. "You sit in a store. 'What would you like? Some pepper? Ten grams? One hundred?' Lots of people would come by. And I would give candy to the children. I would like to be a child, a handsome curly-haired little boy. That would be so wonderful—to sit astride a stick and spur it on, 'Whoa scout, whoa!'"

Skipping, she yanked on his hand. These endless whims exhausted her and sometimes, moodily silent for the whole evening, not having looked at or paid any attention to him, she would, on parting, take his hands and speak longingly, flustering Stepan with her quiet voice, "Ah, divine one, we're so stupid. We're all stupid. You don't understand anything."

He really did refuse to understand anything at all, except the unfortunate fact that this delicate girl had cast a spell over him and tied him to her, occupying an indelible place in his life. Every evening, at seven, he set out from his home and stopped by a candy shop, where, after a week, he began to be greeted with a friendly smile. He, too, had grown so friendly with the shopkeeper that it would have felt uncomfortable not to buy a candy on any given day. Paying for his purchase, he would wistfully surmise, "Indeed, why wouldn't she go out with me? I take her to the cinema and buy her candy. I really am stupid. I really am divine, in fact—divinely dimwitted."

A couple of times he tried to raise his own stature in her eyes, dropping hints about his involvement with literature, although he did not yet dare to speak openly about this to her. But these hints were so opaque that there was probably no way for her to understand them. Besides, she was mostly interested in newspapers and was always showing off her familiarity with the latest political news.

"Did you read the British diplomatic note this morning? It's so long! And it begins so strangely: 'Dear Sir, the Government of His Majesty...' How wonderful! To write such funny diplomatic correspondence."

What did she really want, anyway? In vain, he sought an answer to this question, stealing glances at her face, adorned with blonde curls under her flattened hat. It was strangely animated, every twitch of her soul immediately visible on it. It brightened and faded from unknown clouds that floated in her eyes and, in these eternal changes of mood he sensed first hope, when his eyes caught her affectionate glance—and then despair, when she became dour and descended into ill-omened silence. He would attempt to chase away her unprovoked gloom, telling her stories about his youthful adventures as a soldier and rebel, but she would get excited by something for a moment and then fall immediately back into her gloom, mumbling, "Ah, all this is so boring. Wars are unnecessary. They were invented by people. Are you trying to tell me you were a hero? That's nonsense."

In moments like these, he, too, was overcome with gloom, and the two of them walked together along the

238   THE CITY

slippery streets, infinitely distant from each other but bound together by necessity, shuffling along in silence under the cloudy autumn sky. Once, in a fit of boredom, she threw her riding crop over a fence into someone's yard, saying, "I've grown weary of that—I hate it."

Ten minutes later, she began to pine for it, and Stepan, angered by her fickleness, had to go into that yard and crawl in the mud searching with lit matches for her crop, waking all the dogs and disturbing the residents. Of course, he didn't find it, and as he left the yard, he felt such hatred for his torturess that he might have struck her with his fists.

That night, he experienced a slave's revolt. Turning on the electric lights, he saw, for the first time in a month, the terrible mess in his apartment. His meager furniture was covered in dust, and on the unswept floor there were revolting clumps of trash. Damp, cold air from outdoors was entering through an unsealed window, and gusts of wind rattled the windowpane where the putty was loose and crumbling. In the corner, above the palm with its bent and yellowed leaves, a dark and moist spot was ominously widening. A heavy sadness overcame him, because this dilapidation was a visual reminder of the absurdity of his own life. The devastation in his heart had left its mark on his home as well. Sitting down at his table, where open books and pieces of paper were randomly scattered, he recalled with the sorrow of a convict the vibrant days when he had enjoyed complete serenity in his work and his mind had greedily devoured an enormous meal of ideas. Where were those mornings, full of fresh and irrepressible energy? Where were those quiet evenings, when he fell asleep softly and sweetly, cradled by a feeling of harmony in his soul? They were gone and the paths to them were grown over. But why? He opened a few of his notebooks and examined some notes from his reading like a bankrupt man looking over his former accounts. He felt an autumn within himself, a cold rain and fog.

And what did he now have instead? Nothing but pain and humiliation. What had he become, except a woman's lackey, a plaything in the hands of a crazy girl. If, at least, he had gotten something for it. If he had at least gotten that real treasure, for which it is worth sacrificing oneself for a woman! And how ridiculous were all these candies and visits together to the cinema. Nothing but bourgeois philistinism, the nonsense of the intellectual proletariat.

What's more, he had become poor. The honorarium for the story he had received from the Kharkiv journal had been frittered away a long time ago—the money had disappeared without even leaving a trace approximately commensurate with its origins. His excessive expenditures mercilessly devoured his earnings from the language lessons, leaving only kopecks for his lunch and nothing at all for his dinner. His clothes were looking worse and worse, his socks were worn through, his underwear lacked buttons, and he was a month behind in his rent. Yes, this girl, completely useless and inconsequential, had ruined him not only spiritually, but financially as well, which was just as regrettable. Enough was enough. That's it. He's not going out with her again. Period. It's over.

He knew all too well that the best medicine for any anxiety was work, the pinnacle of human achievement. He felt its happiness with his entire being. He was ready to abandon himself completely to productive effort, but the problem was that some external concern was often tearing him away from this healthful activity. Most concerning was that this distraction would happen entirely unnoticed, as if he were, to his own shame, being blinded by trivial matters that were not only unworthy of his attention but entirely unworthy of even a fleeting thought. But there is wisdom in the saying that it is life's experiences that teach a person the wisdom to govern a lifetime of choices. Furthermore, it's important truly to learn from the experiences of others, particularly of the great ones who serve as examples of the true path and whose names have been inscribed in the honor roll of progress. Of course, you can't adopt their example uncritically. Schopenhauer, for example, liked to have women kiss his hands when they met him on the path to pessimism; Buddha, it is said, died from extreme caution; the moralist Rousseau, who wrote about children's upbringing, had an exaggerated interest in that part of his body on which his educators inflicted punishment; the wise

Socrates expressed an unusual sympathy for his students, showing an unusually delicate sympathy particularly for those who were handsome and well built. Many other famous persons, the heroes of their own nations and of mankind, had various and peculiar faults unworthy of themselves or of their high philosophy, but when this dirt—entirely unrelated to their genius, of course—was brushed off their persons, the remaining image offered a perfect example for unqualified emulation.

No idea occurs suddenly; the most trivial thought has such a complex prehistory in the backstage of consciousness that it requires a very patient researcher to analyze accurately the process of its development. Every thought is like a culinary dish served to us by our consciousness after being fried, one which we consume without knowing the cooks who prepared it, or the miners who dug out the coal on which it was cooked, or the shepherds who cared for the meat-giving animals, or the sowers who tossed into the earth the living seeds of the plants. And only because we know nothing more than fragments, pleasant surprises are indeed possible. One such surprise was Stepan's intention to write a screenplay, which arose in his head one morning, as he awoke and opened his eyes.

With the enthusiasm that was his characteristic trait, he contemplated this new project for a while and, getting up, was ready to bring it to fruition. Clearing his table of the books that had languished there for more than a month, he set off for the library, where, having escaped the late fine with a very sincere declaration about his grave illness, he collected the books on cinema that he needed. Two days were sufficient to gain a sure command of all the principles of constructing a film script—not necessarily a very complicated task. His practical experience of the cinema offered all the appropriate illustrations, and he happily assured himself that nothing in the world passes without some utility—even an infatuation with a girl could produce a variety of by-products, just as the coking of coal results in naphthalene, phenol, benzene, ethanol, ammonia, and various kinds of paint.

Then he carefully constructed an outline for a dramatic film epic about the Civil War. It was in six acts with a prologue, and everything was handled appropriately: 1) social conflict; 2) a love story between the hero worker and a woman from the enemy side; 3) a beautiful woman from the proletarian camp who saves the hero from sudden death and wins over his tender feelings; 4) fire and smoke; 5) victory for the honorable ones—and, of course, a number of smaller matters that do not obscure the significance of the preceding ones. There were comic elements in the drama, too: for example, the character of the *kurkul*, that slouch of a rich farmer, who experienced one difficulty after another in the screenplay and whose failures made the author laugh. He worked on the screenplay for a week, putting all his talents into this simple scheme, giving it a tragic coloring and twisting up the story line to make it interesting. He read over his creation several times, marveling at the compactness of his own construction and, after making a final clean copy, sent it off to the All-Ukrainian Film Administration, VUFKU.

After this, he immediately freshened up his suit, polished his shoes, cleaned his galoshes, threw on his overcoat, and set off for Gimnazia Passage. When Zoska appeared before him, he passionately squeezed her hand and said, "Zoska, I love you so much!"

"Where have you been, divine one? I missed you," she answered, pulling back her hand.

"Work, Zoska—it's that damn work."

He had a brilliant plan. As he was finishing work on his screenplay, he came to the realization that the issue in their relationship was a matter of location. Indeed, as she herself said, she lived in a single room with her parents, and it would be sufficient for just one of them to be present to completely spoil that room. The second point was his conviction that no self-respecting girl would ever go to a boy's apartment on her own: that wasn't proper. The third point was the wet autumn weather. There was a fourth point and, fortunately, he remembered this one precisely from all those novels he had read. Damn it, the solution would be found in the European approach.

"Zoska, I'm hungry. Let's go for dinner," he said.

"I'm hungry, too," she admitted. "But we never go out for dinner."

He lowered his voice.

"Shall we dine in a private room?"

She clapped her hands in joy.

"How lovely, a private room!"

They turned into the first dive they found where one sign, among others, announced "Family Rooms," which, as Stepan immediately deduced, did not differ in any significant aspect from what he had in mind. They climbed down a narrow staircase into the basement. She was laughing at the adventure, curious and excited. He was self-conscious, anxious about the potential consequences, and secretly embarrassed by every step he was taking. When they reached the landing at the bottom, they could see through an open curtain the entrance to a general dining room where music was playing and, directly ahead, a dark door. When a figure appeared before them with a napkin over his arm and an expressionless, blank face, Stepan felt a wave of such embarrassment that, before he could put together his thoughts and words, Zoska spoke up, calmly and naturally, like someone who had often visited such premises, "A private room, if you please."

The figure silently bowed and led the pair through the dark door down a low corridor whose moisture and mold reminded Stepan of the near and far caves of the Lavra Monastery. He shuddered from the oppressively stale air, a strangely common feature of alcoves of worship and debauchery. Letting go of Zoska's hand, he kept to the center of the corridor and lowered his head to avoid accidentally touching the ceiling or the walls, which, he thought, were covered with layers of slime and mold. But the figure soon stopped and, turning a switch in an opening on the right, illuminated the space and welcomed them, "Here you are!"

Stepan now noticed four doors opening onto this corridor, as well as a small grated window, without glass, that likely faced the wall of the adjacent building, since it was as black as a missing eye and no air could be felt coming through it. The corridor curved in a horseshoe shape, which explained why the music made its way down here in a whisper, like a distant sound echoing into the deep cavern of an abandoned, humid mine shaft.

Zoska had already entered the chamber when Stepan warily crossed the threshold. The first thing he noticed were the walls, once covered with wallpaper that had now separated from the wall and hung in clumps with patches where it was completely torn off, revealing the gray plaster underneath. The design on the wallpaper had long since disappeared beneath the dust and grime, untouched and now uncleanable, which itself had formed strange splotchy patterns, darkening in the corners from the moisture and cobwebs. There were no windows. On the right, by the wall, stood a wide canvas sofa, mildewed and faded, sagging and lumpy, all wrinkled and uneven, covered in the muck of human sweat and secretions as markers of its prolonged and diligent use. Above this principal object in the room, the focal point of the desires of the souls who came here, hung an oil painting depicting a group of transported convicts feeding pigeons through the grates of their railcar. A second painting, in a similarly cracked gilded frame, which hung across from the door and above the table, cheered the eye with a depiction of a girl with a kitten on a veranda adorned with roses. Everything here stank of cigarette butts, stale vomit, spilled wine, and sweat. The odors had nowhere to escape and hung in the air of the chamber and the corridor, penetrating the stone and brick of the walls, settling in smudges of dust-covered moisture.

Stepan sat down at the table without removing his coat. Revulsion was brewing within him, and the beautiful plan to solve the problem of location no longer appealed to him. Zoska, on the other hand, was enchanted. To her, everything seemed unusual and magical. She examined the paintings, tried the sofa with her foot to see if it was soft, peered out into the corridor, extinguished and turned on the light, and came to a conclusion: "It's very pleasant here."

"What's the matter with you, Zoska?" Stepan uttered in surprise.

"I would love to live here forever."

The figure appeared again with the menu. Dinner was ordered and the guests took off their coats. From the corridor there suddenly came the sound of the eager footsteps of several pairs of legs, and the adjacent chamber filled with the cries and laughter of a rowdy company of bass and soprano voices. Zoska threw her cigarette to the floor.

"They're having fun," she said.

"We'll have fun, too," answered Stepan.

Indeed, the first glass of wine immediately improved his spirits. An unfamiliar tipsiness sweetly clouded the mind, he felt a warmth in his chest and a lethargy in his shoulders. What was there to be ashamed of? He had, after all, written a collection of very fine stories and a screenplay in six acts with a prologue.

"Zoska," he asked, "who am I?"

"A bum," she answered.

He laughed loudly and turned to the breaded cutlet, which was in no way inferior to a fried shoe sole.

Now, his eyes explored the room with the gaze of a merciful judge who understands human weaknesses and knows how to forgive them. The fact that he was sitting here, drinking wine and chewing a cutlet, made him feel happy, and in this he saw great progress, which excited him.

Suddenly, above the yells and guffaws from the adjoining room, they heard the raspy sounds of an old piano.

"A waltz," cried the girl. "Do you dance?"

"No," he answered, pouring wine for the girl and for himself.

"You must learn."

He sat down beside her with a glass in his hands.

"Zoska, let's drink to our love."

She laughed giddily.

"To love, divine one."

A moment later, they were seated on that sofa and he was embracing her and whispering, "Zoska, be mine! My love, my sweetheart, be mine."

"What do you mean—yours?" she asked.

He was momentarily nonplussed, then murmured, "I'll show you."

"Show me," she agreed.

Befuddled by her consent, by the wine, and by the howl of the cracked piano behind the wall, choking on the prospect of the coming fulfillment of what had gnawed at him and angered him, he resolutely took her in his arms. But the girl instantly squirmed out of his grasp and curled up in a corner of the sofa.

"It's filthy here!" she cried.

The cry brought him up short and he bent over in an uncomfortable pose, leaning with his arms on the canvas cushion. Wilting in shame and weakness, he slid to the floor on his knees and his head fell at her feet.

"Forgive me, Zoska—forgive me," he rambled, lacking the courage to raise his head.

She wrapped her thin arms around his neck and, leaning over, silently kissed him on the lips.

"More, more," he whispered, swooning, blinded by the meeting of their lips, by the touch of her curls on his face, and from the joyful loss of sensation that swept over him with every kiss.

Later, they sat down side by side, cuddling and holding hands.

"You're nice," said Zoska.

"You're outstanding," he said.

In an outburst of unstoppable love, he covered her neck, her hands, her fingers with passionate kisses. He gazed meekly into her eyes, he gratefully put his head on her breast, and he stroked her curly hair, animated by his newfound happiness.

"I look just like that girl," said Zoska, pointing to the painting. "I'd love to have a kitten and a porch covered with roses."

And they laughed like children on a sunny day.

Since Stepan was not yet so cultured as to summon the waiter by tapping a knife against a glass, he stepped out into the corridor to call him. While there, he glanced into the open door of the adjacent chamber, where there was so much laughing and music.

He was surprised to see a familiar male face there, smiling senselessly and drunk. He taxed his memory and recalled what he would rather have forgotten for all time: the kitchen, a shameful conversation, a fight, and then his flight from the house. It was Maksym, son of Tamara Vasylivna Hnidyi. The son of his former lover,

Musinka. He had grown a moustache, which made it difficult to recognize him right away. On his knees, he was rocking a very fat woman whose skirt was pulled up, while he himself was barely visible behind her wide shoulders. Stepan instinctively drew back and pressed himself against the wall to avoid being seen. He was overcome by a terrible disgust over this event from the past, which he had forgotten but which hung over him, nevertheless—it was his, it would be with him forever. At that moment it seemed to him that the heartless past, all his sins and errors, the slings and arrows of bygone times, would remain in his soul forever, like a worm that gnaws at the roots of all other longings. He now felt the overbearing, eternal immutability and irremediality of his past actions, even thoughts and desires that lay the foundations of the future, hiding within themselves potential earthquakes.

In the narrow passage before him, other men and women were circling about, and one of them, stumbling along, closed the door.

Having paid the bill, Stepan grabbed Zoska by the hand and whispered in terror, "Let's get out of here!"

She pressed against him and said wistfully, "But I really like it here."

Nevertheless, he quickly led her out onto the street, where the autumn gloom was deepened by a sharp wind and cold drops of mist.

Chapter Four

The money problem was growing ever more serious. From his cap to his galoshes, he was facing bankruptcy in his entire wardrobe, which, having served him for half a year, was showing signs of a catastrophic, although quite natural, decline that could no longer be disguised with meticulous cleaning. The ritual of getting dressed, once so pleasant for him, now became a source of suffering, since morning, more than any other time of the day, clearly revealed the ruinous state of his underwear, the complete disintegration of his shoes, and the ugly shine of the elbows of his jacket, a sure sign of an imminent tear.

The first months of Kyiv's sloppy winter had begun, and it was very uncomfortable to leave the room unheated, even though he had sealed the window very carefully and precisely, not passing over even the smallest of gaps. The cold air, it seemed, came directly through the walls, and Stepan woke up early most mornings shivering, even though he had put everything he had on top of his well-used military blanket, even his pillow, which he put over his feet, resting his head on a couple of statistics textbooks that he covered with leafy twigs. The poverty of his dwelling and possessions wore him down and sapped his energy. On those evenings, when he wasn't going to the cinema with Zoska, he would lie down on his bed in an attempt to preserve some warmth and comfort himself with the hope that he would come up with an idea for a story. In fact, however, he just lay there, tired and miserable, often nodding off in his clothes, only to awake suddenly at night with a gnawing at his heart.

One morning, having downed a cup of hot tea and half a pound of coarse wheat bread at the communal cafeteria, he sat down at his table, found a pencil among the papers, sharpened it, and began to consider the various ways he might improve his financial status—which is to say, his physical and moral condition—since, quite understandably, he blamed his psychic ennui, at least in part, on the decline of his cash resources. The first step was to assess his needs, the expense side of his budget ledger. First there was Zoska. Considering all the circumstances, he determined that allocating less than ten karbovanets per week for her was simply impossible. Repressing his feelings and secretly regretting that he had started off with the cinema—undeniably an expensive place to take her and, by its very nature, not significantly better than other places—he neverthe-less acknowledged to himself that changing the routine would be shameful, as would be any interruption in the candies he still bought her. He was powerless in this regard, conceding with disappointment that, after the incident with the private room and the sudden burst of intimacy, he was bound to this girl ever more firmly. Abandoning her now was far more complicated than it would have been back when their relationship did not go beyond simple acquaintance.

He himself understood that a new feeling had emerged within him, something deeper and more poi-sonous than desire, something with an aftertaste of obli-gation and significance. On the other hand, his stubborn pride would not allow him to abandon an unfinished enterprise, and a costly one at that, not only in terms of financial losses, which had their own value, of course, but in psychic losses as well—the devastation in the soul, which would have surely frightened him if he had felt any weaker and had a better understanding of the value of human energy, whose wasteful expenditure is one of the unique privileges of the young. In any case, he had invested too much capital into this enterprise to renounce the legitimate earnings. Sometimes sul-len, sometimes happy, he went on making his visits to Gimnazia Passage, which had become the focal point of his life, his thoughts, and his displeasure. In the kiss-es he had begun to receive he could sometimes sense the strange warmth of the first one that had blossomed in the filth of the tavern, the secret meeting of lips that expands the limits of a being in the highest and most profound self-realization, and with its powerful magic pushes that being to search for further intoxication in creativity, in work, in learning, and in struggle.

Often, he told himself that he loved her very powerfully, as he had never loved before, and he took joy in uncovering this strong feeling within himself. At other times, he was annoyed that this feeling was turning him away from the single goal whose distant echo filled his dreams. What surprised him most was that the desire to make Zoska his had somehow faded, and he saw a certain danger in this. But, for the most part, he took a tolerant view of the girl's presence in his heart, somehow convinced that it was perfectly natural and inescapable for a young man to be in love.

So, considering that his usual income from the lessons was eighteen karbovanets a week, that left eight karbovanets to cover food and rent. It was senseless to think that any part of that could be spared for firewood or clothing. Calculating what it would take to fix up his external appearance, he arrived at a figure of 85 karbovanets at a minimum, which is to say that he drew up a budget with a deficit of at least 100 karbovanets.

Thus, he decided to visit the offices of the Kyiv journal that had printed his stories, since, he figured, they owed him a royalty payment. Why hadn't he gone before—only out of embarrassment. He was ashamed to appear anywhere where people would recognize him as an author, let alone where they might see him collecting money. The inspiration that he had put into his stories was entirely incompatible and unrelated to anything connected with money. It was one thing to get money in the mail—that felt like a present—but it was entirely different to get it in person as a payment for work. However, his actual needs—as is their wont—proved stronger than his benevolent meditations: they helped throw his cap on his head and his coat on his shoulders, pushing him out the door to the editorial offices located in a wing of the State Publishing House of Ukraine.

What a surprise! The editorial office of the journal was located in the same office that he had run through in his field jacket and boots, chasing his fortune just after his arrival in the city. He recognized it immediately—the same bookcase, the same black typewriter, the wooden couch, and, on it, a couple of young fellows whom he charitably took to be his potential colleagues. They were smoking, chatting, and laughing, not very loud so as to avoid disturbing the work of this institution. He felt ashamed of his earlier self, for his incredible naiveté and self-effacement, and a thousand small recollections, like an album of old photographs, entered his consciousness and fostered a feeling of embarrassed but nevertheless sweet-tasting pride.

He approached the desk and spoke softly, with humility. He was asked to sit down. Yes, he is owed a payment: 70 karbovanets and change. But why hadn't he shown up for so long? Stepan blurted out the first lie he could think of—he'd been sick. And what disease did he have? And so he had to answer this and answer that and answer something else—and what was he doing now? how was he managing? when had he started writing? He spoke very vaguely, lying at every step and blushing at every word.

"And I hope you've brought us a few more stories," continued the secretary with a friendly smile.

"No, I don't have any, I haven't finished yet," answered Stepan. He had not anticipated such an inquisition and was enduring it as if it were a form of torture. But he couldn't very well just push the money into his pocket and take off. That wouldn't be polite.

Then the secretary introduced him to the young fellows on the sofa. It turned out they were, indeed, all writers, except for one, who was only a courier but whose appearance did not distinguish him from them in any way. Stepan even knew some of them from their writing—these frightened him the most. But from the interest his name elicited among them, Stepan realized his stories had not passed by unnoticed. In the mockingly friendly looks he received from his new acquaintants, he observed something like the glint of envy, or a challenge to a duel, which, in the literary arena, is far more brutal than French wrestling or English boxing.

Here, he was subjected to a new round of questions. Would he be submitting a volume of collected stories? No, are you kidding, that's not in the works! So, what was he writing? Stories... Stories about what? He couldn't answer this right away, since he wasn't writing anything and wasn't even thinking about writing. But he couldn't admit to being completely idle—that would be shameful. Especially since someone threw in a sarcastic comment: "Don't worry, we won't steal your ideas!"

Then Stepan announced, "I'm writing a story about... people."

Everyone laughed but he was satisfied with his answer, which didn't commit him to anything in particular.

The secretary asked Stepan to come again and to submit more stories. Since he did not strike the others as a particularly strong personality, everyone liked him. A little rough around the edges, but on the whole a decent fellow. Maybe he'll even turn into something someday, since his stories, though certainly in need of a little more polish, with many technical errors, some even quite glaring, and also quite mannered—still raw, drawn out, unfocused, confused, completely terrible in some places, weak in imagery, poor in imagination, and uncertain in their lyric tonality—were nevertheless quite original and fresh, offering promise of something better in the future.

That's how the other writers evaluated his work. Then an argument emerged over the question of whose influence he was writing under and whom he was imitating, since otherwise he would have been original and that was simply unacceptable. Among Ukrainians, Kotsiubynskyi and his "Vin ide" (He's coming) was mentioned, as well as Franko and his *Boa Constrictor*. Then came the tests on familiarity with foreign literatures, and soon there was a whole bouquet of names of various scents. Someone even made a pitch for Selma Lagerlöf, whose stories he had read just yesterday.

No doubt Stepan would have been pleased to hear how many previous authors he was judged to be following—and certainly would have been frightened by the number he was deemed to be imitating—if he had not already left the building, carrying in his pocket the money that he regarded as the profit of a brazen fraud. How exactly had he earned this money? Could he really imagine that he might become a writer, like those fellows sitting on the sofa? Could he ever achieve such a level of careless ease, naturalness, self-confidence, and eloquence? No, that was plainly impossible. No, he was not a suitable candidate to become an author.

"I simply will not write," he thought, but, secretly, he felt that this renunciation was merely an attempt to appear even grander in his own eyes, since he would, after all, continue writing, writing well, much better than all these coxcombs.

The payment was immediately converted into a broadcloth suit, though not of the highest quality, into which Stepan changed before delivering his next lesson.

On his way home after dinner, he bought one hundred eighty pounds of firewood. While a grimy worker in ragged clothes hauled the wood on a dolly to his apartment, Stepan decided he would spend this evening in a fully heated home mending his wardrobe. This perfectly suited the mood of quiet contemplation that had washed over him after his visit to the journal's editorial office.

Gathering the articles of his wardrobe that needed attention, preparing a needle, thread, and some buttons, ripping his most tattered shirt into strips for patches, he laid out all these materials in front of the stove and set about lighting the fire. Anticipating the warmth that every particle of his skin longed for, he gazed with excitement as the flames spread, their tongues embraced, and the smoke swirled. Evening was falling, predictably moist and fluffy with clouds, gray, blustery. He didn't light the lamp, and, in the room's twilight, the erupting flames made his shadow lengthen and narrow like the bone of a giant hand.

Spreading a blanket on the floor, he sat down and began to sew. But the languor from the warmth inflaming his face and chest soon poured into his fingers, and the needle fell to the floor. He didn't trouble himself to pick it up but stretched out face down in deep fatigue with his elbows on the floor and put his head in his hands. The fire was now directly before him, vibrant, unsettled, magical. It danced before his eyes with that flaming, sinuous beauty that still conveys the power of the first and unsurpassed god. Fire! He knew it well, because it had marked entire eras of his life. Was it not these flames that had warmed him while grazing the herd on the fields as a child, when the nighttime shadows were dense with ghosts and goblins? Was it not into a fire that he directed his eyes as a young rebel resting after bloody events at the forest's edge, where the tree trunks seemed to be a party of enemy scouts? And now, in new battles, he was observing this flowing warmth on an autumn night in this city, still unknown, unconquered, where perhaps lay hidden even greater dangers than those of a child's imagination or an armed enemy. But, in answer to them, an internal fire burned within him, an indomitable life force that could not be extinguished until the last breath was drawn, the magic lantern of human aspiration that fills the screen with dramatic heights and leaves the swampy lowlands in the shadows, its prophetic voice appealing for ever more and more quests to find the golden, albeit ovine, fleece.

At that moment, caressed by his memories and the warmth of the fire, he felt the profound unity of his life experiences, happily recognizing himself in childhood, youth, adolescence, and as a young man. This recognition awakened in his soul a numb and forgotten organ, an abandoned space where life had already gathered its harvest, and this organ, this space, was spreading far beyond its bounds, further than memory could reach, reaching with its blind fingers into the infinite space of eternity. These reaching fingers set off a trembling in him—he saw before him all the more clearly another eternity, the sister of the one from which he had emerged: the one he, eventually, must enter. In this magical state of excitement and longing, refusing to think or know, forgetting yesterday and tomorrow, he drifted off into a boundless dreamscape, where nothing was accomplished or even possible, where images dissolved in the fading glow of the dying embers.

Abandoning the sewing by the stove, he wearily fell into his bed, full of sorrow and thirst.

The next day, Stepan decided to visit the Bureau of Instructors to see if he could get another group in some institution, since the money he had gotten for his stories was simply not sufficient for the plan he had developed. After all, he still had some leisure time in his schedule, which could best be devoted to the cause of coupling the city and the village both on the national and the personal levels. Oh, this coupling! He often thought about it, considering the difficulties of its attainment, even for himself. He saw the city as a powerful center of gravity, around which orbited villages, like tiny planets, its eternal satellites. The pieces of these satellites that fell into the fiery atmosphere of this sun must adapt to the new conditions of pressure and climate. He experienced this painful process almost subconsciously, absorbed by a blind desire to rise higher and excited like a person who has breathed in oxygen, like a drunk who stops noticing dirt and the lesions on his skin. For the speed and noise of a city affect a person far more than the gentleness of scenic views in the bosom of nature and an uncontrolled interplay of natural forces—forces summoned here to build a new nature, artificial and, therefore, more refined.

Stepan was confident he would be given another group, since he had acquired a reputation as a very good instructor, following the exemplary results of an official state evaluation of his teaching. Indeed, the administrator of the Bureau of Instructors greeted him very graciously and expressed his deep satisfaction at his elegant attire.

"You understand," he said, "that until Ukrainians learn how to dress properly, they will never constitute a true nation. And that requires good taste."

"And money," added Stepan.

"A person with good taste never lacks money," noted the administrator.

As for assignments, the only available openings were evening classes for upper-level employees of the Leatherworkers' Collective. Although upper-level employees, of course, have linguistic preferences that are as firm as their salaries, Stepan didn't hesitate and accepted the task of teaching them.

On the appointed day, fully armed with knowledge and experience, Stepan Radchenko appeared in the grand waiting room of the Leatherworkers' Collective, which had been converted into a classroom.

He organized his introductory lecture on a broad outline, beginning with a discussion of language in general, the factors that led to its appearance and development, the basic division of languages into agglutinative, analytic, and inflectional, the fate of Indo-European languages, particularly proto-Slavic, its varieties, and the foundations for these distinctions. He confidently and clearly led his listeners along, like Virgil leading Dante down through the concentric circles of Hell, each narrower than the previous, ever pointing toward the very center, where sat Beelzebub himself—the Ukrainian language.

Happily observing that he had caught the attention of his listeners and sensing, during his pauses, their expectant anticipation of the next phrase—that anxious silence which is better than applause as a stimulus to eloquence—he turned his eyes to the auditorium, hoping to uncover in the faces of those present the future course of his efforts with this group. Suddenly, in the corner, he encountered a pair of eyes that were following him with scorn and derision, eyes whose gaze he found unpleasant, almost frightening. How could he have forgotten that Maksym was an accountant at the Leatherworkers' Collective! Surely, he would have turned down this assignment! And why did he have to run into him? This was a happenstance, of course, but a mysterious, unfortunate happenstance, like an intentional attack, since his cheeks had suddenly turned red, as if they were again revealing a concealed but unexpunged insult.

While continuing his lecture, Stepan rehearsed the unpleasant memories which he could not repudiate. However repugnant they might be, they were still snippets of his life, deeply painful and, especially, deeply his own. Why is it impossible to clean up one's past? Perhaps because the future, too, can't be fixed. This pessimistic thought kept weighing on him, while he energetically continued the lesson, but the moment he finished he felt fatigued from the lengthy strain on his voice and the secret tribulation. For a while longer, he had to answer inquiries about textbooks, readers, notebooks, assignments, and all the doubly childish questions that came from these adults who had again become schoolchildren, so that, when he finally left, he was sorry that he would have to return. Oh, that Zoska! If it weren't for her, he wouldn't need so much money and thus would not have had to encounter the fellow who had slapped him. Indeed, that girl was just ruining his nerves! Walking along the deserted streets in the autumnal hush of the city, broken by the dull clatter of streetcars, he thought alternately about love and about insults to his honor, and, although he considered both of these to be superstitions, he had to admit, nonetheless, that they were both exceptionally compelling.

While he was thus preoccupied, someone caught up with him and took him by the arm. In the feeble light of the streetlamps he recognized Maksym.

"Excuse me, honored teacher," he said, with an exaggerated bow, "I wanted to express my gratitude for your instruction."

"I haven't taught you anything yet," answered Stepan.

Maksym laughed.

"Precisely. I learned on my own, thanks to you."

They walked on for a while in silence, and suddenly Stepan detected the unmistakable scent of alcohol from his companion.

"Are you drunk?" he asked.

"Are you sober?"

"Absolutely!"

"What a shame! As the Kyivan Chronicle tells us, 'The Rus´ are happy in their cups!'"

And, without further introduction, he slapped Stepan on the back and told him, with the sincerity of a street urchin, how he drank a great deal and often, that drinking was fun, that ladies prefer drunkards, expecting a higher payment—but, of course, they're wrong about that.

"And you say you haven't yet taught me anything!"

He said these words while pretending to be offended, but Stepan found such jokes distasteful.

"I am not the cause of that," he said gruffly.

"No? You don't say! I had a stamp collection. I gave presents to my mother."

Maksym laughed and added with conviction, "Don't believe the Josephs who run away from women, sit behind their books, and love their mothers, but... but their right hands are not clean."

When he said this, a terrible revulsion to his presence overcame Stepan. This was the same feeling of visceral aversion that he had felt back when he saw him in the adjacent room of the tavern, but now enlarged and sharpened by the twilight, which compounded the strength of the reaction. Forgetting about the man beside him, Stepan thought about himself. Who needed this meeting? Sure, it was a natural event now, an accidental encounter following a previous acquaintance, but can't the past be forgotten? Is every misfortune in life recorded in an indelible stain, a permanent brand, which can again and again renew the same pain that accompanied its flaming origin? Everything can be forgotten, he assured himself. But this forgetting was fickle, only surface deep, because even now, with his thoughts turning gloomy, he was experiencing a flood of memories about the harm he had caused others through his life. There were enough of these incidents, but they were always somehow unintentional, and he could not in any case accept any guilt for them. Why were they so unpleasant?

"Are you listening?" asked Maksym.

"I'm listening," replied Stepan.

And the accountant resumed his story or, more precisely, his rambling, which seemed completely otherworldly to Stepan, since he had missed its beginning. Maksym was eagerly describing the comforts of his lifestyle, the frequent parties with girls whose attractions he was painting with drunken colorfulness. Abruptly, he cut short his recitation as if he suddenly remembered something and, changing his voice from that of a scoundrel to that of a secretive friend, he whispered to Stepan, "Let's go to the Lotto Hall. A wonderful experience, you'll see."

"I'm on my way home," said Stepan.

"Don't worry, you'll get there. It won't run away. Come on, do this for me."

And he sharply pulled Stepan aside beneath an archway, where flashing letters blinked on and off one after another in a half circle, spelling out "Electronic LOTTO." At the door of this establishment of urban amusements, Stepan was overcome with a dire premonition of the kind that arises suddenly and without cause, the weight of fear obstructing any efforts to clear the mind and think. After all, he really didn't need to go in there with Maksym. Indeed, he needn't go anywhere with him, but an insatiable curiosity overcame his revulsion and led him on.

Passing through a quiet corridor and past a silver-haired footman, they entered a large hall, flooded with light, where preoccupied men and women sat hunched over rows of tables, while ushers moved through the narrow alleys between the rows of seats, silently exchanging cards for the next round. Above this silence of intense expectation, like an oracle making sacred proclamations, like a chief justice delivering a verdict before a crowd of supplicants, maintaining regular pauses, emphasizing with metallic clarity the monotonously similar words, which raised a quiet whisper of hope and disappointment, the barker sharply and without any emotion called out:

"Forty-one. Twenty. Thirty-four."

And, with every pronouncement, the appropriate number lit up on a giant board along the back wall, weaving a chaotic pattern of illuminated dots.

Maksym stopped at the threshold beside a table where money was exchanged for chips, and Stepan looked at him questioningly, certain that the accountant wanted to try his luck, perhaps even at Stepan's expense. But Maksym whispered, "Over there, in the corner, on the right."

Stepan raised his eyes in the direction and saw by the table a swollen and drowsy woman, in a familiar blue dress that could barely hold back her bulging flesh. With lowered head, she was intently looking at her cards so he could not see her face, but from her posture and the hopeless and insensible concentration, he understood that this table had become her only friend and family, that she had brought into this hall all the remnants of her desire.

"Is that her? It is!" he thought, sickened by the wreckage before him.

Suddenly, after another number was called, the bloated shadow that had once been Musinka jumped up and in a muffled voice, as if holding a fowl between her teeth, called out, "I've got it! I win."

"Twelve. A winner," the barker announced without emotion.

And everywhere there was a buzz and commotion, as if the characters, frozen in a fable, had been awakened from their enchanted sleep by a magic word. The winning card was being verified.

"She always wins," Maksym blurted out angrily.

Her thick and greedy voice, so different from the tender words spoken in the past, animated Stepan's soul, as it had the audience in the hall. But there, too, tranquility quickly returned, emotion subsided, as if all his recollections were again flooded by a magical dream. He felt himself free, distant, and superior. He turned and left the hall. Maksym didn't catch up until they reached the entrance.

"I expect that you will allow me not to attend your lessons," he said when they were out on the street.

His sober and sharp voice echoed with the hatred from the past.

"As you wish," answered Stepan.

They bowed studiously to each other. Maksym left first, disappearing into the twilight just as he had appeared. For Stepan, everything that had just happened immediately took on the quality of an illusion, a painful trick of the imagination. Forcing himself to understand what he had seen as reality and to give it careful consideration, he was frustrated by his inability to do so and angrily jumped on a streetcar, where he gloomily stared at the dark slabs of buildings which seemed to sail past the windows very close to the tram.

At home, he realized he hadn't had supper, but he did not want to go out again. Knowing that he wouldn't find anything edible, he lazily searched his drawers, then lit a cigarette and began thumbing through his notebooks. One page unexpectedly caught his attention. He opened it fully and read:

"Today, I decided to start a diary. There are moments that need to be recorded. My stories have been published! I feel like yelling: 'Published!' And I see an open road ahead of me. I walk—no, I fly, I glide! I'm free, I'm warm, I'm happy. I kiss this day."

He discarded his cigarette and was about to tear out the page, but then he took a pencil and scrawled one word in big black letters across the lines on the page: "Imbecile."

Chapter Five

S tepan Radchenko was growing ever more concerned about the fate of his stories. Enough time
had passed for him to have received a positive response, but he had not heard anything at all from the editorial office. In his eyes, the stereotypical notice on the
inside cover of every journal that the editors do not conduct correspondence concerning rejected manuscripts
now acquired a disheartening significance. In these
words he heard the funereal dirge of his pretentious
hopes, which had suddenly seized him and cast him into
a dark torrent, a strong current that crushed him and
threatened to wash him up onto a deserted shore. Slowly,
first as a bitter taste in his consciousness but then relent-
lessly gaining clarity every day, doubt crept into his heart.

Still unaware of the true cause of his despair, he already felt the bitter disappointment, the sour mood that
pushes aside the true cause and grabs hold of anything

at hand and highlights the trivial, thus justifying its own presence. He fell into a state of helplessness, and the secret forces of the soul, the true guardian angels of man, divinely blind and naive, quietly used any means to divert his attention away from the actual danger to substitute for it some other danger, be it even a multiple one, so long as it was less important, thus protecting him from a possible catastrophe. The instinct for self-preservation, so crude and brutal on the outside, ceaselessly conducted its devious work within, insistently demonstrating that he was troubled only by the minor discomforts of his unsettled situation, which was temporary and would soon pass.

He got the notion that the food in the People's Food Service cafeteria wasn't nutritious enough for him, so he switched over to a private dining hall. It seemed he didn't spend enough time outdoors, so he started taking walks between one and two in the afternoon, regardless of fog or precipitation. Having caught a cold with mild bronchitis, he became terribly alarmed about his health and carefully examined the mucus on his wet handkerchief, searching for signs of tubercular blood. Although he never found a single drop, he nevertheless felt a deep anxiety about his physical state, which he felt had been compromised. Feeling his biceps, he noticed a diminution in their former tone, accompanied by weakness and lethargy. And, indeed, in the course of this painstaking research guided by a fervent desire to find signs of physical decay, his body softened and wilted, dutifully offering the desired evidence of a loss of energy. Then he was overtaken by sadness and an unspecified dissatisfaction.

He made a direct association between this state of exhaustion and his diminished emotional desire for Zoska. And, indeed, the moments of sensual dreaming in the morning, when the entire body fills with a wild desire and yearns for all the women in the world, when arms stretch out to embrace them, when lips radiate a welcoming smile out to them and ears seem to hear from them a heartfelt response, these moments of a morning's rebirth of energy, when the entire world rises in a passionate web of lovemaking—these moments of soundless communication between the sexes no longer visited him, no longer coursed through his veins in currents of excited blood. That's what he had come to! The horror! The shame! And if the list of possible diseases only frightened him, then the weakening of those bodily functions that he considered important stripped him of his self-respect and left a deep gash in his honor.

And so one day, while constructing the outline of his next lesson, he began to leaf through *Fata Morgana*, selecting a passage he would work through with his students. Scanning the pages with pedagogical indifference, he unconsciously began to take interest and started examining various lines with greater attention. The mournful harmony of the images intrigued him.

The words, illuminated by apprehension, uncovered for him the boundless panorama of the secret of their interconnections. Suddenly, like a swarm of active lightning bugs, they began to move on the page, leftwards toward the white margins, where they went out. He sat, mesmerized by the phosphorescent pages, whose sharp rays burned a painful mark on his downturned chest.

He had never read with such passion or experienced such deep immersion in his reading. In this book, not new to him, he found a new, intoxicating enchantment with the majesty of creativity, the power of its chisel, and the thickness of the paint distilled from its impulse. His eyelids trembled and his fingers fidgeted on the table. After finishing, he felt tired, the weariness of the thirsty who drink only to find their thirst grow, and the massive construction of the work, built in front of his eyes brick by brick, now toppled onto him. Bowing his head into his hands, he listened to the echo of the lines growing softer, dying out like the sound of a distant song. And, from there, from that distant place, from the emptiness formed by the silence, a deathly chill blew into his soul.

"I could never, ever write anything like that," he whispered.

Now, he recognized the absurdity of his ambitions. A writer indeed! Who was the sly one who had suggested this word to him? Where did he acquire that insane confidence that had tempted him for so long? Now he couldn't see any reason for confidence. Anyone can dream big, but only an idiot chases those dreams. A cossack riding a broomstick rather than a horse! A dope, a hopeless dope! And to trade an education and the Institute for this illusion, to cast aside years of hard work, carefully formulated plans, and obligations? Obligations to whom? To himself, at the very least!

Failing to understand how all of this could have happened, he anxiously reviewed all the missteps in his descent. Vyhorskyi—there's the one who had led him astray, that's who sent his stories to the journals. And who asked him, after all? Damned seducer! A flim-flam man! And along with this anger, there arose in him a warm gratitude to the severe critic who had chased him from his home without even hearing him out.

But, on the other hand, his stories had proven no worse than the stories of other writers. Some had already been published, though that didn't mean much. Anyone could write something good by accident, somehow once and not again. There was no shortage of such accidental names on magazine pages, appearing just once and never again. And maybe he would be one of those writers, maybe even a prolific one, whose works are forgotten right after they are read, whose works disappear without a trace, forming the immovable foundation on which true masters develop and grow. To become one of them you need to believe, to feel your creative strength, just as you do your physical strength. They don't fall into despair! But he was not going to serve as background for someone else's shining glory, no way! He recoiled from the thought that he might be the ladder on which others climbed to success.

Then he felt tired and pitied himself. Poor fellow! Why was he beating himself up? So he had made a mistake! OK—enthusiasm had gotten the better of him, but he was still young. That's so natural. And now it's over. What should he do now? Stepan got up and enlivened his benumbed hands. How long had he been sitting? An hour? Two? Slowly, he put on his coat and went out on the street.

November. Autumn was entering the period of age-related shortening, its days were numbered, its tears already shed in the face of the inevitable end. It became quiet and cold, tense but calm in the face of a snowy end, and the city's stony echoes seemed muffled in the emptiness of extermination. Feeling relief in the fresh air, happy to escape his room, where the walls smelled of his poisonous thoughts, Stepan pulled his hat down on his forehead and found himself walking to the Sinnyi Bazaar. He passed by it and walked out on to Velyka Pidvalna Street, stopping by the gates of Golden Gate Square, where the silent fountain towered over a pool of green rainwater. The walkways, covered with yellowed chestnut leaves, were lined with rows of lonely benches. No one was about. He yearned to go in and walk along the paths, to rustle the leaves with his footsteps. Over there, in the corner, he had once torn up his short story, but his memory of that was now tender and precious.

He trudged on in peaceful melancholy, desiring to go to sleep. But as he approached the Volodymyr Cathedral, a strange unrest awoke in him. The Institute was just down the street—should he stop in? What for? A moment later, this sudden urge had turned into an unquenchable need. With passionate curiosity, as if he were about to peek at something forbidden, he approached the wide doors of the Institute. The doors were on strong springs and hard to open, and the effort he made to open them reminded him of the countless times each day he had done so in the past.

In contrast to the outdoors, the long corridors seemed dark and stale, with a gray mass of people and the hum of their voices coursing back and forth and up and down the stairs, like living blood coursing through the veins of the building. Stepan felt the peace and chill of alienation. He pulled his hat down even further to avoid recognition and walked up to the glass doors of the auditorium. A class was in session. He looked around the benches, densely packed with students, and at the lecturer, whom he knew well. He observed familiar gestures of attention, indifference, incomprehension. But there was no anxiety or torment, and the regret that had troubled him just a moment earlier withered from the sense of estrangement he now felt from this setting he had once found so appealing. Surprised, he stepped back and looked around with the eye of a wanderer who has returned after a long trip to find that nothing of what he had left remained there, everything had changed and was so different from what he remembered that this deformed reality was not even worthy of regret. Having come in contact with what had been abandoned, he understood that there was no way back to it, that he was forevermore estranged from these walls and that these sounds would never call out to him, never reawaken his interest.

He walked out with the same dreary anxiety that he had felt when he first set foot in the city. The square seemed narrower, the buildings heavier and more severe, the low autumn sky an endless bowed stretch of cobblestones. Suddenly, he realized that beyond the first row of buildings were countless others on the hills and in the valleys, countless glum settlements scattered in a giant ring, with each one hiding a surprise and a threat. He discerned the tangled web of streets where you can wander for hours and days through the same crisscrossed paths, wander until you fall in exhaustion and with tears in your eyes on the naked stones that define the horizon with their jagged teeth. He felt those invisible walls that had arisen for him at the edge of the steppe, and he bowed his defeated gaze, begging for peace. He was tired.

In the evening, when Zoska came out to him, he grabbed her by the hand and began to silently kiss her. She was astounded.

"What's the matter with you, divine one?"

"Zoska," he said. "You're my one and only, there's no one else."

She sighed.

"You're such a liar!"

"There's no one else," he continued. "No family, no friends. I'm alone in the whole world. And today I feel as if this were my first day here. It's so difficult."

"It's difficult for him," she mused gently.

"Don't laugh," he replied worriedly. "You don't know what I'm thinking or how I'm suffering."

"He's suffering!"

Stepan stopped and whispered in despair, "I can't go on like this anymore! What's the point? Is this love? I'm sick of the cinema. The films make me sick. I want to be with you. The two of us, alone. Don't worry, I won't do anything to you," he added bitterly. "I don't need that. I love you anyway. You don't understand me, you don't know me at all. This is silly, this way we are. It would be better for me if we were together, just for an hour, just you and me. I want to sit down beside you and tell you everything."

"And what's that to me?" she cried out.

"Don't say that—that's not how you think," he pleaded. "I can't joke around right now. This is serious. Do you understand? Serious! Zoska, think of something, because I can't think at all. Think quickly."

Zoska thought for a moment and then cried, "I've got it!"

"Let's hear it."

She briefly laid out her cunning plan. She had a girl-friend who worked in the SoRobKop, the Union of Workers' and Peasants' Cooperatives. Her room was unused until four o'clock! You understand? Let's assume that Zoska would like to take the university entrance exams but there's no room in her apartment to study with a tutor.

"Zoska," he cried exuberantly. "You're extraordinary. I'd like to kiss you."

"Really?"

Then she added secretively, "Let's go to Shevchenko Park—it's dark there, we can kiss."

He returned home completely calm. He was thrilled with Zoska's plan. The notion of daylight meetings with a girl so dear to his heart, meetings that would have a secretive character, in someone else's apartment, struck him as a very urban romanticism. The mere thought of such trysts boosted his self-respect and floated above all his other concerns like a sweet song.

In such moments of psychic comfort, he often felt the need to clean up at home, take out the trash that usually accumulated in the corner, and attend to his linens, like any respectable homeowner. When neatness was on his mind, the slightest disorder in his surroundings irritated him. When he had finished tidying up, he felt great joy. He arranged the books in neat piles, wiped down the inkwell, covered the table with a clean white sheet of paper, and there, after his commendable efforts, he sat down to rest.

He figured thus: the young are characteristically ambitious, they dream of extraordinary accomplishments and fame, although only one among thousands ever achieves that. But if you revealed to such a young person his eventual fate, he would stop trying, throw everything to the dogs, and settle into the life of a bum. So, it turns out, deceptions are necessary. But it is sufficient to understand their nature—as, for example, he does—for them to stop being troublesome.

He felt the wisdom of his thoughts and was satisfied. He must live just as others do. A simple, normal life—develop friends and visit them, go out for entertainment, read newspapers and translated novels. What else does he need? All in all, compared to others, he was pretty well situated. His lessons gave him a decent income without too much effort. Ukrainization would continue for, say, three more years—then he'd go get a job. No, wait! He would certainly find a job as a teacher here, in the city—that would be the simplest. He just needed to expand and deepen his knowledge of the language and become a real expert. He was smoking now and in the clouds of smoke he could readily see his future. What could be simpler!

Two days later, at noon, Stepan had his first urban meeting with Zoska. Entering the small room filled with the arousing scents of a woman's apartment—powder and perfume—he felt uneasy. Then, after a few breaths of this intoxicating air, he felt light and exceptionally ardent. Surveying the place he also saw Zoska, whose face and figure were entirely hidden by the newspaper she was reading, as if she had not heard him enter. Only two legs dressed in fine stockings from the knees down hung motionless, sticking out from under the hem of a dark dress.

"Miss Zoska," he began jokingly in a serious bass. "Let's start the lesson."

She was silent. Stepan came forward as if sneaking up to her and tore the newspaper out of her hands.

"Careful!" she cried out.

He stopped for a moment, having long not seen her undressed—that is, in just a dress, without a coat and hat.

"What are you gawking at?" she asked. "Where are the books?"

He suddenly bent down and embraced her knees.

"Zoska, is it you?" he whispered. "Are you mine, Zoska?"

Later, Zoska forlornly said, "You taught me very quickly, divine one."

He was delighted to have discovered that his fears about the performance of the organism were unfounded. He wanted to joke around.

"What's there to teach here?"

"You have spoiled me," she said. "Now I'm spoiled."

"It's your own fault," he said. "What was the point of covering yourself up with the newspaper?"

Zoska waved her hand.

"In any case, you wanted to tell me something."

"Did I?"

"You said that you wanted to sit down beside me and tell me something."

He remembered.

"That was nothing. If you want, I'll tell you."

He sat down and started talking.

"It's silly. Last year I was a student."

"I know," said Zoska.

"I guess I told you. And I foolishly began to write stories."

"I know."

"How do you know that?" Stepan asked, surprised.

"Because you read one at the Institute, at the stage event."

"Were you actually there?"

"I even threw you a flower, but you didn't pick it up."

"That was you? My love!"

He embraced her and drowned the rest of his story in kisses.

In parting with Zoska that day he thought, "Fate itself brought us together. That is wonderful."

Their lessons were strictly arranged: twice a week, on Wednesdays and Fridays. In addition, by separate agreement, they were to go to the cinema, to shows, and to the theater.

Returning home from their meeting, he found an unusual looking envelope waiting for him. Inside he read that his collection of stories was accepted for publication, had passed Glavlit approval, and that an honorarium of 350 karbovanets was being offered. A contract requiring his signature was also included.

Stepan read it over and threw it on the table. He had decided to rid himself of this business of being a writer, but it would not let him go.

"This nuisance again," he thought.

Chapter Six

L iterary life begins when the quantity of people with the talent to talk continually about literature reaches a minimum sufficiency. Actually, these endless conversations are not even about literature as a product of the human desire for understanding: they don't discuss its finest examples, and they don't express the reader's satisfaction or admiration. Instead, they are about trivial details, the mechanics of creativity, its professional side, which, like all things professional, is boring and monotonous.

Literature consists of creativity, and literary life consists of the conversations of literary figures. And through their words, every fact from the life of a writer magically becomes a literary fact, any anecdote about him becomes a literary anecdote; his galoshes become literary galoshes, since, of course, all the parts of his body have the magical quality of endowing anything they touch with literary value. Legends about nearly divine singers who, through their songs, earned the favor of despots and princesses, as well as treasure—in short, a nice honorarium—are nowhere more prevalent than in the subconsciousness of writers who would, without any remorse, scorch the hearts of all humanity with their words. And it doesn't matter that, through the functioning of libraries, these hearts become more and more fire-resistant; writers secretly and stubbornly wallow in the prospect of their own exceptionality, the uniqueness of their talent, the originality of their works, nourishing with past experience the roots of their creative desire. And no matter how boring and nauseating this literary life may be, this unwinding of the ribbon of literary news—who is writing what, who is thinking of writing what, who said what about whom, who is about to praise or attack whom, who is going where for the holidays, and who makes how much—it is precisely from this blather that there arises the inherent spirit of authentic, non-commercial literature, the spirit of hidden competition. And, within the perimeter laid out by the unrolling of this ribbon, lies the place where literary soldiers gather to smoke the peace pipe before the next assault.

The young writer Stepan Radchenko began to take part in this literary life, visiting almost daily the editorial offices of the journal, where at twelve o'clock the bench and chairs were full of well-known, somewhat-known, and not-at-all-known literary figures. After spending an hour or two in their company, he would depart completely satisfied, although he had kept silent throughout, since he did not have the necessary store of trivial knowledge and was too much of a novice to have the right to speak. It's a well-known truth that non-authoritative ideas, no matter how insightful, evoke suspicion, while from the lips of the famous, even foolish utterances earn praise. So, here, as everywhere else, the right to command attention was earned by the quality of one's work or, at least, by persistent attendance. And Stepan was happy to serve out his literary apprenticeship.

After all, he figured, if it turns out that I am fated to be a writer, if I have instinctively already made so many steps in that direction that it would be shameful to stop, then I may as well keep going, and make connections with those others with whom I am destined to act—to show myself among them, remind them of my existence, to weave myself into the circle of literary friendships like a regular writer. At first, he felt annoyed and uncomfortable in this new circle of acquaintances, because no one paid any attention to him, because there weren't enough chairs for him to have one. He was frightened by his inability to follow the conversations he overheard. But, as his attendance continued, he quickly became familiar with the personal accomplishments of the people he met there, accomplishments often quite small and disproportionate to the pretentiousness of their behavior, and so he happily recognized that he was certainly no lesser a literary figure than they were. Now he waited impatiently for the publication of his collection, since only a book could give him a true literary passport, rather than the temporary identity card offered by stories in journals.

At first, he was merely tolerated, then he was seen as one of the usual crowd, and later he even earned some sympathy by his reserved behavior and so might even hear a friendly word upon entering.

"Oh, and here's Radchenko."

This pleased him enormously. Say what you will, but he had, it turns out, won for himself at least a little corner of the literary landscape, a seat that might accommodate at least a portion of his person. One day, in the course of a dispute, in a moment of silence, he even found sufficient courage to blurt out with a blush, "I think so, too."

It wasn't quite clear what exactly he also thought nor which side this remark was intended to support, but he had expressed an opinion, and he was proud of himself for the whole day. He had taken part in a literary conversation!

His greatest interest, of course, was in the literary groups. Each of them had their own name and logo, and he imagined them as something akin to a marketing collective for the distribution of the members' works. He was particularly thrilled that the members of each team defended, promoted, and supported each other without qualification, while mercilessly excoriating their opponents. He, too, needed a firm foundation beneath him. Studying the members and listening to their ideas, he rejected those organizations that did not suit his ideas and style, but he was in no hurry to choose from among those others that were more or less acceptable. He was waiting for an organization to hold a general meeting, so that he would not be signing up unnoticed. This was all the more important a decision since by his choice, he risked losing, in the opinion of the others, not only his sympathetic qualities but his abilities as a writer. That was true everywhere: your choice of friends determined your enemies. But it was not so easy to become acquainted with the internal life of the groups, to see what the situation would be like for you after you joined, because, in the atmosphere of continual intergroup warfare, their meetings were closed. Naturally, for tactical reasons, no group would allow strangers to attend a meeting where the enemy's troop strength was discussed and various attack plans were proposed.

Along with the first snows, the poet Vyhorskyi returned to the city. They met in the street like old friends.

"Let's go," said the poet.

"Where?"

"For a beer."

They went into a dimly lit establishment with plenty of free seats and tables in the center and along the walls. It smelled of stale beer and the dirty rag with which the floor had been washed.

"This is my favorite beer hall," said the poet. "A couple of beers, please!"

"It's spooky in here," commented Stepan as he sat down.

He had not been in a beer hall before and looked around with curiosity at the buffet with its variety of snacks, the portly proprietor who wore a suit and tie with boots, the brewers' advertising posters on the walls, and the juicy illustration of a fresh crab right in front of him.

"I like this beer hall in the daytime," the poet began. "I like the stale air that carries the scent of thousands of people. I like this dampness of spilled drinks. And the quiet. A magical mood comes over me. I see better. If you want to know, I think through my poems here."

He took a sip of beer.

"I missed this place while I was away. I missed Kyiv. On the train, I stood by the window and looked out—the city was spread out wide, like a giant crab. The buildings looked like cardboard boxes on hills. It's gigantic. And fantastic. When I got off the train, when I felt its ground beneath my feet, when I saw myself in it again, I trembled. It's silly, of course, but where else will you find such an expanse, such a mighty web of streets? And, at each step, you find memories, you walk in the footsteps of your ancestors. Yesterday, I walked around examining everything, even the familiar porches. And I saw that everything was as it had been, as if it had been waiting for me. It seems to me that you can't even fall in love with a person as much as you can with a lifeless thing. How many of us have loved dozens of women and have gone through even more friends; but we love veal cutlets all our lives. I visited the Lavra, even went down into the caves. What a difference from 1922 and '23. Back then, it was just old ladies from the villages. Yesterday, even women from the intelligentsia were there. Even a few men! I thought to myself: 'They know the sweetness of prayer, the deep satisfaction of communicating with their god. What about us?' When push comes to shove, all our airplanes, radios, and poison gases are mere rubbish against the lost hope of paradise. To tell the truth, I envied them. Listen, have you ever thought about the terrible paradox of mankind; conscious of the absurdity of its fleeting existence but incapable of immortalizing it? I'm afraid we may be standing at the brink of a rebirth of faith."

"Well—no," Stepan spoke up. "I'll have you know that, back in the village, young people are not at all religious."

"Maybe so. I'm not going to argue about it. All I know is that the big issues have lost their attraction. We're tired of big issues—being or consciousness, form or substance. You just want to say it's all the same and makes no difference. Life does not break down into systems. Each one of us starts life from the beginning, and to each new person life seems new."

"But science and learning are making advances," said Stepan.

"Science and learning have been making advances for a thousand years. You must understand that the accumulated experience of past ages is just the background against which everyone demonstrates his tricks. Another couple of beers, please."

When he unbuttoned his coat, Stepan saw on him the same satin shirt with the same tie that the poet had been wearing last spring when they first met in the offices of the Housing Administration. Vyhorskyi's elongated face had become nervous and it trembled, as if all the muscles beneath his skin were in a heightened state of activity. And Stepan, himself somewhat excited after a bottle of beer, was following his words with interest and attention.

"Drink up," said the poet. "Nothing stimulates our ability to think like beer. Science and learning are nothing. Absolute zero. For a thousand years, it's been spreading and it still can't teach people how to live. What benefit do they offer? You'll say, the revolution. Yes, I agree. Humanity sheds its skin, like a snake. But it sheds its spiritual skin with much more difficulty than a snake sheds its physical skin. Mankind oozes blood while it is shedding. But don't forget—the new skin will eventually shed, too. Progress? Well, that's child's play. I agree, there is progress—but there's no reason in it. The worst mistake is to consider the inevitable as success. Man eats the very same meat, but fried and with a fork. Progress does not increase the sum of all happiness, that's the important thing. The person condemned to death on the rack three centuries ago did not suffer any more than someone being executed by firing squad today. Or do I, perhaps, experience my dirty fingernails more acutely than a so-called savage would a whole filthy arm?"

He slowly finished his glass and drifted off in a reverie.

"That's why I always said that teaching people is just cheating them. There's nothing more shameful than inspiring illusions. And what's even worse—spreading ideals."

"Ideals?"

"Yes, exactly. Mankind, like a woman, likes to listen to compliments in the form of ideals. There are as many curses in the world as there are idealists. Who would follow them, if they didn't scold? But these ideals are like food—while they're on the tongue, they have a variety of tastes, but the stomach makes them all equal. The catarrhal stomach of history, as one poet with excellent digestion put it."

He fell silent and bent over his glass. Stepan lit a cigarette and enjoyed sending smoke into the half-light of the room. Indeed, it was quiet and peaceful here.

"He's pretty smart," he thought of the poet.

"Two more beers, please!" yelled the latter.

"That's all for me," Stepan said. "I'm smoking. Drop already."

"Nonsense! A healthy young fellow like you and you can't handle three bottles of beer? Here you are. But let's talk about those devoted to their ideas. That's always been popular and admired. But what do we do with those people who live exclusively according to their ideas? Those for whom the whole world dissolves into their idea? We lock them up in the Kyrylivka Asylum. So where's the logic?"

"You mean the insane?"

"That's what they're called."

"You know, I remember an incident," said Stepan. "There was this girl in the village—what a beauty she was. And she went insane. They said this one boy was to blame."

"No one owes anyone anything in this world. But there is blame, because there has to be some kind of responsibility. Notice that animals are never insane—they're rabid. Insanity is the exclusive privilege of humans. A marker on the road that humanity is traveling. An image of its future."

The clock struck two. The poet flinched.

"The universe will die from the dissipation of thermal energy," he said. "It will spread out evenly. Everything will be equalized and wiped out. Everything will cease. This will be a beautiful sight that no one will see."

After the third bottle, Stepan felt a sadness in his soul, as if the universe were going to die within a few days. But the clock reminded him of his lessons at the Leatherworkers' Collective.

"Maybe we should be going?"

"Sure, let's go. Who's paying? You? Actually, I'm a little short at the moment."

But for Stepan money was not a problem. A week earlier he had gotten an advance from his publisher for 50 % of his honorarium for the collection of stories, already at the printer's. He immediately acquired a felt hat and ordered a stunning suit, for which he was waiting so as to impress Zoska. He was now all the more inclined to treat clothing as an artistic arrangement of his body. Since he liked his body and appreciated its strength and symmetry, he could not but take an interest in clothes intended to display that body in a favorable image, since displaying it in the nude was prohibited. Clothing became for him a formal consideration, a question of taste and even influence, since he fully understood the different impressions made by a person with a torn shirt and one in a stylish suit. This was, of course, entirely a matter of convention, but it takes an extraordinary degree of spiritual charm to overcome the effects of carelessness in clothing.

When the suit was ready, Stepan felt a wish to give Zoska a present, too. His feelings for her had taken root in his being and sometimes, quite unexpectedly, at home or during a lesson, her smiling image would flit airily before him. Zoska! What a beautiful name! It was a pleasure just to pronounce it, because the sound of it carried the echo of her playfulness, the sensuous cadence of her kisses that evaporated on his lips, his eyes, and his chest. Beyond that, he felt toward her that peculiarly masculine gratitude with which the experience of secret assignations augments romance. And she, too, approaching with him the dark wellsprings of existence, consuming with him the eternally fresh fruit of the tree of knowledge, had become more judicious and friendlier towards him. She lost the capriciousness of her earlier desires; what remained was only some kind of nervousness that manifested itself in sudden bouts of longing.

Then she would gaze at him with a look that made him anxious, as if her glance penetrated his soul and agitated its most secret chambers. She would lie, then, with her hands under her head, distant, pensive, alien, and silent. Later, she would come to life again.

"Is it bad for you at home?" he asked.

"Yes, it's bad. But there's nothing that can be done."

Her father, a minor bureaucrat, earned too small a salary for their domestic life to be attractive. And she herself had no luck finding a job. Stepan tried hard to cheer her up as best he knew how. He bought her chocolates, candy, flowers, and illustrated magazines that they looked at together. And now he wanted to make her a present. But what should he get her? Having considered a large number of possibilities, he settled on a fragrance, because he liked scents but was ashamed to use them himself.

At the perfume shop he asked for a fine scent.

"Would you like Coty?"

"The very best!"

"Paris? L'Origan? Chipre?"

"L'Origan!" he said, because that name pleased him more than the others.

He paid fifteen karbovanets for the bottle, but he was satisfied. It must be a very fine scent if there's so little of it for so much money.

On Friday, dressed in his new suit, he appeared at their meeting in good spirits.

"Zoska," he said. "Look what I bought you."

"Coty!" she cried, like a child receiving an unexpected but long-dreamt-of delight.

"This is the most expensive perfume," he said. "I'm glad you like it. And I have a new suit."

"Really? Stand up! Walk over there! Come back! You're divine!"

"Wait," he said, glad to see the impression made by his present and by himself.

He picked up the vial and opened it, carefully removing the film from the glass stopper. In a fit of tenderness he began to apply the perfume to Zoska with his moistened palm—on her neck, her arms, her face. She meekly endured, sitting still with only slight tremors from the touch of his cold hand and the scent on her body.

"Enough, enough," she whispered excitedly.

"No—the legs, too."

A wave of fragrance slowly spread through the air, forming into an invisible halo around Zoska's figure. The fine, gentle scent altered the room, transforming it from a common dwelling into a fairy-tale setting for lovers, evoking dreams of love in a flowering garden with gentle whiffs of celestial wind, as if the magic of secret essences, ointments, and oils from the distant past had penetrated this space through unseen cracks in the walls.

But where had he felt this intoxicating scent before? Why did it agitate him? Why did it burden his soul? And then he remembered. It was the scent of that woman, the woman he had once encountered at the window of a store. Suddenly a wave of recollections arose in him, countless memories spread out before him, like a disturbed pile of shimmering stones, radiating the shine of bright diamonds and cloudy rubies, tickling the eyes with their bright rays and touching the skin with a troubling shiver. His entire life passed before him in this play of light and shadow—an unexpected life, not the one that had to be, but the one that was.

"I'll put my head on your knees," he whispered. "May I do that?"

"You are allowed everything, unfortunately," she replied.

Agitated, he pressed his face into her scented thighs, wrapping his arms around them as if on a sturdy support, and felt calmer. Then he asked, "Zoska, have you ever loved anyone?"

She was stroking his hair, burying her hand in it, disheveling it.

"I did," she answered.

"Tell me about it."

And, while still stroking his hair, she told the story of her first love. She was nineteen then, so it was three years ago. She was enrolled in stenography courses. One of the students always walked her home. Then he disappeared one day.

"But he was really strange," she said. "He didn't kiss me, even once."

"Did you want him to?"

"Every girl wants that when she's in love."

"But you didn't want me to kiss you, at first."

"You didn't love me."

"Do I love you now?"

She pulled back her hand.

"Now I don't care," she said.

Lulled, he felt the urge to talk, to ask about their feelings for each other, to finally understand their origin. Under the influence of the scent and tenderness, he was enveloped in a mood of quiet observation, the kind that awakens a need to explore and understand the flow of life.

"Do you love me?"

She became pensive, as if considering the question.

"I love you terribly much."

He embraced her again in a sign of gratitude.

"For what?"

"You have a nice voice," she said. "I close my eyes and it cradles me. And your eyes."

"...and your eyes," arose a dreamy echo in his heart, "...and your eyes."

"And what else?" he asked.

"Your soul is bad," she added suddenly. "It's a bad soul."

"How do you know?" he asked, taken aback.

"I just know. But I like you. You're handsome."

"Do you think I'm a thief?"

"Oh, if only you were a thief! You would bring me Persian rugs, like the bandits in songs. And then you would kill me or sell me into slavery."

"Zoska," he said, rising to his feet. "You're extraordinary. How fortunate I am to have found you."

"I let you find me."

And they talked on, speaking words that, when taken out of their romantic context, seem banal and stupid, naive words without meaning, senseless, like a deck of well-used playing cards that acquire powerful symbolic meaning in the hands of each successive group of players. They were bound together by words spoken in whispers and in cries, old as the gray earth itself but vibrant, reinvigorated on the lips of lovers, reborn into their original brilliance by the power of undying feeling. They sat, enchanted by their own proximity, their boundless commitment, the tender touch of souls that, in moments of extreme longing, ring with the silver bells of spring. On parting, he looked at her for a long, long time, remembering her image, to take it with him into his hopes and dreams.

Chapter Seven

Stepan's collection of stories was published in early January of the new year, even earlier than he had expected. Holding it in his hands for the first time, he experienced a moderate joy. This was something useful and valuable for him, he thought, like a trump card in his hands, but he did not experience any extraordinary satisfaction, since he had already had this thought earlier, awaiting its publication, and had gotten used to the idea of the book's appearance. He was not one of those people who strive for something methodically, approaching the desired goal step by step, and knowing how to rest at appropriate stops along the way. His wishes were always an unquenchable need that burned him from inside, propelling him directly through difficulties that might have been avoided by patience and planning. In the struggle with inevitable doubts, he needlessly sacrificed the joys of success. His soul was a chiseled millstone, an unstoppable millstone that grinds everything together equally—grain, weeds, and the grass of life.

On the second day, he leafed through his book, examining the typeface and the cover. He perused the titles of the stories in the contents, but he did not have the courage to read over a story. He felt uncomfortable before himself for what he had written. Had it been worthwhile to write this? While he was writing he had had no idea why or for what purpose he was writing. What value could you ascribe to such unconscious work?

He showed Zoska the collection, expecting her praise and suggestions.

"Did you write this?" she exclaimed. "People are so comical. They're always up to something, trying this and that."

"Should I stop, then?" he asked.

"Well, no! Once you've started, keep writing."

He understood this perfectly himself. Once you've started, you must keep writing. For him, this book turned writing into an obligation, a duty, a solemn pledge that he must keep. But with that, it stopped being a mere game he played with fame, a way of putting himself ahead of all his peers. Now, it acquired the sense of being responsible work—too responsible for him to allow himself to write any-which-way about anything he liked. Why? He couldn't determine this himself. He could not trace the convoluted path of his relations with literature, from a childish prank to an ulcer on the soul. In playing around carelessly, he had cut himself and unintentionally severed those veins through which the heart pumps a river of blood. So, now, he had to be creative under a dual burden: obligation and responsibility.

He must write. This thought would not give him peace—not at home, nor at his lessons, nor in conversations, nor in his meetings with Zoska. He smoked and ate with it, as with a best friend, or worst enemy. He must write! But about what? He chose and arranged a couple of plotlines about the life of an insurgent, including plenty of action, but one by one he rejected them all, sensing in them an unscrupulous repetition of what he had already written. No, that field was already exhausted for him. Actually, it had pushed itself away. It had become an illusion, one that no longer elicited the same interest that could force him to search and select new beads to thread onto the string of a new story, and so he was not at all worried that he was no longer able to find material on *this* topic. He vaguely yearned to write about what he saw now, to work out his most recent impressions—impressions of the city. Here, only here, was the fertile ground that he should cultivate, because it was only here that he experienced the unknown, the understanding of which is the motive and the joy of creativity. And it didn't matter that these impressions were lying around his soul in a pile of raw fibers: life never offers anything all wrapped up, it is just hints and fragments, the elements of the montage that need to be arranged, spliced, and refined into that final product called a work of art. Life only offers the clay that needs to be shaped by the hands and vision of an artist. He knew this, but he could not find the core.

Then he remembered inspiration, and he tried, doggedly and cleverly, to catch some, starting with simple naive methods and ranging all the way to complex endeavors. At first, he tried to stimulate his conscience, putting himself into situations where it would be shameful not to write: he sat down at his table, eagerly pulled out a clean sheet of white paper, opened his inkwell, and took his pen between his fingers. And then waited. But, instead of the desired concentration, all manner of trivial nonsense stole his attention. His eyes inadvertently rested on advertisements in the newspaper, on the cigarette label, on the knuckles of his own hand, examining everything with great interest, seeking any place they might focus other than the deceitful piece of paper that was the surface intended for their attention. His ears listened to shouts, crashes, and echoes beyond the walls, while, in his head, disordered thoughts wandered freely, disappearing without a trace in the clouds of cigarette smoke that hung over and choked him. And nothing came out.

That being the case, he decided systematically to remove any distractions that might divert him, to isolate himself completely and force himself to concentrate.

First, he got rid of his pen, since it had to be dipped in the inkwell, then he discarded regular pencils, since they needed to be sharpened, settling on a mechanical pencil. He moved his table away from the window, where a gentle breeze perturbed his face, and moved it by the stove, in a corner, which also required rearranging the electrical connections. And to escape the exasperating din of the neighbors, he tried to write at night when everyone was asleep. But here, too, between four and five in the morning, when no one was yet up, he experienced defeat. The results of all these attempts at deprivation were always the same: on paper—a few lines of text crossed out, among innumerable drawings of trees, houses, and faces; in his heart—bitterness and fatigue.

Sometimes, on returning home, he would imagine that he was in a great mood and so, playfully, would tell himself: "Well, it's time to write something for income."

Something light and cheerful—the hell with all those serious topics. Why shouldn't he be a humorist? Here's a great topic, for example: A teacher is conducting anti-religious propaganda as part of his lesson, choosing the story of the Great Flood as his whipping boy. Do you really think, he says, you could fit all the extant creatures of the time into an ark? A pair of them, no less! And he impresses the students with a zinger: You can't get a pair of whales into an ark. The whales weigh more than a ton each and would drown the ship with a swipe of their tail. But then one student, a wimpish kid with a high-pitched voice, asks: Why take the whales on board? They can swim in the water themselves! And then you can even add that the teacher himself is a religious man, prays to God for forgiveness before each lesson. Or wait—this one's even better: A professor, a stately man with a family, a well-known economist, is answering a question for a newspaper about his view of the economic situation in the Soviet Union. His view is clear and simple, but "unspeakable." So he sweats, and rewrites, and gives it to his wife and close friends to read over. He edits, deletes, avoids, obfuscates, squirms, and is left with something ... well, something beyond time and space, with ideas that are neither here nor there but everywhere. Or take Ukrainization! How many dramas, comedies, farces, anecdotes you could find there! And who could know them better than he did. Damn it, why didn't he think of this earlier!

But it wasn't so easy to fool oneself. The primary power in the mechanism he was trying to put into motion was likely a lazy donkey, unresponsive to anger or seduction. The central management of this creative enterprise was apparently in the hands of a mindless bureaucrat who always required something more, refused to approve anything, and always gave the same answer: "Come back tomorrow!" Slowly, Stepan felt superstitions arising within him. Maybe this house was uncreative? Maybe this year was unpropitious, because it's an odd number and he was born in an odd-numbered year...

Fearing despair, he instinctively began to imagine that he had already written something extraordinary, written a great many very interesting works, unmatched by anyone, whole piles of books that grew on his table into a substantial library. He could hear whispers of admiration all around him; he set out on distant trips; he conducted correspondence with his fans in which he explained his views, his beliefs, his opinions; he held public readings in huge auditoriums full of mesmerized listeners. And these dreams gave him comfort, they feasted on his accumulated doubts for their own nutrition, they left a strange satisfaction and a desire for more. But they didn't result in any progress.

On the other hand, external literary circumstances were, it seems, very favorable. First of all, the published collection secured him a place in the literary world; it granted him the rights of literary citizenship that he was seeking. He noticed this when people started asking him for his opinion, when he was addressed not as Radchenko but as Comrade Stefan, more like an old friend in familiar company. He heard a few verbal tributes about his stories and understood that he had become an equal among equals. His self-esteem was singing, but his soul was silent.

Evenings he began to meet quite often with the poet Vyhorskyi at the beer hall, where the poet was a constant fixture. Stepan now entered here as a regular, feeling relief and relaxation at the door of this large hall, converted from a dingy basement by a bright flood of light. He easily dove into the friendly din of the patrons who sat by the white marble tables in colorful groups of two or three, punctuated by the clatter of dishes, the pop of bottle caps, laughter and cheers, all enveloped in loud music that streamed from the dais in the corner, uniting the diversity of faces and clothing into the plurality of a human collective, maintaining the unity of the motley group, which in moments of silence immediately dissolved into individual persons and words, distinct and distant, carried here from unfamiliar haunts, from unknown lives and fates. But, after these brief intervals of alienation, the gray mass of beings coalesced in a new crescendo of sounds and melded together again, enchanted by what they had in common, as if the song coming from the instruments were their song, rising together from all their lips, exhilarated by the feeling of togetherness.

Stepan felt the striking effectiveness of this beer hall music fully on his own person. It removed layers of worries from his shoulders, liberated the suppressed portion of his soul, which suddenly stretched its wings in a confused but passionate effort. He himself became sharper, more attuned to the fluttering hearts of others, consumed with the selfish certainty that he would write something, that he would succeed in expressing that something, still unreachable, that lived within him, and reacting in a faint echo to the wild winds of life.

He looked around, spotted Vyhorskyi, and, smiling, approached him, threading his way through the labyrinth of tables.

"There's a jazz band today," said the poet. "Let's listen."

On the dais, instead of the usual threesome, there was a quartet, with a piano, violin, viola, and a Turkish drum with cymbals, spreading throughout the hall an animalistic roar that drowned out the melody.

"What thieves!" complained the poet. "They call this a jazz band? And for this we must pay an extra five kopecks per bottle! But have a look at the new violinist."

The new violinist was young and wore a tie that he had artistically configured into a big bow. His gestures resembled those of an epileptic. He bent over, jerked his head, stuck out his tongue, winked, frowned, and made faces, jumping up and down once in a while, as if the drummer's strokes were accidentally falling on his stomach.

"He is solving the problem of how to conduct a musical ensemble when your hands are otherwise occupied," Vyhorskyi explained. "What sensitivity! Please give them each a glass of beer."

Swaying his torso in keeping with the rhythm, he dreamily hummed along.

"What's new in the literary world?" he asked.

"Nothing much," Stepan replied. "I was praised in *The Red Path*. They published a review. Nothing new."

"Who was it?"

"Guess!.. It was Svitozarov."

"Svitozarov's chief quality is to be different from everyone else. If no one else has praised you, then he will offer praise. In the opposite case, he will criticize you, from an instinct for self-preservation. They all see us as some kind of racehorses that they're playing in a betting pool. Because to be a critic you have to be a very good critic. In any case, avoid them like the plague."

"But, in the end, I suppose I'll have to join one of the literary groups," ventured Stepan. "It's hard for a novice without some support."

The poet frowned.

"It's all the same: either you have talent, in which case you don't need any support, or you don't have talent, in which case all the support in the world won't help you. So what's the point?"

"To tell you the truth," Stepan replied, "I've grown accustomed to community service, whether at the village hall or in student leadership."

"Then why don't you join the International Organization for Aid to Revolutionaries?" the poet said with irritation. "Join the Volunteer Society for Cooperation with the Army, Aviation, and Fleet, or the Society for Aid to Children, or to cripples, or to the unemployed. What's this got to do with literature?"

Nervously he tapped on his bottle with a fork, to indicate he wanted another round of beer.

"To be perfectly frank," he continued, "I don't understand why these literary groups exist. People try to explain, but I don't get it. I just can't understand. For me, their existence is an incomprehensible and sad mystery. If these are crutches for crippled writers, I'm glad that we two have good strong legs. And here's the beer, at last."

He poured it into the glasses energetically.

"To literature! We have to honor what gives us an income. But tell me, honestly, why did you start writing?"

"From envy," said Stepan, blushing.

"In my case, it was a sense of frailty. That's the same thing. But the problem isn't in the fact that our literature is plain, like bread without fixings. I always compare a writer to a baker. From a little ball of dough he creates a loaf of bread. He has a good oven, he uses good yeast, and he's industrious enough to knead his dough for a month, a year, or even a few years. But if he's timid, if he's afraid of what he himself thinks, and of what others think, then it's better for him to close the bakery and take up teaching village bumpkins."

The music came to life again, with the drum pounding. This time, the melody reverberated clearly, unraveling in a fine thread from beneath the fingers of the violinist, who was bowing every which way in what looked like a religious seizure. It was a melancholy motif of unfulfilled desire, a luminous stream of anguished reproach, craving, and unrest.

"What is that?" asked Stepan.

"A foxtrot. In our world, it belongs to the genre of dances that is condemned as debauchery and degeneration. Some people call it a bedroom dance, although it is really nothing more than a minuet. It's denounced for being sensuous, but what kind of dance is not sensuous? After all, the whole point of dancing is the pleasure of touching each other. On the whole, the issue of dancing has met a strange fate in our country. In the first years after the Revolution, it was persecuted as a form of religious ritual, but now it's encouraged in civic clubs as a form of cultural expression. The processes of life are the processes of self-contradiction, my friend."

"I can't write," whispered Stepan, overcome by the wistful tension of the melody. "I keep trying but I can't."

"You can't write? Don't worry! When it starts to hurt, the writing will flow."

When the music stopped, Stepan felt a strange excitement, a deep agitation of some kind, because the motif died unfinished in the noisy hall. The motif just suddenly came apart, cradling in transparent shards, petting and irritating the ear, and he felt an irresistible urge to gather together this acoustic swarm. The ache from his unsuccessful efforts to write was reborn in this urge, rekindling his longing for what had become inaccessible to him in his hour of triumph. In his memory, he quickly reviewed the various segments of his urban path thus far and, bending over to Vyhorskyi, he recounted the story of their first meeting, not in the offices of the

Housing Administration, but in another office, where the poet had commented on his leaving with words that he did not then fully understand.

"Strange, isn't it?" Stepan asked.

"I don't remember that," said the poet, "but that's not the point. Back then, you showed up hungry, tattered, and without a place to live. Now, you've got a nice coat, a suit, some money, and a collection of stories. But are you any happier? You're already complaining: 'I can't write!' Here you have a perfect illustration of my ideas about progress. That's why I always say that happiness is impossible. Today, you eat; tomorrow, you're hungry."

"It's unnatural, all this," sighed Stepan. "Everything in the city is somehow unnatural."

"Once the super-natural has been negated, the un-natural remains our only joy," said the poet. "Any talk about happiness—that is, about complete satisfaction—elicits disgust. It's the most animal-like of all human illusions precisely because it is the most natural."

He poured two more glasses.

"Listen to me," he continued. "All those people who go on about naturalness have as much understanding of life as pigs do about oranges. Ever since the human mind began to formulate abstract thoughts, man has irrevocably abandoned the path of naturalness, and the only way to return him to that path is to cut off his head. Just consider this: how can man destroy the natural around himself without destroying the natural within himself? Every tree chopped down on the planet shows that something has also been chopped down in the human soul. When man abandoned natural caves for constructed dwellings, when he began to sharpen natural stone, that's when he chose the path of artificiality, which has come down to us as an inheritance. Is it natural to admit the imperfection of life at a given moment and to yearn for new forms? Or to condemn our life altogether? It would be natural not to notice its faults and to trumpet its glory regardless, as various panegyrists do. That's why all progress is progress away from nature in our environment, our thinking, and our feelings. Your smoking is also artificial, since it would be more natural to breathe fresh air."

"But I'm not going to stop smoking," asserted Stepan.

"I'm not berating you," said the poet. "I just want you to understand that man is the *reductio ad absurdum* of nature. In us, nature destroys itself. We are the last phase on one branch of the evolutionary tree, and there will be no others after us, no super-man. We are the last link in a chain, which may perhaps unroll again on this earth, but down different paths, in different directions. The brain—there's the greatest enemy of mankind. But, my friend, don't stare so much at that woman in the blue hat, although that's very natural."

"That's just incidental," Stepan excused himself.

"On the contrary, listening to me is very unnatural."

"You're always talking about the end of the world," Stepan interjected uncomfortably. "It's so depressing."

"I'm always more interested not in how things are developing, but how they will end."

"So, that's why they call you a spineless intellectual!"

These words visibly offended Vyhorskyi.

"Spineless intellectual?" he grumbled. "And what's the point of having a spine if it's topped off with a dunce cap?" Then, after getting up, he added, "We're all just petit bourgeois, because we all have to die. Give us immortality and we'll all become new, great, consummate. As long as we're mortal, we're risible and inconsequential."

Chapter Eight

When Stepan got home that evening, he was told that someone had come to visit him and promised to return tomorrow morning. Who could it have been? Stepan was deeply concerned by this. The simple fact was that, in all the time he had been living on Lviv Street, no one had ever visited him here. He could not even remember whether anyone at all knew his address. He lived just like the little mouse behind the wall, in a horrible place where he couldn't write at all. And this knock by an unknown hand on the door of his apartment awoke in him the wish to have visitors, to welcome guests, and to chat with them in his leisure time.

"I must develop some acquaintances," he thought.

Indeed, he needed to simply live for a while, to enjoy the minutiae of city life, to rest and rebuild his strength after the strenuous months he had just lived through. That's likely why he can't write—because he's debilitated.

An enervated soul, like an exhausted ox, is incapable of pulling any load.

This was the plan that he formulated while lying down to sleep: not to visit the editorial office, because the literary conversations only aggravated his helplessness—in general, to stay as far away as possible from literature while developing a social circle unrelated to literature, even drinking beer with Vyhorskyi no more than once a week. Actually, after his initial enchantment with the manifold complexity of Vyhorskyi's thinking and his insouciant attitude toward the cosmos, Stepan was beginning to have doubts about him, since he himself lived without sophistry and embraced the world without the filter of abstract categories. He was not dishonest with himself, neither in thought nor in deed, and he retained his concrete materiality; and, for him, life did not cease being a fragrant, if sometimes bitter, almond.

In the morning, the mystery of yesterday's visitor was resolved very simply. True, Stepan did not immediately recognize his face, which was now decorated with an English moustache, nor did he recognize his person in the wide deerskin jacket and the tan leather gloves, but the moment his guest uttered his greeting—"Hello there, Steffi, I've come to visit you"—there was no longer any doubt that this was his old buddy from the Institute, Borys Zadorozhnii, who had left this room to Stepan when he himself moved out.

"Sit down, Borys," Stepan said. "It's good you came for a visit."

Borys Zadorozhnii had certainly changed in the year since he finished the Institute, not only in his clothing but in his behavior and in the tone of his voice. That first cheerful exclamation coming from his lips by way of greeting at the door was but an echo of the old student days. His further conversation showed signs of the confident superiority typical of a man of business who does not scatter words needlessly and knows their value.

Taking off his coat, he revealed to the light of day a Tolstoy shirt of gray cloth with ivory buttons. He pulled a folding cigarette case from his pocket and graciously treated his host. "Please, have a smoke."

Then he examined the apartment critically.

"So, you live here, it seems."

"Yes, I do, thanks to you."

"Nothing to thank me for. It could do with a facelift. Put up some wallpaper, and maybe paint the ceiling. Have you got money?"

"Sure, I have some."

"Then get some wallpaper, for sure. It's not expensive right now. I recommend the Leningrad cooperative store."

Stepan agreed, then asked, "How are your studies at the Institute?"

Borys let out a cloud of smoke up to the ceiling.

"My studies? I left after a week. Not for me this dry academic sh... Now, I'm the senior instructor in cooperative sugar-beet agriculture for the Kyiv region. Where's your ashtray? You probably flick the ashes on the floor, right? You're a student, after all."

And he began to talk about the general state of cooperative sugar beet farming, about last year's harvest, about combating pests. A whole lot of problems, but we're moving forward, that's for sure. The bureaucracy is stifling. They're restoring the sugar-processing plant near the Fundukliyivka station, which he often passes. So, what's happening? The labor is there, the materials are there, the money is ready, but, while they procrastinated, the construction season has passed. It's the old guard "experts" who hold things up.

"They haven't got any fire in their bellies," he said. "Chase them out with a rusty poker, these gentlemen bureaucrats! So, when do you finish?"

"I dropped out," Stepan admitted sheepishly.

Borys grimaced.

"So, you got caught up in something? Literature, no doubt."

Stepan nodded.

Then Borys didactically explained to him that literature was, of course, a very nice thing, but an uncertain one. In life, you need a secure source of income, a profession, and rewarding work for the common good.

"And for whom are you writing?" he added. "Take me, for example. I have no time to read."

"So, how's your wife?" asked Stepan, changing the topic. "Nadiika, isn't it?"

He really had to dredge up this name, as from a deep cave.

"Nadiika's wonderful," beamed Borys. "She's a great housewife, I couldn't be happier."

"Still at the vocational college?"

"I talked her into quitting."

Of course, he was not against education for women, or equal rights, but the most important thing for him was family and a peaceful home after all those damned business trips. Besides, experience teaches us that women are only qualified for secondary work—copying and registration—but could not be trusted with responsible tasks and leadership.

"Plus it's time we had a son," he added.

"So what's the problem?"

"Money," Borys admitted, "though abortions aren't free either. In a word, we'll see."

"Couldn't you go on without children?"

"Then what was the point of getting married?"

"What about love?"

"Love, Steffi, is a temporary phenomenon—a two-week vacation for a working man. But you have to live, too. I see you haven't changed a bit."

As he was leaving, he told Stepan, "I'm hoping to see you at my place, that's 38 Andriyivskyi Descent, Apt. 6. It's a two-room place. Come visit."

After seeing his guest off, Stepan sat down on the bed, as he always did when he wanted to concentrate on something and have a comfortable smoke. Borys's visit had produced a generally unpleasant sensation, but nevertheless he felt a certain envy of his old friend. While the conservatism of Borys's views and his bourgeois philistinism in the area of high culture were deeply offensive to him, on the other hand, Borys's practical inclination, his love for his work and certainty about its utility, which rang out clearly in the words of the young agriculturalist, impressed Stepan with their solidity. Into this room, the scene of many disappointments and successes, Borys had brought the spirit of a real builder, the eager vitality of mundane, unnoticed creativity that ceaselessly changes the world. It is only thanks to him and to others like him, the constructors of the material foundations of human existence, that higher creativity becomes possible. Isn't it then his right to consider that creativity a mere reflection of his own work, and to reject it, if he doesn't have the time to enjoy it? His work is simple and unrewarding. It will not bring him fame, and his name will not be inscribed in any history book, so he seeks his reward in money and finds comfort in family, where he can enter eternity at least through his children. Does that mean he should be condemned with the label "philistine"? Careful! It is not yet clear who should condemn whom. It is not yet clear who the real movers of life are: those who create its structure, or those who create its songs while sitting on that structure.

Stepan threw away his cigarette butt. Yes, Borys and he don't smoke the same tobacco. Yes, they are different people.

So, Nadiika had quit the vocational college! He talked her into it, he says. It's pretty clear what kind of talking that was. Administrative decision for the greater good. But so what—it's none of this writer's business. These are all trivial matters.

But a sense of disappointment remained, as if Borys had offended him somehow. And the more he tried to justify his friend in his own eyes, the guiltier Borys seemed, and the more estranged. A speck of bitterness, rolling down the hill of emotions, grows wider, gains substance, increases in size like a giant snowball, and drops into the heart like a giant block of ice. And then it takes many, many calories of warmth to melt this unexpected burden.

It was half past twelve, time for his meeting with Zoska. Getting up and stretching, he felt hesitation, not because he didn't want to go, but because he didn't like to abandon any thought unfinished, not fully thought through and thus left behind like a knotted ball of wool. He got dressed and went out, shuddering from the frigid air after the quiet comfort and cigarette smoke. It's cold!

He turned up his collar and stuck his hands into his pockets. The blinding whiteness of the packed snow on the street, the dry crunch of his own footsteps and those of others, the soft shush of sleigh runners were all bothersome to him, disturbing him with their irrational clarity. He walked quickly, overtaking other pedestrians.

He arrived early, Zoska wasn't there yet. Stepan sat down, urgently lit a cigarette, which quickly died out in his fingers, and stretched out on an arm of the chair. This single armchair in the room, once upholstered in blue silk but now covered with a motley rug, was Zoska's favorite place, and he occupied it now, enjoying the feel of its softness. He wanted to dive into something warm and comfortable, to stretch out his entire body and forget about it, abandoning himself to those slow thoughts that penetrate into the depths of the soul and uncover its treasures for examination. He wanted to descend into the dungeons of the heart, to remove the forged locks from the trunks of experience, to open their lids and thrust his hands into memories, old and dry, like flowers between the pages of a book. Maybe Zoska will be late today. Perhaps she won't show up at all.

But he waited for her. He examined the furnishings in the room with interest, even more interest than when he had first entered this room that had provided him with unexpected shelter. The furnishings were meager: a bed, two chairs, the armchair, and a small table. There wasn't even a wardrobe to house the dresses that hung on the wall in cloth coverings. But the unknown girl who lived here had formed these paltry things into an attractive harmony, infusing their arrangement with a woman's grace, sprinkling their gentle simplicity with the magic of youthfulness. He could sense her adept hand in the straight line of the comforter, in the fluffy pillow that coquettishly raised its top corner, and in the series of photographs and glasses that stood on the doily-covered table. This is where she took action, where she lived, where her heart beat with all the usual human desires, where she had decorated the walls with the invisible pattern of her dreams. And this borrowed residence, fixed up perhaps for someone else, tidied perhaps in the expectation of someone else's kisses, had become the scene of his own activity, the shelter of his most intimate feelings, the location of his lovemaking. Why?

Finally, Zoska showed up, cheerful and red from the frost, her brisk walk bringing with her the liveliness of the cold air.

"You're here already?" she wondered.

"I left too early," he said, laughing, "to see you sooner."

"You're such a little liar."

She took off her coat and hat and ran over to him.

"Warm me up," she said. "Zoska is very cold today!" And in that moment she noticed that he was worried. "The divine one is sour? Why is the divine one sour?"

"A bad mood," he answered. "It will pass."

She embraced him.

"Where's this bad mood? Is it here? Or here?"

She kissed him on the forehead, the eyes, and cheeks, just as children have their fingers kissed so they stop hurting.

Then she took her place on the armchair, and Stepan sat down on a pillow by her feet. "At the feet of a queen," he joked.

Lighting a cigarette, Zoska crossed her legs with her elbow on her knee and began to talk as if thinking out loud, expressing all her thoughts just as they unraveled in her mind, with all the gaps and jumps. Certainly Zoska, too, has bad moods occasionally. Why? Because people are so terribly comical, they don't want to simply live, they're always up to something, imagining this and that, and then afterwards they suffer. She's been looking for a job, visiting the job lotteries and the union offices, but everyone there is so full of themselves, so serious, that she just feels like sticking out her tongue at them. Father spends his evenings writing some kind of reports; she once drew a doodle at the end of one, because he's writing these silly reports that no one needs or cares about. She really likes airplanes, because they fly so high, but they will never give Zoska a ride because they're for dropping bombs. She would like to poke all fat and self-absorbed people in the stomach, so that they would stop thinking.

But the strangest thing for Zoska was lovemaking between people. Everyone lives in pairs and performs these pleasant debaucheries in private, but no one wants to admit it. They even say it's indecent—well then, don't do it at all. All this riding on their high horses!

"Have you fallen asleep?" she asked suddenly, poking him.

"No," he said.

He sat leaning against the chair and listening to her words, which he had heard more than once in various combinations on various occasions. He was silent and it seemed to him that everything in the room was silent, that all the furniture had bent over, wistfully wondering why they were here, and not somewhere far away. He didn't even notice when Zoska fell silent, falling back into the armchair and closing her eyes. He didn't ask what she was thinking about, since he knew he would not understand, just as he would be unable to convey to her his own ruminations, sensing that she had unconsciously crossed the limit where verbal communication between people ends. They sat in the room, mindless of each other, submerged in something endlessly their own, concealed behind the margins of the heart that suddenly grow into impervious walls of otherness.

Stepan woke up first and rose awkwardly.

"Are you sleeping?" he asked.

She opened her eyes without saying a word. He stood beside her and did not know what to say.

"We're not cheerful today," he said finally. "Are you OK?" he asked worriedly.

She was silent.

"Maybe something has happened?"

In their intimate conversations, this "something" designated the price that nature tries to impose for the enjoyment of pleasure despite the ingenuity of the participants.

She raised her worried eyes. "Will we all die?" she asked.

"Of course," he answered, relieved. "Everyone dies."

"Is it possible not to die?"

His heart melted at the sincerity of her voice. She wasn't joking, she was asking candidly, as if she had some doubt, some secret hope of becoming the exception to the idiotic fate of the living. He kissed her, comforted her, overcome with a mournful sympathy for her and for himself.

"You shouldn't think about that," he said.

"It comes on its own," she whispered.

They went out together and stopped on the corner where they usually parted.

"Don't go," he said.

"You're silly."

She nodded to him, and then he stood watching her slight figure weaving amid the passersby, getting progressively smaller, disappearing more and more until she completely dissolved in the crowd. He kept standing, hoping that she might still appear for a moment, from a distance. Then a torment began to grow: with her departure was he also losing hope of ever seeing her again? Never had she been so close to him as she was now, and he had never felt such longing on parting with her. It was as if he had not told her what he had wanted to tell her, what he had to tell the only person who was dear to him, and he felt the weight of the unsaid words on his heart. Like an old miser, she had systematically taken from him everything that was hers, taken all his memories, like the presents he had once given. The thought that they would see each other again seemed strange to him.

Although it was still early, Stepan stopped at a cafeteria along the way to have dinner. Food did not find particular favor with him, and his attitude toward it was strictly utilitarian. He certainly did not belong to that category of people who, on their way to dinner, consider what they will have for the first course, the second, and the third, and can taste the anticipated dishes on the way there. Even his strongest appetite was completely bland, lacking the colorful additives of sensation. Desserts didn't tempt him at all, no matter how appealing they may have seemed at first. He had purchased bags and bags of candies and chocolates, but he never ate any himself. At first, the inscrutable names of certain dishes on the menu intrigued him, but later, when he learned that roast à la broche is nothing but ordinary beef on a skewer and that the mysterious omelette is just scrambled eggs, he stopped paying any attention to these inventions, these strenuous efforts to introduce variety into eating with the help of exotic names and the imagination of the consumers. He had developed a taste for the scent of tobacco and for better clothing, but his skills in fine dining were making no progress, still stuck at the level of a primitive villager.

Looking around at the cafeteria, its customers, and the settings in front of him, he thought suddenly, with no connection to anything preceding, "Nadiika is a great housewife. Borys couldn't be happier."

This was a terribly bitter thought for him, as if his now ancient acquaintance with this girl had left an undigested stone. It seemed a horrible crime to turn that blue-eyed Nadiika into a cook, cleaning woman, and defender of the domestic comforts of this young petty bourgeois. Does that lout Borys have any sensibilities, does he even know any pity? He'll just mangle everything he takes into those sinewy hands, be it a sugar beet or a woman. That's just the cruel personality of this priest's son.

After splashing around in his borsch with a spoon and leaving almost half the bowl, he had begun picking over some *varenyky* with meat when a person entered the cafeteria in a tattered coat and red hat, pushing something large and strange in front of himself. It was a harp, and its owner asked permission to entertain the honored company with his playing. Permission granted, he sat down in the corner on a chair and set the huge instrument between his legs. Amid the sounds of clatter and chatter, he struck the first chords on the thick, straight strings.

The harpist played a familiar aria from Kalman's *Silva*, and the dull sounds of his instrument, suitable only for accompaniment, gave the love song a sad depth and tenderness, expressing only a portion of the entreaty, leaving the rest hidden in the quiet trembling of the notes. But Stepan was looking at the performer. Where had he seen this elongated, cold but passionate face, these sharp black eyes that seemed ready to ignite with a fire hidden within? Maybe he had caught a glimpse of him on a street wearing this strange garb? Maybe this musician had traveled in the villages during the years of tumult, trading his music for bread? Or maybe he had never seen him before but this strong first impression had created an illusion of earlier familiarity.

Who was he? A Crimean Tatar? A Greek? An Armenian? What kind of fate had sent this strong, swarthy fellow on this sad journey and had hung a triangular weight on his shoulders, concealing his passion in the melancholy sound of the strings? And how could this beggar retain the pride that shone in his eyes, that calm indifference to the public, to which in a moment he would be stretching out his pleading hand? Stepan sensed that this vagabond had his own separate world, like Stepan's, his own human fate, his own suffering and hopes, like all the others here, whom he only sees but doesn't know or understand. And Stepan felt his excitement growing, like the excitement of someone who is about to travel from earth to another planet. He was excited by the sudden transformation of the people around him into mysterious beings. He was as excited as a child who discovers the hidden mechanism in a toy.

He realized that people are all different. He gained this understanding in the same way that any understanding of the known is gained, when that understanding penetrates your heart like a sharp blade, when it breaks out into the open like the music of a seed of grain from beneath the ancient husk of words. No, he did not comprehend—he perceived, as love can be perceived as pain by those who love, as despair, and desire can be perceived by those who are overwhelmed by them without clearly distinguishing between them. People are different! He had anticipated this, but now he knew. He had felt it, and now it had become real.

There was a new world within him, the world of a new idea that tickles the brain, sweeps out the corners, and rearranges the furniture so that it may find its own place there. He had, it seemed, found that magic sentence that would open the door for his talents, exhausted after long wandering outside the walls. And, like a researcher with an insight, intoxicated by his brilliant discovery and fearful for its veracity, needing to further test and strengthen his conclusions with wide-ranging observations, he went out into the loud wide streets, where there were people, masses of people, whom he could observe without impediment.

He went out onto Khreshchatyk as if into an alley in a large park, sprinkled with cold tufts of clouds, these large puffy birds from the blue heights who had flown yesterday above the slopes of chiseled cliffs topped with colorful hats. The sun, hovering in the sky as a cold disk, threw down an abundant shower of blue, red, and yellow sparks beneath feet, hoofs, and wheels, scattering on streets and rooftops a shiny dust of trembling frost, which, at this very moment was softly and lovingly setting eyes alight with spontaneous happiness, painting lips with the unconscious smile of a being that sees the sun. Everything looked blacker and whiter, contours became deeper and narrower in the airy glow, the clamor rose a few notes higher in welcome to the rays, and the cheerful crunch of packed snow beneath ceaseless footfalls became more audible. The street was teeming, people returning from work came out in rows, from doors with wide signs above them, blending into the crowd, into the brightness, which they pulled into themselves and returned to the air in puffs of opaque steam, the warm evidence of their living spirit. So many eyes! So much motion!

Stepan moved along among them with a passionate flutter, as if all eyes were focused on him and all motion was at his behest, as if he were reviewing this lean, energetic, song-filled parade of heroes, nonentities, and those in-between who were passing in front of him. And they felt so dear to him and among themselves, so simple and familiar. Yet soon they would go off each to their own home, their own love, their own thoughts, inclinations, cleverness, and stupidity. There, on their own turf, they hoe the rows of their past existence, grow the happy and forlorn flowers of their puny little lives. There, something waits for each of them that waits for no other, perhaps similar but expressed in different feelings, colored in different tints, poured into glasses of a different type, shape, and quality. For each of them, the world begins and ends, appears and disappears in the narrow slit between their eyelids. People are different! Crazily different, despite their outward similarity. And he could see them as a single being that has disintegrated into a diverse multiplicity, like a single face that is divided and altered in the shards of a mirror into thousands of faces, each of which has retained its riddle, the riddle of a human being.

The crowd stimulated him; it stimulated not only his vision and hearing, but also his nose, dilated to take in the scents; his fingertips trembled to touch this moving, rumbling crowd. He longed to feel it with all the senses, collectively and individually, to pour it in through every connecting channel into that enormous workshop where impressions are melted in the fires of blood and forged on the anvil of the heart. All the floodgates of his being were raised, and the frothing streams of the world poured into them, merging into a single turbulent flow along a narrow flume that turned the wheels of the creative mill. And this first shudder of the long-idle mechanism felt like pain, like a fearful anxiety, an unspeakable rapture that was overpowering him, pulling him to the side, carrying him out of its own element where it had arisen until, moving slowly, blinded and deafened, he was himself among the crowd, alone with his fire. Then he set off for home, carrying this fire carefully and anxiously, like the faithful carrying candles on Maundy Thursday.

When he entered his room, dark after the brightness on the street, moist after the dry chill outside, Stepan felt only fatigue. Everything within him had come to a halt, and the flame that had been burning within him but a moment earlier had suddenly died out, quietly and without a trace. Where had it gone? What had all this been for, this excitement and then its disappearance? He sat down without undressing, insulted and depressed by the sudden evaporation of his drive, immeasurably saddened at the loss of his confidence to write. Just a short while ago, he had been certain he would write; he did not know what and how he would write, but he felt within himself that flood, that churning of emotion ready to break out and overflow the narrow confines of the soul. And here it had dried out, like a trickle across the sand. It had burst like a colorful soap bubble. And, once again, as before, he was barren; once again, in his room, this coffin of his expectations; once again, by his table where he had watched the nights and mornings pass, a slave to his own quest. Would it always be so?

Was he condemned forever to this punishment, expiating his ill-considered notion, his mindless, unplanned notion to write a short story? Condemned to these flare-ups that would agitate and scorch his soul, casting him into endless sorrow, eliciting a ruinous loathing of himself, of life, of people? Because the creative drive in an individual is indomitable: once it has taken root, it takes over the whole person, makes the person an extension of itself, a meek servant carrying out its instructions. It ruins the purity of feelings by its intransigent demands, it turns life into a strange and permanent refuge, cheering the person with unimaginable dreams, oppressing him with unimaginable despair; it stings the heart, inflicts distress on the mind like a tumor on the tissues of the brain, envelops the person like a vine, and there is no desire more powerful, because all others seek something external to the self, but it alone seeks something within, because the fount of all other desires is transient, but only its source is bottomless, since it is the entire world!

Meanwhile, behind the back of the writer Stefan Radchenko, who was unable to write anything, there were developments preparing a pleasant surprise for him.

It was a matter concerning literary life, that endless turmoil which, in the context of the battle between literary organizations, leads to the accumulation of explosive material. Amid the daily quarrels and conflicts, occasionally—once or twice a year—real literary skirmishes erupt where the battle becomes explicit and public, a battle for privileges, for influence, for the first spots in the line to the printing press and publisher's pay office. There are internal literary competitions, creative rivalries, which give value to literature, and there are external competitions, which give value to the writers themselves but have about as much to do with literature as backstage intrigue does with an actor's performance. And, while creativity itself is a silent and sedentary thing, the battle for its consequences, on the other hand, is very boisterous and athletic, with the peculiar feature that it produces a whole cadre of combatants, whose connection to literature is limited to the mere fact that they take an active role in these gymnastic exercises.

The immediate cause of the conflict was very simple: there was an opening in a journal's editorial office and each of the groups had advanced its own candidate. A real parliamentary crisis developed, with meetings and dealings, telephone calls, coalitions created and then broken, demands put forward, attacks mounted, sieges endured, all in keeping with the finest examples of strategic thinking. This had lasted for a month and everyone had been bloodied, but no one was ready to retreat. Then, as the only solution in this irresolvable situation, an idea born from hopelessness was advanced: to reject all the candidates put forward and to issue an invitation to some Varangian who was not involved in any of the bloodletting. Somehow everyone immediately agreed on Stepan Radchenko, because they had tired of the continual warfare and, on the other hand, the new candidate had never given anyone any offense and behaved mildly, giving everyone the hope that they could easily influence him.

Thus, Stepan got to sit at a chair behind a desk marked, "Editor. Office hours: Tuesdays, Thursdays, and Saturdays, from 11:00 am to 1:00 pm."

Chapter Nine

Work, work, and more work!

During the month of literary skirmishes, chaos had, of course, descended on the editorial office. And so, Stepan rolled up his sleeves and got to work, attacking each matter in a full-scale assault, an approach he owed in part to his military service and in part to his innate character. The archive of manuscripts, for example, was completely disorganized. Correspondence was in a hopeless state. The library did not have a catalog and three-quarters of the books were missing. And a person only has two hands!

In the first days, he considered it a matter of sacred duty, of preeminent importance, to examine the manuscripts, some old, some resubmitted, since he himself had experienced the excitement, despair, and hope that were infused into these manuscripts—some of uneven quality, some even illiterate—by the distant young writers who yearned, as he did, for a ray of that literary light, who longed to display their own thoughts and feelings, which they considered most valuable, and to express their own understanding of the world above, below, and around them, which was, of course, the truest understanding. He meticulously read over the abundant notebooks and loose pages, written in the finest penmanship, sometimes adorned with naive sketches, sometimes with complete illustrations for possible use, and the cover letters that came with them. Their authors had spent perhaps weeks considering, searching for the most polite and modest words to express the pride and satisfaction that was overflowing their hearts. Somewhere out there, in far-off villages, towns, and cities, these countless authors waited, in distress or defiance, awaiting the appearance of their work, an answer, some comments. Sensitive to this waiting, Stepan turned the pages of their works for hours on end, filling his evenings with papers of various quality, from wrapping paper to the finest sheets, with inks of various kinds, and various styles of handwriting, always careful not to overlook anything that might turn out to be valuable in the pile, feeling an immeasurable sympathy for the failures and expressing in his heart a kind word of encouragement to all.

But, after a few days, he had come to understand how little talent there was out there, how hopeless a task it was to search for pearls in this ocean of paper. After a week, he was tired of it all, feeling irritation at the silly pretense of these hopeless writers with their silly stories and their even sillier poems. In the end, he became what everyone must become, what the jailkeeper becomes among the prisoners. That is, he laughed at the miserable wannabes and used their worst errors as comic anecdotes among his friends and acquaintances. Sometimes, the authors themselves would stop by, perplexed or stately, like an anxious accused waiting for the jury to reach a verdict, entering this land of milk and honey where fame and glory lie right on the surface, ready for the taking. And Stepan listened to them with a serious demeanor, answered them politely and pleasantly, but in his soul he was laughing at them, because they really were funny in their diffidence, devotion, and concealed disdain. Among those who came were unrecognized geniuses bitterly complaining of injustice, swindlers pretending to be extremely naive, and even an insane man who identified himself, with documentary evidence, as a well-known writer who had long since died.

In a week, Stepan had brought order to the manuscript archive and even arranged the library, working on it with a peculiar sensory satisfaction, because he loved this work, he loved books. Those for whom their first experience of the world and their fascination with it came from books will always see them as eternal, protean, and living benefactors. He wanted not only to read books but to feel them around him, and so he envied anyone who had a library and secretly hoped that some-how, somewhere, he would have one of his own con-sisting of thousands of volumes stacked floor to ceiling among which he could live. In general, despite all his passions, he never lost hope in a kind of quiet, simple life among his books and his friends, a hope he guarded and protected against the possibility of various failures, as if it were a psychic life preserver, not particularly comfort-able to swim in but nevertheless better than drowning.

The new editor was unfailingly and calmly polite with everyone, although they were always waiting for him, seeking him out for conversations, turning to him with requests, trying to find his soft spot. He was reli-able in his promises, true to his word, understanding perfectly what can and must be said to whom in the always heavy literary atmosphere, to which he tried to bring a breath of fresh air. He found himself buffeted by an enormous variety of mutually contradictory in-fluences, and, through their interaction, he developed his own ideas and views about literature. They were not even views, not a thorough system of literary rankings, but a living relationship to the written word, a thirst and respect for it, a skill in understanding it and in finding within it the golden seeds of nourishment.

His lover's assignations continued without change, twice a week as scheduled previously. But now, preoccu-pied with literary matters that cling to a writer like tar, at his meetings with Zoska, he could not stop himself from launching into descriptions of his conversations, meetings, and business, giving voice to his need to express that overflow of impressions that had accumulated in him over the last few days. In these stories, there was, aside from their inherent interest, a certain dose of bragging, a hidden impulse to highlight the role of his own person and thus to elicit amazement that it was no one else but he who was at the center of all this activity. He praised as if to suggest that he could praise, he criticized as if to emphasize that he had good judgement, and he conjectured as if to recall that he was capable of thinking wisely. This was innocent preening before the girl, an expression of his need to please his girlfriend also with his spiritual qualities, a need to take delight in himself on her account, to demonstrate to himself that he deserved her attention, and to demonstrate to her that, in choosing him, she had, after all, chosen well. And Zoska understood this, since, from time to time, interrupting him at the most interesting moments, her hand stroked his head and she exclaimed with a smile, "In a word, divine one, you're enthralled."

He laughed and assured her that he was enthralled only with her.

Aside from his work in the editorial office, he was also responsible for seeing the journal make it through the printing press. This colossal enterprise, which spit out hundreds of thousands of offprints a day, conjured entirely new though familiar feelings in him.

Upon entering the premises, he immediately loved the sharp pungent scent of ink and lead dust. Waiting for the proofs, he was fascinated by the wide rows of type cases where workers in blue shop coats, some talking and laughing, and others silently focused, snatched the elongated letters in their nimble fingers, snatched them quickly, seemingly carelessly, and arranged them into lines and then the lines into columns that would later be divided into the even rectangles of pages. Here, before his eyes, was the strange and simple process of the materialization of human thought. Having flashed into existence elsewhere, it came to rest in this expansive, bright hall under the incessant clatter of ventilation fans, in an infinite row of dumb signs, maintaining its insight and clarity. He could feel it being woven in the hands of the typesetters, how it poured forth from under the keys of the linotype machine, continually gaining strength, preparing to be reproduced on paper thousands upon thousands of times under the pressure of the press. Here, the thought achieved its innate goal—to spread out without limit, as gas spreads, but without thinning out, in its original clarity and density. It entered this place as a small manuscript, only to emerge in packages, wagons, boxcars of books, replicating, like a living cell, into an infinite series of clones.

But it was the print shop that he loved best—a long, curved corridor where the squat presses stood in single file stretching out a heavy jaw with each turn of the flywheel. Here, the odor of the fumes from the inking rollers was strong, and you could hear the faint rustle of the paper squeezed between metal, the rhythmic sighs of the rollers, and the whine of the motors in wooden frames. In the midst of this variety of endless noise that drowned out speech and footsteps beat the mighty heart of the city. Here, in the breast of the city, he could see the steel weave of the city's fabric, hear its voice, and apprehend its secret being. Enchantment and reverie overcame him and, listening to the disparate knocking, drawing together its component parts, he slowly internalized this shining motion, became one with it, entered into it, endowing it with lightness and energy. In that moment, there awoke in him an old recollection of the boundlessness of the steppe at night, of the deadened stillness of the plains beneath the vast and shifting heavens that he had observed with wonder and trembling as a solitary child. Now, as then, vague desires surged within him, like the splash of a small wave against the rustling sand.

He frequented the beer hall as often as before. One evening, the poet Vyhorskyi threw down on the table before him a copy of his new collection of poems, *Metropolis and Moon*. It was a book about the city, the city in darkness, the city asleep, the city that lives a magical life at night. On its pages, with almost no rhymes but with sharp, taut lines of verse, unfolded the interminable meetings of the government, the passionate dreams of the love-struck, the shadowy figures of thieves, the serenity of a scholar's study, the illuminated vestibules of theaters, lovers on the streets, the casino, twenty-four-hour factories, the train station, the telegraph office, streetlights, and policemen on the corner.

"I've read it already," said Stepan, "At the printer's. It's a wonderful book."

"What of it," grumbled the poet. "I don't feel that way anymore."

Later, he added, "There's too much sympathy in it."

The evening threatened to be rather silent because the poet was in a bad mood. But, suddenly, he said to Stepan, "My friend, you're getting on my nerves with your constant staring at that woman in the blue hat."

"But she's here almost every evening," answered Stepan nervously.

"And where should she be? And your staring says much more than you think."

"You're making that up."

"She's a whore," said the poet. "A *restaurant whore*, as opposed to a *street whore* who finds her clients in the great outdoors. It's very sad that you don't know how to distinguish them from honest women. Of course, I'm talking about distinguishing them practically, since a theoretical distinction can hardly be made objectively, without using such slippery and relativistic concepts as decency and honor. In any case, every good beer hall like this one has three or four dames working in collusion with the owner who clears all their competition from the premises, sometimes with considerable force. In the bowels of the premises, there are a couple of rooms where they practice, as Heine put it, their horizontal craft. The price per episode is from three to five karbovanets for a single pleasure, not including the cost of the meal, where the proprietor makes his money. Now do you understand the essence of this symbiosis? But, in this world, there is nothing bright without its shadow—in this case, the police. The proprietor risks a 500-karbovanets fine and the closing of the establishment. But there is a well-developed system of signals, and the girls disappear from their rooms through back doors in a truly fantastic manner. And here we go. Your friend has just gone behind the screen."

"Indeed, she has," said Stepan.

He drank some beer and lit a cigarette.

"She's cute," he added. "I'm sorry for her."

"I'm sorry for them, too," answered the poet. "But only because they lose their appeal too quickly. Even singers are luckier in that respect, and singing is honorable, besides. The street whores are not so refined, but they're less expensive and more numerous. They're unpretentious, so you can't expect very much of them. But they all categorically call themselves simply *women*, thus very aptly emphasizing the very essence of their profession."

"How do you know?" asked Stepan.

"I'm the one who should be wondering that you don't know!" answered the poet. "Leave it to the poets to expound on theoretical ideas and lyricism. A prose writer who doesn't know people isn't worth a fig."

"But you can't really know people," said Stepan.

"It only seems that way. Life is so simple that it seems in the end to be secretive. Relax. People, like numbers, are put together from a few basic figures—in various combinations, of course. People are not even pictogram puzzles; they are equations that can be solved with four arithmetical rules. What is the essence of a beer hall? People come here to take a break from their work, from politics, from their family, and from their problems—to live without care for a half hour or so, and to dream a little. The guy sitting across from us over there is an official of X rank who can only allow himself to come here and have a beer and a couple of salt pretzels once a fortnight. He thinks about if for half a month, and then he comes here and stretches his pleasure out for two hours, dreaming about heroic adventures, love, glory. He's happy. The fellows on the right are a bunch of NEP businessmen celebrating a good contract with a government ministry. From here, they'll go to Maxim's, which is open 'til 3 am. Over there is a young couple whispering about how their lives will not be like that of the old couple next to them, who have also come out to have a good time but are feeling uncomfortable about it."

"And who's that?" asked Stepan, his eyes indicating a figure sitting beside them, his head sorrowfully bent over and staring intently at an empty glass.

The poet looked carefully.

"That," he said, "is a white-collar worker who was fired in a cost-cutting reorganization."

"No," said Stepan. "That's probably a young writer with writer's block."

"Let's check!" the poet said dryly.

They moved over to the next table. "Don't worry, comrade," said the poet, as the stranger looked up at them in amazement. "It could happen to anyone."

"That's true—to anyone," he answered with a scowl.

"You'll write something yet," said Stepan.

"You'll find another job," said the poet.

"No, I have a business of my own," the stranger blurted out. "Over on Vasylkivska Street… Aw!"

And he lowered his head into his hands again.

"So, why are you so upset then?!" Stepan called out.

"How can you be happy when your stomach is churning! Damned liver paté! And they call that fresh?"

Outside, the poet said to Stepan, "Mistakes are always possible! What's strange is how a stomachache looks just like a spiritual ache."

His regular salary as an editor allowed Stepan to quit his job teaching Ukrainian language at various institutions, even though payments for that had increased. To tell the truth, he had long since grown tired of those courses. They had become nothing more than a source of income, without any discernible satisfaction. They had held his interest only as long as he was still learning something from them himself and had become intolerable as they became a bland repetition of abhorrent facts. Endlessly rehearsing iotated and sibilant sounds, sucking on nouns and digging up verbs and impersonal constructions—what a horribly boring task. So he left this linguistic cubbyhole with the same joy that he had once entered it.

His material circumstances stabilized and his time was occupied without those unpleasant gaps that force a person excessively to examine his own person and to arrive at negative conclusions. During the day, work and lovemaking, in the evening, the beer hall, theater, cinema, and books—read now not with youthful enthusiasm but with a sober seriousness. The period when books seemed more important than readers had passed for him, and he now turned the pages with a calm equanimity. He might be surprised by them, or moved, or even taught by them, but not belittled. His life had once again found balance, an unconscious satisfaction with himself, thanks to the constant demands of his work. This sense of equilibrium reduced the intensity of his worries about his creativity.

Somehow, always doing and thinking about something else, he would forget about writing. Once in a while, he would think of it, but vaguely, as if about the distant past or the future, though time and again he sensed within himself the indistinct presence of something extraneous, hidden, like the barely audible gurgle of a stream in the silence of a brightly lit forest. But, sometimes, quite unexpectedly, there would appear in his head an image, part of a phrase, a fragment of a description that hovered in his thoughts for a moment without beginning or end, filling him with a great, inexplicable joy. These were brief, almost contentless letters from the unknown. They were incomprehensible but gratifying messages from a distant, sunny land where he had abandoned forevermore a part of himself, only to long to be reunited with it. He painstakingly gathered these precious crumbs, reflected on them, sometimes even wrote them down on pieces of paper, and entered them into his memory, a store of provisions without a specific purpose. Enough, enough of this childish futility and despair. He had, in the end, done everything he could to chase creativity—let it now chase him, let it try hard to please him, to entice him to allow his attention to be turned back to it.

In this mood of peace and comfort, he finally received word about his film script. One thousand five hundred karbovanets in honorarium! One hundred fifty of those white chervinets notes with their magical power to be transformed into desired objects. He was richer than Croesus or Rockefeller ever were, because he felt that, from this day forward, his material problem was solved, that he had managed to secure his life on a solid economic base. The only questions that remained concerned the superstructure.

That evening, he bragged to Vyhorskyi about the fortunate and comfortable beginning of his career in cinema.

The poet frowned.

"Just don't confuse cinema with art," he said.

"On the contrary, only two art forms have grown into industries: cinema and literature."

"Arts need to be valued not for the size of the industries necessary for their development, but by the degree of abstractness of the medium they employ. This is the only way to establish an objective ranking of their value. Beyond any doubt, first place belongs to an art that does not exist, although there have been efforts to create it—the art of smell. Its medium is so refined and sophisticated that the organ of its perception in humans is incapable of making fine distinctions. That's also why our language doesn't have independent terms for the basic categories of smell, as we do, for example, for colors. The ultraviolet band of the arts—the art of sounds, music—is the highest of the arts that actually exist. In third place is the art of words, because its medium is far more definite than sounds and requires only average sensitivity for artistic perception, but it is nevertheless refined and subject to profound modeling. The crude arts begin with painting, which is locked in a single dimension and cannot be distributed for widespread dissemination, as were the two previous arts. Its medium, paint, is very concrete and limited, since light is a precondition of its effectiveness. Darkness is inaccessible to it, and so, too, is change. So, you understand how successively more concrete media begins to limit an art form? This is most evident in sculpture, which can only reproduce something in three dimensions. But the crudest form of art is the art of action, theater, which combines the concrete elements of all the preceding arts.

"And that's good," said Stepan.

"And last," continued the poet, deeming it unnecessary to answer, "the infrared band of arts: the art of living, an art form that is exclusively concrete, but just as undefined as the art of smell. To experience it, one only needs to know how to eat. So, here I have given you a logical ordering of the arts according to a definite principle. There's no room for cinema here. That's just a gimmick, not an art—a magic lantern plus the work of actors, not the other way around. It's entertainment, which is why all films have a happy ending. But, if you've made some money on it, then you're buying me dinner today."

"It will be my pleasure!" said Stepan.

And they held a little banquet at the beer hall with a bottle of white wine.

"I envy you, though," said the poet. "The difference between a person and a plant is said to lie in the fact that a person is capable of moving around. But is a person allowed to take advantage of this quality? Are we not chained to our cities, our villages, our employment? Are we to be content with dreams? I can't be! Life is tolerable only so long as you can change its location. If you can't go somewhere tomorrow, you're a slave. For that, one needs money, and you have it."

"But I have no wish to go anywhere."

"That's why I'm jealous of your money," said the poet. "But don't worry, I won't ask for a loan. This spring, I'll come into 500 karbovanets. And I'll leave. This summer, I will wander on foot across Ukraine, like the famous Ukrainophile Skovoroda. I hate the city in the spring. Why? Because we have not quite escaped nature. When she awakens, she calls us like an abandoned mother. It's a blessing to live beside her, but she's much too distant to spend too much time with her. For us, nature is recollection and relaxation."

"You mean the forests and the fields?" asked Stepan thoughtfully.

"The forests and the fields. We have to remember them at least once a year. Life is a miserable thing, we are justified in our complaints about it, but, in choosing between life and death, there isn't any choice. I raise a toast to Grandma Nature: although the present she gave us was meager, it was the only one at her disposal."

Chapter Ten

The first order of business for Stepan Radchenko after he had become very wealthy was to change his room. He couldn't wait to send his tattered apartment off to the archives, feeling a dull enmity toward it for all that he had endured there, because a person's room knows their most intimate desires, spies on their vacillations, absorbs their thoughts and becomes, over and over again, the evil and odious witness of the past, always somewhat paralyzing their willpower and undermining their wishes with its eternal and annoying "I know you."

So he engaged a broker and explained his wishes to him: a spacious, bright, and private room in a large building somewhere in the central district. Steam heating, unfurnished, and he was willing to pay a release fee. The tenant will be quiet, single, and neat.

The broker heard him out and said, "In a word, you want a *real* room."

Gradually, his circle of acquaintances was expanding. From his colleagues at work, his handshakes now extended to their families and friends and even further, into the depths of the city, to representatives of the most diverse characters, professions, and ideas. He was tipping his hat ever more frequently on the street, in response to greetings from young scholars, party members, union activists, and just ordinary people of both sexes, undistinguished workers at various institutions where they were paid. In the theaters, in the smoking rooms, he could freely join a group where the play, the actors, and impressions were being discussed. He could stop by some place for a cup of tea, he could spend a half-hour walking around and chatting with someone on the street about important and trivial things; he attended events where new works were read and criticized over a glass of wine, as well as events where people goofed off and told love stories. So, he could certainly find the relaxation that all souls, fatigued by their daily obligations, find in meaningless diversions.

He felt free and at ease in social circles, taking pleasure in the thin threads that he had woven among people, like an industrious spider. He felt an insatiable curiosity about everything, an unquenchable thirst to know and understand every new person he met, trying to understand them completely, asking inconspicuous questions about them, about their circumstances, their views, their work. He observed their wishes and pleasures, he longed to enter that secret museum that every person makes of themselves, a museum of used-up ideas and buried feelings, a museum of memories, of anxieties experienced and hopes dashed, to enter into that archive of a person where endless drawers hide operational plans and the ledgers of the past. He was attentive to those little things through which a person appears more clearly than when speaking on stage, attentive even to gossip and rumors, and he was so persistent in his curiosity that, if someone was not home when he came to visit, he would ask to leave a note and then take the opportunity to rifle through the person's desk, examining their notebooks and letters as if overcome with an unconquerable intrusiveness, a kleptomania for the tokens of someone else's existence. Like a true maniac, he knew how to hide his prying beneath an unflappable composure and politeness. Like an accomplished thief, he carried with him everywhere an assortment of sophisticated picks and hooks which he used to perform, undetected, the most complex operations on his acquaintances. He had dozens of acquaintances but no friends, he walked side by side but felt an immeasurable distance from everyone, because there was always glass between them, the magnifying glass of a researcher. And often, returning from a well-attended function, he felt lonely, empty of all thoughts, and tired.

His official duties were supplemented by work in the cultural section of the union's local committee, to which he had been elected. As usual, he took on all the work himself, injected new life and spirit into it, fulfilling his own appetite for community work, his need to work on behalf of people and to stir them into action, for that other, malicious attitude toward them could not absorb all his energy or exhaust the breadth of his interests. He was a responsible citizen, as decisive in public matters as he was tentative in personal ones, as dedicated in the former as he was self-serving in the latter, because these were different affairs that he handled in different manners, although with identical fervor. First as a rebel, then in the village hall, in the KUBUCh, and now the union's local committee, everywhere he found—because he had to find it—a niche where he could satisfy his innate inclination to civic activity. Meetings of the cultural commission, meetings of the local committee, workshops, roundtables, conferences, appearances, fundraising events, reports, development plans, accounts, and estimates—all of these whizzed through his hands like the colorful balls of a juggler. You could rely on him, and you could pile on more. He could pull a full load like a racehorse, and the more pressure he felt, the more efficiently he allocated his time.

The greatest difficulty in this atmosphere of relentless activity was to block off a few hours each week for his assignation with Zoska. They were harder and harder to fit into his schedule, since the busiest time was always before lunch. Before their meetings, he fretted, almost grudgingly, that tomorrow he would have to drop various business, put off some smaller matters, run across to the other side of the city, and then come back to pick them up again, necessarily somewhat tired, and then go for a late dinner, throwing off his accustomed schedule all the way into the evening. But he could find little time to devote to the girl in the evenings either, since he could never quite be certain if he would be free the next evening, and he would, for the most part, go to the theater with his colleagues, rarely having the opportunity to invite his girlfriend to join them.

For him, the room where they met became a small waystation, where he could get off the express train, with his suitcase and his watch in hand, listening for the whistle of the next train. He kissed her hastily—indeed, he did everything hastily, adding a certain sense of anxiety to their assignations, which destroyed the earlier serenity of their romantic dream. The moments of quiet enchantment when they sat close, happily leaning toward each other, had passed; the passion of caressing hands, always searching and finding something new, had faded; impassioned whispering about love had melted; and words no longer combined in stimulating sequences but sputtered into familiar platitudes. On the eve of spring, leaves were withering on the tree of knowledge in their Eden and slowly falling day after day, leaving the branches bleak and bare.

The girl sensed this painfully and apprehensively. He had completely brushed her aside. What could you do? He had business to attend to! But wasn't she worth attending to as well? Then he would talk about the priority of public matters over private ones, emphatically lecturing her about a boring moral code he hardly believed in himself. But he assured her that, when spring came, he would have fewer obligations, he would have more free time, and then they would be able to abandon this room and move outdoors into nature where they would not be constrained by the time of day. They'll move their assignations to the evening, because they always seemed unnatural for him in the daytime, for reasons that are well understood, and every man, unfortunately, feels this much more acutely than women do. What's more, he would have some vacation time in the summer and, if she wished, they could go somewhere together. Surely, they would go! He spoke so convincingly, the sound of his voice was so comforting that she unwittingly followed him on this imaginary journey where there would be only the two of them again, without any cares or obligations, happy and enchanted. Where would they go? He was adamant about water. Either the Dnipro beyond the rapids, or the sea between Odesa and Batumi. Maybe they could wander in the mountains some, too. He would buy a camera. But now, he had to go.

"Stay! Just five more minutes," she said.

He grumbled, but he stayed. She sat in her chair with her legs tucked in beneath her, silent and thoughtful, feeling a weariness that displaced her laughter, joking, and coquettishness. After a moment, she sullenly whispered, "Go, already."

It was an awkward parting.

One day, Zoska mentioned that, to celebrate the coming spring, one of her girlfriends was organizing a potluck party. But the problem was, this would necessarily involve dancing. Just a foxtrot would be enough, but she wasn't sure the divine one could learn to dance in so short a time. He would have declined the invitation, no doubt, but since the matter concerned his physical prowess, he answered, "Nothing to it! Show me."

First, he needed to learn the waltz, the foundation of all other dances. Lifting her skirt, she showed him the necessary steps.

"One, two, three! One, two, three."

He stood with his hands in his pockets, carefully observing her steps.

"One more time," he said.

Then he tried on his own. He took off his jacket and forced his unwilling legs to move with his arms outstretched. Zoska stood beside him, quietly clapping her hands, so as not to arouse too much interest from the neighbors.

"Yes, yes," she repeated. "That's wonderful."

With the movements now familiar, he asked that they practice together.

"You must embrace the woman," she said.

"That I know how to do," he answered.

Time passed unnoticed. Zoska predicted he would have a great future as a dancer.

"You're very nimble in your dancing," she said.

"I'm very nimble in everything I do."

"So our lessons will continue?"

"Yes, but now we've switched roles."

The next time, they danced the waltz again, quietly humming a melody. He was more confident in his movements and was better able to keep the beat.

"I'm tired already," said Zoska.

"More, more!" he said. "We have to work on this. There isn't much time."

In the end, he admitted that he had been practicing at home with a chair.

After the waltz, the foxtrot seemed very easy. He was even somewhat disappointed in its simplicity.

"You just walk around like this?" he asked.

Zoska explained that the opportunities for variations were endless, that you could add acrobatic elements or your own inventions. But holding the woman is far more serious here than it is in the waltz, so this cheered him up. He immediately imagined that this would lead to squeezing quite a few women, tall and full-breasted women, stepping between their legs and feeling their breasts and tight abdomen through clothing. So he doubled his practice time.

The business of finding a new apartment was progressing very poorly and occupied a great deal of his time. He couldn't find a suitable room. When Stepan visited his broker, expressing his disappointment, yelling and cursing, and repeating his conditions regarding the room, he always heard the same obsequious response. "In a word, you want a *real* room."

Stepan would get ten new addresses, but the same thing would happen without variation: some of the rooms had already been rented even as long as a half a year ago, some would be free at an unknown time in the future, some were not for rent at all, and the two or three that were actually for rent were real hellholes, the tattered homes of bedbugs. He viewed with revulsion the dirt that a person leaves behind after moving, the piles of trash and the slimy wallpaper thrown aside like manure. He was repulsed by the air in the empty spaces that reeked of sweat and the smells of life, and he would emerge from these visits with forlorn thoughts about the depravity and animal-like character of people, among whom the finest are clean only because they wash and change their underwear.

In the end, he told his broker that he had no intention of climbing all over buildings for nothing, and the agent agreed to come over personally to inform him when an appropriate room was available. He took three karbovanets for this.

But Stepan had long since said goodbye to his own room and he entered it in the evenings as if it were a hotel. To all his doubts about the creative process, he found a simple, formulaic answer: as soon as he found a new apartment, he would begin writing. Indeed, he had gotten into the habit of tying various expectations to his new room. Thus, although his housing crisis did trouble him somewhat, it did not disturb the equanimity of his spirit.

Be that as it may, trouble was stalking him from a different direction. On the distant horizon of his young spring sky, which was growing deeper and bluer under the influence of the enthusiastic rays of the sun, dark clouds had appeared, still barely visible, still transparent, but sad, like the first teardrops from the icicles hanging off the roofs of tall buildings.

Actually, spring was just getting sketched out, but it was certainly imminent. The snow wasn't melting as yet, but it had turned gray, lost its luster, and shrunk into heaps piled along the edges of the streets, while, on the cobblestones, continuous traffic had chopped it into a dark, reddish mush and the constant hammering of horses' hooves had pounded it into a series of uneven potholes. On the sidewalks, during bright days, it turned into a thin jelly but, during the cold nights, it hardened into inconvenient lumps. Everywhere, it was being cleared off roofs in giant snowballs, which hit the ground with a dull thump, like a soulless body. On the street corners, girls in fur coats were selling bunches of snowdrops that had sprouted on nearby hills where the ground had already thawed. Five kopecks a bunch. Five kopecks!

There were sunny mornings, mornings with a warm wind that carried the scent of moist soil and last year's herbs from distant fields, the seductive aroma of rye shoots and bursting apple blossoms. There were quiet, dreamy days when, in response to nature's rebirth, a powerful, simple joy of life awakens in the blood, when the soul succumbs to that mindless desire that led our ancestors to the altars of the god of spring. On days like these, Stepan liked to wander and observe.

With his heavy portfolio under his arm, he meandered the streets in the afternoon without any evident destination, avoiding greetings and feeling a need to be alone among strangers after tedious meetings at work or in civic organizations. For a while, he did not himself understand this sudden urge to go out on the street and that sense of comfort and satisfaction that enveloped him amidst the bustle and laughter of the spring crowds. He thought he was just passing the time, the way everyone else passes the time on a sunny day, for rest and relaxation.

But once, returning home late, nervous and excited, he had to admit to himself that he was wandering in order to look at women. He now understood that his gaze rested only on them, on their smiling faces, on their seductive legs, and on the warm clothing that hid their bodies, which he could almost feel; it was only at them that he looked with ardent desire, as if each one had her own, unique secret, her own garden of passions and delights that she tended for his benefit. From each of them flowed a voluptuous cloud of her female essence that intoxicated and energized him. His soul wilted in a steamy fog when he saw a shapely and good-looking woman, capable of love and worthy of love, and he would fall in love with her immediately for a moment, overcome with gratitude that she exists, that he sees her, that he can caress her with his passionate gaze. Some of them turned and looked, greeting him with a barely visible, provocative smile. This made his heart jump and sing. But now, having understood this, he did not feel shame, but rather fear and happiness at the realization of the wild force burning within him, a fraction of the powerful craving that moves the world. A new, bright feeling awoke within him—not lust, not desire, but a reflection of them: the certainty that he was capable of desire and that he would desire.

He approached the window and opened it, tearing the paper pasted over it. With the cold air that entered the room came the bustle of the inexhaustible street and, along with it, the jingle of *their* voices, the rustle of *their* footsteps and skirts, the motion of *their* bodies and lips. He stretched out his hands. What was it with him? Was it spring? Where did this intoxicating premonition of an intimate, unexpected encounter come from? He fell on the bed and curled up from the cold air that continued to flow into the room, abandoning himself to that ardent dream that appeared before his open eyes in a numberless swarm of apparitions. The apparitions filled his room, appearing and disappearing with the unfettered flight of his imagination. He wandered in hot foreign lands, rambling across fragrant fields and through thick leafy forests, he climbed a mountain from where he could see the endless horizon of the earth, and everywhere, from various hiding places, slender hands stretched out to him, enchanting faces bent down toward him, and he felt their touch as if these were really kisses. He was dreaming. And suddenly, in this strange journey across the bright land of lovemaking, a small pale figure stepped out toward him. She was bent over and sorrowful, like a roadside beggar. Zoska. He stopped in surprise, and the bright illusion he was experiencing faded in proportion to the growing clarity of this figure, until he was alone with her, face to face in an empty room, confounded by the sudden interruption. Zoska! A terrible sorrow crushed him at the recollection of the girl who was used up as far as his feelings were concerned, who was no longer on the path that his soul was following. Her image called forth a worry, not an impulse, a discomfort over the preposterous order of life that required penance for past happiness, a protest against the stickiness of feelings and people that have to be peeled off of oneself, like a bandage.

He got up and closed the window. It was only nine o'clock—he could still catch Vyhorskyi in the beer hall.

As usual, a crowd of people was there, which calmed him. Smiling, he approached the table where the poet was sitting.

"Too bad you're a little late," said the latter. "You just missed a little scandal. They had to escort a drunk out the door, but he slipped out of their hands and managed to smash two platters of fish over by the counter. It was a great scene. Unfortunately, they didn't let him continue."

"Shall we have dinner?" asked Stepan.

"As long as you're buying," said the poet.

They ordered chicken fritters, and the poet filled their glasses.

"Do you know the relation between alcohol and the astral world?" he asked. "It's an inverse relationship. Theosophists tell us that mankind will progress from its current intellectual phase into a spiritual phase. The nervous system will get refined into a truly psychic one, but for that to happen you must abstain from meat and alcohol. The center of the highest spiritual activity resides in the pituitary gland of the brain, which cannot tolerate alcohol. The pituitary gland is the focal point of all theosophy."

His hand stroked his shaved head.

"What about the astral world?"

"It will be accessible to the race of beings that develops this gland. But I think we're not missing much in this astral world by drinking beer, because human beings have had trouble wherever they appeared."

"I don't believe in old ladies' fantasies," said Stepan. "But I'm anxious today. Spring, maybe?"

"Remember that every spring ends with frost," said Vyhorskyi. "Better not to bloom, to avoid withering."

"Well, excuse me," said Stepan. "It's better to die than to think like that."

"I have no wish to die," answered the poet. "To wish for what must come anyway is sheer lunacy."

Suddenly, he cheered up.

"My friend, I haven't yet told you my latest good news. Happiness on earth is possible!"

"You don't say!"

"Yes! I thought about happiness for twenty-eight years, and I came to the conclusion that it did not exist. But, in my twenty-ninth year, I have changed my mind. By the way, did you notice when I turned twenty-eight? It was the day before yesterday. Time is such a cheat—always working conscientiously."

"But it brought you happiness!" said Stepan.

"It would have been better if it had not come," sighed the poet. "I'm not afraid of old age, or of death, but everything that is unavoidable is annoying."

He planted his chin into his palms and silently stared for a moment at the room full of people in front of him, throbbing with voices and motion. His overgrown, unshaven face looked completely exhausted. Then his fingers began to move, scratching his rough cheek.

"Happiness?" he said directly. "Even happiness doesn't satisfy me. The problem is that I was happy and didn't notice it."

He filled their glasses with his peculiar sharp motion.

"The problem is that happiness has nothing to do with satisfaction. If it were otherwise, we could never understand people. Victories in the realm of our emotions or our reason are too fleeting to bring happiness, which is a permanent sense of joy at a higher, that is, an abstract order. Happiness is a higher quality of spiritual life, as health is of physical life. Happiness is spiritual health. Particular pains and wounds cannot undo it. What is happiness? It is the aesthetic delight we have from ourselves, our own 'self.' The aesthetic function derives from the perception of harmony, or of greatness. The harmony of the 'self,' that is, this equilibrium within a person, is static, a stoppage at a given spiritual state. In our case, the aesthetics of harmony are a happiness of non-yearning, a happiness of acquiescence with life, a submission to it—that is, the happiness of a slave. It exists, it is happiness, but a miserable quality of it. Do you understand?"

"I understand, but not so fast, if you please. You've been inventing this for twenty-eight years, but I have to comprehend it in ten minutes, don't forget."

The poet smiled.

"You weren't so witty when we first met. Now, I'll continue. The aesthetics of greatness are the elevation of one spiritual element above all others, its dominance over the others, its active struggle against them, and thus action, yearning. The happiness of greatness is dynamic while the happiness of harmony is, in the final analysis, nothing but a pleasant dream. And now, the most important thing: the happiness of greatness can develop from the elevation of either feeling or reason.

The former is evident in the example of any religion you may choose. The latter—happiness from the consciousness that the soul is ordered on the principle of reason and is subservient to it—this is the highest form of happiness, at least for now, and maybe for all time, if the prophecies of the theosophists do not come true. I don't believe in them either, but we know so little that, in the future, all kinds of nonsense may come true. I can't even be sure that I won't end up in paradise."

"Not to mention hell?"

"I'm willing, if they have beer there and the devils are as friendly as you are. Therefore, we must put reason as the first principle of life. It is good. It accepts everything, and it is forgiving. It knows how to rely on causes, while feelings destroy them. The happiness of the greatness of feelings is the happiness of negation, while the happiness of reason is affirmation. Feelings are irritation, reason is tolerance; feelings are enthusiasm, reason is sharpness; feelings ultimately leave only ashes, reason only wounds. That is the full picture of happiness. Which do you choose?"

"The happiness of feelings, even though it is limited."

"Everyone chooses what they can. As for the limitations, don't forget that our entire lives are limited by a particular time, place, and conditions which are, under the best of circumstances, hardly dependent on us. Personally, I assume it's even worse. When someone talks to me about the independence of nations, or of women,

I want to answer, 'My friends, there is only one independence—the independence of our lives from us.' So there is no reason to fear limitations, because the inclination to the unlimited always leads to emptiness."

"It's midnight already."

This was spoken by the barman with a pleasant smile. Of course, this was an hour when even some children weren't in bed, but he, as an honest citizen, took it as a personal obligation to adhere to the prescriptions of the law, particularly since the fines were enormous.

He made a bow at the door.

"It was a little noisy today, please excuse us."

He was alluding to the scandal with the plates.

"Use aluminum tableware," advised the poet. "It doesn't break, and the metal itself is very fashionable right now."

Then he turned to Stepan. "You want to walk around? It's a beautiful Ukrainian night."

Stepan hesitated. "I'm pretty tired," he said.

"I promise to be silent."

They walked together to the Opera, where the performance had already ended and the unsuccessful coachmen were slowly dispersing down Lenin Street. On reaching Shevchenko Boulevard, the friends turned back. The poet indeed kept silent, pulling down his hat and sticking his hands into his coat pockets, while Stepan, intoxicated by the cold glow of the moon, took off his galoshes and slid on the frozen sidewalks.

On the way to his next assignation with Zoska, Stepan was nervous, even somewhat fearful. What words would he need to find to express that heavy, complex feeling of regret and parting that gnawed at him? The stereotype of love suggested that breaking up required a sufficient reason: jealousy, infidelity, at least an argument, or the gradual cooling of feelings over a long period of time. And would he have the courage? Would she understand?

Zoska was already waiting for him. Having kicked off her shoes, she was sitting on the chair in a puffy blue jacket. She smiled at him as he walked in.

"I've missed you so much!" she said.

Hesitantly, Stepan stopped by the door and looked at her with restless eyes.

"I missed you, too," he answered.

There was so much longing in these words that even to him they sounded surprisingly sincere.

"Come here," she whispered.

He threw his coat and hat on a chair and approached her with the timid walk of a criminal.

She sat him down beside her on the rug and lifted his head up with her hands.

"Shall I kiss you?"

"Kiss me!"

"Do you want that?"

"I want it," he whispered in desperation.

She barely touched his lips with hers, and then, shuddering, fell on him with such a long and passionate kiss that he began to gasp for air.

"That's how much I love you," she said.

He sat in silent mortification, stroking and kissing her hands.

"These two days when we didn't see each other seemed so long, like two endless years," she said. "I don't know what's happened to me. I even wanted to come visit you at the office."

"Springtime," he mumbled.

"Yes, of course—springtime. How could I have forgotten."

And she began to sing quietly, rocking a leg back and forth:

As I walked out one morning,

In the springtime of the year.

Stepan watched her, taking delight in her petite figure, enchanted by the happiness that rang out in her voice. He wanted to take her by the hand and lead her through fields of flowers and have her sing like this, sing for him, for the sun, for the beautiful horizon dotted with white puffs of cloud.

He squeezed her hand and said, "Zoska, shall we go out in the fields when the snow melts?"

"Yes, we'll go, and I'll plait a wreath."

He could not hold himself back. In a sweet burst of repentance, in a flood of memories of all their times together, he embraced her and began to kiss her slowly, madly, on the eyes, hair, lips, choking on the happiness of contrition, as he had never kissed before.

"Zoska... you're... I can't live without you, I can't," he whispered.

When he calmed down, she stroked his head.

"You're divine."

But these kisses were not enough for him. Something inexhaustible and inspired still remained in his soul. He wanted to do something unique just for her, he wanted her always to be happy when she was with him, as she was now. He wanted to bind her to himself forevermore.

"Zoska, I've been thinking about something for a long time," he said enthusiastically.

"About what?"

"Let's get married!"

She gasped.

"You're insane!"

No, he was not at all insane. With inventiveness at the speed of lightning, as if he had really been thinking of this for a long time, he seriously began to expound his arguments. First of all, they were already married in all but name. They weren't thinking of breaking up, were they? Good! Well then, it's time to draw inferences. He's living like a beggar, with no peace or comfort. His life is in such chaos he can't even write. And you can't go on relying on someone else's apartment forever. They know each other quite well already. Why steal hours here and there to be together, when they could be together all the time? Her life will also be better—if she actually loves him, of course. Everyone else gets married. It's somehow strange they haven't done it yet. The financial side is completely secure. He'll even help her find a job, if it comes to that.

He calmly weighed all the arguments "for" and couldn't find any "against." Then he asked, "So tell me Zoska, do you want to?"

She answered slyly, "Of course, I want to." And then she added sorrowfully, "If you only knew how difficult it is to be a mistress. How much I've suffered."

He kissed her in gratitude.

"This will be the end of your suffering. But what about your parents?"

"Why would I ask their permission? I'll just get married, and that's that."

Now, she sat down on the rug next to him, and they began an exuberant exploration of their future life together. They would visit the marriage bureau when the room Stepan was searching for became available. But maybe they should be looking for two rooms? They considered this for a moment and decided that a two-room place was harder to find and more complicated to furnish. Maybe over time. Stepan expounded ambitious plans for work and leisure. Zoska immediately developed a woman's instinct for putting things in order. Instantly, she could see herself as a housewife with unchallenged authority in the home. Two rugs, or you can forget about marriage! Breakfast will be eggs, of course.

"That's very nutritious, and tasty, too," she said.

He hugged her and whispered in her ear, "And we'll have a little one."

"A little what?"

"A baby—a little boy."

"Oh, a little boy. That's very nice!"

Finally, Stepan remembered to look at his watch. Five to four. What a cheat time is!

When they were dressed, the girl remembered and added, "Tomorrow is that party. Shall we go?"

He politely kissed her hand.

"Why not and, if you like, we'll announce our engagement there."

"Oh, that will be something!"

Zoska took six karbovanets from him for their contribution to the party, his and hers, gave him the address, and told him to show up at ten. She had to go earlier, to help set things up.

But he did not want to part from her until tomorrow.

"Shall we go to the theater tonight?"

"Only if we come home in a carriage!"

Chapter Eleven

The next morning, Stepan woke up in good time, but even before he had gotten out of bed, he felt a gnawing in his heart. As if everything he saw around him was very ugly. He lay in bed with his eyes open in that half-diseased state when you don't want to move or think, when blood barely flows in your veins, as if the body were still sleeping, though the mind is awake. Then, suddenly, he jumped up, realizing what a stupid thing he had done yesterday.

He tried to force himself to reimagine yesterday's events calmly, to understand the confusion that had led him into a trap, but one thought kept ruining his recollections, piercing the surface of every reflection he tried to develop. He was getting married! But he wasn't just getting married: he had to get married, because he had asked for it himself—like a complete idiot he had made this senseless request, which, when fulfilled, will imprison him in chains. All the horrors of married life immediately appeared before him, searing his heart with revulsion, like a vision of a jail cell or a coffin into which he had volunteered to lie down with his hands bound.

He felt the unshakeable presence of what is usually called "someone close," with whom he would have to share his thoughts, his joys, and his sorrows, diluting them between two hearts. Someone who would put his thoughts and plans under invisible and tender control, who would become the permanent partner of all his hopes and actions, a required addendum, chosen once but forged together forever. Someone who would always be in the same room with him, who would always eat with him at the same table, who would breathe the same air. And it would always be she, everywhere it would be she; at night, he would hear her breathing; in the morning, he would see her face; during the day, she would be the one waiting for him; in the evening, she would be waiting at the door. He imagined the lazy sleep of a couple in bed, the gradual familiarization of passionate encounters, which become regular and monotonous in the end, like tea or dinner; the intimacy with a different soul that no longer holds any secrets, the permanent availability of a body, which destroys the fire of desire; the boredom of inevitable quarrels that uncover the depth of incompatibility between two beings, and the even greater boredom of making up afterwards—evidence of powerless obedience to fate.

Thus rose the curtain on the reality of marital life, this bottomless pit into which fall those who are blinded by a fading love that has played out, and he struggled, like a little insect caught in the web of a giant spider, fluttering the transparent wings of its soul to tear itself free of the deadly threads. But this is foolish, to ruin oneself for nothing! A deep sorrow, an inexhaustible self-pity enveloped him. He wanted to hug and comfort himself, calm himself with the kindest of words, as a credulous victim of human relationships.

On the other side of the wall, his neighbors were also getting up; the door to the kitchen creaked, the stove whistled, women's raised voices rang out along with the cries of children. He listened to this and clearly felt the danger at close quarters, just beyond the door of his room, with its menacing hand on his doorknob, ready to enter. "That's how my child will cry. That's how my wife will yell. And there's my booming voice grumbling about something or other." And how is he going to be able to write in wild circumstances like these? And the voice of his soul answered without hesitation: "No, you won't—certainly not! My boy, you won't be able to write a damned thing—it's the end of all your hopes and dreams. And it's a shame, because, say what you will, you do have talent." So now he must say farewell to his dear inner world, like a monk's parting from the bright world outside before entering the darkness of a monastery.

And would his creativity be the only sacrifice on this monstrous altar of matrimony? Isn't he offering a futures contract at wholesale prices for all his lifelong kisses? Isn't he buying love on a promissory note without terminal conditions—a note that obliges him to pay an outrageous rate of interest in self-restraint. There are countless women he hasn't known, countless charming faces and sculpted bodies—to pass over them is to experience a loss. And, from the depths of his memory, there suddenly appeared lithe figures seen somewhere, glimpsed at some point vaguely on the street, figures who captivate the eyes for a moment and imprint themselves in memories like quiet invitations to the future. In the imagination, they combine into dreams containing singular bits and pieces, gathered by the senses and assembled into a single image that appears before the mind as a creation from another world. Longing tortured him—until now he had loved only random women, women whom he met accidentally on his urban journey. But he had never searched for a woman. At that moment, he thought that perhaps somewhere there waits for him a woman who is identical to the one in his dreams: slim, charming, and beautiful, who would kiss him in the dark on a spring night in the park, who would walk with him arm in arm along the slumbering streets, raising her radiant eyes beneath the streetlights. And now he would be cutting off the paths leading to her!

Stepan got up and sat on the bed, his hair disheveled from sleeping, his shirt unbuttoned, his bare legs hanging down to the floor. He took a cigarette from the chair by the bed and smoked gluttonously, inhaling its smoke continuously until he had burned it down to the end. Then he lit another and began thinking again.

How could it have happened? He could no longer find the thoughts that he had expressed so eloquently yesterday. But they were, of course, only a reaction. The essence of the matter was that he had felt sorry for Zoska, the sorrow and pity of parting, and he had carelessly gotten carried away with these feelings. Now, he had to pay, not for a sinful act, but for his own goodness. And he was overcome with the angry wish to force himself to marry, to teach himself a lesson forevermore. Next time, he would know better—to feel sorry for someone is to punish oneself!

And how could *she* have been so treacherous as to take advantage of his noble impulse? Didn't she have enough judgment to turn down the offer? To see that such offers are only made in desperation? How could there be any respect for her now? An absence of the most ordinary sensitivity—that would be the most charitable way to put it. And, in the worst case—a craftily calculated game, a woman's masterful hunt for a husband. And what's more, she has no job. She is probably unfit for any kind of work. She's bored, and doesn't have the money for clothes—so why not get married? Particularly when you find a nice young man, an honest fellow who doesn't have too much experience in life and with women's trickery!

Indignant, he got up and walked barefoot to the table where his pants lay. What a cheat that Zoska is! But he wasn't going to be duped quite so easily!

Remembering his obligations at the office, he began to dress quickly. A personal tragedy did not give him the right to ignore his duties, and he immediately abandoned his unfinished thoughts without reaching any conclusions. Only while washing up, the thought occurred to him that maybe she really did love him and would be distressed to hear all the things he was planning to tell her. But, noticing again the signs of pity within himself, he angrily splashed water into his own face. What a dope! And even if she does love you, it's foolish of her to do so—she should have stopped a long time ago. It was not his function to provide a lover's equivalent of unemployment insurance.

Grabbing his portfolio under his arm, he ran out to the street, buttoning his coat on the run, and jumped on a streetcar, which took him to the Regional Executive Committee building. Having gulped down a cup of tea with marzipan at the cafeteria, he appeared at the editorial office only a half hour late. But he was embarrassed even by that.

"I've got to keep ahold of myself," he thought.

And there was plenty of business to attend to. Over the course of an hour or so, he had to walk over to the telephone at least a dozen times and answered a whole pile of letters. Then he rode over to the print shop, came back to the editorial office, drew up the statement of honoraria for the most recent issue of the journal, and signed off around four o'clock. The staff nodded or shook his hand as they dispersed to go home, and he wanted to tell them, by way of a pleasant joke, "You know, I almost got married! What a joke, eh?"

He had his dinner, read over a few newspapers in the reading room, and, at five, he went to the meeting of the local committee of the writers' union. The topic for discussion was the policy for summer holidays—an important and substantial matter. Spring was coming and it was time to plan for writers to get some rest over the summer and to replenish their creative juices. The meeting ended at eight, but someone suggested the cinema and they all went in a big group. It was ten thirty before Stepan Radchenko returned to his room that day.

At home, his anxiety, which had been sidelined by the extraneous business of the day, awoke again. Damn it, this marriage thing has to be cancelled! And then there's this party. Anger choked him when he recalled that this was to be the party where their engagement would be announced. How wrong can you be?! But, after hesitating for a while, he decided to go anyway. He won't let that little cheat think that he's a coward. He'll tell her straight to her face, you can be sure of that! She had not earned any leniency with these sneaky tricks.

The address was in his notebook. Great! And why let his money go to waste? And tomorrow's a holiday to boot, the day after is Sunday. So, let's have a good time. In the end, he just wanted to dance a little, make use of the skills he had worked to acquire. But he changed slowly, washing up and brushing his clothes carefully, to make sure he arrived as late as possible. Let her worry a little, too!

Around twelve, he rang the bell on the third floor of a big building on Piatakov Street.

The door was opened by a girl he had never met before, but Zoska came out to the vestibule right away. No sooner had he glimpsed from a distance her little figure, thin face, and the tip of her nose on it than it became perfectly clear to him that not only any notion of marriage but of any relationship with this canary was just some kind of misunderstanding. What could he have seen in her? He all but blushed in shame for his poor taste.

Meanwhile Zoska introduced him to the girl who had opened the door. She was the hostess and Stepan graciously kissed her hand.

"Take off your coat," she said invitingly. "We've been dancing for a while already."

Stepan bowed. Through the half-open door of the living room came the loud rhythm of a dance, the rustle of feet across the floor, and indistinct conversations.

"Why so late?" asked Zoska apprehensively when the other girl had left. "I was worried. I thought you might be sick."

"Nope. Perfectly healthy," he said.

While he hung up his coat, Zoska, reassured, rambled on happily. Well, it's great that he showed up. Everyone's here now. How wonderful! The parents had been sent out of the house, because parents are such a bore. Nothing can spoil a party like parents!

Then she took him by the hand to lead him into the living room. But he pulled back his hands and coldly said, "Wait, I need to talk to you."

Zoska stopped, startled by the severity of his voice.

"I knew that something has happened with you!" she cried.

"Zoska," he began, "Yesterday, I said a bunch of stupid things to you. I admit my mistake. But forget them, once and for all."

She was silent for a while. Then she quietly answered, looking him straight in the eyes, "You made it all up yourself. Well... all right. Let's go back to how it was before."

The reproach in her eyes angered him. Nervously, he shrugged his shoulders.

"No, not how it was before. Nothing. Not at all. You understand?"

Zoska whispered, shaking her head, "So, you don't love me?"

"Stop with this love already!" he yelled in despair. "I'm sick and tired of you. Leave me alone!"

And, turning away, he walked into the living room.

He stopped for a moment at the door, examining the apartment. It must belong to a doctor, judging by the illustrated journals scattered on the round tables and the medical smell that lingered in the air despite the tobacco smoke. The tables and chairs were pushed up against the walls, to make room in the middle for dancing. Further on, in the next room, glowed a soft red light, and over on the left, behind a closed door, there was a clatter of dishes and silver. Altogether, there were about twenty people, and he immediately noticed that there were more women than men. Only four couples were dancing, the others sat against the walls amidst the displaced furniture. By the piano in the corner was a thin Jewish musician, who looked up at Stepan as he walked in with the careless gaze of a professional who was otherwise uninvolved, except for his hands.

Having carefully examined the place and the people, he walked up to the hostess with an easy, friendly smile and asked her to introduce him to the guests.

"Where's Zoska?" she asked.

"Off somewhere."

The music died down, the dancers separated, and everyone was available to him. He slowly walked around the whole room with the hostess, stopping by every chair and pronouncing his name clearly and confidently, carelessly looking at the men but closely examining all the women, as if they were citizens brought before a court. His torrid gaze eagerly explored their faces, floating easily over their hair, cheeks, and neck, mercilessly uncovering any blemish in their appearance, as if his was a superior gaze with unlimited rights to choose. His were the ardent eyes of a passion seeking its object. His handshake was firm and inviting, his body was limber and taut for, while making his own examination, he was putting himself on show as well. He had the sweet feeling of being the handsomest of the young men, but, having made the entire round, he was disappointed—none of the women were attractive.

"We haven't visited the 'red' drawing room yet," declared the hostess.

"So, let's do that," he said.

There, in the reddish half-lit room which he had entered without much hope, were two men and a woman sitting in soft chairs by a table. All the plants from the apartment had been brought into this room—a large rubber plant, an oleander, broad-leaf cactuses, prickly clover—and, in the dim light of the lamp, wrapped in translucent colored paper, the room seemed a secret garden. There was a large rug on the floor—the soft soil of this enchanted copse, which rustled softly beneath footsteps in languid sensuousness. Here was that quiet hideaway, that languorous atmosphere that makes one speak in whispers and stifle laughter.

The woman had a calm and almost static elongated face, framed by a rectangle of evenly cut straight hair with straight bangs over the eyes that resembled something ancient, refined, and fixed, eternally young, confident in its beauty, and regal, like the faces of ancient Egyptian women who carried fans behind the pharaoh. But her eyes were alive, filling her face, vibrant and smiling—large beguiling eyes that shone in the twilight like the eyes of a kitten. She was dressed, as far as he could see, in a dark velvet dress that hung on a narrow strap across only one, otherwise bare, shoulder.

The hostess departed. Stepan pulled up a chair, sat down across from her between the two men and without waiting for the conversation, interrupted by his arrival, to begin again, offered his own comment.

"This could be a photographer's laboratory."

"That's just what we're missing, a photographer," she said.

From these words, their cheerful tone, he understood that he pleased her.

"Rita, I, too, am an amateur photographer," spoke up the fellow on his left, a young man with a girlish appearance.

This answer showed Stepan that this fellow's chances were exceptionally poor.

"I, on the other hand, am a master photographer," Stepan declared.

Calmly, with a deep sense of confidence, he went on to add that he was a writer and that his art lay precisely in photographing human souls.

"Only their souls?" she asked.

"The pathway to the soul lies through the body," he answered.

The conversation turned to literature. Stepan lit a cigarette and very capably played the leading role. Naturally, none of the others could match him in knowledge of the subject and the accuracy of his judgments. But his neighbors kept trying to keep their own in the conversation by any means possible, particularly the one on his right, the somewhat chunky fellow with a moustache and signs of a legal education. Does she really like moustaches?

Finally, the girlish fellow gave up and left after making his excuses. From the other room oozed the longing sounds of a foxtrot, dropping the wilted petals of a giant ardent flower over the rug, the furniture, and the plants in the room. In the bright rectangle of the door, dancing couples shimmered and some, crossing the threshold into this room, destroyed the sacred stillness of the bower by the sharp clatter of their shoes. Stepan spoke about contemporary literature, their own and foreign. He recited poems of passionate poets to suggest to this beautiful Rita the feelings and atmosphere of love, to draw toward himself her bare arms, which lay on the table and looked so dark and tempting in the dim, suggestive light of the red lamp. Sometimes, she rested her shining gaze on him in passing, intimating mutual understanding and consent, and then Stepan felt a heavy and burning sensation in his blood, as if it were not her gaze but her shoulder that had touched him.

"There really are a whole lot of new writers," she said.

The lawyer's moustache laughed haughtily. What's there to wonder at? Everybody keeps a diary and writes poems as a child, but, when they grow up, they stop this silliness. Yet some just remain the children that they were.

Stepan flushed and without raising his eyes to him added acerbically, "A moustache is not a sign of adulthood."

Then he got up and asked Rita, "Would you like to dance?"

He figured she'd either agree or he'd leave.

"I'd love to," she said.

She took him by the arm and led him out onto the dance floor.

Now, under the light of six white bulbs that hung from the ceiling, he could get a better look at the rest of her. She was composed of two shades, without any transition between them: the black of her hair, eyes, dress, and shiny shoes and the swarthiness of her face, hands, shoulders, and stockings. This simple combination gave her figure a proud charm. There were no curls or combs in her straight hairstyle, there were no decorations or embroidery on her simple dress, which widened somewhat as it fell from the waist and seemed to be cut off at the bottom, just like the bangs across her forehead. Everything black sparkled on her, highlighted by her shining eyes, while the swarthy part was still. Life was in the clothing—the body was dreamy.

Before them, excited couples moved fluidly around the floor, and Stepan suddenly saw that Zoska was very energetically dancing with the girlish-looking fellow. He thought smugly, "She's having a good time already. A perfect match, those two!" Then he took his own lady in his arms and, finding the beat, set off into the crowd of dancers. She moved supplely and suddenly; her entire body, from breasts to knees, pressed against him, given over entirely to him and to the dance, while he stared into her eyes with an imploring gaze, all tense in this passionate embrace. Their ardent heat met, passing through the weave of their clothing. A wave of enfeebling languor, powerful and sensuous, quivered in their blood, and Stepan lost all sense of feeling except for the rhythm of the music and the woman's body pressed against him, which, in that moment, he possessed more completely than he might ever expect to control in reality.

"Time for supper! Food's ready!" the hostess called out.

The music stopped, and Stepan, with painful regret, opened his arms. A doleful annoyance overcame him, leaving behind longing and unconscious energy. He took her by the arm, just to feel her body. She, as if feeling his anxiety, quickly squeezed his hand and he, immediately relieved, whispered, "Shall we sit together?"

"Of course."

Everyone poured into the dining room with loud cheer, eager for refreshment after the lengthy exertion. In the doorway, he ran into Zoska, and, taking advantage of his partner's diverted attention, quietly but cheerfully whispered, "Sorry and goodbye, Zoska." She looked at him with her deep, slow, familiar gaze that no longer irritated him and said something quietly in response, but he did not catch what it was as he walked past.

The table, extended to its maximum length, was densely covered with simple but tasty dishes—canned foods, cheese, herring, ham, marinated fish, vinaigrettes, and smoked sausages of various kinds. Among the bowls and platters holding these foods were some flowers, three baskets of sliced bread, the green necks of wine bottles, and the transparent beaks of vodka carafes. When everyone had sat down, it became quiet for a moment as everyone took their first bites. Then a breeze of quiet, reserved conversations blew among the guests.

Stepan was diligent in filling his own and Rita's glasses. She drank patiently, slowly, choosing her wine deliberately—no doubt she knew the varieties—but somehow lazily. He observed her and did not recognize her. There was something inert, completely indifferent in her features, and it was only when she raised her eyes to him that he again perceived the woman with whom he had danced.

"Rita, dear Rita," he whispered. "What a wonderful name!"

The faces of the guests seemed friendlier now, under the influence of the continued consumption of alcoholic beverages. The mustached lawyer, who was sitting across from Stepan and was enthusiastically wooing a blond with a beautiful bust, at first met his gaze severely, but then, quite unexpectedly, winked and smiled, like a partner in an enterprise. How satisfying! Stepan could approach any guy or girl and speak with them like an old friend, because everything that makes people distant had melted in their drinks, and everyone was equal—all carefree animals who only wanted to laugh and joke.

Zoska sat at the end of the table, engaged in a friendly conversation with the girlish young man, whose round face was glowing with satisfaction. Stepan looked attentively at this couple a few times, expecting to meet the girl's gaze and shame her. But she stubbornly did not turn around toward him. So much for love! Now she's running after the first guy she sees, as if nothing at all had happened with her! It's a shame he hadn't rubbed her cheating nose in the dirt a little harder.

Eventually, he stopped noticing her. Voices were getting louder and more shrill, pouring out in a stream of disordered speech, in which only occasional drunken exclamations and laughter were discernible. It seemed to Stepan that he was moving faster and faster down an enormous hill on a small, light sled. He found that his neighbor's leg was alongside his and he squeezed it as hard as he could.

"Careful there, you'll soil my stocking," she said calmly.

"I'll launder it in my own blood," he answered.

"You have so much excess blood?"

"Twice what is needed."

He tried to give these words of his the deepest of meanings. After this, he spoke to her in clear and bold hints and related suggestive anecdotes, about which she made very appropriate comments, since she already knew most of them.

Finally, his inebriation reached the point where a person becomes sad and worried. He had already reached the bottom of the hill and was standing alone on a gray field. From there, he glanced at his neighbor in fear and despair. Will this just be the same game of love all over again, that nauseating give and take between a man and a woman? Love is a complex algebraic equation where, after all your efforts, simplifications, and eliminating parentheses, you're still left with zero. The next equation is the same. And on and on they continue, always equivalent. The variables change, as do the operations and the signs, but the outcome is always the same, and it's always empty. And he despairingly felt that yes, he would get all excited, he would seek her, grab on to her as to a lifejacket, which even after reaching the shore he would still have to wear, because it will have swollen and shrunk, all the wet straps eating into his flesh. Nausea overpowered him, like a person who is about to see the same show for the tenth time but still, inexplicably, came to the theater.

He fell deep into thought. Suddenly, she put her hand on his knee.

"Stefan…"

"What?"

"Give me your hand."

He gave her his hand and then immediately tore it away, jumping back from the sharp pain. She had stabbed him mercilessly in the palm. He instantly flared up, as if her pin had burst the soap bubble of his contemplation.

"Hold on there," he said, laughing. "I'll poke you, too, one of these days."

Her eyes were fading.

"You'll run out of time."

He leaned over and told her an amusing story from Catulle Mendès about a blind grandmother who sewed her granddaughter to her skirt to protect her from evil but became a great-grandmother nevertheless, even though she had let the girl go off alone only twice, once for fifteen minutes and the second time for five minutes. "How did you manage to find a lover in fifteen minutes?" she had asked in anger. And the sinful girl had meekly replied, "No, grandma—it was the second time."

"A foolish grandmother—to force the girl to such desperation," said Rita.

"But I assume there's no grandmother in your case?" he asked.

"There's no grandmother, but there is a train."

And she informed him that she was here by chance, having come to visit her parents, but actually lives in Kharkiv, where she dances in the ballet. She's leaving in the morning.

Never had Stepan felt such gratitude to a woman as he did now. She's leaving! So, there won't be any romance! How fortunate! He was ready to get on his knees before her and sing a hymn of praise to her. God, what a wonderful world this was, after all!

"It's two o'clock," she said. "I have to go. Would you like to walk with me?"

He wanted to very much.

He waited in the vestibule while Rita said goodbye to the hostess. When she came out, he grabbed her by the hand and pulled her to himself.

"Kiss me," he said.

She laughed quietly and sang:

> The girls were washing their feet in the stream,
>
> The boys were fishing just upstream,
>
> La la la la, la la la la
>
> La la la la la, la la la.

Then she pushed herself against him as if dancing and, for a moment, he felt the sensuous touch of her tongue.

"The fire of love is sweet only for a moment," he cried in delight. "Later they cook borsch on it."

"A moment is not long enough for a woman," she said.

"I was speaking allegorically."

A terrible racket of moving chairs came from the apartment. They were getting up from the table.

He went out into the street without his coat, despite her protests. Since it was cold, he immediately fell into a reflective mood.

"The sky is the color of a five karbovanets note," he said.

"Are you such a materialist?"

"Absolutely! And you?"

"Yes, we've already endured too much for the sake of ideals."

"The ideals have endured a lot, too."

Getting into a carriage, she said, "Farewell, mischievous one."

"Farewell, my dream."

He watched joyfully as the danger disappeared around the corner. He waved to it. Goodbye! The end!

He could have gone home at that point, but he had left his coat. Fortunately, the door had not been locked behind him, and he could easily get back into the vestibule. Here he found the fellow with the thin girlish face pacing anxiously.

"What's the matter?" Stepan asked him.

"Well, it's..." he muttered, "Zoska is not feeling well."

"So take her home."

"Sure, but I can't carry her there in my arms."

Stepan pulled three karbovanets from his pocket. "Here!"

The fellow hesitated but then took the money and disappeared.

In the living room they were still dancing—lethargically, ponderously, frequently colliding, but dancing. Stepan casually walked along the wall into the red drawing room, sat down beneath the rubber tree, stretched out his legs, and immediately fell asleep, coddled by the music, the whispers around him, and the stolen kisses.

He awoke in complete silence. The red light had been extinguished, and only a single bulb was burning in the other room, barely illuminating the corners. He got up, walked to the vestibule on tiptoe, took his coat, and left, walking out into the long deserted streets of the city, which slept under a leaden sky as dawn approached.

Chapter Twelve

He got home in a state of warm drowsiness, which had enveloped him from the moment he got up from the chair under the rubber plant where he had fallen asleep. All the way from Piatakov Street, across the empty Jewish Bazaar, which at night looked somewhat like a cemetery, he felt as if he had never completely awakened from the very deep sleep that had suddenly overpowered him after the spiritual and physical tension of the evening. He walked along listlessly, without thinking, seeing only what was necessary to keep walking. Throughout his body, his mind, and his heart, he felt a pleasant fatigue and a need for something like total forgetfulness. In his room, he undressed mechanically and stretched out on the bed, forgetting even to remove his socks.

At one o'clock in the afternoon, he woke up and squinted in the shining deluge of light that flooded his room. Through the window opposite his bed flowed the first warm rays of spring sunlight, tracing patterns on the walls and tickling his face. He got up and stood on his bed, surrendering to the mindless joy of warmth and the expectation of a close, unreachable happiness. And so he stood, body taut, bathing in the bright streams that washed over him like healing waters. Then he jumped down from the bed, ran over to the window, opened it, and stuck his disheveled head outside. The first wave of air from outdoors rolled over him in a shiver, the second was more pleasant, and the third was already familiar, cheerful, and enchanting, as if a giant sunny hand had stretched out toward him and stroked his hair, patting him on the chest. A new energy was flowing into his soul, a primitive power, filling out his chest and pumping up his heart with fervor. He sensed that his past had melted away after a powerful dream and sunny awakening, that he had no memories, that he had been born just now, in the arrival of the spring, immediately born an adult—experienced, wise, full of a new strength and an unshakeable faith in it.

He got dressed hurriedly, grabbing at things as if every wasted moment was a great loss. He washed and went outside. Happy people were splashing in the dying puddles of winter, melting under a smiling sun. And everything was like a happy ending in a tragic movie.

He walked straight ahead, without a goal, without any wish to get anywhere or to stop. An intoxicated sense of freedom was driving him forward, a feeling of complete independence, an animal-like satisfaction of liberation from what he had seen, thought, and wished yesterday, from how he had lived yesterday, from all the pains and all the troubles from all the days that had come before. At the corner of Volodymyr and Sverdlov Streets, where girls stood with baskets of flowers for sale, he bought two bunches of blue snowdrops and, unwilling to pin them to his coat, carefully carried them in his pocket.

At home, he set the flowers in a glass of water. They smelled of vegetation, the usual rawness of plants, but it was an awakened scent that had sprung from the impenetrable depths of the earth, from the darkness and cold into the thirsty glow of warmth, and these humble flowers smiled at him with their little flags of the greatness of life. He put them in the center of the table. Then, from the pile of books, he unearthed his own collection of stories.

He could only dimly recollect what it was he had written about, and so he read with enthusiasm, as if this were something unknown, unrelated to him. He marveled at the unexpected images, the construction of the sentences, at individual words, which he seemed to anticipate, which were placed precisely as he would place them today. And everything he read came to life for him under his assiduous observation, allowing him to experience again the joys of his past creativity, resurrecting the past zeal in anxious trembling and sweet languor over the lines of text. A deep amazement came over him as he read the last page. Had he really written this? Certainly, he had! The cover had his name on it. But his soul reacted coquettishly, refusing the earned praise, putting on airs, and retreating in modesty, like a fifteen-year-old girl receiving a gorgeous bouquet of flowers from someone she likes. Perhaps they're not for her? But, suddenly and shamefully, reversing one hundred and eighty degrees, without hiding the wish to possess what she was getting. It's you, he felt within his breast. It's you, it's you, echoed his heart. He was hearing a symphony sung by a giant choir singing him a song of self-love, and he was overcome with self-respect for his artistry. And he wanted to go out again, to roam the streets, smiling at everyone and everything, but he quelled this expansive urge and read over his collection from beginning to end once again.

Now he was left somewhat disenchanted. Specific faults troubled him: substantial flaws in construction and a terrible embarrassment over the contents. What, exactly, was he writing about? Nowhere in the space of hundreds of pages had he encountered a person—one who suffers and struggles, who generates insane impulses out of pain, who languishes and soars, crawls and scales heights. He didn't find in these pages a sad dwarf with great wisdom, a tiny animal that carries on its narrow shoulders the eternal weight of consciousness; he didn't find a charming child who cries and laughs sweetly among the colorful toys of existence, or the ruthless warrior who knows how to kill and to die for his dreams, the stern defender of days long gone, or the tireless messenger into the future. And this absence distressed him. What good are these works if the human heart does not beat in them? They now seemed dead to him, these stories in which people disappeared under the weight of things and ideas, created by them and for them.

He got up from his chair listlessly and lay down on the bed, his hands under his head. Indeed, he had not encountered a single person—and what was worthy of attention other than people? Without a person everything else loses its meaning, becomes a soulless mechanism, a bell in a vacuum. The naive belief of the past that man is the measure of all things, that the world came into existence and the stars began to shine for people, this idea now appeared to him the only truth in the world, greater than all other truths or theories. He had spun the initial threads of his heartfelt creative tapestry from a longing for this past misunderstanding, from a clear appreciation of the first principles of life, from a glowing feeling for people.

He would write a novel about people.

When he formulated this thought, a terrible fatigue overcame him from his helplessness before such an enormous task, whose weight he felt sharply and clearly, unconsciously magnifying in his imagination the actual difficulties of the work ahead of him. How to combine the innumerable facts that he had managed to accumulate and experience, how to weave together the mass of observations about others and about himself into a single flawless artistic expression, accurate and well tuned, like the mechanism of a clock? How to convey in a few thousand lines of text the endless variety of people, the mad incongruity of their thoughts, moods, wishes, and actions? So that the person appears complete, without improvements or omissions, just as he or she appears in struggles, in love, or in work, with all the usual noble and depraved urges, with criminality and sympathy, with baseness and with honor? No, this was entirely beyond his abilities! He must immediately forswear such a grandiose intent and must protect himself from the enormous pain of failure. And he should give up this writing altogether, which, as far as he could remember, repaid his efforts only with bitter disenchantments.

But he lay with clenched teeth, attuned not so much to his own hopeless thoughts as to something barely discernible, indistinct, and distant, like the memory of a dream. Hope? No, something larger than hope arose in him. Suddenly, he forgot about everything, about himself, about his intentions. He seemed to have stopped existing, to have dissolved into passionate visions that carried him off on powerful waves. Unfamiliar figures filled his room—light, airy creations of his stimulated imagination, among whom he did not recognize anything either real or his own. They moved before him in the quiet evening twilight. Without the slightest effort, he gave life to countless bodies, clothed them, christened them—heaven knows why—submerging himself into the sweet dreamscape from which this captivating kingdom of shadows was born. He could not feel the activity of his will nor the sensation of his feelings in this unconscious, imaginary game, nor even any satisfaction from this creative expression. He shrank down and became numb and still, so as not to cut off with an inept interruption the shiny parade of his incarnations. And, suddenly, these strange figures, these unexpected guests in his humble and forsworn home, began to laugh and cry, demand and struggle, then to set off into the distance on responsive sailboats, buffeted by breaths of hatred and love.

He sprang up in bed. Was he going crazy? A trick of the visual imagination he could understand, but he had clearly heard their voices. He sat motionless, listening to the fearful beats of his heart, the only sound that remained real for him in the silence of the dark room. It seemed he was alone within a vast noiselessness at an immeasurable distance from the world and from people. He felt that he was not connected to life but was close to it, as never before. And, in this feeling of terrible solitude, of a complete loss of contact with the surrounding reality and a new unity with it, lay an incomprehensible certainty of victory. A certainty! He was beginning to realize the depth of his own strength. He really was going crazy, but from joy.

This secret inebriation lasted a whole week. From what he saw and heard, from what he observed within himself and around him, he now cut out characters, thoughts, and landscapes, and sewed them together with the nimble threads of plot. He wasn't writing yet, just inventing. He wasn't even thinking about having to write all this down—such was the burning, sensuous satisfaction that he had merely from imagining, the unforced labor that was transforming itself into a self-rewarding goal and was occupying all of his interest and enthusiasm.

At work and at meetings, he became something of a well-tuned machine. Everywhere outside his room, he felt like a wound-up mechanism that performs a given number of necessary actions, reacts in a familiar way to its environment, and has the capacity to respond. All of his sensitivity was concentrated in his dreams, putting a chill on his life.

In connection with this, he changed his attitude, most importantly, toward himself. Now, he no longer allowed himself to eat whenever he wanted and whatever he wanted. He had breakfast, lunch, and dinner at prescribed times and consumed nutritious foods, primarily vegetables and grains. When he went outside, he carefully wrapped his neck in a scarf, something he hadn't done previously, even in the coldest weather. He routinely aired out his apartment and reduced his consumption of tobacco during the day, so that he could smoke more in the evening, without, however, crossing the limit beyond which, in his opinion, nicotine began to have a negative impact on health. And, in the morning, he began again to practice the system of calisthenics of the nerves as introduced by Dr. Anokhin. Once in a while, quite unexpectedly, he would speak to himself in the second person: "Well, it's time for you to go to sleep," or "Go outside and relax a little." He was courteous with his colleagues, as always, but secretly he felt a sense of his own superiority over them. It was even somewhat comical that they continued to greet him and talk to him just as they had yesterday and the day before. To tell the truth, he even felt some disdain for them—no one had noticed the great impulse that had entered his life. For them, he was just as he had been before. Incredible! Too bad for them! Sometimes, submitting to the sweet tide of self-admiration, he smiled, dreaming of the majesty of the wonderful work that he would write, and how it would amaze all of those who had noticed nothing at all.

The poet Vyhorskyi, worried by Stepan's long absence from the beer hall, came to visit him at the editorial office.

"You've probably started writing something, haven't you," he asked.

"Almost," Stepan answered. "I'm thinking it through."

"Oh, that's the happiest time, the springtime of creativity," the poet sighed. "It's like Platonic love, so to speak, and then comes the tiresome boredom of family life."

And then he suddenly asked, "Do you know the mistake that most people make when they use the word 'Platonic'?"

"I do indeed, except that hardly anyone uses that word anymore."

And then Vyhorskyi informed him that, on April 20, in the morning, he would be setting out on a trip, and asked him to come to the beer hall the night before so that they could mark the occasion.

That day, Stepan had another visitor, whom he certainly did not expect at all. It was Maksym Hnidyi, accountant at the Leatherworkers' Collective, dressed in a rather tattered coat but wearing a very nonchalant smile. He spread himself out on a chair next to Stepan's desk and, when Stepan looked up at him questioningly, he declared, using the familiar pronoun, "I'm happy to wait until you have a free moment."

At first, Stepan thought he had misheard, but, when he finally shook off the young writer who brought a lyrical short story to the editorial office every week and entered into conversation with Maksym, he found that the accountant not only addressed him with the familiar pronoun, but actually called him Stiopa. Stepan chose not to cut off this unexpected assertion of some kind of camaraderie but spoke to the accountant using indirect, third-person constructions.

Significant changes had occurred in the Hnidyi family. Everyone lived together now. At least they had achieved a modicum of normalcy in their old age, Maksym observed. The fish merchant's store had suffered a setback—it was liquidated to pay those damned taxes. But old Hnidyi now hawked fish from a stand at the Zhytnyi Bazaar, and Tamara Vasylivna helped out with a haberdashery stand. So, they made do, somehow. He, Maksym, was the only one who wasn't working. The problem was that, at the Leatherworkers' Collective, where he had been an accountant, there was a little misunderstanding over the cash account, and he had to quit his job to avoid any unpleasantness. But that was just a trifle. He was actually happy it turned out this way, because he had had enough of this number-crunching already. It dried up your soul, particularly for a vibrant and independent person, like him. So, he had decided to change jobs.

"Stiopa," he said, "you know I always liked books. Remember my library? It's a shame, but I had to sell it! Life has its ups and downs, as you know."

He smiled slyly to underscore the hint. But Stepan still didn't completely understand where this was heading. Soon enough, everything became clear. Maksym had his eye on a position as a bookstore manager for one of the state publishing houses, or at least as assistant to the manager, and it was up to Stepan to help him, through his contacts.

"You're a well-known person," he added. "You probably know plenty of Communists, and nowadays without connections you're not going anywhere. You know, without a little help you may as well give up and kick the bucket."

Again, he smiled with a sly insinuation. Stepan grudgingly acquiesced, angry at himself for letting this cheat assert any kind of rights over him. Maksym added, "I'll write an application and give it to you, and then you'll pass it along into the right hands and put in a good word for me."

He wrote the application, but still he didn't leave. He asked for a cigarette and lit it.

"This is really nice tobacco you're smoking," he said, knowingly. "Remember when I was the one treating you? Well, what the hell—no matter."

He twitched his head nervously.

"I have another matter for you, a personal one," he said, lowering his voice. "I have five albums of stamps I've collected. My situation is such that I must sell them. But I don't want to sell them to just anybody—they mean a lot to me. Buy them from me. I won't take much—a hundred karbovanets, which is like giving them away for free. Do this for me as an old acquaintance."

"No. I don't need stamps," answered Stepan.

Maksym sighed. Well, then maybe he would loan him thirty or so, for a week? Stepan gave him five karbovanets and stood up decisively.

"OK, I'm leaving, I'm leaving," said Maksym. "When will you come visit us? You know, it's not nice to forget your old friends, not nice. And things are so cheerful now.

We all get together, we sing. Mom has put on so much weight, she looks just grand. Come over! And when shall I come to ask about the job?"

"A month and a half," answered Stepan. "There won't be anything sooner than that."

Maksym bid him farewell like an old friend, but with a strong infusion of precautionary respectfulness. At the door, he turned and said with some embarrassment, "Maybe you're still angry at me, Stiopa, but that really was stupid of me back then... I regret it myself."

"All right. It's all right."

When Maksym had finally left, he shrugged his shoulders. What a comedy! The very thought that there once was this woman named Musinka, and these little tragedies, and even a fight! A whole millennium has passed since then. And now this unnecessary, ridiculous, completely useless snippet of the past suddenly comes walking through the door and stretches out its hand to you. What the hell! The past should have some self-respect, it should know its place and not go pushing in where it isn't wanted. He tore up Maksym's letter of application and threw it in the trash.

Finally, he was done with the novel. That is, he had thought through the whole thing along with all the details. The novel appeared in his head like a transparent color photograph. True, it had come out a little different than he had originally conceived it. At first, he had sketched out a colossal work in three sections, with over a hundred characters and the action taking place over a period of ten years. Then he had shortened it to two sections and thrown out around thirty characters. Finally, he had shortened it by another section, and what remained was a novel that would stretch in print to four or five signatures and encompass twelve characters. What had forced him to shorten so much? An inescapable inner command. Forced out of the original plan under the weight of this creative press were all the liquid, all the accidental matter, all the cheap effects and tragedies, all the unnecessary conversations and actions, leaving only a solid thick mass that no longer lost its shape under the pressure of a further turning of the press's screw. This was a painful process, like cutting out living flesh that wanted to live and clung to life in every possible way. But, like a stern surgeon, he caused this pain in the name of future health. He was conscious that he was capable of accomplishing only a tiny portion of the enormous challenge that now stood before him, since even the life of a single person was worth more than volumes of short stories. Even more, he was conscious that, over the course of his entire life he would accomplish only a small portion of this challenge, because the human soul is immeasurable and unfathomable, even if it suddenly fits into a few bursts of energy. But he used the material he had cut to cobble together a plot for a movie script, as well as a few themes for future novels. Now, he was well provisioned for at least a year of intensive work. All he needed to do was write! Having bought a half ream of ruled paper, he sat down one evening at his table and picked up a pencil with the sacred trembling of a prophet who has raised his knife over the sacrificial victim. This was the moment he had feared. Oh, happiness! He wrote the first chapter, then a second, then the third. He wrote easily, without stopping, and even without feeling any anxiety. The words poured forth from him, a stream of vivid, disciplined words that knew their own places and connections. He threw down his pen, clenched his hands in satisfaction and got up. Enough, enough for one day. Gradually relaxing, he counted his pages—if he kept up this pace, he would have the novel finished in two weeks. Wonderful!

But the second day he didn't write anything at all. He sat, he paced, he even lay down and tried to dream, but he couldn't squeeze out a single word of the next chapter. As if the entire spring flood of his imagination had suddenly dried up with only dead clumps left behind, which the heat of his despair could not melt. He knew *what* to write and he knew *how* he should write it, but a chasm had developed between his intentions and the paper. He felt a terrible disinclination to writing itself, an unfounded hostility to the very act of moving pen across paper. At first, he was irritated with himself, then he tried to convince himself, and finally he became contemplative. Where had this crisis come from? Was the written word unwilling to come to him, or was he unwilling to write it?

Maybe the remaining chapters were defective in their construction and this stoppage, an intuitive projection of the creative instinct, was a warning about that danger? And behind every thought of his stood the well-known terror of all vain attempts at creativity.

Finally, he decided he needed to rest. He needed to protect himself. He was simply weary in his soul. You can't push yourself without mercy. The right thing to do was to take a break from his work for a few days, to entertain himself and renew his energies. But how?

Suddenly, the memory of Zoska filled him with a pleasant warmth. Zoska! That lovely, smiling girl, the faithful companion of so much of his wandering. He remembered her slight figure, her unflappable smile and sudden melancholy, her naive, joyful philosophy, and her passionate kisses. He wanted to see again the curls on her forehead, her wonderful face, animated by emotions, to hear her wonderful whisper and to sit on the rug by her feet, "at the feet of a queen." He felt as if she had just left the room and was about to return at any moment. He jumped up and looked at his watch. It wasn't yet six. He could still go with her to the cinema, and then... and then invite her over to his place. That would be wonderful! They could have a nice little party here after their separation—and the hell with what the bourgeois neighbors would whisper about them in their little burrows.

Stepan hastily began to put on his best suit while stringing together a series of pleasant thoughts. True, there was that misunderstanding between them. Getting married was, of course, a silly idea, but he had been somewhat harsh toward her. He didn't deny that. But he would apologize. He sensed that there was a link between his novel and the breakup with Zoska, one that he did not fully understand, and now he regretted that he had not arranged with her a temporary, half-month hiatus. Because now it was a little unpleasant.

"But if she really loves me," he thought, "then she should not be very angry."

He quickly walked over to Gimnazia Passage and rang at the familiar doorway. An elderly woman in an apron opened the door.

"May I see Comrade Zoska?" he asked.

Surprised, the woman asked, "Which Zoska? Holubovska?"

"Yes," he confirmed.

The woman clapped her hands together.

"Good God! But she poisoned herself!"

"She's dead?" asked Stepan.

"Indeed, she is no more," the woman answered sorrowfully. "Lord have mercy on her soul." She made the sign of the cross.

"And you... How do you know?" he asked.

"What do you take me for?" the woman exclaimed, offended. "We're neighbors, and we share their grief. Would you like to visit them?"

"No," said Stepan.

They stood silent for a moment, looking at each other. Stepan was crushed. The woman was curious.

"And who might you be?" she asked.

"Stepan, Stepan Radchenko," he answered.

"A relative?" she continued.

"An acquaintance."

"You won't see her anymore," she sighed. "May she rest in peace."

He walked away slowly, while the woman continued to follow him with her eyes for a while, then loudly closed the door.

Crossing the street, he stopped. "I should visit the parents and ask about the details," he thought. "Maybe she left me a note? Where is she buried?" But these thoughts were so vague that he could barely distinguish them. They moved so slowly that, by the end of each, he had already forgotten the beginning. And they seemed strange, completely foreign, absolutely unconnected to him. Someone was thinking for him, stringing together fragments of thoughts in a boring and frightening manner. And he himself was completely empty. He lost the feeling of his own person and of the world beyond him. As if he were nothing, nowhere, never. He feared raising his eyes lest he see the emptiness around him.

He shuddered, shriveled, and set off, experiencing his own motion with trepidation. Then he began to consider what one could use to poison oneself. Arsenic, mercuric chloride, strychnine, prussic acid, opium? What was the difference in how these poisons worked? Which of them is used to poison flies on those dark sheets that are purchased at the pharmacy, with the label in large letters and an exclamation mark: Death to Flies! And what is death? How can a person just disappear, so that she is never seen again? How can a person die, not for a day, not a week, not a year, but to be no more? So, he could also die? How ridiculous! What a terrible misunderstanding!

"This is impossible," he told himself. "It's just completely impossible!"

It seemed to him in that moment that he could freely lie down in front of a streetcar, thrust a knife into his heart, drink any kind of poison, and still remain alive.

He raised his eyes, unconsciously expecting to see someone familiar and walk up to him. But all the faces he saw were those of strangers and seemed not to be alive. Yes, as if they had long since died, had long since drunk poison. And, suddenly, he felt that he was the only living creature in the vast kingdom of death.

Finally, he managed to think: "Maybe it was an accident?" Instead of an answer, he experienced an overwhelming sense of loss. He wanted to run, shout, crawl on his knees, beg, and howl. To receive his punishment. To receive forgiveness.

Then sorrow moistened his eyes. He wanted to sit by a grave in the freshly sprouting grass, to wreathe it with cornflowers, to bow down and cry. Clearly, painfully, he felt that incomprehensible link that develops between a soul that has departed and a living soul that yearns for the otherworldly with a mindless longing. *She* was now accessible to him through his heightened sensitivity, she entered his soul like a warm breeze. The feeling was indescribable, but healing. He thought in sorrowful joy, "Zoska, you are gone, but I am yours forever. I shall come to you every year, when the earth flowers. You have died for everyone, but not for me."

At the doorway to his building, he was struck with nausea again—a fear of the evening and the coming night.

On the stairs by his door, he ran into the agent who was doing such a poor job of providing him with addresses of possible apartments. The agent stopped, glowing with satisfaction.

"Well, there's a room," he said mischievously. "But not just any room, a *real* room. In short, you won't..."

"I no longer need any room," replied Stepan wearily.

The agent was very surprised. A nice room is always needed! Why had he run over here himself? Why had he wasted a month running around across the city like a hound dog, only to find out suddenly that the room is no longer needed? If the comrade will just have a look at it, he'll move in there right away.

And Stepan suddenly agreed. Just to do something. Just not to be alone. And, in the long run, he did actually need a room.

"All right," he said. "Just wait so I can get some money."

And they rode out together to Lypky.

"Just wait 'til you see the building," the agent rattled on, excited, as they got off the streetcar. "It's a gem, a real treat. You won't be able to turn it down."

The building was indeed very impressive. It was seven stories tall, with countless windows that were just being illuminated.

"This way, if you please," said the agent.

They got into the elevator, and this mode of transportation, experienced for the first time, greatly appealed to Stepan. While still in the elevator cabin, he decided to rent the room. But the room sold itself without any help from anyone. It was a smallish, bright, and well-ordered study, with parquet floors and central heating. It was hung with new blue-gray wallpaper and had two windows offering an unlimited view of the city and the distant horizon beyond the river. This was exactly the kind of room he had dreamt of. And he immediately imagined where he would place all of his future pieces of furniture and how comfortable it would be to work on them.

"I will certainly be able to write here," he thought.

They were asking too much and he bargained ferociously. In the end, they agreed to a one-hundred-and-fifty-karbovanets release payment, plus expenses for the renovations they had made, plus ten percent for the agent. Stepan turned over the money and documents and was to move in the next day.

He was the last one to leave the room, and, as he was turning out the electric lights, the sickening anxiety that had melted for a while in the face of financial concerns and the satisfaction of an acceptable agreement returned again in this dark emptiness, where the windows gleamed like two giant dead faces. Clenching his hands in despair and despite himself, he said almost aloud, "Forgive me, Zoska."

Everything was silent around him, but silence is the sign of consent.

He quickly walked out of the frightening darkness, carefully and timidly locking the door behind him. The agent, having received his payment, disappeared without even saying goodbye. The property managers bowed to him very graciously. He had made arrangements with them about morning coffee and a separate key to the building's main door. Then he summoned the elevator and softly descended.

On the street, he was again alone, and a terrible anxiety rolled over him. It was only eight o'clock. In the two hours since he had left his apartment, two unusual and unique events had transpired. Unwittingly, he set them side by side. But was there any connection between *that* and the fortunate resolution of the housing question? And, suddenly, he felt that he had made a step forward, upward, having abandoned someone on a lower level. But, in response to this secret rationalization, which had barely resonated in his head, his soul began to whimper even louder.

On the streets down which he walked, he again did not meet anyone he knew. There was nothing unusual in that, but it seemed to him that everyone had abruptly abandoned him. And, suddenly, he remembered that today was April 19, the evening that he was to meet the poet for a parting drink. He cheerfully shook off his gloom and quickened his steps.

Chapter Thirteen

The traveler had not yet arrived at the beer hall. Stepan limply sat down at a table in the middle of the floor, surrounded by people and voices that evoked a feeling of disgust in him. For the first time since he had begun frequenting it, he found the beer hall repugnant. Now, he could see the banality of the merriment that he heard around him, the artificiality of the alcohol-stoked laughter, the cheap gilding of the local variety of entertainment. The music, the jazz band with snares, drums, and cymbals that had always lifted his spirits and relieved his tension now oppressed him with horrible riffs and irritated him with intolerable clanging. He would have left immediately if he weren't waiting for someone, and so he sat with his hat pulled down low and his head resting on the table beside the still untasted bottle of beer that had been placed before him. Then he began to smoke nervously, breaking matches in agitation.

Finally, Vyhorskyi showed up in a rubberized jacket and with a cap on his head. He was struck by Stepan's expression.

"So, why the Childe Harold face?" he asked in greeting.

"You must mean your face, not mine. You're the one who's leaving."

"I may be leaving, but I'm not cursing anyone."

"Well, I'm cursing, but I'm not leaving."

The poet carelessly waved his hand.

"Stop. The world only gets worse from cursing."

Vyhorskyi volunteered that today would be his treat.

"But please note," he said, "I've become a vegetarian."

"Out of conviction?" asked Stepan.

"No, just for variety."

When the meals and the wine were served, the poet again asked Stepan, "So, why this dour melancholy? Is it because I'm leaving?"

"No," smiled Stepan. "It's worldly sorrow."

The poet sighed in relief.

"At least that's completely safe."

He was very pleasant, cheerful, and gracious. At first, Stepan wanted to admit everything to him, to spill out his pain and sorrow and their most secret sources. But he only said, "If you want to know the truth, it's just a really bad mood. Sometimes you get the feeling that you're an animal, a wild, blood-sucking animal, and you feel sad. Life is cruel. You know that there's nothing you can do, but you regret it nevertheless. Then you begin to understand more clearly that everyone around you is also a wild animal—miscreants, lowlifes, criminals—and you are frightened by the fact that you're just like them, and they're like you."

"Where do you see such horrors?"

Stepan smiled despondently.

"Where? Right here, all around us."

"The people around us are lovely, pleasant people."

"You're always joking," said Stepan.

"Not at all. Just look!"

The poet leaned out of his chair and touched the shoulder of the person sitting behind him. The man turned around.

"Excuse me," said the poet. "I think you're a very fine fellow and I want to shake your hand."

The fellow hesitated, but he offered his hand and even said, "Well, thank you very much."

"You're a strange one," sighed Stepan.

Then they ate and drank, each one focused on his own thoughts. Stepan, suffering from a need to express his sorrow, raised his glass and announced, "My friend, let's drink to love."

The poet was surprised.

"What's the point of drinking a toast to this horrible sentiment that robs people of their peace of mind?"

Challenged, Stepan answered, "It robs you of your peace of mind, it robs you of your life. It really is terrible, this love."

"So you agree with me?" asked Vyhorskyi with uncertainty.

"Absolutely!"

"I can't stand being in agreement with people," grumbled the dissatisfied poet. "Agreement is death. What's more, I must tell you that the power of love emanates exclusively from tradition. The golden age of love has passed, knights and maidens have melted into the fog of ages. In the twelfth century, women divided their persons in two parts: the body went to the husband, the soul to the lover. In the ninteenth century, it was the other way around. In the twentieth century, they've completely lost the sense of any difference between these two parts. Love has plummeted—by about a half-yard from the heart. Which is to say, it has returned to its point of origin. If you truly want to understand its contemporary, let's say international, situation, then you must understand that love is not an inherent quality of human beings at every stage of development. Savages did not know love, and our age is the age of enlightened savagery, of savagery in a sublated appearance, as the dialecticians would have it. Thus, love is also sublated. The music of love has been played out. Love stands beside the muses and along with them inspires only old-fashioned poets. However, what was foremost among savages now rises again as the preeminent value—work. The true poet today is only the one who is a poet of labor."

"You, for instance?" asked Stepan.

"I am a sad phenomenon. In the transition between two ages, there inevitably appear people who are stuck precisely on the boundary, from where they can see far into the past and even further into the future. So they suffer from the disease that members of either party will never forgive—the acuity of their vision. The most desirable servants of life are those who are blinkered and partially blind. They eagerly move forward because they see what they imagine. They see the newness that they want to see. Life is governed by will, not by reason."

"Heaven only knows what's governing it," said Stepan gloomily.

They soon left, because the poet planned to get a good night's sleep before his trip.

"Yes, I'm going, I'm going," the poet cried out on the street. "Tomorrow, I won't see any of this anymore. What joy it is, not to see tomorrow what you see today! And you, too, my friend. I've put up with you long enough."

"The same is true for me," said Stepan.

"Admit it! It wasn't really so boring, was it? But don't even think of seeing me off tomorrow at the train station. A friend at the train station is just a nightmare."

"I don't even know which train you're leaving on!" Stepan assured him.

"I don't either!"

At the corner of Velyka Zhytomyrska Street, they stopped.

"Farewell, my friend," said the poet. "I say farewell because we might not see each other again. Don't forget that it's just as easy to die in this world as it is to be born."

The poet left, and Stepan suddenly felt that he was alone in the street, in the harsh, merciless city, alone in the infinite starry cosmos that glittered above him before the rising moon.

A string of ordinary days followed, which, for Stepan, passed like the endless circle of beads through a monk's fingers. He could not rid himself of a profound distress. Although its sting had been dulled—its cause was now shrouded behind the mists of many days—the sadness he felt was unchanging, infiltrating all of his thoughts, cutting off every desire that would arise from time to time in his breast. The world seemed to fade before his eyes, his soul became numb to sensations and the warmth that grew more pronounced every day. Like everyone else, he took off his coat, but he was not aware of the difference.

He settled in to his new apartment very quickly. After a week, it acquired the appearance and comfort that he had once dreamed of, when dreaming was still interesting. He put an American-style brown wooden writing desk by the window in the corner, a mirrored dresser against the wall across from the door, a dark red sofa across from the windows, and, next to the table, a bookcase with glass doors for his library, the heart of which were the books on statistics and political economy once given to him by Maksym Hnidyi, and also a complete run of the *Literaturno-naukovyi visnyk*, as well as the works of Fonvizin, which he had never returned to his old village friend, the mild-mannered agricultural student Levko. The length of his possession allowed him to think of them as his own. After all his great and small expenses, with the rest of the money from his filmscript honorarium, he bought a rug for the floor and a half-dozen chairs.

But the more improvements Stepan made in his apartment, the more alien it felt to him. Every new thing he brought into the room filled him with a strange sense of anguish. He would set it in its intended place and then look at it in surprise, as if it were something foreign that had audaciously intruded into his life. After a few days, he would get used to its presence, would use it when needed, but the sense of the incongruity and hostility of the furniture would remain hidden somewhere deep within him, bursting forth suddenly when he turned on the light after coming home in the evening. It was as if the furniture all led their own life apart from him, even talked and whispered about him amongst themselves, having overheard his thoughts, only to fall silent suddenly as soon as he opened the door. From the door, he could see himself in full stature in the rectangular shiny mirror and this was unpleasant for him, as if he had unexpectedly encountered his double who stayed behind here at all times and conspired with the morose furniture against him.

But most of all he feared the desk. There, in the top drawer on the right, lay hidden the beginning of his novel. He never pulled it out, but he sensed that the manuscript was hiding there, like a guilty conscience. He could not write further. The vacuum that had opened within him when he stepped away from Zoska's door was invisibly expanding, ruining his soul more and more, capturing ever deeper regions where human memories are preserved and, in this expanding destruction, his past was disappearing into oblivion. It was disappearing without trace under the poisonous influence of his anguish, and, along with his past, he was losing his support.

Generally, he awoke at eight, drank some coffee and, after a half hour, made his way to work. These were the happiest hours of his life, when his former strength, enthusiasm, and persistence awoke in him. He worked energetically and eagerly, immersing himself in his tasks, racing all over town, cheerful, witty, efficient, always indispensable. But, at eight in the evening, having finished his work and attended all meetings and obligations, he was left alone with his own private life whose threads had fallen out of his hands. This transition was terrible, as if he were divided in two parts, one for everyone else, the other for himself, and this second one was unfulfilled. On the way home from work, he crossed one of life's great borders.

Evenings filled him with a fearful anxiety, a feeling of terrible loneliness oppressed him. And he endured the debilitating pain of a person who has lost the personal, all those, perhaps, trivial things—those human joys and sorrows that give life flavor and allure.

All his efforts to find something were in vain. Conversations with friends seemed pointless. Women's views—disgusting. The courtesy of hosts—ridiculous. At the lectures he began to attend from time to time, he did not hear anything interesting or new; the plays in the theaters were monotonous, the films at the cinema—disgusting. He could not bear to visit a beer hall. On one occasion, he went into the casino and put one karbovanets on number twenty. He won thirty. He put the whole sum back on the same number and lost, after which he walked out impatiently. Everywhere, it was much too crowded, too bright, and too loud. And everywhere, a gnawing loneliness kept following him.

Sometimes, he remembered his former friend from the beer hall, the poet Vyhorskyi, who was wandering about Ukraine with a bag of provisions slung over his shoulder. Now that he no longer saw him, he felt even more deeply the qualities they shared that had attracted them to each other. His feelings were as agitated as his reason. He and the poet were both immensely restless, changeable, and insatiable. So where was he? What was his address? Maybe he could write him an enormous, heartfelt letter. And he was stricken with a deep jealousy toward this person who had no address. He sometimes thought about taking a vacation himself and heading off to a sunny seaside. But he always put it off. He had some kind of antipathy to everything that might give him any happiness.

Finally, he received at the office an envelope written in the poet's hand. He ripped it open impatiently. Inside were two poems for the journal, but not a word for him. That was when the poet ceased to exist for him.

One evening, as Stepan was walking slowly in the dark along Khreshchatyk, near its end where a concentration of stores sell mechanical equipment and there are few streetlights, he was accosted by a woman of the type that asks for a light or expresses an interest in what time it is. She chose the first method and he struck a match for her. She made a suggestion.

"Shall we go?"

He agreed. Then the woman took him by the arm as a sign of their partnership and turned into Triokhsviatytelska Street, where she led her client into a dark yard through a wooden gate latched with a chain. Stepan had to double over to fit under the low opening. Here, the woman whispered to him, "Don't make so much noise! You know, people now stick their noses into everyone else's business."

And he heard the woman use the kind of obscenity that is considered a male privilege. Finally, at the end of a fetid basement corridor, her keys jingled and she led him into a room of some sort whose odor was a direct extension of the corridor. Looking around, in the corner he saw the faint light of a small lamp that barely illuminated a dark icon.

The woman turned on a small light and could now be plainly discerned against the background of her setting. She was fat, swollen, and no longer young. She had angry eyes and a colorless, large mouth from which emerged crackling sounds like those from the cone of an overused gramophone. There was a bed in the room, covered with a gray sheet, and a few simple pieces of furniture appropriate to the simplicity of the activity that took place here. The Mother of God in the corner bent her head down over her Son and did not pay attention to what went on around her.

Most importantly, the woman sternly demanded a karbovanets in advance for one "hit." When she received it, she asked somewhat more graciously, "How do you like it? Naked?"

He replied that he would rather see her with her clothes on.

"Like a soldier on the march," she laughed.

And she added that she had worked in the army, too, on the German front.

Stepan was looking at the photographs that hung on the walls, without frames, dusty, and sprinkled with the stains of flies over many years. And, suddenly, he developed an interest in this woman. He wanted to know how she lived, her views, her tastes, her legal status, her opinion of the government, and that secret inner life of her soul beyond the usual routine of her trade. He offered her a cigarette and sat down at the table. From the pack he offered, she took at least a half dozen cigarettes, but said with displeasure, "Are you trying to marinate me? Let's have two more karbovanets, for the whole night."

He pulled out his wallet and spilled out all the change—sixty five kopecks.

"You're lying!" she said in disbelief. "Let me look... What's this?"

"That's two more kopecks."

"Add them to the pile."

Having turned the wallet inside out, she finally settled down and began, gruffly but willingly, to answer his carefully formed questions, frequently using words that she felt were sharp, appropriate, and refined to describe the activities and objects that informed her occupation. She wistfully looked back at the period of war communism, when she could bring home stockings full of money. But now people are just thieves—miserly, and tyrannical. Sure, she has plenty of suitors, but she's not interested in them.

"You get married for love," she said. "But I can thump around even with you."

Then she told him some of those invented, stereotypical stories that they all tell to amuse their clients and themselves, stories that slowly get transformed from dreams into half-real memories, into unconscious self-deception, to which their soul clings in its mechanical search for happiness. In particular, she emphasized a story about a Denikin army colonel who begged her on his knees to escape with him to England.

"And why would I go?" she dreamily asked. "I don't even speak English. So, over there I'd step out onto the street, and I wouldn't understand anything... He didn't know English either," she added comfortingly. "This English guy would come see me, and he also said he didn't know English."

But, as his questions became more exact and more demanding, she began to get restless. Suddenly, she stopped him in mid-sentence.

"Why are you interrogating me? What d'you come here for?"

He answered self-consciously that he had come mostly to let his soul communicate with another soul, and she became terribly offended.

"So, it's my soul you want? For a single ruble you want me to open my soul for you? For you, my soul is under my skirt."

He barely managed to calm her down, swearing before her that it was not his intention to offend her.

"And isn't it all the same to you what we do?"

"It certainly isn't all the same to me. Take what you've paid for. Don't touch my soul."

Their conversation failed to continue. She coolly bid him farewell, as if he had done her a terrible outrage, and he left, filled with respect for her, somehow moved by the realization that the woman can be put up for sale, but the person cannot.

Mostly he spent his evenings reading, lying on his sofa. There was some kind of imperative in this endless turning of pages in the absence of that living interest that makes the eye stop over the lines. Between him and the book, there was always glass, like the pane of a window that stands before the view of the landscape, letting it be seen but blocking its sweet smells, bending its outline, and muting its colors. Often, having read to the last lines, he would without noticing stop at an empty half-page and thoughtfully weave an extension of the concluded events that were slowly dimming, fading from his imagination, and suddenly disappearing. For a moment, he felt that he was no longer thinking, and this feeling was magical, somehow joyful, unusually peaceful, unchangeable, as if he had fallen into a state completely different from life, a state of pure observation, of complete independence from his surroundings.

He read an equivalent volume of newspapers, not skipping even the most boring sections, carefully going over every story, note, and announcement, even including the various notices of meetings and conferences that are found on the last page in small type. He was a diligent but eclectic reader of magazines, which are published for the general public and can be interesting to an individual reader only on condition of skipping over very many articles.

Just at that time, the Regional Congress of the Sugar Beet Industry was taking place and, among the names,

Stepan noticed in the report was that of his former friend from the Institute, Borys Zadorozhnii. The latter had given a presentation on some new system for selecting beets. He had been elected to the resolutions committee and as a delegate to the All-Ukrainian Congress. Stepan learned a great deal from these sentences! They became a bitter, painful reprimand to him. He read them over again. Yes, Borys Zadorozhnii, this young bourgeois, tyrant over a beautiful girl, was moving ahead, acting, working, making progress. An old, suppressed enmity to him surfaced in Stepan's heart, and he threw aside the newspaper in order to avoid seeing his name again.

The Sugar Beet Congress had a bad effect on him, awakening in him a line of sad thoughts about himself. Would this last a long time? Even if he had done something wrong, even if he had wronged someone, the penance had been sufficient by now. According to the calendar, three weeks of loneliness had passed, but, in his imagination, these were years. It was time to get out of this slump. It was time. It was time!

He yelled this like a horseman over a horse that had fallen in the road and was unable to get up on its own. But where would help come from? From whom? And he began to hope that a deep and sudden change would come over his life, and his despair, having reached a certain level, would transform into expectations. As if he were expecting a letter, and that letter was already on its way, getting closer, perhaps containing horrors and terrors, but also possibilities. His presentiment did not deceive him, since it was not so much a foresight of events as a herald of an inner need projected into actuality. It is a mystery of the human soul that, in moments of hunger, it focuses so strongly and brightly on certain trivialities that they, previously unknown, suddenly become an event long fostered in the heart, the answer to sad dreams, the realization of unconscious desires. The mysterious soul of man, the essence of his simple being, having hesitated at the edge, suddenly takes off down an incline from the slightest push, automatically transforming the boredom of inactivity into kinetic energy.

Now, he always had dinner in the big dining room of the People's Food Service cafeteria on Khreshchatyk, which he had chosen only because it was on the way from his office to the Bessarabka Market, where he got on a streetcar to go home. He particularly liked a small table against the wall where he could sit alone with his meal and a beer, which had become a staple element of his menu. The greatest drawback of the People's Food Service cafeteria, as with all cooperative cafeterias, was the very long wait and the minimal attention to the client—these were of no matter to him now, since dinner, usually very late, was the last event of his day, the boundary between day and evening, and he had nothing against the possibility that this hour, when his heart still beat in the rhythm of the working day, might not turn so quickly into the deadening hours of silence in his room.

Thus, it was all the more disheartening to find one evening that his table was already occupied. This was almost an insult to him, an attack on his usage-established rights, maybe even an attack on his person, which, from persistent use, subsumes lifeless things into inalienable parts of itself. But, after examining the invader more closely, Stepan ran up to him and warmly took him by the hand.

"Hello, Levko!" he cried. "It's you, Levko!"

The surprised guest raised his eyes without recognition.

"It's me, Stepan from Tereveni, remember?" he said, leaning over to his friend. "Remember, we traveled together on the steamship to Kyiv. Do you recognize me now?"

Levko recognized him, but was all the more surprised.

"Stepan?" he muttered. "I would not have recognized you. Not at all."

The young man's soul was submerged in sorrow by these words.

"Why not?" he asked quietly.

Levko was now smiling with his comforting, a-million-pardons smile.

"You've changed," he said. "Look at you, so dressed up, all decked out, a real dandy."

Stepan hastily took off his hat and sat down at the table. The unfamiliar agitation that had awakened in him on meeting Levko now grew stronger, reaching into the far depths of his soul with a hot echo. He looked at his

friend with joyful, almost loving eyes and, with unconstrained delight, discovered in his face the same features,
the same motions, the same smile and softness that he
had abandoned long ago and now found unchanged.

"Levko, I'm so happy to see you," he said. "You can't
even imagine how happy I am. Ah, Levko. Everything is
strange here. The people—the life."

"Life?" cried Levko. "This isn't life, it's a meat grinder.
And look at what they feed us!"

"And I eat this every day!" added Stepan.

"They feed us like kittens."

He laughed, pointing at the portion of meat on his
plate. And to Stepan his smile seemed pleasing, his
thinking—sound, his expressions—masterful, his behavior—unparalleled. And he was suddenly jealous
of this fellow, who had managed to remain unchanged,
to stay the same over the years. And he was sorry for his
own futile choices, desires, and inclinations. Before this
friend, whom he had abandoned and considered inferior,
he was now ashamed like a schoolroom prankster who
has noticed the teacher looking at him.

"So, how are you getting on, Levko?" asked Stepan
cheerfully.

"No, you tell me about yourself first."

And Stepan told him, briefly, blandly, and hesitantly,
about the time that had passed since their last encounter. He mentioned his short stories and his job without

sensing in his own words or in the events they described any reflection of the rays of life's rainbow.

"Heigh-ho, heigh-ho!" laughed Levko. "You must be pulling down a hundred fifty karbovanets at least."

"More or less. Plus the honorariums. A few months ago I sold a screenplay for a thousand five hundred."

Levko smacked his lips.

"That's damn good!"

But there was not the slightest hint of jealousy in his voice, only admiration. Then another idea struck him.

"So, it seems you're a Ukrainian writer!"

"So it seems, indeed," said Stepan with a sad smile.

Levko thought for a moment.

"So, there really are living writers?" he asked.

"Of course."

"And is there one like Shevchenko?"

"No, there's no one like Shevchenko."

Levko sighed in relief, as if contemporary literature did not yet pose any danger to him.

Then, taking his time, he talked about his own affairs and plans for the future. He had finished the Institute and served as an intern for a year at the Nosivka station. Now, he was picking up his diploma and setting off to Kherson province, where he had been appointed regional agronomist.

"That's nice. And what about that teacher and Latinist in whose place you used to live? The one who offered us tea," asked Stepan. And he felt an anxious satisfaction at touching in this way some of the past, which suddenly came to life within him, though still hazy, like the morning mist that will soon disperse under the sun's bright rays.

"It's not so good with him," laughed Levko. "He killed himself, the poor sot—slashed his own wrists. And with his own knife. He had said he would kill himself like some famous philosopher, but we thought he was just raving. But he went and did it. We had a mess of trouble."

"What about his wife?"

"She's a champ, that old lady, even if she is toothless. She can cook and bake like nobody's business. Restaurants can't hold a candle to her. They sure knew how to eat, those old bourgeois. I'm planning on taking her with me to Kherson province."

"You're not married?"

"Are you kidding? Once I get settled in my new job, then I'll find myself a dame. Or I'll manage without one."

"You're a strange one! What are you going to do without a wife out there in the wilderness?"

"There's great hunting out there," said Levko. "And I love the steppe."

The steppe! Stepan loved it, too. A bright and warm memory surfaced within him, a recollection of a still night and the dreamy expanse of plains, of the endless reaches of the sky and the earth, the blue silence of the moon's rays. Lying face up in the grass, with arms outspread, without a hat, barefoot and looking at the golden, azure, red, and green shimmering of the stars scattered across the sky by someone's benevolent and powerful hand. To feel that hand in the air blowing faintly across your face. To fall asleep tired from observing the infinite space, secretly in union with it. And, in the morning, from behind the mounds, sunrise—a ray of light from the red ocean, a terrible, giant icicle of cold fire, flowering slowly into a searing ball.

Levko finished his meatballs and wiped his hands on the paper napkin.

"I'm off to the cinema right now," he said. "I like to watch people hopping around. Just think—how people manage to make money. Let's go together."

"No, thanks—I'm busy," said Stepan.

On the street, they embraced warmly. Stepan was moved.

"Levko, write to me from your Kherson wilderness," he said.

"There probably won't be anything to write about," answered Levko. "It's for you writers to do the writing. And we'll read it someday."

Chapter Fourteen

I n autumn, dry corn rustles apprehensively on the steppe—whole fields of even yellow stalks, as if someone were crawling on the ground, pushing aside its hanging leaves. In autumn, along the trails, weeds spread their seeds: the tall, overgrown, ungainly goose foot, spurge, thistle, wormwood, and mugwort. Plants are ungainly in the fall, they've lost their green life. In autumn, the winds blow, strong and unexpected. In autumn, the winds are sly and prone to attack. They surprise and disappear. The gullies in the steppe unexpectedly collapse into the deep, uncovering the clay below. At the bottom of the pit are clumps of pea-shrubs offering shelter to snakes, insects, and millions of lizards. There are countless roads and paths in the steppe—intersecting, curving, doubling back. It seems they have been purposefully intertwined to allow for endless walking and wandering. And you want to enter the steppe.

You want to turn off on a side path. Where does it go? You walk slowly in the steppe, and it feels strange when you reach a destination. The roads are uneven, with deep depressions that hide a person completely, while the paths wind over hills and mounds, running straight across meadows and orchards. And the stubble breaks beneath your feet.

Stepan stopped suddenly. As far as he could make out, this was Pavlivska Street. He had been walking for maybe a half hour since he parted with Levko at the door of the cafeteria. He had been walking, deeply immersed in thought, happy and in that unintelligible serenity that envelops people at the most responsible moments of their lives after painful difficulties and disenchantment. He sensed that he was preparing for something, that something unique was about to happen, something long expected but frozen in the soul by an accidental vision. He had a premonition of his liberation, and the recollections that flowed endlessly into his consciousness kept throwing him back, again and again, into his wonderful childhood, into the unforgettable period of his first apprehension of the world. He was walking the magical path of the past, breathlessly searching for his earlier wellsprings. In the middle of a spring day in the city, he was passionately dreaming of the autumn warmth of the steppe.

He glanced at his watch. A quarter to nine. It wasn't late yet. He could still see her. And what difference does the time make? He *must* see her!

He turned and walked quickly, formulating his intentions equally quickly. He found them already formulated, luminous, chiseled deeply into his heart.

He would return to the village.

This idea, wild and sudden, did not frighten him. It did not even surprise him. It was born unexpectedly, bright and wonderful, full of vibrant joy, strength, and hope. He would return to the village. To the steppe. To the land.

He would abandon forever this city, so foreign to his soul, this stone, these enervating streetlights. He would forswear forever the harsh entanglements of urban life, the poisonous dreams that weigh down the noisy cobblestones, the stifling fervor that gnaws at the soul in the narrow confines of apartments. He would discard the insane desires that fester in a mind locked in between the walls of a city. He would go out to the peaceful, sunny expanses of the fields, to the freedom he left behind, and he would live as the grass grows, as the fruits ripen.

The bell of a streetcar made him stop. And he was cheered by the thought: "Tomorrow, I won't hear you anymore."

And all the pain that had accumulated for a year and a half, the festering disappointments so typical of people with ardor, all the bitterness of daily strivings, and the exhaustive dreaming that he had experienced in the city were now transformed into a happy fatigue and a painful yearning for tranquility. He saw himself tomorrow not as an activist of the Village Hall or a member of the Village Council, not as a teacher or union official, but as an ordinary farmer, one of the countless gray figures in peasant garb who pull the eternal plow across the soil. Welcome, moist sunrise! The freshness of the first rays of light! The wonderful gleam of silent dew! May the hour when the light of life is born be forever blessed! The spirit of the past, petrified and powerful, awoke in him, the spirit of the ages that sleeps in the soul and awakes only in the moment of agitation, encouraging stillness and silence—that invincible, though subdued voice that whispers fables about the lost Eden and sings the hymns of naturalness.

But this was not where his greatest problem lay. Tomorrow, he could find someone to buy out his lease on the apartment and furnishings, and he would submit his resignation from his job. Sure, they would try to keep him! But, tomorrow evening, he would get on a train heading south to join a commune or a workers' brigade. That wasn't important. That was simple and easy. There was nothing there to think or worry about. But!.. But he would not go alone!

Just thinking of this made him lose his breath. There was something absolute about this sudden animation of a rejected and trampled love. From the tiniest ember, half-extinguished and turned into ash, as if in revenge for the cold horror of going out completely, this passionate fire erupted and illuminated him with a new ardor. The path before him was bright, straight, and happy, and he would follow it together with Nadiika.

"Nadiika, my little Nadiika," whispered Stepan.

He now understood that she had always been present in his soul, like a distant bell calling him. With her breath, she had awakened anxiety in him, she had appeared in his dreams, but he did not recognize her until now. In others, he had loved only her and, in her, he loved something infinitely distant, an unrecognized memory, a barely audible echo from beyond the hills of consciousness. He now felt that he had never forgotten her, that he had always been searching for her in the maze of the city, and she was that flame that burned within him, urging him forward into the distance. In returning to her, he was finding himself. In returning to her, he would be resuscitating what had died, what had disappeared because of his mistakes, what he had ruined in his blindness.

Nadiika! You beautiful girl! Fair-haired water sprite of the twilight meadows. She answered his call with a quiet trembling that entered into him, having come from over there, where she lived, where she waited for him, trampled and suffering. She seemed to turn her head toward his plea and her eyes lit up in joyful consent and her hand stretched out toward his forehead. She was forgiving him! Could it be otherwise? She would come! And that, too, was inevitable. In the flowery valleys that awaited them, he would look ceaselessly into her eyes, where he would find the world and life; he would take her by the hand in radiant submission and feel in his palm the inexhaustible warmth of her body, which he would never approach. At night, he would keep watch over her dreams, the wonderful dreams of a somnolent beauty, and he would understand them, just as he understands human speech. And he would drink, drink forever, the sweet poison of her divinity, and he would slowly die at her feet in fatal intoxication. That's how it must be! Her resurrection, along with the song-filled allure of the steppe, flowed together into a single urge for sensual penance, a longing for eternal slavery, in which he felt all the joy of renewal.

At the corner of Volodymyr Street he stopped, worried. Had he forgotten their... that is, her address? No! 38 Andriyivskyi Descent, Apt. 6. The name of the street and the numbers immediately flashed in his memory, although he had heard them only once. And the only surprise was how close it was, how easy it was to get there. All the better, since he would have gladly crossed a desert in hunger and thirst, or wandered in underground tunnels, or in a jungle with otherworldly dangers. He would have conquered anything in her name.

He repeated to himself, "Andriyivskyi Descent, Andriyivskyi Descent."

He soon recalled this curved, inclined street, his former path from the Podil to the Institute. And he would meet her again on this path, where he had lost her, and he would now find her again.

"How wonderful! How wonderful!" he thought.

A new idea suddenly came into his head, born of his recollections and the wish to renew the past that up 'til now had lived only within him. He wanted to see that little building in Bessarabka, to go into it just as he had done earlier, when he had seen Nadiika in the company of her village friends. Where were they now? Where is the bashful Hanusia and young Asha? Where is the full-bodied Nusia and the instructor of club work? Suddenly, they became very dear to him, almost family, and very interesting. A vague expectation overcame him that he would meet them all in a moment around a table and that he would sit down beside Nadiika who was waiting for him. And why, indeed, wouldn't she happen to drop by here? If he could run into Levko whom he hadn't seen for an even longer time, why not her? Stepan turned to the right and quickly walked down to Khreshchatyk.

His heart was beating wildly as he knocked on the rickety door of the squat shack. He recognized everything around him, the old-fashioned porch, the fenced-in yard, the wooden shutters. Nothing had changed. How fortunate! Well, it hadn't actually been so long ago—only a year and a half, which now seemed to him like one night of very deep sleep.

The door was opened by a man with a heavy voice who seemed somehow disappointed, uninviting.

"Do the girls still live here? The ones who lived here a year and a half ago?" Stepan asked.

Unfortunately, he could not put the question differently, since he had forgotten their surnames.

"There aren't no girls here," answered the man in a tone as if to indicate that there were only honest people living here. He was about to close the door but Stepan, in confusion, began to explain. He was actually looking for his sister, whom he left in the city a year and a half ago. The only people who would be able to tell him were the girls who had lived here. Did they move out? If he doesn't find them, he won't find his sister, who has gone off somewhere. He's already visited the address bureau, but they couldn't tell him anything.

"Yeah, they just take your money," grumbled the man, softening. "That's the Soviet way, for sure!"

"Yes, the bureaucracy's terrible... One of the girls was a seamstress. A small girl."

"There's a seamstress living over through the courtyard. Just go through the gate."

They parted on friendly terms and Stepan went into the shadowy courtyard—a narrow space with a few trees between the neighboring tall buildings. At first, he couldn't see where there might be any habitable space, but then he noticed a tiny shed that seemed to be attached like a mushroom to the blank wall on the left. A faint ribbon of light from the crack between the shutters was hardly visible in the darkness of this enclosure.

Tripping over clumps of earth and bricks, Stepan approached the window and knocked carefully.

"Who's there?" he heard a woman's voice.

He trembled and then answered, "Open up, it's me, Stepan. Remember? I used to come visit when Nadiika lived here."

"Stepan?" the voice from inside asked in surprise.

"Sure, Stepan from Tereveni. Hanusia, open up."

There was a sudden laugh inside.

"You bet, but my name is Yivha."

Stepan recoiled in horror. Her name is Yivha? Yivha? That's a useless name for him. He was ready to fall on the ground right here, close his eyes, and forget everything. But when he got out to the street, the memory of Nadiika swept over him again and he began to think about her once more.

But his thoughts were no longer the sweet dreams that had thus far warmed and cheered him, but an extrinsically imposed, painful necessity, a terrible, inescapable need, whose causes were not even remotely known to him. Now, he was considering the matter more with his reason than his desires and evaluated his intentions from the perspective of their actual realization. That Nadiika was waiting for him seemed an undeniable fact. A sense of his exclusive rights to this girl had, indeed, never left him. If she was not with him now, that was only because he had not wanted that until now. Today, he would explain to her that life was only possible in nature, which they had abandoned and to which they must now return. The city, suffocating and nauseating, was a terrible mistake of history. He understood that these ideas were not particularly new, but that was only further proof of their veracity. But she would understand this even without words. At the moment, he was not worried about her at all. But she's married! And that Borys was such a stubborn fellow, he'd probably be hard to convince. What will it take to explain all this to him, to convince him? And he'll probably disagree and contradict! It will probably be necessary to mention that Nadiika's virginity belonged to someone else. How unpleasant! He glanced at his watch. It was twenty to ten. A little late, but this had to be done today!

Feeling terribly tired, he called a cab and set off, drowsily leaning back in the seat. The flickering streetlamps and the evening rush of the crowd annoyed him, accelerating his fatigue to complete exhaustion. He closed his eyes and a longing for sleep, like a warm and heavy quilt, covered his thoughts in a motionless fog. He felt the stiffness of his body, a tight swaddling of his soul, and the soft swaying of the carriage on its springs rocked him further and further from the troublesome bustle of life.

Suddenly, the coachman stopped.

"What?" asked Stepan, awakening.

"We've arrived," said the man.

Stepan shook himself and jumped to the ground.

"Shall I wait?" asked the coachman.

"Yes, wait. I'll be right back," answered Stepan.

He nervously opened the door of the building on whose gate he saw an illuminated sign with the number he sought, but he climbed the steps slowly, lighting his way with matches. Finally, he stopped on the third floor and rang. His soul was filled with tranquility.

He leaned against the doorjamb and began to think about the fact that he had left his home today with his portfolio but did not have it with him now. Obviously, he had lost it. And, although the portfolio, fortunately, held nothing of great importance, Stepan nevertheless felt a deep disappointment. "What a dolt I am," he thought.

Footsteps behind the door interrupted his thinking. He felt nervous again. Will she open the door, or will someone else? No, it was a woman's voice, but not hers, that asked, "Who is it?" Stepan suddenly thought that maybe they had moved somewhere else. This possibility encouraged him, and he answered loudly, "May I see Comrade Borys?"

The door cracked open on a chain and, through the crack, he was observed by a teenage girl.

"Borys Viktorovych isn't home," the girl responded earnestly. "He's on a business trip."

"That's a shame," grumbled Stepan. Then he added, nonplussed, "I'll leave him a note."

"Please come in," said the girl, inviting him in.

In the vestibule, he hung up his hat on a hook and patted down his hair before following the girl into a room where a lamp with a wide lampshade of orange lace stood on a table covered with a bright oilcloth. He sat down at the table and, before the girl brought him a pencil and paper, he stealthily looked around the apartment. The windows were covered with embroidered drapes and there were flowers on the windowsills. In the corner was a fabric sofa with a small rug beside it. Against the wall were simple chairs arranged very neatly. And, unexpectedly, off to the side, an enormous bourgeois sideboard with engraved panels—the heavy centerpiece of the apartment, disproportionate to the size of the room. The room was simple and clean—all the furniture stood in its duly appointed place, keeping to the principle of symmetry. The sideboard seemed to be the chief guardian of order, the stern representative of the unchangeable foundations of life in this home.

Something touched his leg—a cat was rubbing against his shoe. He caught it and put it on his knees, focusing his attention on writing.

"Dear Borys, I finally decided to pay you a visit, but—such bad luck! I thought we would spend the evening talking about old times…"

A side door squeaked and, raising his head, Stepan saw a woman at the door, with a broad red shawl that covered her figure down to her knees. Stepan got up, embarrassed, deducing that this woman had likely been observing him through the crack when he was petting the cat.

"Is it you, Stepan..."

"Pavlovych," he added, realizing why she had paused.

And no sooner had he heard her voice than he recognized her. It was she! But terribly changed, almost disfigured, but he could not immediately tell in what way. Even her voice sounded different, somehow irritating, confident, and proud. She frightened him with her sudden entrance, with her appearance, with her formality and disdainful look. Shaking her hand, he thought, "I really am a dolt!"

"Have a seat, Stepan Pavlovych," said the hostess.

And he suddenly realized that she was pregnant.

"Thank you," he said, overcoming his horror, insult, and pain.

She sat down on the sofa by the door and called out, "Natasha, put on the samovar."

"Is that for me?" asked Stepan, concerned. "Thank you, I've had my tea. I just drank some."

"But I haven't had any," she answered.

An uncomfortable silence ensued, and Stepan thought this silence was humiliating him and perhaps pleasing to her, but he could not find any words. The round, heavy belly paralyzed him.

Finally, the hostess broke the silence.

"You are a very rare guest in our home, Stepan Pavlovych."

"Indeed," he mumbled. "It's hard to find the time. And Borys is always away on business."

He wanted to stop, but his fear of the silence squeezed a few more sentences out of him.

"I wanted to suggest… That is, if Borys were around… That we all take a trip somewhere together tomorrow… Somewhere distant… Into nature, as they say…"

"That's a wonderful idea," she replied. "But I'm not feeling very well."

And Stepan observed with chagrin that silence was falling between them again, a boring, irritating silence between people who would have done better not to meet. Every thought that arose in him immediately came crashing down on her belly and fled back into nothingness.

Suddenly she said, "They say you write short stories."

"Yes, I used to," he answered sadly.

"And now?"

"I'm not writing now."

"Why?"

"There's nothing to write about."

She smiled.

"Were there really no adventures in your life?"

He gave a start. Was she allowing herself too much liberty in making fun of him? He proudly answered, "There were, but they were minor. Too ordinary."

Then he solemnly looked at his watch and got up.

"Please excuse me, Nadiya…"

"Semenivna," she added.

"Nadiya Semenivna, I have to go. Please give my best to Borys."

"Please come visit us again," said Nadiya Semenivna. "We will always be happy to see you."

On the stairs down, he let his anger loose. What impudence! And who is this person, asking pointed questions? Is she the one he chased away from himself like a whore? She assumes that, now that she has a husband, she's something special. And her husband is just a thief. You think he could purchase such a sideboard on the salary at a cooperative? So, of course, he's stealing! He's heading for a stay in the slammer. As for her, she's just a city girl with a fat belly. He repeated this phrase a few times with sensual pleasure, and that calmed him down.

Out on the street, he decided to descend down to the Podil and then take a bus back up to Khreshchatyk. But he hadn't made more than a few steps downward when someone yelled.

"Comrade. Comrade!"

It was the coachman who had been waiting for him. As he paid him off, regret overwhelmed him. So, why did this coachman wait for him? And why had he come here in the first place?

Descending the dark, curving street, Stepan contemplated the broom of life, which swept up the footprints of the past after the fact—that great sacred broom, always new and always unerring. But, nevertheless, he was not at peace. This evening was pulling him back toward those crumbs of himself that he had once left behind and these crumbs, scattered along the path, now tempted him inexorably. He wanted to gather them, to pick them up, to return them to himself, to undo the depletion of his being. So when he reached Revolution Square, illuminated with streetlights and the moving lights of streetcars, he slowly turned to the left, into the narrow streets of the Podil. And here was Nyzhnii Val Street, and here was the Hnidyi home, his first urban settlement. He was on the opposite side of the street, looking from the shadows at the familiar yard, the shed, the porch where he once sat in the evening, and the house. How strange! All the windows were illuminated and strange sounds emanated through the walls into the dreamy silence of the street. Inside, there was dancing to the vibrant rhythm of mandolins. The somnolent, decaying building had opened its eyes and emerged from an oppressive stupor. The little house had come to life, stepping out of a coffin-like silence and, in this deferred resurrection, there was also, perhaps, a sign of his path in the world, the path of someone whose steps are marked with death and life.

Suddenly, a deep tranquility enveloped him. How comical it was to remember! Because everything in the past gets covered with geological layers and transforms into incomprehensible strata compressed by the oppressive action of time. Anyone who tries to infuse memories with a new existence is simply mad! Because the past decomposes, like a corpse.

But, as he walked away from that house, he slowly realized that his conceived composure was only the quiet beginning of a deceptive longing. It was growing every year, expanding, and becoming heavier, like a pregnant belly and, along with it, an ever deeper, an ever more painful anxiety was suffocating him. He felt a terrible hunger of all his senses, a wild ardor, a powerful excitement of life's energy within him, breaking through the morbidity of his recent thinking. This terrible force churned within him in a white noise and, choking in this renewed maelstrom, he conjured, in fear and hope, that, from now on, his life would be somehow new, not at all like what it had been, entirely different from what he had already experienced. May it begin all the sooner!

On the square named for the Third International, he made his usual purchase of newspapers and, as he was leaving, a surprise stopped him in his tracks. This really was a fairy-tale evening! Approaching him directly, face to face, was a glowing pair of unforgettable eyes, smiling at him from the still mask of a woman's face. He recognized them immediately and threw himself at them, as if they were the rescue beams of a lighthouse.

"Rita, my dear Rita," he whispered, squeezing her hands.

The wound she had once made on his palm he now felt in his heart. And he was ready to clasp this woman to him right here, in the middle of the street, passionately and mindlessly, to feel her as he had felt her then, dancing.

She responded, smiling.

"What a surprise to meet you here."

"Is it only surprising?"

"And desired," she added.

He was devouring her with his eyes.

"Where are you heading?" he asked, finally.

"To Mala Pidvalna Street."

He took her by the arm.

"Let's go."

But, behind the Regional Executive Committee Building, in the darkness of the alley, he stopped and sensually grasped her around the waist.

She squirmed out of his embrace and whispered, without much dissatisfaction, "You're insane!"

"I'm always like that," he replied happily, taking her by the arm again. "Lean over towards me. Closer—don't be so miserly! Today, I've been searching all evening. If you must know, I even lost my portfolio somewhere. But I found you. You can't possibly understand me. After you left back then, I could not do anything. I lived only in recollections of you, in the hope of seeing you."

"Really? I didn't forget you completely either."

"All the better! But, even now, I'm not completely sure it's you. Do you understand? You're dressed differently, and it seems to me that maybe it's no longer you."

"You need proof?"

"You've guessed, precisely," he cried out.

For a moment, just a moment, she touched his lips with her former kiss.

"Is it me?"

"Yes, it's you," he replied, subdued. Then he asked, "Are you in Kyiv for long?"

"Until the fall."

He squeezed her hands in gratitude. He had been afraid she might say "forever."

"I love you madly," he whispered. "You are unique, you are just amazing."

All of his sorrows suddenly poured out of him in a lover's whisper, in poignant expressions, in tender pet names, in bold, arousing comparisons in which flowed all the depth and variability of his feelings.

Suddenly she stopped.

"That's enough, you little rascal. I'm home."

He cried out impetuously, "And I will follow you! I'll come home with you!"

She wagged her finger at him.

"No, you won't. As you know, I live with my parents."

"Oh, that's not very convenient," said Stepan with a pout. "What shall we do?"

"Tomorrow, we dance at the Opera. Wait for me."

"Only tomorrow?"

"Only tomorrow! But I want flowers."

"You shall have them."

In the dim light of the entryway, barely illuminated by a lamp on the second floor, he kissed her passionately and inquisitively, insistently, uncontrollably, as if searching in the depths of her lips the answer he had been searching for all his life. And he left quickly, elated by the joy of discovery.

He had never before felt such powerful emotions. The ground seemed to flow beneath his feet in a velvet carpet, and the roofs of buildings greeted him like giants tipping their hats. And, in his head, in that beautiful, unconstrained head, row after row of invincible thoughts marched in ebullient excitement.

Without waiting for the elevator, Stepan ran headlong up the stairs to the sixth floor, entered his room and threw open the windows onto the dark abyss of the city.

It lay submissively below, in cliff-like waves marked with dots of fire, and out of the darkness of its hills, sharp stone fingers stretched out to him. He stood immobilized in sensual contemplation of the magnitude of this new force. Suddenly, in a grand gesture, he threw an enchanted kiss out below.

Then, in the silence of the lamp on his desk, he went on to write his novel about people.

1927
Kyiv

Recent Titles in the Series
Harvard Library of Ukrainian Literature

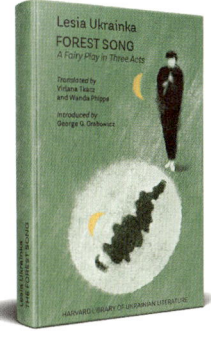

Forest Song:
A Fairy Play in Three Acts

Lesia Ukrainka (Larysa Kosach)

Translated by Virlana Tkacz and Wanda Phipps
Introduced by George G. Grabowicz

This play represents the crowning achievement of Lesia Ukrainka's (Larysa Kosach's) mature period and is a uniquely powerful poetic text. Here, the author presents a symbolist meditation on the interaction of mankind and nature set in a world of primal forces and pure feelings as seen through childhood memories and the re-creation of local Volhynian folklore.

2024 | appr. 240 pp.
ISBN 9780674291874 (cloth) $29.95
9780674291881 (paperback) $19.95
9780674291898 (epub)
9780674291904 (PDF)
Harvard Library of Ukrainian Literature, vol. 14

Read
the book
online

Love Life: A Novel

Oksana Lutsyshyna

Translated by Nina Murray
Introduced by Marko Pavlyshyn

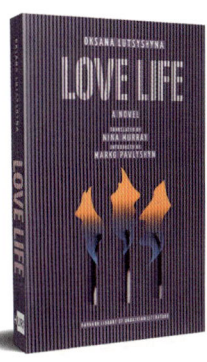

The second novel of the award-winning Ukrainian writer and poet Oksana Lutsyshyna writes the story of Yora, an immigrant to the United States from Ukraine. A delicate soul that's finely attuned to the nuances of human relations, Yora becomes enmeshed in a relationship with Sebastian, a seductive acquaintance who seems to be suggesting that they share a deep bond. After a period of despair and complex grief that follows the end of the relationship, Yora is able to emerge stronger, in part thanks to the support from a friendly neighbor who has adapted well to life on the margins of society.

2024 | 276 pp.
ISBN 9780674297159 (cloth) $39.95
9780674297166 (paperback) $19.95
9780674297173 (epub)
9780674297180 (PDF)
Harvard Library of Ukrainian Literature, vol. 12

Read
the book
online

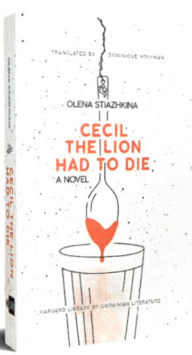

Cecil the Lion Had to Die: A Novel

Olena Stiazhkina

Translated by Dominique Hoffman

This novel follows the fate of four families as the world around them undergoes radical transformations when the Soviet Union unexpectedly implodes, independent Ukraine emerges, and neoimperial Russia begins its war by occupying Ukraine's Crimea and parts of the Donbas. A tour de force of stylistic registers and intertwining stories, ironic voices and sincere discoveries, this novel is a must-read for those who seek to deeper understand Ukrainians from the Donbas, and how history and local identity have shaped the current war with Russia.

2024 | 248 pp.

ISBN 9780674291645 (cloth)	$39.95
9780674291669 (paperback)	$19.95
9780674291676 (epub)	
9780674291683 (PDF)	

Harvard Library of Ukrainian Literature, vol. 11

Read the book online

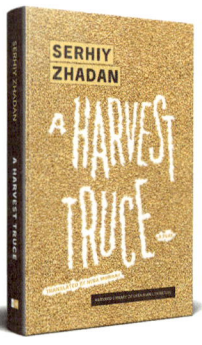

A Harvest Truce: A Play

Serhiy Zhadan

Translated by Nina Murray

Brothers Anton and Tolik reunite at their family home to bury their recently deceased mother. An otherwise natural ritual unfolds under extraordinary circumstances: their house is on the front line of a war ignited by Russian-backed separatists in eastern Ukraine. Isolated without power or running water, the brothers' best hope for success and survival lies in the declared cease fire—the harvest truce.

Spring 2024 | 196 pp.

ISBN 9780674291997 (hardcover)	$29.95
9780674292017 (paperback)	$19.95
9780674292024 (epub)	
9780674292031 (PDF)	

Harvest Library of Ukrainian Literature, vol. 9

Read the book online

Cassandra:
A Dramatic Poem,

Lesia Ukrainka (Larysa Kosach)

Translated by Nina Murray, introduction by Marko Pavlyshyn

The classic myth of Cassandra turns into much more in Lesia Ukrainka's rendering: Cassandra's prophecies are uttered in highly poetic language—fitting to the genre of the dramatic poem that Ukrainka crafts for this work—and are not believed for that very reason, rather than because of Apollo's curse. Cassandra's being a poet and a woman are therefore the two focal points of the drama.

2024 | 263 pp, bilingual ed. (Ukrainian, English)

ISBN 9780674291775 (hardcover) | $29.95
9780674291782 (paperback) | $19.95
9780674291799 (epub)
9780674291805 (PDF)

Harvard Library of Ukrainian Literature, vol. 8

Read
the book
online

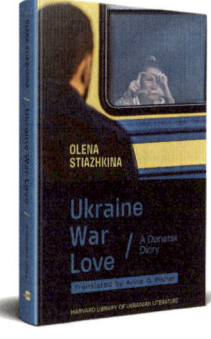

Ukraine, War, Love:
A Donetsk Diary

Olena Stiazhkina

Translated by Anne O. Fisher

In this war-time diary, Olena Stiazhkina depicts day-to-day developments in and around her beloved hometown during Russia's 2014 invasion and occupation of the Ukrainian city of Donetsk.

Summer 2023

ISBN 9780674291690 (hardcover) | $39.95
9780674291706 (paperback) | $19.95
9780674291713 (epub)
9780674291768 (PDF)

Harvard Library of Ukrainian Literature, vol. 7

Read
the book
online

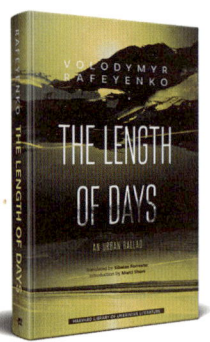

The Length of Days: An Urban Ballad

Volodymyr Rafeyenko

Translated by Sibelan Forrester
Afterword and interview with the author by Marci Shore

This novel is set mostly in the composite Donbas city of Z—an uncanny foretelling of what this letter has come to symbolize since February 24, 2022, when Russia launched a full-scale invasion of Ukraine. Several embedded narratives attributed to an alcoholic chemist-turned-massage therapist give insight into the funny, ironic, or tragic lives of people who remained in the occupied Donbas after Russia's initial aggression in 2014.

2023 | 349 pp.

ISBN 780674291201 (cloth) — $39.95
9780674291218 (paper) — $19.95
9780674291225 (epub)
9780674291232 (PDF)

Harvard Library of Ukrainian Literature, vol. 6

Read
the book
online

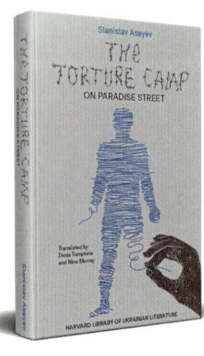

The Torture Camp on Paradise Street

Stanislav Aseyev

Translated by Zenia Tompkins and Nina Murray

Ukrainian journalist and writer Stanislav Aseyev details his experience as a prisoner from 2015 to 2017 in a modern-day concentration camp overseen by the Federal Security Bureau of the Russian Federation (FSB) in the Russian-controlled city of Donetsk. This memoir recounts an endless ordeal of psychological and physical abuse, including torture and rape, inflicted upon the author and his fellow inmates over the course of nearly three years of illegal incarceration spent largely in the prison called Izoliatsiia (Isolation).

2023 | 300 pp., 1 map, 18 ill.

ISBN 9780674291072 (cloth) — $39.95
9780674291089 (paper) — $19.95
9780674291102 (epub)
9780674291096 (PDF)

Harvard Library of Ukrainian Literature, vol. 5

Read
the book
online

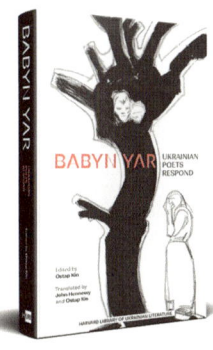

Babyn Yar: Ukrainian Poets Respond

Edited with introduction by Ostap Kin

Translated by John Hennessy and Ostap Kin

In 2021, the world commemorated the 80th anniversary of the massacres of Jews at Babyn Yar. The present collection brings together for the first time the responses to the tragic events of September 1941 by Ukrainian Jewish and non-Jewish poets of the Soviet and post-Soviet periods, presented here in the original and in English translation by Ostap Kin and John Hennessy.

2022 | 282 pp.

ISBN 9780674275591 (hardcover)	$39.95
9780674271692 (paperback)	$16.00
9780674271722 (epub)	
9780674271739 (PDF)	

Harvard Library of Ukrainian Literature, vol. 4

Read
the book
online

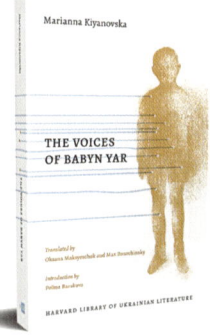

The Voices of Babyn Yar

Marianna Kiyanovska

Translated by Oksana Maksymchuk and Max Rosochinsky
Introduced by Polina Barskova

With this collection of stirring poems, the award-winning Ukrainian poet honors the victims of the Holocaust by writing their stories of horror, death, and survival in their own imagined voices.

2022 | 192 pp.

ISBN 9780674268760 (hardcover)	$39.95
9780674268869 (paperback)	$16.00
9780674268876 (epub)	
9780674268883 (PDF)	

Harvard Library of Ukrainian Literature, vol. 3

Read
the book
online

Mondegreen: Songs about Death and Love

Volodymyr Rafeyenko

Translated and introduced by Mark Andryczyk

Volodymyr Rafeyenko's novel Mondegreen: Songs about Death and Love explores the ways that memory and language construct our identity, and how we hold on to it no matter what. The novel tells the story of Haba Habinsky, a refugee from Ukraine's Donbas region, who has escaped to the capital city of Kyiv at the onset of the Ukrainian-Russian war.

2022	204 pp.	
ISBN 9780674275577 (hardcover)	$39.95
9780674271708 (paperback)	$19.95
9780674271746 (epub)	
9780674271760 (PDF)	

Harvard Library of Ukrainian Literature, vol. 2

Read the book online

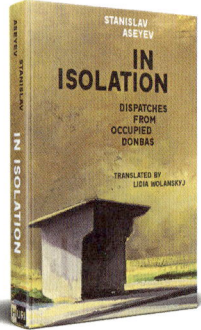

In Isolation: Dispatches from Occupied Donbas

Stanislav Aseyev

Translated by Lidia Wolanskyj

In this exceptional collection of dispatches from occupied Donbas, writer and journalist Stanislav Aseyev details the internal and external changes observed in the cities of Makiïvka and Donetsk in eastern Ukraine.

2022	320 pp., 42 photos, 2 maps	
ISBN 9780674268784 (hardcover)	$39.95
9780674268791 (paperback)	$19.95
9780674268814 (epub)	
9780674268807 (PDF)	

Harvard Library of Ukrainian Literature, vol. 1

Read the book online

Recent Titles in the Harvard Series in Ukrainian Studies

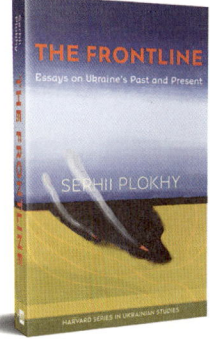

The Frontline: Essays on Ukraine's Past and Present

Serhii Plokhy

The Frontline presents a selection of essays drawn together for the first time to form a companion volume to Serhii Plokhy's *The Gates of Europe* and *Chernobyl*. Here he expands upon his analysis in earlier works of key events in Ukrainian history, including Ukraine's complex relations with Russia and the West, the burden of tragedies such as the Holodomor and World War II, the impact of the Chernobyl nuclear disaster, and Ukraine's contribution to the collapse of the Soviet Union.

2021 (HC) / 2023 (PB) | 416 pp. / 420 pp.

10 color photos, 9 color maps

ISBN 9780674268821 (hardcover)	$64.00
9780674268838 (paperback)	$19.95
9780674268845 (epub)	
9780674268852 (PDF)	

Read all chapters online

Harvard Series in Ukrainian Studies, vol. 81

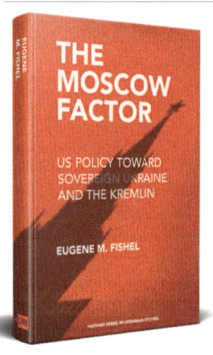

The Moscow Factor: US Policy toward Sovereign Ukraine and the Kremlin

Eugene M. Fishel

Russia's war on Ukraine did not start on February 24, 2022 with the full-scale invasion. Over eight years ago, in 2014, Russia illegally annexed Crimea from Ukraine, fanned a separatist conflict in the Donbas region, and attacked Ukraine with units of its regular army and special forces. In each instance of Russian aggression, the U.S. response has often been criticized as inadequate, insufficient, or hesitant.

2022 | 324 pp., 2 photos

ISBN 9780674279179 (hardcover)	$59.95
9780674279186 (paperback)	$29.95
9780674279421 (epub)	
9780674279193 (PDF)	

Read all chapters online

Harvard Series in Ukrainian Studies, vol. 82

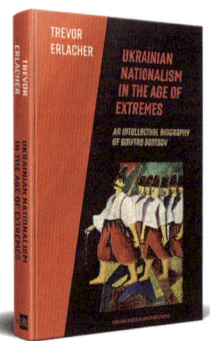

Ukrainian Nationalism in the Age of Extremes: An Intellectual Biography of Dmytro Dontsov

Trevor Erlacher

Ukrainian nationalism made worldwide news after the Euromaidan revolution and the outbreak of the Russo-Ukrainian war in 2014. Invoked by regional actors and international commentators, the "integral" Ukrainian nationalism of the 1930s has moved to the center of debates about Eastern Europe, but the history of this divisive ideology remains poorly understood.

2021 | 658 pp., 34 photos, 5 illustr.

ISBN 9780674250932 (hardcover) | $84.00
9780674250949 (epub)
9780674250956 (Kindle)
9780674250963 (PDF)

Read
all chapters
online

Harvard Series in Ukrainian Studies, vol. 80

Survival as Victory: Ukrainian Women in the Gulag

Oksana Kis

Translated by Lidia Wolanskyj

Hundreds of thousands of Ukrainian women were sentenced to the GULAG in the 1940s and 1950s. Only about half of them survived. With this book, Oksana Kis has produced the first anthropological study of daily life in the Soviet forced labor camps as experienced by Ukrainian women prisoners.
Based on the written memoirs, autobiographies, and oral histories of over 150 survivors, this book fills a lacuna in the scholarship regarding Ukrainian experience.

2020 | 652 pp., 78 color photos, 10 b/w photos

ISBN 9780674258280 (hardcover) | $94.00
9780674258327 (epub)
9780674258334 (Kindle)
9780674258341 (PDF)

Read
all chapters
online

Harvard Series in Ukrainian Studies, vol. 79